Notes
from the
Cove

BOOKS BY JENNIFER BARDSLEY

Notes
from the
Cove

JENNIFER BARDSLEY

bookouture

Published by Bookouture in 2024

An imprint of Storyfire Ltd.
Carmelite House
50 Victoria Embankment
London EC4Y 0DZ

www.bookouture.com

ISBN: 978-1-83790-779-3
eBook ISBN: 978-1-83790-778-6

To my sorority sister, Kalee Magnani, and our joint belief in the motto "do good."

ONE

It was the five words that struck fear into the soul of every mother: "This is the principal calling." Brittany's heart stopped as she held the phone to her ear. Was Jeremy okay? She stepped away from the senior center kitchen and sheltered in the walk-in pantry for privacy. The seniors loved to gossip, and her life was one of their favorite topics.

"I'm Brittany Thompson," she said, clinging to the phone. "How can I help you?" Jeremy might not have been a brilliant student, but he certainly wasn't a troublemaker. She was enormously proud that he was graduating from high school in thirteen days. Brittany's relationship with her son was precious to her, especially considering that so many of her other family connections were strained.

The principal cleared her throat before speaking. "Your son and two other culprits played a highly inappropriate senior prank on Sand Dollar Cove High."

Senior prank? Shivers ran down Brittany's arm, leaving a trail of goosebumps in their wake. Her brother Paul had died playing a senior prank.

Thirty years later, she was still afraid of the ocean.

She'd never forget the night they got the call about Paul's accident. Her father's face draining of color. Her mother throwing the telephone against the wall. Piling in the car so fast that nobody brought coats. Standing on the dock, screaming Paul's name into the wind, the rain pelting them so hard that it felt like the entire family was drowning along with him.

"What prank?" Brittany whispered, barely able to get the words out. "Is Jeremy alright?"

"Yes. He's sitting in my office right now waiting to be picked up."

Relief flooded through her, but the goosebumps remained. Brittany focused on breathing.

"If it weren't so close to graduation, I'd expel him," the principal continued. "But the state looks at our graduation rates, and—"

"What did he do?" Brittany stepped out of her Birkenstocks for a moment to feel the grounding sensation of her wool socks touching the floor, and then slipped into her sandals again.

"He put a toilet on the roof. It's taking our entire custodial team to remove it."

"Seniors play pranks all the time," Brittany said, her momentary relief shifting into defense mode. It didn't matter if Jeremy was in the wrong or not; she was on his side.

"Be that as it may," said the principal, "Jeremy is receiving an in-school suspension tomorrow, and we need you to come in and collect him immediately."

"I'll be right there." Brittany said goodbye and ended the call. Idly, she wondered if the principal had also called her ex-husband Ian. If so, Ian probably hadn't bothered to answer, the selfish jerk.

Squeezing her eyes shut, Brittany took a deep breath before she opened them and looked at the neatly stacked rows of canned goods in the pantry. As the registered dietitian for the Sand Dollar Cove senior center, it was Brittany's job to make sure members ate nutritious meals. It was a role she was good at. But when it came to parenting Jeremy through his teenage years, she struggled with how to guide him.

Sometimes, in the dark of night, when she pulled the covers up over her head and still couldn't fall asleep, Brittany wondered if it was possible for *any* male to be a truly decent human being. Of course she loved her son with every cell in her body... Of course she wanted him to grow up and become a person of character... But was that possible? Did good men exist, or were they something only found in fairy tales, like giants who climbed beanstalks or wizards who transformed into dragons?

The only man she'd ever trusted was her brother Paul. Calling him a man was stretching the truth—he'd been a seventeen-year-old boy when he'd died. But Paul had been her knight in shining armor. If only Paul was here now, to help her with Jeremy. He'd have good advice, Brittany was sure of it. Instead, she'd have to keep doing what she always did, muddling through somehow and hoping for the best. She looked longingly at the embroidered flowers on her jeans, wishing she could be as carefree as the lilies that grew there.

Brittany left the pantry and picked her hobo purse up off the kitchen desk. Today she was filling in as chef since the cook had called in sick. That's why her curly brown hair was pulled up high, away from her face.

"Keith?" she called, as she walked into the main room. She paused at the doorway, scanning the scene for her current boss and former boyfriend. Their recent breakup was still raw. Eight years her junior, with a thin frame and wiry glasses, Keith had an intelligent look that masked his controlling behavior. He had a vindictive streak, too, that she'd experienced frequently. She spotted him by the shelving unit that stored board games, carefully lining up the corners of the boxes. Brittany hurried over and made her case. "I have to rush over to the high school.

Would you please take the chicken out of the oven when the timer rings and serve lunch?"

"You're leaving?" Keith glared at her with disapproval. "In the middle of the workday?"

"Yes." From the corner of her eye, Brittany saw seniors sitting at a table nearby, playing cards, watching her interaction with Keith. "The principal called saying I need to pick Jeremy up."

"What did that animal son of yours do now?"

"He's not an animal!" Brittany didn't have time to debate, nor did she want to, yet again. Keith had always been jealous of her relationship with her son.

"Is he sick?" Keith asked.

"No."

Keith snorted. "He's in some sort of asinine trouble then, and putting your job in peril to come bail him out."

"I will only be gone an hour," Brittany protested. She wished she could go back in time and dump Keith, instead of Keith dumping her. "I've never left in the middle of a work shift before now. This is an emergency."

"That's a stretch, isn't it?" Keith raised his eyebrows. "If he were dying in a ditch somewhere, *that* would be an emergency."

"How could you say such a thing?" Brittany's palms sweated.

"I'm not trying to be harsh." Keith pushed his glasses up the bridge of his nose. "I'm just explaining what a genuine emergency is, one that would warrant you abandoning your job in the middle of the day. That's grounds for termination, and—"

"You go do what you need to do," boomed a voice from the card table. It was Cheryl Turner, Brittany's octogenarian housemate. "Don, could you please pass me my walker?"

"You bet, dollface." The man sitting next to Cheryl stood and angled her walker into position.

"What do you need help with to get lunch on the table?"

Cheryl asked as she steadied herself with the walker. "I'm at your service."

"So am I," said Don. "Put us to work."

"There's no need for that." Keith pressed his palms down in the air, like he wanted Cheryl to sit. "Seniors aren't supposed to help in the kitchen."

"Don't tell me what to do." Cheryl inched her walker forward. "I'll work in the kitchen if I want to."

Brittany's phone buzzed with an incoming text, and she looked quickly at the screen.

Mom, are you coming? Jeremy texted. *Please???*

Omw, she answered.

"It's settled then," said Cheryl. "We'll handle lunch."

Keith pointed at the chairs. "I invite you to sit down."

"You can't boss us around," said Don.

Brittany's phone buzzed again.

Home school communication from Sand Dollar Cove School District. Your son, Jeremy Willis, has been assigned an in-school suspension starting— Brittany didn't bother reading the rest of the message.

"Thank you for handling lunch," she said, smiling gratefully at her friends. "I really appreciate it."

"Just go," said Cheryl. "And tell that lovable son of yours that I'm rooting for him."

Brittany nodded, her emotions tender. She charged out the front door without looking back. The June day was chilly, and the salty scent of the Pacific Ocean stung her nose as she bolted through the parking lot. The foghorn sang in the distance, an ever-present reminder of the sadness that shadowed Brittany's life like an impermeable mist.

It's just a stupid senior prank, Brittany told herself as she opened the door to her SUV and climbed inside. *He probably meant it as a joke.* She pressed the ignition button and her Subaru roared to life. But as she reached for the steering wheel, she noticed her trembling hands. No senior prank was ever smart. All of them were stupid. Misguided machinations of brains that hadn't fully developed. Brains that would never have the chance to fully develop if poor decisions interfered and—

Stop! Brittany ordered her thoughts to quiet down. Thinking about Paul wasn't helping right now. Thinking about her brother never helped, in fact. It only served to pull her down into a whirlpool of tragic what-ifs. What if Paul and his friend Ryan hadn't taken the boat out that day? What if the *Carpe Diem* hadn't sunk? What if Sand Dollar Cove High had never had a tradition of painting class years on the lighthouse rocks?

Lost as she was in thought, the ten-minute drive to school passed quickly. After checking to see that her bra strap wasn't showing underneath her floral peasant blouse, she stepped out of her SUV. She hurried toward the double doors that led into the office and pulled on the handle with all her might, only to end up yanking on a locked door. Brittany rubbed her aching shoulder joint. Of course the door was locked. This wasn't the olden days when she'd been in high school, and nobody knew phrases like "lockdown drill" or "school shoot-ing." Gah! What a horrible world for her son to grow up in. She pressed the doorbell and waited for the secretary to buzz her inside.

"Hi," Brittany said, as she smiled at the secretary in what she hoped was a friendly manner. "I'm here to pick up my son, Jeremy Willis."

"Sign the clipboard and wait in one of the blue chairs," the secretary told her, before looking back at her computer screen.

Brittany signed in and sat down. She crossed her ankles, rested her purse on her lap, and stared at the wall beside her. There was a collection of student artwork, as well as a group shot of the current school board. The principal's face was up there, too, looking professional and all-knowing. But it was the faded color photo in the corner that spoke to her heart. The familiar blue eyes looking right into her soul.

Hopping to her feet, Brittany crossed the room and found herself face to face with Paul's senior photo. His birth and death year were engraved beneath it, along with a photo of him in his letterman's jacket. Every player on his basketball team had autographed the mat around the pictures. Without realizing what she was doing, Brittany raised her fingertips up to the glass, as she searched for the name she most wanted to avoid: Ryan Osborne. There it was, in inky black. Paul's best friend and fellow prankster. It had been Ryan's fault they had sailed on the *Carpe Diem* that night. Ryan was the one to blame for Paul's death. He thought everything was a joke, and that high school was one caper after another, until it wasn't. Ryan's irresponsible antics had brought forth deadly consequences.

Bitterness bubbled in her heart like a scalding hot poison. She'd never forgive Ryan as long as she lived. If it weren't for him, Paul would be alive.

"I see you've spotted young Paul Thompson's photo." The secretary clucked her tongue. "Such a tragic loss for the whole community. One minute he was full of life and the school's star basketball player, and the next he was gone."

Brittany blinked back the tears that were forming and tried to push away the awful memory that came with them, but it was too late.

Paul! she remembered shouting into the storm until it felt like her lungs would burst. *Come back to me!* The cold had rattled her bones so badly that her whole body shook with icy terror. She'd scanned the choppy water and spotted the overturned hull of the *Carpe Diem* floating listlessly in the water. The next thing she'd seen was the Coast Guard vessel inching toward them, like the Grim Reaper.

Brittany swallowed hard and forced herself back into the present.

"Mrs. Willis," the secretary said, waving to get her attention. "The principal is ready for you now."

Brittany turned slowly. "It's Ms. Thompson," she said stoically. She'd shaken off Ian's surname like it was a bad cold. "Paul Thompson was my brother."

The secretary shook her head. "Oh, I'm so sorry, dear, I didn't realize."

Her phone buzzed with an incoming text from Keith and she glanced down to read it.

You're fired.

Brittany lifted her chin. Holding onto her purse strap like it was a life raft, she walked into the principal's office.

Jeremy sat in the corner, his head hanging down. He looked up at her, hopefully. "Mom," he said in a soft voice, before his posture drooped.

She smiled bravely for him. But inwardly, her heart panicked. The teenage years were fraught with peril and survival wasn't guaranteed. She wanted her son to have a rich life full of purpose and wise choices. But she didn't know how to help him accomplish that.

She didn't even know how to accomplish that for herself.

TWO

Thank goodness for lawyers. It was two months later, and one of the last Saturdays in August. Brittany held the keys to her very own, brand-new cafe. Over the summer, Brittany had sued the city for wrongful termination and sexual harassment. So many seniors wrote witness statements on Brittany's behalf that the city got scared, and settled quickly out of court. The windfall of money was just enough for a down payment on a storefront, with some extra to install a kitchen and make her long-cherished dream of running her own place come true. Brittany was opening a cafe that would be a welcoming space for residents, as well as the tourists who flocked to Sand Dollar Cove. Maybe this would be a chance for her to finally do something worth remembering.

The little beach town was one of Washington State's most popular vacation destinations. Situated on the Olympic Peninsula, smack-dab against the Pacific Ocean, Sand Dollar Cove boasted expansive beaches, sand dunes, tide pools, and the best fishing south of Alaska. Airbnbs had become popular, and the fifty-cottage property called Seaside Resort delighted visitors with fine dining and a spa. Tourists weren't the only invaders.

Remote workers came too, gobbling up the housing market and making it so that Brittany no longer recognized half the people she saw at the town's only grocery store.

The only thing Sand Dollar Cove didn't have was a casual dining option that focused on sandwiches and salads. Brittany had dreamt of owning her own restaurant ever since she was a young girl, and Paul had always told her that she made the best sandwiches in town. Now at last her dream was a reality, thanks to the settlement money.

"Have you thought of a name yet, for the cafe?" Mary asked. The young woman stood next to her with her blonde hair tied in a bandana and her sleeves pushed up, ready to clean. Brittany rented rooms in her house to Mary, her sister Hannah, and their grandmother Cheryl, but she thought of them as close friends more than just housemates.

"No name just yet," said Brittany. "I've been mulling it over for weeks, unable to decide on anything." Turning the key, Brittany unlocked the door and flipped on the light.

"It looks amazing," Mary exclaimed. "Quaint and cozy at the same time."

"I couldn't have done it without you as my interior designer." Brittany walked across the room and flicked another light switch that illuminated the counter, refrigerated display case, and sneeze guard. Two stainless steel sinks and loads of shelving completed the space. A doorway led to a tiny back room which provided storage, a refrigerator, and an industrial dishwasher.

"We just have some finishing touches to do, like replacing these blinds." Mary pushed a wooden chair next to the windows and stepped onto the seat. "When is your soft opening again?" She wrestled the blinds off the frame.

"Four days from now. I know that's rushing it, but I wanted to catch some of the summer foot traffic before this place becomes a ghost town after Labor Day."

"Raking in the tourist dollars makes sense," said Mary. "This place just needs a good deep clean before you can open."

Brittany grabbed a spray bottle of disinfectant. "My folks are coming to help. Separately, of course, since they can't stand each other."

That was putting it lightly. Cynthia and Alan Thompson had been married for thirty-five years and divorced for fourteen and still managed to loathe each other as much as they did the day they signed the separation papers. Brittany's father was an orthodontist and habitual cheater. He was brilliant at braces, and wonderful with patients, but didn't have a clue about running a business. The success of his orthodontic practice was due in large part to Cynthia, who was his business manager. They kept up a cool veneer of professionalism in the office, but that civility didn't extend outside of work, where Cynthia's hot temper led to nasty fights.

When Paul had been alive, things had been different. He'd been the family peacemaker. The only thing Cynthia and Alan had agreed on was how exceptional their son was. They cheered for him at every basketball game, beamed with pride at his Eagle Scout Court of Honor, and complimented him on his stellar report cards. Brittany had always felt ordinary compared to her brother, but that had been okay, because she'd hero-worshiped him too. Once Paul died, every argument between her parents had morphed into a verbal boxing match.

"Is your dad bringing his fiancée with him?" Mary asked. "I want to see if she lives up to my gold digger expectations."

"If you mean silicon, Botox, and hair extensions, you won't be disappointed. I told you Tansy and I went to high school together, right? She was one year behind me." Brittany sprayed the chair rail with cleaner and wiped away grime. "I'm not expecting my parents to actually help that much either, but Jeremy promised to stop by this afternoon and lend a hand. My goal for this morning is to de-gunk the place by noon."

"And make it shine." Mary kicked the old blinds. "Where should I put these?"

"There's a dumpster in the alley. I'll get them for you."

"No, that's okay. I can do it." Mary picked up the broken mini blinds and hauled them away.

Brittany squirted cleaner onto her rag and paused for a moment, gazing around the space. The brickwork was original, as were the exposed wooden beams overhead made of old-growth cedar. Lumber like that couldn't be purchased anymore. The timber industry was still active in Washington State, but old-growth trees were now protected. The floor was unusual too, made of fir boards with knots. It wasn't something you could buy at a big-box store like The Home Depot. No, this building was special.

"We should give the floors a good scrubbing with Murphy's Oil soap," Mary said, when she came back. "Then we can protect them with a gloss finish."

"I like the sound of that."

"We might also want to spray down the brickwork with a light vinegar solution."

Brittany flipped her rag over and used the clean side to keep scrubbing. "I have a mop, and I have floor cleaner, but I don't have vinegar or polish."

Mary looked at her watch. "I can run to the store really quick."

"Thank you." Brittany smiled. "Just be sure to collect the receipts so that I can reimburse you, okay?"

"Will do." Mary picked up her purse. "See if you can do the mopping first, because the floors will need a chance to dry before the gloss coating."

"I'm on it."

Five minutes later, Brittany was mopping the floor, and lost in thought. Was this a huge mistake? Starting over with a brand-new career at forty-five years old? Brittany used to be free-spirited, but that was a long time ago. She wasn't the same young woman who'd spent nearly a year backpacking alone through Europe after college. Now, instead of designing jewelry and dreaming of her next getaway, she was more likely to be found on the couch playing Wordle. The only thing she felt confident about was her carefully planned cafe menu.

"Yoo-hoo!" A voice called from the front door. "Are you open yet?"

Brittany would recognize her mother's nasal-toned voice anywhere. She picked up the mop and bucket so they wouldn't stain the wood floors and crossed the room to greet Cynthia. "Hi, Mom," she said, as she held open the door. "Thanks for coming."

"Like my new shades?" Cynthia took off her sunglasses, revealing blue eyes that were an icier tone than Brittany's. "I picked them up at Walmart in the sale bin."

"Nice." Brittany pointed with the mop handle. "That part of the floor is wet, so be careful."

"I'm not surprised to see you hard at work. Like mother, like daughter." Cynthia was seventy-one and in good health. She remained in charge of billing, scheduling, and other admin tasks for the orthodontics practice and primarily worked from home.

"I'm really glad you came," said Brittany. "Mary will be here any minute with the floor protectant. I need help with the prep work."

Cynthia brushed a lock of gray hair behind her ear. "And I wish I could help you with that, but I'm doing something more important." She opened her tote bag and pulled out a computer. "I wiped the hard drive of my old notebook for you, and have it loaded up with accounting software. I'll get your books set up by the end of the day."

"Thanks," Brittany said, feeling overwhelmed. "But I was just going to create a spreadsheet, or something."

"Oh, we can do better than *that*," Cynthia said with a

wheeze of laughter. "I assume you've been keeping track of your expenses?"

"Yes. Absolutely. All the receipts are in an accordion folder in my desk."

"Okey-dokey, then." Cynthia clutched her bag. "I'll get right to it."

"Watch out for the wet floor!" Brittany cautioned. "Parts of it are slippery." Over the years Brittany had learned that it was best to stay out of her mom's way.

"Why are these receipts stapled?" Cynthia called out a few minutes later. "That makes them harder to file."

"Sorry!" Brittany said before she went back to mopping. She always apologized to her mother, even if she really shouldn't. It was easier not to make waves. That was a lesson Paul had taught her; not that Paul had ever had to apologize for anything. *Unless that damn Ryan Osborne was involved*, she thought bitterly.

Looking back, Brittany was ashamed of her teenage crush on Ryan, her brother's best friend. It had been puppy love, nothing more, but knowing how much she'd cared for him made her angry. She'd thought everything about Ryan was swoon-worthy, from the way his dark hair flopped over to one side, to the way he always sneezed three times in a row. All Ryan had to do was look at her, and her knees turned to jelly. On the rare occasion that he said her name, she melted into hearts and rainbows.

Cynthia had never liked the Osbornes, and called them trashy, but Brittany couldn't care less about what her mother said. It didn't matter to her that the Thompsons had money and the Osbornes did not. Even Ryan's beat-up truck had enchanted her. Ryan and his father Frank had fixed it up together. Brittany had thought it was so cool that Ryan could repair things. She'd been impressed at the time, but now she realized that thinking of him so highly had been stupid.

Ryan's recklessness had caused Paul's death. Ryan thought he was made of Teflon and nothing dangerous would ever stick. There's no way in hell Paul would have stayed out so long on the *Carpe Diem* that night without Ryan egging him on. That's why, even if the authorities claimed Ryan wasn't to blame for the accident, Brittany knew, deep in her soul, that he was. He should have turned the boat back the moment the weather soured.

She gave the mop an angry swish and took out her angst on the floor. Twenty minutes later, she was cleaning out the bucket in the bathroom sink when Mary returned.

"It looks great in here!" Mary said, popping up behind Brittany. "Well done."

"Thanks." Brittany whacked the bucket against the counter to drain the last drops of dirty water. "The floor should be dry by now, too. The back of the shop, at least."

"Is that you, Mary?" Cynthia called, poking her head out of the back room.

"Hi, Ms. Thompson. Nice to see you again." Mary waved. "How handy are you with floor polish?"

"Not handy at all." Cynthia wrinkled her nose. "But I'm a whiz at QuickBooks." She darted back into her cubbyhole.

"Cleaning is up to you and me, I'm afraid." Brittany tucked a strand of curly brown hair behind her ear. "But Jeremy should be here eventually, and my dad promised to come after..." She glanced behind her. "After my mom left," she whispered. "I'm supposed to text him."

"Wise plan." Mary lifted two bags from the hardware store. "Let's clean the brick first before we polish the floors."

"Sounds good to me," said Brittany.

It was over an hour later, when the whole place stank of vinegar and wet brick, that inspiration struck.

"The bricks look so much fresher," Mary commented, as she squirted the last spray of cleaner from the bottle.

"They sure do. We're really getting this place shipshape." As soon as she said it, Brittany felt a tingle of excitement. The word shipshape had triggered a vision that was the perfect name for the shop. She put down her bottle and looked at Mary. "What do you think of calling the restaurant Safe Harbor?"

"Yes!" Mary clapped her hands. "I love it! Nautical themes always work well, this close to the beach."

"Speaking of decorations, I had something—"

"Is it safe to come out now, or will vinegar fumes attack me?" Cynthia emerged from the back room and interrupted Brittany.

"We're all done cleaning the brick, but it's going to be floor polish fumes next," said Mary.

"Sounds like my cue to leave, then." Cynthia slung her purse over her shoulder. "How about I swing over to McDonald's and order lunch to go? You two must be starving by now."

"I wouldn't say no to a burger." Brittany reached for her purse. "But my treat, as a thank you both for your help."

"I'd like a burger *and* a milkshake." Cynthia tapped on her phone screen. "I think the app has a coupon right now."

"Sounds delicious," said Mary.

Brittany was just fishing bills out of her wallet when the back door opened.

"We can park in the alley, right?" boomed a familiar voice. "I've always wanted to do that."

"Dad," Brittany said, her face freezing into a fake smile. "You're here early."

"And we brought you lunch from the T Bone Bluff," said a breathy voice behind him.

Brittany felt the back of her neck tense up. "Tansy came, too. How... lovely."

Seventy-three-year-old Alan sauntered across the freshly mopped floor wearing crisply pressed linen shorts and a polo shirt. Tansy, his forty-four-year-old fiancée, tottered behind him wearing high-heeled espadrilles and a snowy-white sundress that was only a few shades brighter than her platinum-blonde hair.

"Are you here to work, or to enter a golf tournament?" Cynthia asked with a sneer.

Alan put the food on the counter. "I'm here to make sure my baby girl is well fed and knows that she's the second most important woman in the world to me."

"Thanks, Dad." That did it; Brittany's face was in danger of cracking, her smile was so frozen. She managed to soften it when Tansy gave her air kisses.

"I love what you've done with the place," Tansy gushed. "It's so... rustic, and open for possibilities."

"It'll look more complete once the rest of the furniture arrives tonight," said Mary, who was unscrewing the lid to the floor polish. "You must be Dr. Thompson and Tansy. I've heard a lot about you."

Cynthia sniffed. "I bet you have."

"Dad, Tansy," Brittany said, ignoring her mother. "This is my housemate and interior designer, Mary Turner. She's the genius behind the renovation."

"Nice to meet you." Alan pumped Mary's hand in a bone-gripping handshake. "I hope you haven't already designed around a sound system, because that's what we've come to install."

"Huh?" Brittany asked.

"I think the plan was to use a streaming service and a couple of speakers," said Mary. She looked at Brittany for confirmation, and Brittany nodded.

"That'll still work, but wait until you see what we bought you!" Tansy jumped up and down, causing her gravity-defying cleavage to shake. "The best speaker system money can buy, one for each corner."

"Surround sound." Alan nodded. "It'll be incredible."

"Nobody talks about surround sound anymore." Cynthia rolled her eyes. "This isn't the 1990s."

"But you'll swear you're at a concert with Kenny G once you hear his saxophone belting from this system we bought you," said Alan.

"You can hook it up to Spotify, no problem," Tansy added. "I can help you if you don't know how to do that. I used to work at Best Buy."

"I know how to use Spotify, Tansy, but thanks for the offer," said Brittany. "And thanks, Dad, for the present. That was really, uh... thoughtful of you."

"I knew you'd love it." Alan beamed. "Let's go get the boxes from my car." He headed out the way he came.

"I'd help, but..." Tansy waved her hands across her lacy white outfit. "I'm wearing the boating outfit I bought at Ann Taylor. Your father and I are going sailing after this."

Brittany winced. Alan's boat was a triggering subject.

"I still can't believe Alan bought a boat when our only son died on one," Cynthia exclaimed. "It's like he has no feelings at all."

"Alan has plenty of feelings." Tansy put her hand on her hip. "You're just a bad listener, is all."

"I am not!" Cynthia protested.

"Tansy, I hear you're redesigning the house," Brittany said, trying to change the subject.

"That's right, I am." Tansy looked at Mary. "I do want to hear more about your interior design services. Our house is so dated, I groan every time I walk into the kitchen."

"*Your* house?" Cynthia paled.

"Oh, that's right." Tansy flipped her hair back. "I forgot that you used to live there, too. Was that ugly purple tile in the kitchen installed before you moved in? That must have been awful, having to live with that for so long."

"I picked the tile out myself." Cynthia's face had transformed from ghostly white to eggplant purple, which, ironically, was the same shade as the kitchen.

"Okay then." Mary grabbed Tansy by the arm. "Why don't you come with me to my car, and I'll show you my design portfolio. I always keep a duplicate in my trunk."

"Shove her in the trunk, while you're at it," Cynthia growled.

"Mom!" Brittany said. "That's not nice."

"You're taking *her* side?" Cynthia jerked her finger toward Tansy, even as Mary dragged the woman out the front door.

"I'm not taking anyone's side." Brittany felt her neck become hot, like she was having an allergic reaction to stress.

"Of course you're not. You never stick up for me. All your father has to do is bribe you with expensive presents and you immediately forget how awful he is."

"That's not true," Brittany protested, thinking her mother was pretty awful, too.

"Isn't it? Have fun with your surround sound, and your overpriced meal from the steak house that's probably soggy by now." Cynthia kicked the empty mop bucket and marched out the door.

Brittany was so rattled she hardly noticed when her phone rang. It buzzed three times in a row before she realized what the noise was and that she needed to answer it. She fished it out just in time. "Hello?" she asked weakly. Her skin felt clammy, like it often did when people yelled at her.

"Hi, Mom."

Hearing Jeremy's voice helped her calm down for a moment, until she immediately worried about why he was calling instead of texting. Jeremy only called when something was wrong. "Is everything okay?" she asked.

"Things are great," he said excitedly. "It's only that... I'm sorry, but I can't come and help after all."

"Oh." Brittany's pulse was beginning to settle. It was still elevated, but she was calmer now. "You can't? Why not?"

"I was offered this amazing opportunity to do a ride along on a firetruck. It'll be so great for my prep to become a firefighter. The shift starts in an hour."

"That's great." The back door opened, and she saw her father walk in carrying an enormous box.

"I knew you'd understand," said Jeremy. "I'll be sure to help later this week. Maybe I could clean out the rain gutters on the house or something."

"That's nice of you to offer." Brittany hated climbing up on the ladder and she couldn't afford to hire professional gutter cleaners. "Good luck tonight. I love you."

"Love you too, Mom."

Brittany ended the call, feeling like she was at her limit of what her nervous system could endure. Then her father spoke up.

"Was that my grandson on the phone?" Alan asked, as he sliced open the speaker box.

"Yup." Brittany nodded. "Jeremy says hi." He hadn't, but it was easier to pretend like he had.

Not wanting to elaborate further, she walked over to the cloth-covered bulletin board she'd been meaning to show Mary earlier and lifted it up for comfort. Brittany had seen a board like this at a coffee shop in Seattle and always wanted to have one of her own. Colorful fabric and padding covered a small corkboard, with satin ribbon crisscrossing the board in a diamond pattern. Up at the top in elegant script was a message:

Angel Board
Your chance to do good. Gift a $5 credit for coffee to someone who could use some lifting up. Pay at the register and we'll give you a card to write an encouraging message.

Next to the bulletin board was a box with blank notecards. Brittany had already pinned one to the board as an example:

For a mother whose firstborn is heading off to college. You're not an empty nester; you're a bird launcher. Fly, little bird, fly!

Brittany felt perked up just looking at the board and knowing all the good it could do. This was exactly the type of heartfelt community building that she'd envisioned for Safe Harbor's future.

"What's that?" Mary asked as she came back inside without Tansy.

Brittany showed it to her and explained how the board worked. "What do you think?" she asked, hesitantly.

"That's brilliant!" Mary exclaimed. "I love it!"

"Really?"

"Absolutely." Mary gave her a side hug. "And don't worry about whipping this place into shape. I've called in reinforcements."

"You have?"

Mary nodded. "Hannah's coming as soon as her shift is done at Seaside Resort, and Guy and Steven are coming, too."

Relief washed over Brittany like a cool spring. Knowing that her housemate Hannah, Hannah's fiancé Guy, and Mary's boyfriend Steven were on their way to assist gave her hope that she might actually be ready for the soft opening in a few days. Her family might have been less than helpful, but her family of friends would save the day. "That's amazing," Brittany said as tears welled up in her blue eyes. "Thank you so much."

But even as she said it, Brittany's mind went back to worrying that she'd made a huge mistake. She was forty-five years old and felt like a failure. Her marriage to Ian had gone kaput. Her relationship with Keith had ended in flames. She couldn't afford her mortgage without renting out rooms, and it was impossible to spend ten minutes with her parents before all hell broke loose. Her shop was probably doomed before it opened. This was pure hubris! She was a grown woman trying to make a childish dream come true, nothing more. It didn't matter what she called this building, safety and calm would never be possible for her. Turmoil had been part of her life for thirty years, ever since Paul had died. Her brother had been her anchor. Without Paul's steadying presence, Brittany had lived her life adrift.

THREE

As a little girl, one of Brittany's favorite things to do was go tide-pooling with Paul. Together they would creep along rocks, peering down into shallow water, searching for signs of life. Dungeness crab scurried across seaweed and urchins waited with prickly spines. But Brittany's favorite creatures to encounter were sea stars. She adored their vibrant colors and laughed at their whimsical names. Paul seemed to know them all: bat star, slime star, gunpowder, spiny red, and many more. Brittany hadn't seen a sea star in ages since she was too afraid to go near the ocean. But six days after Safe Harbor's soft opening, she felt like she'd become a sea star herself. It was like her arms were stretched out, clinging desperately into position, as waves of customers washed into her shop.

It turned out that residents and tourists alike had been yearning for a place that offered sandwiches and fresh salads. Safe Harbor's soft opening had gone better than anyone could have predicted. People were whispering those magical words, "overnight success" about the place. But Brittany was cautious. She worried that this first week of sales had been a fluke. Her shop was still a novelty, after all. But still... she'd sold out of everything she'd made three days in a row and had earned twice as much as she'd predicted on brewing fancy coffee drinks. The tourists from Seattle really liked their alternative milk lattes.

Yesterday had been Labor Day, bringing with it the last burst of out-of-town visitors before summer ended. Brittany's calves hurt from being on her feet all day. She might need to hire a part-time employee—or buy more comfortable shoes, at the very least. Now it was five o'clock on Tuesday morning, and Brittany was unloading groceries from her car. She'd parked temporarily in the alley, so it would be easier to carry bags into the kitchen.

The shop wouldn't open for two hours, but Brittany needed this early morning time to prepare food. Brittany slung the grocery bag filled with eggs on one arm and carried a ten-pound bag of flour on her hip like it was a baby. Safe Harbor didn't have an oven, but she had two bread machines. Hopefully, the scent of freshly baked cinnamon bread continued to reel customers in.

She was so focused on balancing the flour, she didn't watch where she was going. Five steps away from the car and *bam!* She walked into what felt like an iron wall. The flour bag thrust forward in a cloud of white dust. Brittany stumbled backward, limbs flailing, trying to steady herself before falling. She just barely stayed upright, but unfortunately, the two dozen eggs she was carrying weren't so lucky. The carton slipped out of the bag and landed on the asphalt with a *crack.*

"What in the hell?" asked a gruff voice.

"Huh?" Brittany asked, still dazed by the impact. Looking up, she saw a ghost.

A literal ghost.

At least, that's what the flour-coated figure in front of her appeared to be. Every inch of the person was covered in a powdery white film. As for Brittany, she hadn't been spared either. Luckily for her, only her left arm was hit. Still, the encounter unnerved her.

"You should watch where you're going," she exclaimed.

"No, you watch where *you're* going," growled the ghost, before sneezing three times in a row.

Three times in a row.

Tickles crept up her spine. Throughout her entire life, Brittany had only known one person who sneezed three times in a row like that: Ryan Osborne. But there was no way it was him. Ryan hadn't set foot in this town in over thirty years—at least as far as she knew.

"I *was* watching where I was going," Brittany said stoutly, even though that wasn't exactly true. She looked at the figure carefully.

The man wiped his sleeve across his face, brushing away the fine particles, and glared down at her.

Brittany gasped. It *was* him! The person responsible for Paul's death.

Ryan Osborne stood in front of her, looking as angry as he had been on the day of Paul's funeral.

Only she wasn't a devastated teenager anymore. She was a grown woman ready to unleash her fury.

"What are you doing here?" Brittany demanded.

"Do I know you?" He brushed another bit of flour out of his eyes.

"Sure, pretend like you don't know me," she said, feeling insulted. Brittany knew she'd aged considerably over the past three decades, but that didn't mean she was unrecognizable. "Once an asshole, always an asshole. And it wouldn't be the first time you ignored my existence like a self-important jerk. The only difference is that nobody cares how many points you shot at the last basketball game, and I'm not baking you cookies." She stooped down to clean up the egg mess.

"I don't—"

"And you didn't answer my question," she continued, glaring up at him. "What are you doing here, sneaking up on me like this? Wrecking my groceries." *Destroying my life.*

"Brittany?" he asked. "Brittany Thompson? Is that you?"

"Took you long enough."

"I've got flour in my eyes."

"And whose fault is that? You should look where you're going."

"I could say the same thing about you." Ryan bent down to pick up the fallen flour bag. "It's not safe for a woman to walk alone through dark alleys without being aware of her surroundings. Someone could have attacked you."

"This isn't Seattle, it's Sand Dollar Cove." *Idiot.* "And I don't need your advice about anything." Brittany stuffed the gooey egg carton back into her canvas grocery bag. "Save your mansplaining for someone who cares."

"You used to love my advice."

"Yeah, well, people are dumb when they're teenagers. You of all people should know that."

Brittany trembled, her memory rewinding to the past. Ryan was correct. Back when she was the younger sister tagging after Paul and his best friend, she'd hung on every word Ryan uttered. Her tender crush on him had been powerful, and all-consuming. She'd written her name linked with his in her notebook and drawn a heart around it. She'd memorized his class schedule at Sand Dollar High so she could happen to walk past him in the hall when he collected books from his locker.

She'd done other dumb stuff, too, like bake his favorite cookies—chocolate thumbprints—every time he came over to shoot baskets in the driveway with Paul. She had hoped, pitifully, that Ryan would finally notice her as someone other than his friend's little sister. That he would wake up and realize that the two-year age gap wasn't insurmountable. But with Ryan it was always the same-old, same-old. He would chat with her if

Paul was around, and he'd gobble up her freshly baked cookies, but in the school hallways he barely acknowledged her existence.

"I don't need to be reminded of teenagers doing dumb things." Ryan dusted flour off his arms. "That's my lived experience."

"I bet," she said nastily.

"It was an accident," he blurted.

That word—accident—hovered between them like a mist. *What accident is Ryan talking about?* Brittany wondered. *Bumping into me just now, or killing my one and only brother?*

"I was looking for bats," Ryan clarified. "I'm sorry I bumped into you."

"Looking for bats?" Brittany repeated, because that didn't make any sense. "Why were you looking for bats? Who does that?"

"Lots of people." Ryan took a step back. "Some people watch birds, I'd rather observe bats. Dawn and dusk are the best times to spot them."

"Oh."

"I saw some flying into that building over there." He pointed to the roof of Safe Harbor.

Brittany looked to where he was directing her. "That's my cafe. Damn, the property inspector was right."

"He warned you there was a colony before you moved in?"

"The word 'colony' wasn't mentioned, but yeah." Now that Ryan had taken the blame for their collision, she felt slightly guilty. She hadn't been looking where she was going either, but she wasn't ready to admit that. Instead, she extended an olive branch. "Why don't you come into my shop and clean up in the restroom? That way you keep your eyeballs gluten-free."

"Thanks," he muttered. "I'd appreciate that. Maybe I could get a look at the bats while I'm at it."

"That's unlikely. I've never seen any vermin, flying or otherwise, in the working space of my building. There's no risk of food contamination."

"Whatever you say." Ryan kept his head down and followed her.

They didn't speak while she unlocked the back door and led him down the tiny hallway toward the front of the cafe. "Here's the batroom," she said. "I mean bathroom," she corrected herself. "I'll bring you a couple of dish towels from the kitchen."

"Thank you. I'll try not to make too much of a mess." Ryan turned on the faucet.

"Good luck with that." Brittany glanced down at his floury footprints. "I'll go find the mop." She came back a minute later with three towels and a bunch of questions. "I still don't understand why you were looking for bats. Do you run a pest control business or something?"

Ryan chuckled. "No." He used the first towel to brush additional flour into the sink. "I'm just fascinated by them." Ryan held the towel underneath the stream of water, before using it to wipe his face.

Once the chalky whiteness was cleared away, Brittany got a better look at him. He was still the handsome heartthrob she remembered. Wavy brown hair. Square jawline. Dark eyes that pierced your soul. But now he had a weathered look, like a cowboy who'd just come back from the range. It wasn't fair how good he looked. It was sexist, really. Why should Ryan look weathered, and she wrinkled? Did he worry if his retinol cream was a high enough percentage? Brittany doubted it. Probably Ryan washed his face with bar soap, when he remembered to, and headed off into the world looking like Pedro Pascal.

So unfair!

"Why are you staring at me like that?" Ryan asked. "Did I miss a spot?"

"No." Brittany felt embarrassed to have been caught checking him out. She quickly changed the subject. "Your dad liked bats, right? He sold bat boxes at the county fair." It had been one of Frank Osborne's multitude of side hustles.

"He did," Ryan nodded. "He built them, too."

"Your dad was always good at fixing things." It was the kindest thing she could think of to say about a man whom Paul had called a drunk and Cynthia referred to as a louse.

"He was handy with a lot of things." Ryan used the last bit of clean towel to wipe off the bathroom counter.

"I'm sorry about Frank getting Alzheimer's," Brittany said, in a somber tone.

"It's a cruel disease." Ryan wadded up the soiled towels. "Look, I apologize that I can't stay and mop the floor for you, but I've got a work call with a team in India. I need to hurry home, or I'll be late."

"That sounds important. What do you do?"

"I'm a director of marketing."

"Oh. That's impressive considering..."

"Considering what?" He narrowed his eyes.

"That... you know..."

"No, I don't." Ryan folded his arms across his chest.

"Considering that you weren't planning on applying to college at all until Paul forced you to take the SAT your Junior year." There, she'd said it. She'd named the elephant in the room. *Paul.*

"He did." Ryan brushed past her in his haste to leave the restroom. "I need to be going."

"You said that already."

"Uh-huh. Bye, bye, Britt."

"Later," Brittany managed to respond, her voice hoarse. She felt like she'd been sucker-punched.

Bye, bye, Britt...

That's what Paul used to say to her too before he and Ryan would go off on one of their adventures. Ryan had no right to echo her brother's words. Or had they been Ryan's words all along, and Brittany couldn't remember? It had been so long, after all, and she'd worked so hard to push those memories away. It wasn't that she didn't want to remember her brother, but thinking about Paul made his absence hurt even more.

The back door shut, signaling that Ryan had left the building. It was a relief knowing that he was gone, but there was an emptiness there, too. It had been impossible for Brittany to look at Ryan without feeling Paul's presence sticking to him like flour paste.

Why was Ryan here in Sand Dollar Cove? She should have asked him when she'd had the opportunity, instead of rambling on about bats. Hopefully this was only a temporary visit, otherwise she would be constantly looking over her shoulder, worrying he'd sneak up on her again. She didn't need that painful reminder of everything she'd lost hanging around.

Brittany swallowed her grief and got to work, tidying up the bathroom. She turned on some music before she washed her hands and began cooking. Since the business wasn't open, she could pump up the volume on the surround sound speakers her dad had installed. Nineties pop songs always boosted her mood.

Work like this, so early in the morning, was difficult for Brittany, who had never been an early riser. But she was a breakfast-and-lunch joint, not a fine dining establishment. When she closed up shop at four p.m., she'd have the whole evening to herself to do things she enjoyed, like walking along the beach at a safe distance from the water, watching travel shows, or indulging in a glass of wine on her back deck by the canal.

Paul would have kayaked, she thought, before she could stop herself. *Kayaked, or paddleboarded.* That realization came to her unprompted, as she pictured the canal.

Built in the 1960s to be a tourist destination, Sand Dollar Cove featured human-engineered canals that allowed homeowners to sail from their personal docks to the beach. "The Riviera of the West," the promotional brochures had called it.

Sixty years later the canals were a maintenance nightmare for homeowners' associations, but they still worked as promised.

Paul would have loved my house, Brittany thought, as she peeled carrots. It should have made her feel happy, knowing that she was living in his dream house, but it didn't. What would have made her happy would have been Paul, stopping by her house after work for a barbecue. Paul, helping her fix her untrustworthy garage door opener. Paul, parking his boat on her private dock. Paul, celebrating his forty-seventh birthday and insisting that he couldn't blow out all the birthday candles without her help. Tears splashed on her cheeks, and it wasn't because she was slicing onions.

Seeing Ryan brought back memories of Paul, alright. She wasn't strong enough to keep them at bay. Before she could stop herself, the worst memory of all floated across her subconscious like tangled seaweed.

Brittany, standing on the pier, screaming Paul's name into a jet-black storm.

Alan, sobbing beside her.

Cynthia, railing at her husband that this was all his fault.

Praying as the Coast Guard surfmen navigated their motor lifeboat through churning water, toward the sinking hull of the *Carpe Diem*.

The surfman captain later told them it was the spotlight that found Paul first. It caught a tiny patch of orange floating dangerously close to the lighthouse rocks. That was Paul's body buoyed by his life vest. Ryan had clung to the straps and waved frantically for help that arrived too late.

Brittany took a deep breath, trying to calm her rippling emotions. But then the 1990s pop station she was listening to played a Celine Dion ballad, and she totally lost it. They had played 'My Heart Will Go On' at Paul's funeral service. It was the only thing about the day that her parents had agreed upon. Brittany had thought it was a horrible choice, especially since

Titanic was a movie about drowning, but there was no reasoning with either of them.

The clock was ticking, and the time crept closer to opening hours. There were only twenty minutes left to finish her prep work, and stock the grab-and-go fridge. Once Celine stopped singing, Brittany blew her nose on a paper towel and washed her hands in the sink. She finished the salads robotically and snapped on the plastic lids. Then she carried them over to the front of the shop and put them in the refrigerated display. Ricky Martin was on the station now, and he was a lot easier for her to deal with.

After she'd stocked the salads, Brittany looked around the room, grounding herself in the space's serenity. Scattered across the middle of the floor were tables and chairs, in various configurations, as well as a communal table near the back that could accommodate a crowd. Brittany's favorite element was the bookshelf decorated with fairy lights along the side wall. Board games lined the top shelves, and books stocked the rest of it. It was a lending library that invited people to pull up a chair, or gather around a table and stay a while.

"Paul would have loved this place too," she murmured. "If only he could have been here now."

If only he could have been there all along...

Maybe with Paul's help she would have been able to convince Ian to go to marriage counseling with her earlier. Her marriage could have been saved, or perhaps her divorce would have gone smoother. Or maybe Paul would have seen red flags about Ian from the very beginning. Ian's selfishness and workaholic tendencies. The fact that they had so little in common.

Brittany had met Ian when she came home from Europe and needed a reliable car for her job as a roving convalescent hospital dietician. She was young, naive, and hungry for affection. Ian sold her a used Toyota Corolla that was within her budget and asked her out to dinner. He was cute and had given her a great deal on her car, so she said yes. But as soon as Ian got what he wanted—a live-in girlfriend who did all the cooking and cleaning even though Brittany worked full-time too, he stopped nurturing their relationship. He wasn't cruel like Keith; Ian was indifferent. Which was maybe worse...

Perhaps Paul would have warned her against marrying Ian in the first place. At the time, marriage seemed like the logical next step since they had lived together so long. But their marriage was like a plant Ian failed to water that died slowly of neglect. Of course, if Brittany hadn't continued her relationship with Ian, that would have meant not having Jeremy. Her son was her life's biggest blessing. But in less than two weeks Jeremy would be gone!

First her brother, and now her son. Brittany would be all alone in the world. Sure, Jeremy wasn't dying, but when her son moved away, he'd take another chunk of her heart along with him.

Dammit, the tears were falling again. What she needed to do was lock these emotions up in the tight box that contained them and shove them out of her mind. Her eyes drifted to the Angel Board, and she thought of a way to do exactly that. She had already penned a card for someone whose child was going off to college. Now she'd write one in honor of Paul.

Brittany walked back to the counter and plucked one of the notecards she kept underneath the register. Using her best handwriting, she wrote from the heart.

For someone who lost a brother. Every day without him hurts like hell, but the pain is precious because it's the only thing you have left.

Brittany pinned the card to the board, forced a smile on her face, and unlocked the front door.

FOUR

"I thought this line would last forever," Cheryl said, as she pushed her walker up to the register nine days later. "For a place that's only been open for two weeks, you're really bringing in the foot traffic."

"Sorry to keep you waiting." Brittany tightened her apron strings. "Today's been madness." She looked at Cheryl with concern, knowing that her housemate's osteoporosis made it difficult for her to stand too long. "Next time please jump to the front of the line. You're my one and only customer who gets to cut."

"I'm not above cutting, but I was trying to figure out what type of criminal activity the couple two spots ahead of me were up to. Did they pay in cash?"

"They used a credit card." Brittany's eyebrows shot up. "Why?"

Cheryl pointed discreetly behind her. "The man said free charging stations were the best, and then the wife said Seaside Resort had several. As soon as I've ordered, I'm calling Hannah to let her know the hotel is about to be robbed. They must be credit card fraudsters, or something."

"Or maybe they're driving an electric car." Brittany looked past Cheryl to the long line behind her. She knew her friend loved detective shows, and sometimes let her imagination get away with her, but she didn't have time to indulge her now. "Better talk it over with Hannah, just to be sure," she said kindly. "What can I get you?"

"I'd like the Gobble Gobble: turkey and cranberry cream cheese on white bread. But with none of those sprout things, like you put on last time. They got caught in my teeth."

"A custom order. You got it." Brittany rang the transaction up and made change from the twenty Cheryl gave her. "You can take a seat. I'll bring your plate to you."

"Thank you, dear. I'll try to sit next to the credit card thieves so I can gather more information before I call Hannah."

"Good plan." Brittany put on disposable gloves and picked up two slices of bread. "I'll be with you in jiff," she told the next customers in line. Custom sandwiches took longer but were an important part of her menu. She'd just barely plated the food when the bread machine behind her beeped. Brittany hurried to deliver Cheryl's lunch and then raced back to her spot behind the counter. She tore off her disposable gloves and replaced them with oven mitts to lift the loaf out of the machine.

"It's about time," said the next customer when Brittany stepped behind the register. "I can't believe the manager's having you work the lunch rush on your own." It was a woman with long black hair wearing yoga pants and a designer fleece jacket.

"I'm the manager," Brittany said in a pinched voice. "What can I get you?"

"Oh," the woman pouted. "My bad. Well, don't worry, hon, my order's easy. I just want a coffee to go."

"Great. Dark roast or medium?"

"Drip?" The woman laughed. "No, thank you. I'll take a 12

oz double cappuccino with extra foam, but only if you have one percent milk. You have one percent, right?"

"We have two percent or whole." Brittany said calmly. "As well as oat, soy, and hemp."

"Oh." The woman pursed her lips together. "Well, in that case, I'd like a 16 oz oolong green tea with two bags. It's organic, right?"

"That's right." Brittany nodded. "I'll get that for you now." The second bread machine beeped on her way to prepare the order. How did she think she could ever manage the counter by herself? She'd envisioned a slow trickle of customers her first few weeks of ownership, not a gush of hungry people waiting to be fed.

"Here's your tea," Brittany said, as she passed the cup to the woman. That'll be $3.80."

"What a bargain!" The woman whipped out her credit card. "I love how cheap things are around here."

"Cheap is a relative term," said a deep voice behind her. It was Don from the senior center, along with Patti Osborne, Ryan's mother.

Patti's presence made Brittany flinch. She'd developed a respectful working relationship with the woman since she'd interacted with her for several years at the senior center. But seeing Patti now reminded Brittany of her floury encounter with Ryan last week. Thankfully, Brittany hadn't run into Ryan since. But he was always there, in the back of her mind, waiting to smack into her again and destroy everything she held dear.

"Cheap is accurate," said the woman with the tea. "This would cost seven dollars in Seattle, at least." She adjusted the cardboard sleeve on her paper cup before walking away.

"Thank goodness we're not in Seattle," Don muttered, as he stepped up to the counter. "I'll take a Prosciutto's a Pesto, and the little lady here will have La Grande Dame."

"I've never tried ham and brie before," said Patti. "Is it good?"

"My son Jeremy loves La Grande Dame," Brittany said as she slipped on a new pair of gloves. "He taste-tested the entire menu for me. I developed most of the recipes based on places I visited in my twenties when I used to travel."

"I remember you taking off for Europe after college," said Patti. "I always admired your gumption."

"I had a few scrapes, but I really got my use out of the Euro-rail pass my dad gave me as a graduation present." Brittany laid out the slices of bread. "You're the fifth and sixth people I've seen from the senior center today. I appreciate you coming."

"Thank you for providing an alternative to neon-yellow macaroni and cheese," Don grumbled.

"Neon yellow?" Brittany layered a slice of brie over the bread and popped it into the toaster oven. "What was the other meal?" When she'd been in charge of nutrition, she'd always included two options, with at least one of them being a good choice for diabetics.

"There was no other option," said Patti. "Since you've left things have really gone downhill."

"I heard there had been some employee turnover." Brittany spread pesto on a slice of white bread.

"It's gotten so bad that I've contemplated cooking at home, only I don't know how to cook." Don poked Patti gently in the arm. "Maybe you could give me private lessons later?"

Patti giggled. "That could probably be arranged."

"I don't understand how the food at the senior center could have gone downhill so fast." Brittany laid a pickle on each plate.

"It's because the new nutritionist thinks we should all live on frozen meals," said Patti.

"And they're gross." Don clucked his tongue. "Ann had to be rushed to the hospital after her blood sugar went haywire."

"Oh, no!" Brittany exclaimed. "Is she okay?"

"It was a close call." Patti stepped nearer to Don, and hugged his arm. "I took her poodle home with me while she was in the hospital, and then when she came back to the center again, Keith told her that dogs were no longer allowed."

"Ann purchased one of those therapy dog certificates off the internet for Nugget, but Keith said they were bogus," said Don.

"And that means that our plans for a dog fashion show are completely off the table." Patti shook her head. "Even though I've spent the past month on pattern development."

"I want to hear all about it, but your lunch is ready, and I should help the next customer." Brittany plated the sandwiches and took off her gloves.

"And I want to hear about how you're doing now that Jeremy's going off to college," said Patti. "That's a big change."

Brittany's muscles tensed as she contemplated Jeremy's upcoming departure. All her family relationships were like scar tissue building on top of each other. Life without her son was impossible to even think about.

"How's that fine boy of yours settling in?" Don asked.

"He hasn't left yet," Brittany managed to say. "His classes don't begin until mid-September."

Jeremy would attend a community college in Seattle and live with Ian. He would earn his two-year fire science degree and also train to be an Emergency Medical Technician. After that, his path was less clear. There were multiple routes to becoming a firefighter in Washington State, but it was such a competitive profession that it depended on what current hiring trends would be like.

"My heart goes out to you as you deal with Jeremy leaving." Patti shook her head sadly. "I know how hard it is when your only child goes. Of course, that's why I'm so pleased that—"

"I'm so sorry, but I have a line of customers waiting to be served," Brittany interrupted. She didn't want to hear any news of Ryan *at all*, even if it meant finding out what he was doing searching for bats in her alley last week. She passed them their meals and tapped on the register. "Would you like separate checks?"

"No need for that." Don whipped out his wallet. "I couldn't let a lady as beautiful as this pay for her meal."

"Oh, Don," Patti said, blushing.

After Brittany sent them off it was time to transfer the second loaf of freshly baked bread to the cooling rack.

"Heads up: I got the last two sandwiches from the fridge," said the next customer, a hiker who was carrying an enormous backpack. He didn't smell that great, but he wore a winning smile. The man shoved two grab-and-go sandwiches onto the counter along with a bottle of kombucha.

"I hope you enjoy them," Brittany said as she rang up the order.

"I'm sure I will. I've been eating freeze-dried packages all week."

"This should make a pleasant change then." Brittany smiled.

Unfortunately, the next customer wasn't nearly as friendly. "This is the worst customer service in the world," said the woman, with a huff. She was about Brittany's age and wore a "Gonzaga Mom" sweatshirt. "The restroom's out of toilet paper, the water station is almost empty, and the place is so crowded there's no place to sit." She handed Brittany a prepackaged Caesar salad and a bag of chips. "This better not be mushy."

"I made it fresh this morning." Brittany felt her cheeks turn pink. "And I'll tidy the restroom just as soon as I ring up your order."

"I should have gone to the Starbucks in Aberdeen, and I *hate* Starbucks." The woman sneered. "At least they'd have a clean bathroom."

"She said she'd take care of the toilet paper situation," said an older lady standing behind the rude one. "Give her a break."

Brittany recognized the woman as a repeat customer named Nancy. She had curly gray hair that fell softly to her shoulders and wore a cable-knit cardigan sweater over navy-blue slacks.

"I didn't ask for your opinion, but thanks," said the Gonzaga mom.

Brittany processed the transaction and read the total. "That'll be $14.27, please."

"For lettuce and potato chips?" The woman plucked a twenty-dollar bill out of her wallet. "I guess you can get away with highway robbery out here in the sticks."

"You mean in Washington's favorite vacation town," said Nancy. "There's no need to be rude."

"I'll speak however I want to, lady."

"No, you will not." Nancy's face turned as red as her cardigan. "This is a local business, and here in Sand Dollar Cove we respect our business owners."

"Who says I wasn't respectful?" The customer ripped her change out of Brittany's hand and as she did so, the receipt fluttered to the floor.

"I'm sorry about the toilet paper," Brittany said quickly. "I'll go deal with that right now."

"There's no need to apologize to people who are rude to you," said Nancy. She pointed to the woman. "Aren't you going to pick up your trash?"

"What trash?" The lady grabbed a huge wad of napkins from the dispenser.

"Your receipt!" Nancy exclaimed, pointing at the ground.

Brittany didn't hear what happened next because she was darting off to restock the toilet paper in the restroom. When she returned, the Gonzaga mom was gone, and Nancy was clearing dishes away from empty tables and depositing them into the bins of soapy water on the cart by the trashcan and recycling bin. Brittany had hoped that most patrons would clean up after themselves, but not everyone did.

"Thank you so much," she told Nancy. "That's really kind of you."

"It's no bother at all." Nancy returned to her spot at the front of the line. "I can see how hard you're working."

"I need to hire an assistant, but I've been too slammed to post the position." Brittany washed her hands at the sink behind the counter. "What can I get you?"

"I'll try the Blue Bird on whole wheat today, and I wouldn't say no to a part-time job, if you're hiring."

"Really? Are you serious?"

"About the sandwich, or the quest for employment?"

"Both."

Nancy stood straight. "I'm definitely serious about the sandwich. Blue cheese and chicken breast sounds like a winning combination. As for the job, that kind of slipped out when you mentioned you needed help. The whole reason I've been coming here so often is to escape my beloved husband of forty-three years who has recently retired. I love Herman with every breath in my body, but didn't realize he was a sixty-seven-year-old man-child until he was at home all the time, asking me to fix him a snack."

"That would annoy me too." Brittany dipped a knife into the blue cheese spread. "I can only offer twenty dollars an hour, but the job's yours if you want it."

"How about I eat my sandwich and think about it?" Nancy took her wallet out of her purse. "In the interest of full disclosure, I haven't worked outside of the home in several decades. But I'm organized, prompt, and detail-oriented. Herman brags to his friends about my cooking all the time."

"I bet he does." Brittany laid sliced chicken on the bread. From the corner of her eye, she saw Cheryl shuffling toward them, pushing her walker.

"Nancy," Cheryl said, once she arrived at the counter. "I'm so glad to see you."

"Hi, Cheryl." Nancy smiled brightly. "It's good to run into you too."

"You two know each other?" Brittany asked.

"For years and years," said Cheryl. "Her husband Herman was the manager of Seaside Resort where I used to work."

"Cheryl's granddaughter Hannah is the manager now," said Nancy. "I'm so proud of that girl."

"I adore Hannah." Brittany added lettuce to the sandwich. "Hannah, Cheryl, and Mary are my housemates."

"You're their landlady?" Nancy clasped her hands. "How did I not put two and two together? This is excellent. The answer's yes, then. I'll definitely take the part-time job."

"What job?" Cheryl asked.

"Working here at Safe Harbor," said Nancy.

"I could really use the help," Brittany admitted.

"I think that's a fine idea." Cheryl nodded her approval. "By the way, Nancy, do you think you could give me a ride home? Mary was supposed to pick me up, but her interior design appointment is running late."

"It would be my pleasure," said Nancy. "Why don't you go save me a seat and I'll join you as soon as I've paid?"

A couple minutes later, Brittany watched Nancy go, sandwich in hand, and felt an enormous sense of relief. The older woman seemed quite capable and had Cheryl's vote of approval. This might be exactly the solution Brittany needed to help keep her head above water.

The lunchtime rush kept at it until around one thirty and then trickled down until the high school let out at two. Clusters of teenagers arrived after that, all of them ordering expensive coffee drinks that Brittany didn't know how they could afford. All of them, except for one girl who was so young that she was probably a freshman. She wore her thick brown hair in two French braids down her back, and arrived on her own, rather than in a herd like the other teenagers did. But that's not what caught Brittany's attention about the girl; it was how she paid for her drink.

The girl stepped up to the counter with solemn eyes. "I'd like a small golden milk latte, please," she said somberly. Then she slid a notecard from the Angel Board.

Brittany looked at the card and read her handwriting.

For a daughter whose parents are divorced. It can be hard feeling like you are caught in the middle.

"Coming right up," Brittany said, with an empathetic smile. Safe Harbor had been open two weeks now, and this was the first time the Angel Board had done good.

FIVE

This was it. Jeremy was really leaving her. Brittany had known this time would come from the minute Jeremy was born, but now, eighteen years later, when her one and only child was about to depart for college, she felt like a wound was forming in her heart that would never close. This would be another layer of scar tissue toughening her up. Paul's death... Her parents' divorce... Ian ignoring her until their marriage busted up... And now this, Jeremy growing up and moving away. But it wouldn't do to let him see how worried she was—about his future, and her own without him, so Brittany put on a brave face. At least she had one night left to cherish him living under her roof. Jeremy wouldn't leave for Seattle until tomorrow morning.

"My last home-cooked meal before I'm fending for myself," Jeremy said from his spot at the kitchen table. His chair cushion had torn ties and there were scratch marks on the wood floor he'd caused by tilting the chair back on two legs. The whole house would be easier to maintain after he moved out, but that thought made Brittany sad, instead of relieved.

"I'm sure you'll find lots of good food to eat in Seattle," she said.

"Yeah," Jeremy nodded. "Dad told me there are some great restaurants near him. I promise not to starve. But still... thanks for making paella." Jeremy helped himself to another serving from the piping hot dish at the center of the table. "I know it's a complicated recipe."

"It's absolutely delicious," said Mary as the rich aroma scented the air. "Especially the crusty part on the bottom."

"I agree." Hannah nodded. A brunette in her mid-twenties, Hannah spent most of her time at her fiancé's apartment but had made a point of being here for Jeremy's going-away celebration.

"Everything's tasty except for the weird sausage." Cheryl picked up her water glass. "It's a bit too spicy for my taste."

"That's the chorizo," said Jeremy. "It's supposed to have a kick to it."

"It's not as good as what I ate in Spain," said Brittany. "But I did my best." She was speaking to the whole table, but her gaze lingered on Jeremy, whose blue eyes were the same color as her own. *The same color as Paul's.* Their mother–son relationship hadn't always been smooth. They'd had their share of butting heads, especially during the earlier teenage years. But they had a deep bond that could never be replicated. Brittany turned her head for a second so Jeremy wouldn't see the tears that were forming. "You deserve a grand send-off," she said as she looked back at him.

"Aw, thanks." His smile wobbled a bit. "I'm going to miss your cooking," he said before taking another bite.

"What's the story with this pan?" Mary asked. "It's gigantic."

"Ian gave it to me for our ninth wedding anniversary," Brittany said. "It has a special non-stick coating." Ian might not have been the best husband or father, but he was always good about purchasing presents for special occasions, especially if she circled what she wanted in a catalog and taped it to his bathroom mirror. He reminded her of her dad, in that way. Alan gave splendid gifts, too. "Does anyone want seconds?" she asked.

"I've already had seconds, but I'll take thirds." Jeremy picked up the serving utensil. "You're going to have to roll me out of here."

"That'll make for a long trip to Seattle," Cheryl joked.

"He wouldn't need to roll," said Mary. "As a future fire-fighter, I expect him to run."

"All the way to Seattle?" Jeremy asked, with his mouth full.

Everyone laughed.

At first, when Jeremy had explained his career ambitions to her, Brittany had been terrified. She didn't like the idea of her son running into burning buildings. But the more she thought about it from Jeremy's point of view, the more she realized why that type of job appealed to him. He was smart, but not in a scholarly way, and would have hated a desk job indoors. Working on a team and helping save lives was a much better fit for his personality.

"Promise me you'll text me every day and call me once a week," she said, after he had swallowed. "Or you can call me more than that. Calling me every day is fine, too."

Jeremy chuckled. "I'm not going to call you every day. I can't promise to text that often either, but I will call you when I remember."

"Gee. Thanks."

"I'm not the type of person who will get homesick." Jeremy patted her head like she was a puppy. "But I will miss you. Probably."

"You're going to do great in Seattle," said Mary. "I can't wait to hear all about it when you come home for Thanksgiving."

"Why not come home earlier than that?" Hannah asked. "It's only a couple hours' drive away."

"I bought him brand-new tires for a graduation present to make that journey easier," said Brittany.

"The new tires are great." Jeremy scooped rice onto his spoon. "I might come home before Thanksgiving, we'll see. But even with the new tires, my car has 167,000 miles on it and gas is expensive. Plus, I'll be super busy what with school, and getting a job, and—"

"Spending time with that girlfriend of yours at the University of Washington," Cheryl said, interrupting. "Will Kenzie have a car, too?"

"No. Her parents didn't think she'd need one."

"She won't need one," said Hannah. "Unlike here, Seattle has a good public transportation system."

"Good, if you like being mugged while you wait for the bus," said Cheryl, who hated the city. "You know what I always say—"

"A bad day in Sand Dollar Cove is better than a great day in Seattle," Mary and Hannah both said in unison.

Brittany looked at Jeremy to see if he'd be offended, but he was used to Cheryl's antics, and grinned.

"I'll remember that, Cheryl," he said. "Thanks for that bit of life advice."

"How are things going at Safe Harbor?" Hannah asked, changing the subject. "You've been open a little over two weeks now, right?"

Brittany nodded. "Yes, and business is booming. I had no idea it would shoot off like a rocket, like this."

"Everyone at the senior center is talking about how good your food is," said Cheryl. "People would eat there every day if they could afford it."

"I wish I could lower my prices to accommodate that, but my margins are slim." Brittany blotted her mouth with a napkin. "There's just barely enough money to pay Nancy, who starts on Tuesday."

"Nancy?" Hannah asked. "*My* Nancy?"

"You know her, too?" Brittany asked.

"She's practically my fairy godmother," Hannah said with a grin. "Nancy used to pick us up from school when we were sick, and Gran had to work."

"She was our emergency contact person," said Cheryl, who had raised the sisters while their mother had served time in prison and struggled afterward.

"Nancy took care of me when I got my wisdom teeth removed," Hannah continued. "And she's helping to plan my wedding."

"I thought *I* was helping you plan your wedding," said Mary. "I'm your maid of honor, after all."

"You are, sis. But I'm counting on you for style decisions. Nancy's helping me figure out the guest list and the seating charts."

"Oh." Mary wrinkled her nose. "That sounds boring."

Hannah looked at Brittany. "Nancy will be a great addition to Safe Harbor. You're going to love working with her, and I think this will be good for her, too, because her husband was getting on her nerves."

"Herman gets on everyone's nerves," Cheryl said with a harrumph.

"Herman's my friend, too," said Hannah.

"Friend or not, Herman's an idiot." Cheryl put her palm on the table. "Once Nancy starts working, he'll probably be so clueless that he won't be able to operate a can opener to heat up a can of soup."

"He can't use a can opener?" Jeremy asked.

"Probably not," Hannah admitted. "But I bet Nancy will compensate by opening it ahead of time and leaving it in a microwave-safe bowl."

They all laughed good-naturedly.

"Hannah, tell everyone your big news," said Mary. "And by big, I mean mammoth."

"Oh, I don't think now is such a great time for that." Hannah gazed down at her plate. "This is Jeremy's night, not mine."

"Well, now you've got to tell us," said Jeremy. "This is possibly my last chance to hear it before Thanksgiving."

"Yeah," said Mary. "Spill it."

"Why don't I know your big news already?" Cheryl asked. "What are you girls keeping from me?"

Brittany was curious too.

"Guy and I have bought a house on Sand Piper Lane," Hannah blurted.

"A mansion," Mary corrected. "It's 8,000 square feet."

"It's a crumbling house," Hannah clarified. "It needs a ton of remodeling. The previous owners built it in the 1970s and then went bankrupt, so there's a lot about the interior that's wonky."

"I know that house!" Brittany exclaimed. "Oh, my gosh! Are you telling me you bought the house with the turrets?"

"That's the one." Hannah nodded.

"The architect must have been in love with Renaissance fairs or something," said Mary, "because there's also a draw-bridge in the garden over a moat."

"It's not a moat, it's a muddy koi pond," said Hannah. "But yes, to the weird Renaissance fair obsession. The kitchen has a brick fireplace with a meat spit that has definitely got to go, especially since Guy's vegetarian."

"Tell Gran the best part," said Mary.

"What's the best part?" Cheryl asked.

Hannah took a deep breath and looked at her grandmother. "We're remodeling the entire house, and it's going to take at least a year or so to do, but one of the ways we're remodeling it is that we're adding a ground-floor apartment for you."

"With an accessible bathroom," said Mary. "I'm going to help design it."

"Oh, my word." Cheryl brought her hand to her mouth as she gasped in astonishment. "My own apartment? Right there in your house?"

"Mansion," Mary said. "It's a mansion."

"It's not a mansion, it's only a really large house," said Hannah. "But yes. It'll be your own apartment with a doorbell and everything."

"That's wonderful," said Brittany. "I'm so happy for all of you." She was, too. It meant that her own shared housing situation would need to change, but that would have happened eventually, anyway. Maybe she could renovate the attic in Safe Harbor, move in there and rent out her house to help save for retirement.

"I hope you decide to keep the turrets and the moat," said Jeremy. "Maybe you could add some suits of armor by the front door."

"Now you're talking like an interior designer," said Mary. "An awful one, but I appreciate your commitment to a theme. As for me, I would get rid of the turrets, because I think they're ridiculous, but to each their own."

"I'm sorry to change the subject, but you got your car tuned up, right, Jeremy?" Brittany asked, suddenly getting anxious again about Jeremy's impending departure.

"Yeah, Mom. No need to baby me. I got it handled." Jeremy gulped down half a glass of water. "But that tune-up can only do so much. On Reddit it said that cars like mine usually crap out at 160,000 miles, and I'm already 7,000 miles past that. I'll need to save for a down payment on a new one soon, or I'll be screwed."

"Or you could take the bus," Mary suggested.

Honk! Honk!

The sounds of a car pulling up in the driveway caught everyone's attention.

"That must be Grandpa Alan and Tansy." Brittany pushed her chair back from the table. "They're bringing apple pie and vanilla ice cream."

"I'm going to need a bigger stomach," said Cheryl.

"Don't get too excited," said Brittany. "I'm sure the pie is from the grocery store."

"Tansy doesn't strike me as much of a baker." Mary chuckled. "She wouldn't want to ruin her manicure peeling apples."

"That's a sexist assumption," said Hannah, whose fiancé Guy loved to cook. "What if it's Brittany's dad baking the pie?"

"The only thing my dad can prepare is dental molds," said Brittany. "My mom's not much of a chef, either. That's one reason I learned to cook in the first place—self-preservation."

Honk! Honk! Honk! The car horn beeped again.

"I don't know why they don't come inside already," Brittany wondered aloud.

"Maybe they need help bringing in groceries." Jeremy stood. "I'll go see."

"I might as well come too." Brittany put her napkin next to her silverware. "I should turn on the porch light."

"Girls, why don't you load the dishes in the dishwasher, to make room for pie?" Cheryl began stacking the plates.

"Will do," said Mary.

"I'll put the leftover paella away," offered Hannah.

Brittany followed Jeremy out to the driveway but was three steps behind him on account of her flicking on the porch light. She heard his shout first and saw what he was shouting about second.

"No way! Grandpa, this is unbelievable! Thank you so much!"

Looking across the porch, Brittany saw a fire engine-red

Ford Mustang convertible parked on the driveway with a gigantic white bow attached to the hood. Alan stood in front of the driver's side door dangling a key fob, and Tansy stood next to him in a skimpy dress and high heels, with her hip jutting out.

"Happy graduation!" Alan said, a huge smile on his face. "I thought you should roll into this next phase of your life in style."

"Dad, you shouldn't have," said Brittany, her eyes popping out of her head. Giving a teenager a sports car was a horrible idea, and a convertible was even worse. What if Jeremy rolled the car? What if the top got stuck down and rain destroyed the interior? He was moving to Seattle, after all, one of the rainiest cities in the entire country. She was furious with her father for not consulting her before he surprised them like this. But she also knew that if she told everyone this was a terrible idea and that Jeremy could not, under any circumstances, accept the car, then that would cause an irrevocable rift between her and her son, who was eighteen years old now, and technically an adult.

Jeremy threw himself at Alan in an enormous hug. "Thank you so much!" he said, before giving Tansy a hug too. "Thank you to both of you."

"I picked out the color," said Tansy. "The dealership tried to unload a blue model on us, but I insisted they order the red."

"They had to ship it from Georgia," said Alan. "That's why it didn't get here in June. We meant to give it to you after your graduation ceremony, but at least we made it in time before you head off to college."

"I don't understand why you did this," Brittany said, still trying to wrap her head around what was happening. She felt a sting of jealousy among other things. Would he have given Paul a car if he'd lived to see graduation? Was this some sort of father–son fantasy Alan had long cherished that he'd never been able to turn into reality until now?

"Because I love my grandson, obviously." Alan handed Jeremy the key. "Hop on in."

"He doesn't have his license with him," said Brittany, still trying to stop this madness.

Jeremy pulled his wallet out of his back pocket. "Yes, I do."

"Our car insurance will go through the roof," Brittany worried aloud.

"I'll sell my old car to help pay for that." Jeremy clicked his seatbelt.

"He'll save money on repair fees, too," said Alan. "This baby is brand new."

"You never gave me a car," said Brittany. That feeble protest just slipped out, before she could stop herself.

"I *would* have given you a car," said Alan, wearing a pained expression, "but you know what a tightwad your mother is. She said no."

"Oh." Feeling a little better, Brittany softened her stance. She saw how happy her son and her father were over this purchase and realized that she'd better course-correct fast or else they'd hold her lack of enthusiasm against her. "This was really generous of you, Dad."

"It was Tansy's idea too," Alan said. "She deserves some of the credit as well."

"Uh... thanks," Brittany told her.

Jeremy was already revving the engine. "Can we take it for a spin now?"

"Sure," said Tansy.

"Well, my dear," Alan said as he opened the passenger door for Tansy. "Why don't you and I sit in the back and let this fine grandson of mine chauffeur us home?"

"Drive safe." Brittany stared after them as they drove away, and then went back inside.

"Where's the apple pie?" Cheryl asked, as Brittany entered the kitchen. The table was sparkling clean, and Hannah and Mary had already set out plates and forks.

"There isn't any." Brittany washed her hands at the sink absentmindedly and explained what happened.

"Wow." Mary plunked down in a chair. "Wow. Wow. Wow. Jeremy must be thrilled."

Brittany nodded. "He's over the moon." She dried her hands on a towel, wishing that it could have been in her power to make her son that happy.

"I'm excited for Jeremy, but bummed about the pie," Cheryl admitted. "I was really looking forward to that."

"Same." Mary nodded.

"Don't worry, ladies, I have a solution." Hannah walked over to the freezer and took out a cardboard box. "This evening calls for cheesecake."

"I hope you don't mind if I eat half of it," said Brittany. "The only thing that will make me feel better right now is sugar."

Sugar, or turning back time.

SIX

Four days later, Brittany was sharing a pot of tea with Cynthia at Safe Harbor while Nancy ran the register. Brittany had hoped that a visit from her mother would help her process the grief she was experiencing as a brand-new empty nester now that Jeremy was gone. She'd been trying to stay busy, and running the cafe helped, but Brittany felt wounded inside, like a piece of her heart had been ripped away. Unfortunately, instead of consoling her about Jeremy's departure, Cynthia was hyper-focused on his getaway car.

"I can't believe the nerve of your father," said Cynthia. She wore a crisply ironed blouse over twill pants. "That's so like Alan. Wanting to look like a hero even if it means doing something idiotic and dumb."

"It was an overly generous gift, to be sure, but Jeremy was thrilled with the car." Brittany squeezed a lemon slice over her mug, being careful not to splash the embroidered tunic she wore. "I was against it at first, but now I'm glad he has a new car with advanced safety features."

"But it's a convertible." Cynthia sniffed. "How safe can it be?" One wrong corner and..." She shuddered.

"I'm not going to think about that."

"Alan's made my graduation gift to Jeremy look pitiful. It was so practical, too. Much more practical than a car that doesn't even have a normal roof."

"Jeremy likes that raincoat you gave him a lot. North Face is a good brand."

"It has zippered pockets." Cynthia sipped her tea.

"Which I'm sure Jeremy will appreciate when he's in the middle of his first Seattle rainstorm."

"I don't think you should have allowed Jeremy to keep it."

"The raincoat?" Brittany asked.

"No, silly. The car. You should have made him give it back to Alan and that floozy of his."

"I didn't really have a choice in the matter," Brittany said, trying to defend herself. "I—"

"Was too much of a daddy's girl to stand up to Alan and that trollop."

"I'm not—"

"Which is rich, considering your father did the bare minimum when it came to child-rearing." Cynthia set her mug down so hard that tea splashed over the rim. "He never signed permission slips or showed up to parent–teacher conferences. He would have forgotten every birthday unless I reminded him. And he never once, in all your years of schooling, bothered to help you with your homework. He was too busy being handsy with cocktail waitresses at the T Bone Bluff."

Brittany sighed, and her posture slumped. There was no use in arguing with her mom about any of this. Cynthia was right, Alan wasn't father-of-the year material, but then again, Cynthia wouldn't win any medals for mothering, either. Her uncontrollable temper meant that Brittany and Paul had spent their childhood walking around on eggshells, constantly afraid their mother would explode. That was one of the reasons Brittany loved television so much. It had been her way of escaping, especially into travel shows.

"Let's not talk about Dad anymore." Brittany warmed her hands on the mug. "What do you think of my shop now that it's up and running?" Brittany knew it was highly likely her mother would have at least one critical thing to say about her business. Cynthia could only be supportive up to a point.

"This tea is excellent. Nice and hot." Cynthia picked up her mug and looked around the room. "The furniture you picked out is fine too, although I bet those easy chairs will be difficult to keep clean if someone spills something on them."

"I bought the ones made with outdoor fabric, so they are tougher than they look."

"Smart girl." Cynthia nodded her approval. "I'm glad to see those old board games on the bookshelf are getting some action." Her gaze narrowed as she looked at the communal table. "I hope those teenagers don't trash the place."

"What?" Looking around the shop, Brittany saw quite a few regulars including a cluster of high school girls that she knew to be harmless. The tallest was Scarlett Mathews, the daughter of Brittany's friend Stephanie from high school. Thirty years ago, Brittany had been super jealous of Stephanie because her parents had gifted her a Volkswagen Rabbit to drive when she turned sixteen. Sitting next to Scarlett was Gabby Santos, whose parents taught at the local elementary school. Jeremy had given Mrs. Santos a lot of trouble in third grade. Then there was Lana Shields, whose father owned a fishing boat charter and whose mother was Brittany's dental hygienist. Brittany was so focused on the high schoolers that she didn't realize Nancy had approached until she felt Nancy tap her on the shoulder.

"I'm sorry to bother you on your break, but I have a question about this." Nancy waved an Angel Board card in the air. "I don't know how to enter it in the register."

"Oh. That's no problem at all." Brittany stood and pushed in her chair. "I'll be right back, Mom."

"I love the idea of the Angel Board." Nancy pushed up the sleeves of her purple sweater. "It's such a great opportunity to do good."

"Thanks. I'm glad you like it." She took the card from Nancy and read what it said.

For a woman who is brave enough to take risks. You are an inspiration to everyone around you.

When Brittany looked up, she saw the dark-eyed girl with the two French braids standing in front of her. The same girl who had used an Angel Board card last week. How unusual for her to have used two cards in a row. Brittany wondered if everything was okay in the girl's homelife.

"This is how you enter the free credit into the register," she told Nancy, before walking her through the process.

"That seems easy enough." Nancy looked at the girl. "What can I get you, sweetie?"

"I'd like a golden milk latte." The girl gripped tightly to her backpack straps. "And could it be a medium?"

Nancy looked at Brittany for confirmation.

"Sure." Brittany nodded. "The cards are good for up to five dollars." Feeling curious about the girl and her situation, Brittany dug for more information. She picked up a Sharpie and a paper to-go cup. "What's your name for when your order is ready?"

Nancy glanced sideways at Brittany. During training yesterday, Brittany had told her that the only time they'd write down names was if both of them were working, or if they were creating multiple drink orders at the same time.

"You didn't need my name last time I ordered a latte," the girl said in a sullen tone.

"This time I do." Brittany poised the pen above the cup.

"Since Nancy and I are both working today, the orders might get confused."

"Isabella," the girl mumbled. "My name's Isabella."

"Coming right up, Isabella." Brittany wrote her name and capped the pen. "I'll make it myself."

Later, after she had given Isabella her latte, Brittany returned to her tea with Cynthia.

"I'm glad you hired someone to help you with this place because you look worn out," said Cynthia.

"Gee. Thanks, Mom." Brittany pulled a lock of unruly hair behind her ear. She'd woken up the night before with a nightmare about Jeremy falling off the observation deck of the Space Needle. Brittany shuddered. She hadn't been sleeping well all week, from the stress of him leaving.

"I didn't mean it like that." Cynthia patted her hand. "You look fine. The only reason Tansy looks younger than you is because she's part vampire."

"Okay, let's—"

"And the other part of her is plastic."

"Yeah, um..." As Brittany's mind scrambled for a way to get out of the conversation, she saw Isabella sit in a chair that was slightly adjacent to the communal table, where Lana, Gabby, and Scarlett sat. "I should probably get back to work since it's only Nancy's second day. It's been lovely chatting with you, though."

"I agree." Cynthia smiled. "This has been nice." But then her smile morphed into a frown. "Oh no," she groaned. "Will you look who's here?"

Please, not my father and Tansy, Brittany thought to herself. But when she turned toward the front door, she saw Don and Patti. *Shoot! This was almost worse!*

"What is *that* woman doing here?" Cynthia hissed.

Brittany looked back at her mother and pushed the breakable teapot out of Cynthia's way. It wasn't that Patti would do or say anything inappropriate, but Cynthia was a lit fuse. She blamed the entire Osborne family for Paul's death: Frank, for purchasing a derelict boat, Ryan for captaining it that fateful day, and Patti for sticking by Frank all those years even though he was clearly a deadbeat.

As for Brittany, she pinned the blame directly on Ryan. It wasn't Patti or Frank's fault that Ryan didn't turn the boat back to shore when the storm picked up. That was Ryan's horrible decision-making and gigantic ego at work.

"Patti's my customer," said Brittany. "She was my client at the senior center, too." From the corner of her eye, she saw Isabella grab her backpack and slink away from the teenagers, who didn't seem to want anything to do with her. It was sad, really, but that was the least of Brittany's concerns.

"How can you stand to be around that woman after what she did?" Cynthia demanded.

"She didn't do anything." Brittany leaned forward and whispered hoarsely. "It's not her fault that Paul and Ryan took the boat out that day."

"But it *is* her fault that she stuck by that louse of a husband of hers. And it's also her fault that she knew your father lost big to Frank playing poker but didn't tell me. Frank never would have had the funds to buy the *Carpe Diem* in the first place if it wasn't for those winnings."

"We don't know their financial history, and it's none of our business." Brittany wished that Cynthia would keep her voice down.

"It wasn't a boat, it was a death trap waiting to happen, and Frank knew he didn't have the skills to repair it! Don't tell me that Patti didn't know it too. I can't look at that woman without thinking of Paul. There were two sons on the boat that day. Why did she get hers back and I didn't?"

"I don't know." Brittany felt like her heart was breaking all over again. "What happened was tragic and unfair. But since

I've interacted with Patti so much over the years, I've gotten to know her as a sweet woman who's has a difficult life. Frank has dementia now, you know. He requires round-the-clock care in a memory home."

"I hope Frank forgets every last thing except for what he did. He's—"

"Suffering from an incurable disease, and let's try to remember that," said Brittany.

"I don't care what—" Cynthia paused, her face splotched, red with emotion. It must have taken every ounce of self-control she had, but she smoothed her expression to a neutral one.

Her mother's change of course confused Brittany until she saw Patti and Don approaching. Don wore jeans and a hunter-green fleece, and Patti wore a knit dress with a wide belt cinched at her waist.

"Hi, Cynthia," Patti said, halting a good three feet away from the table. "I thought I should come over and say hello."

"Hello to you, too, Patricia." Cynthia nodded her head. "You are looking well."

"You, too. Lavender is a lovely color on you." Patti waved her hand toward Don. "This is my friend Don, who moved here almost two years ago."

"Came up from the city," Don said. "After my wife died of cancer."

"I'm sorry to hear about your late wife." Cynthia picked up her empty mug. "It's good to meet you." She looked at Patti. "How's Ryan doing?"

Sneaking around alleys and ruining groceries, Brittany thought angrily. She'd been actively trying to not think about him ever since their floury encounter.

"Great." Patti smiled, ever so slightly. "In fact, he's moved back to town."

"He has?" Brittany gasped. There went the hope that he'd only been in Sand Dollar Cove on a quick visit home.

Patti nodded. "Ryan's a director of marketing for a company that makes robotic vacuum cleaners. He's been with them for over twenty years, and he's doing well. He'd be vice president if he was willing to travel more, but he isn't."

It irked her to hear that Ryan was doing so well for himself, but not as much as it did knowing he'd moved back to town. She wondered what had changed Ryan's mind about traveling. Back in high school, he'd talked non-stop of going on a cross-country road trip after high school graduation. That was one of the inspirations for her backpacking across Europe after college. She loved the idea of an epic journey.

"I ran into Ryan last week," Brittany confessed, omitting the detail about literally smacking into him with a bag of flour.

"That's great!" Patti brightened. "I was hoping you two would reconnect. He brought my little granddaughter with him, too. She's a darling."

"I remember you mentioning he had a daughter," said Brittany. "What made Ryan move back to Sand Dollar Cove?"

"It's on account of my husband's dementia." Patti's smile faded. "Most of Ryan's work can be done from home now because of all the online meetings. He can live anywhere he wants, really, so he's moved back to Sand Dollar Cove to help me with Frank."

"That's good." Cynthia sat ramrod straight. "It must be nice to have a son who can help out like that."

"Yes, well..." Patti shifted her weight to her other foot. "We better get going. We ordered our coffee to go."

"How's your husband doing these days?" Cynthia asked, looking pointedly at Don.

Brittany wished her mom would zip it, but there was nothing she could do.

"Not so well, I'm afraid." Patti looked down at her feet for a second. "But he's being taken real good care of at the memory home. I visited him this morning, in fact."

"Come on, dollface. It looks like our coffee and cupcakes are waiting for us." Don held Patti's hand.

"See you around," said Cynthia.

"I appreciate you coming in," Brittany added.

"So, is that man Patricia's boyfriend, or what?" Cynthia asked after the couple had left.

"Something like that. I think she feels a bit conflicted about the relationship since Frank is still alive."

"She should feel like a tramp, that's how she should feel."

"Mom!"

"The nerve of that woman, parading around town in a red dress, showing off her boyfriend, and bragging about how successful her son is. Paul would have been successful too, if he'd had the chance to live."

"I know, Mom." Brittany felt torn. She understood the anguish behind Cynthia's bitterness but hoped that her mom would control her temper and not make a scene.

"The anniversary of Paul's death is coming up," said Cynthia. "Did you know that?"

Brittany nodded. "It's this Monday, September twenty-second. Paul will have been gone thirty years now. We should have a memorial, or something."

"No way. Even if it was a private memorial with only the two of us, Tansy might show up wiggling those fake tits of hers. Paul would have hated that woman. He would have let your father know he was making a fool of himself." Cynthia folded her arms across her chest and leaned back in her chair with a huff.

"I don't know about that. Paul was patient, and kind, and tolerated everyone."

"That's right. A kinder soul never walked this earth. Your brother's only fault was befriending that jackass Ryan who always got him into trouble."

"I couldn't agree with you more, on that count. Ryan was trouble."

"And that awful father of his. Frank and his get-rich-quick schemes. That man could never hold a steady job a day in his life. That boat was destined to sink, and it was hubris on Frank's part to think he could refurbish it." Cynthia picked up her empty mug and clenched it tightly like she might throw it.

Brittany held her breath. It wouldn't be the first time porcelain had met its death in Cynthia's clutches. She jumped to her feet. "The dishes go over here in the tubs of soapy water," she said as she guided her mother over to the self-service station.

Patti and Don were just leaving. "Have a nice day," Patti said, with a little wave.

Cynthia narrowed her eyes. "I haven't had a nice day in thirty years." She dropped the mug into the tub so hard that the handle fell off.

Patti shrank back, and Don stood in front of her protectively as Cynthia stormed past them and slammed the door.

SEVEN

There were some moments that were better spent alone. Sometimes solitude was required to truly commune with the gravity of a situation. As Brittany stepped onto the wooden boards of the boat dock on the following Monday, the anniversary of Paul's death, she was relieved her mother had turned down her suggestion to accompany her this morning. Brittany zipped up her fleece and stuffed her hands in the pockets. The foghorn crooned in the distance. It took all her concentration to manage walking across the dock without triggering a panic attack. That's what had happened the last time she'd been here nine years ago.

She had only had one panic attack in her life, and it was when she'd signed up to chaperone Jeremy's fourth grade whale-watching trip. The teacher had been desperate for volunteers, so even though Brittany was terrified of the ocean, she'd signed up to help. Her doctor had given her anti-nausea medicine in case she needed it, but it had been so long since she'd been on a boat that Brittany didn't know if she'd get seasick or not.

She never got the chance to find out.

In fact, she never made it aboard the vessel at all.

Brittany had followed the group of students and parents onto the dock, to board the whale-watching boat, and while standing there in line had become dizzy.

Her pulse raced.

Her hands became clammy.

Before she knew it, she'd been gasping for air, unable to breathe.

The adults in the group worried she was having a heart attack, and the teacher dialed 911.

It was so bad that Ian rushed to the hospital to meet her, and he never left work early at the car dealership.

The ER doctor diagnosed her with a panic attack, which was a much better outcome than heart troubles, but that didn't make it any easier to explain to Jeremy when they got home. His entire class had returned to school since they didn't have enough chaperones to run the field trip.

"I can do this," Brittany told herself in the chilly morning air. "I can be brave for my brother." Nobody else was watching. If her nervous system went haywire, nobody would witness her humiliation. She'd just creep back up the dock to solid ground and honor her brother from there. But that's not what her goal was. Her goal was to stand on the last place Paul had stood, the slip where the *Carpe Diem* had been moored. She wanted to root her feet in that spot and stare out across the harbor to the lighthouse rocks where the foghorn blew every three minutes, warning passing ships of danger.

Using every ounce of willpower at her disposal to push herself forward, Brittany walked across the wooden planks one by one. She passed sailboats and rowboats, fishing boats and catamarans. One of them was the *Moonstruck*, her father's current motorboat. Brittany had only sailed on it one time, when Jeremy was three. It was a more modern version of the *Lovestruck* that their family used to cruise on. She hadn't always been afraid of the water. Some of her happiest memories were waterskiing from the back of the *Lovestruck*, her father at the helm, her mother smiling, and Paul cheering her on.

Why did happy memories from the past have to hurt so much?

When Brittany got to the dock's edge, she stood her ground and breathed in the salty taste of the ocean. Gray skies made the water look even darker. Wind whipped her curly brown hair across her cheeks. The cold bit her nose ring as the metal chilled. Brittany looked straight out across the water, staring at the lighthouse, counting the seconds until the foghorn blew. It sounded a minute later, and she relaxed slightly, her memory drifting back to that fateful day, thirty years ago.

"Come with me," Paul had said, holding a can of paint. "It'll be fun."

"But she's not a senior," Ryan had argued. "This is supposed to be a senior prank."

Alan and Cynthia had been attacking each other all weekend. Paul knew Brittany didn't want to be stuck at home in the middle of the conflict without him there to make peace. "Brittany can keep a lookout," he'd said. "There's plenty of room on board."

"Maybe another time," Ryan had said, shaking his head.

Her pride stinging, Brittany had come up with a retort right there on the spot. "I can't come with you anyway," she had told them. "I have a date." She kept watch over Ryan from the corner of her eye, hoping he'd be jealous. Sure, he was two years older than her, but she had on her tightest pair of jeans, and her cropped white fisherman's sweater that skimmed above the navel. Brittany had just discovered jewelry making and had hammered the copper buckle of the belt she wore, as well as the delicate earrings that danced across her shoulders, and she'd hoped Ryan would notice.

"A date?" Ryan had asked. "With who?"

"A sophomore you don't know," she'd bluffed. "He's in my science class."

"Then I probably don't know him either," said Paul. "He better not be a douchebag."

"He's not." Brittany had slipped her hand in her back pocket.

"Take a quarter with you just in case you need to call for a ride home." Paul picked up the paintbrushes. "I'll check the answering machine when I get back."

"Thanks," said Brittany. "Do you have water?"

"Water, and a jumbo-size bag of peanut M&M's." Paul pulled a piece of candy out of the bag, tossed it in the air, and caught it in his mouth.

"Nice." Brittany laughed. "Good luck out there."

"I don't need luck." Paul flashed a smile. "That's what Ryan's for."

"Har har." Ryan looked sideways at Brittany but didn't say goodbye. "Let's go," he grunted.

"Aye, aye, Captain." Then Paul turned and high-fived her. "Bye, bye, Britt."

With one last smile, Paul walked out of her life forever.

If Brittany had insisted on coming that day, would it have made a difference? That was one of the things that tormented her over the years. Maybe she would have noticed the boat taking on water. Maybe she would have complained about the weather and insisted they turn back—her crop top sweater hadn't been very warm after all.

Or maybe she would have died in the icy cold sea, with Paul.

There had been days, especially in her late teens, when she had wondered if that would have been better. A lifetime without Paul, the one man in her life who had never disappointed her, was difficult to bear.

"*Carpe diem*," Brittany murmured, as she stared at the light-house. The foghorn blew, and she shuddered.

If Paul were alive today, or if he could hear her, wherever he was, what would she tell him? *About Jeremy, of course.* She'd tell him all about his nephew. Maybe she still could.

"You have a nephew who looks nothing like you unless he smiles," Brittany said quietly. "He's strong-willed, and fearless, and has a good heart, just like you."

Nobody was listening but two harbor seals sleeping on a buoy.

Brittany spoke louder. "I ended up getting divorced, which I swore I would never do, and boy, could I have used your shoulder to cry on when that happened. I could have used your help dealing with Mom and Dad all these years, too." She took a deep breath and tried to stop rambling. "Mainly, I would have loved having you here on my side, as the one person I could always count on. Now I have absolutely no one because Jeremy's left me as well." Brittany took a ragged breath. "I still need you, big brother. I really do."

She clutched the necklace she'd made, the one she'd worn to Paul's basketball games and at his funeral service. She'd hammered a thin piece of silver into an X, the Roman numeral for the letter ten, which had been Paul's jersey number, and had threaded the beads with blue and gold, the colors of Sand Dollar Cove High. Brittany rarely wore this necklace anymore, preferring to keep it draped over Paul's picture on her dresser. But there had been a time when she'd worn it every day for years, including the six months she'd spent traveling through Europe.

Ian had been the one who had convinced her to stop wearing it. He bought her a new necklace to replace it, a stupid silver heart on a chain. At the time, she'd thought that was a sign of true love. Now she realized it had been a sign of Ian's total lack of empathy for her grief. If Paul had been alive, he would have pointed that out to her, that Ian was a poor choice in life partners. But then, she wouldn't have gotten Jeremy out of the bargain, so Brittany didn't have any regrets.

"Love you, Paul." Brittany kissed her fingertips and then blew on them, sending the kiss out to the water. When she turned around to walk back to her car, she saw a lone figure walking through the mist, straight down the dock. It wasn't until the person drew closer that she saw who it was.

Ryan strode forward wearing a long brown raincoat almost as dark as his eyes. His hair glistened in the mist, and his sturdy hiking boots pounded with each step. Despite everything she knew about him, Brittany felt butterflies in her stomach. Her lingering attraction to him was as powerful as ever.

When his eyes met hers, he nodded slightly, but didn't say one word in greeting. He just walked up to the edge of the dock, stood beside her, and grunted.

Why was Ryan there? Did he realize it was the anniversary of Paul's death, or was he out here on one of his morning nature walks again? Brittany shivered in the cold. The sun had risen, but had done little to burn away the marine layer. Why wasn't Ryan saying anything? The whole thing felt weird.

But then she watched as Ryan pulled a jumbo bag of M&M's out of his pocket. Not plain M&M's, but the peanut version. Paul's favorite.

Still not speaking, Ryan ripped open the package and offered her some. Brittany held out her hand. Several pieces of candy plopped into her palm, her fingers too cold to melt the chocolate.

Ryan tumbled some M&M's into his own hand and tossed one piece up into the air, before catching it in his mouth, like Paul had loved to do.

Tears filled her eyes knowing that he remembered that tiny detail about her brother. Or maybe it was a coincidence. *Probably it was a coincidence*, she told herself. Ryan was an early morning walker who didn't make good choices about breakfast. That had to be it.

But then Ryan ripped the bag open all the way, held onto the plastic, and threw every last piece of candy into the water.

That's what gave Brittany the courage to ask the question that was burning on her heart. "Do you think about him?"

"Every damn day," Ryan answered in a husky voice, before turning to walk away.

Brittany didn't follow him. She stood at the edge of the dock, staring at the tiny bubbles where the candy had fallen. She hugged herself, trying to keep warm in her too-thin fleece. Then she mustered her courage once again. "*Carpe diem,*" she whispered, before charging after Ryan.

"Why'd you do it?" she demanded. "Why did you keep my brother out on that boat in rough water? It's your fault he died! You were the captain! Why didn't you turn the boat back as soon as the weather got bad? It was stupid to stay out so long."

"You're right," Ryan said, slowly, his voice weighty. "It was my fault. All of it. Paul would never have been out on the water that day if it weren't for me. I take full responsibility for his death, and that's a grief I carry with me every moment."

"As you should." Brittany shivered.

"You're cold." Ryan took off his jacket and handed it to her.

Brittany tossed the coat right back at him. "I don't want anything from you."

Ryan picked his jacket up off the dock and handed it to her again. "Take it anyway, so you can stay warm. Paul wouldn't want you to be cold." Then he stormed off without looking back to see if she put it on or not.

Brittany stood there for a full minute, watching him go. "Damnit, Ryan," she muttered as she clutched his coat. "I hate that you're right." She slipped her arms into the warm sleeves, and it was as close as she'd gotten to a hug from her brother in decades.

EIGHT

"We need to make more grab-and-go sandwiches," said Nancy, as she pointed to the line out the door. "We're out again, and it's only eleven thirty."

"I think we might run out of bread, too." Brittany rinsed lettuce and dropped it in the salad spinner. "It looks like half of the senior center is waiting in line." She ran back to the counter and put the lettuce in its bin underneath the sneeze guard. "Thank goodness both of us are working today."

"We'll keep this line moving." Nancy rang up her customer.

It had only been a little over a week since the older woman had joined her at Safe Harbor, and already Brittany felt an immense sense of relief. Nancy was efficient, prompt, and had a no-nonsense attitude that she appreciated. So far Nancy was working Tuesdays through Fridays, so Brittany's weekends were still a challenge, but she could deal with that later. One step at a time.

"Next customer, please," Brittany said, standing in front of the counter. She smiled when she saw her friend Ann from the senior center and pretended to ignore the tiny pop of poodle fur sticking out of Ann's purse. Brittany didn't want

Nugget in her dining establishment. She couldn't risk the health department's wrath. But she felt too uncomfortable to speak up for herself. "Hi, Ann," she said. "What can I get you?"

"Something that won't mess up my blood sugar levels." Ann's unnaturally red hair was set in an elegant French twist. "What do you recommend?"

"Why don't you try the Grilled and Chilled? That's a chicken salad sandwich on whole wheat with a side of coleslaw."

"Perfect!" Ann clapped her manicured hands together. "I suppose you heard what happened to me last month at the senior center with my diabetes. My blood sugar went haywire and I landed in the hospital. That was a close call."

"I *did* hear that, and I'm so sorry you were unwell." Brittany sidestepped to the left, down the sandwich line, and started Ann's order. "I always cross-checked your blood sugar levels to make sure what you ate at the senior center wouldn't hurt you." She winked at Ann. "Of course, I couldn't predict what you'd do when you went to your granddaughter's bridal shower."

Ann held her hand up like she was guilty. "They were homemade meringue cookies. It would have been rude to say no."

"That was a close call, too, if I'm remembering right."

Ann nodded. "Which is why I've been good since then. Really careful. It was a shock to me when I woke up in the ambulance after eating those chicken strips. I thought that what I ate at the senior center would be safe."

"It *should* be safe for you. I'm sorry that it wasn't."

"If this sandwich tastes as good as it looks, I'd come here every day if I could afford it." Nugget barked and Ann fed him a nibble of sandwich bread. "Living on a fixed income means dining out has to be a special treat, I'm afraid."

Brittany, who'd had her share of financial pressures in the

past, nodded with understanding. "I totally get that. Thanks for coming in."

"Excuse me, ma'am," said Nancy as she rushed out in front of the counter and approached Ann. "I'm sorry, but we don't allow dogs."

"Dogs?" Ann pushed Nugget's head down inside her purse. "I don't have a dog with me."

Nugget yapped, and Nancy looked at the poodle pointedly.

"We love that you are here," said Nancy. "But next time, do leave your dog at home. We don't want the health department to shut us down."

Ann looked over at Brittany. "I'm sorry, sweetie, I wasn't thinking. Next time I will leave Nugget at home."

"Thank you." Brittany nodded.

"Why didn't you say anything?" Nancy asked, after Ann had walked away. "This is your restaurant. You're allowed to maintain order."

"I know, but Ann's my friend and—"

"You're allowed to have rules."

"But what if she'd argued? You saw how she pretended Nugget wasn't in her purse."

"Then you politely but firmly argue right back." Nancy looked at the long line of customers. "All these people waiting to order lunch deserve to do so in a canine-free environment, unless that dog is helping someone with a disability."

"You're right," Brittany agreed, not wanting to argue.

Nugget's presence was only one factor in her interaction with Ann that captured Brittany's attention. A couple of hours later, once the lunch rush had ended, she was still chewing on what Ann had said about the seniors on fixed incomes not being able to afford her prices on a regular basis. She relayed the conversation to Nancy while they tidied up before the high school crowd arrived. "I wish there was some way I could offer food at a more affordable price, like they do at the senior center, but they have government subsidies helping lower costs."

"And you aren't a not-for-profit." Nancy wiped down the counter. "It's okay to make money. That's your goal."

"One of my goals." Brittany restocked a napkin dispenser. "I also want this to be a safe and inviting place for the community to gather."

"Which you are doing. You've created a charitable support program with that Angel Board of yours." Nancy disinfected the register. "Although I worry about it being abused. Have you noticed that girl with the braids taking a card down every single day and eating for free?"

"Isabella? The golden milk latte girl?"

Nancy nodded. "She's practically cleaned off the whole board."

Brittany looked over at the Angel Board and saw that Nancy was right. "I've been so frazzled, I hadn't even noticed."

"Maybe you could set up a one-card-per-customer limit."

"What if she really needs help, though? And the Angel Board is her only option?"

"Nobody's that desperate to drink turmeric. I don't know what that girl's story is, but something doesn't add up. Her backpack is expensive, and so are her shoes. I bet she can afford to buy her own drinks."

"Maybe those were donated."

"Could be." Nancy put down her cleaning spray. "Still, it doesn't seem fair that she's monopolizing the whole Angel Board and not leaving cards up there for others to enjoy."

"You're right. I'll monitor the situation."

"By the way, that's a pretty necklace you're wearing. Blue looks good on you. It picks up the color of your eyes."

"Oh. Thanks." Brittany fingered the blue and gold beads and glanced down at the number X. She'd worn Paul's necklace three days in a row. "I like what you've done with your hair. It looks pretty, clipped back like that."

"Do you think so?" Nancy checked her reflection in the toaster oven window. "Herman says it makes my ears look big."

"Your ears look perfect."

"I'll tell him you said so when I get home." Nancy put her supplies away. "My shift's over, but I could stay if you need me."

"It's pretty quiet now, and the after-school crowds shouldn't be so bad. Thank you so much for your help. Things have been a lot easier since you came aboard."

"Easier for me at home, too. This gives Herman a chance to be excited to see me, big ears and all." Laughing, Nancy waved goodbye and headed out through the back door.

A little while later, the high school let out and teens streamed in. Some students were younger friends of Jeremy, and Brittany enjoyed chatting with them, cherishing that faint but real connection to her son. The group of teen girls that usually claimed the communal table came too, Gabby, Lana, and Scarlett. Brittany couldn't remember if they were freshmen or sophomores. The girls kept her busy making sugary cappuccinos for a while. She was so preoccupied that she didn't notice Isabella pluck the last gift card off the Angel Board until she stood in front of her at the register, pushing it forward.

"I'd like a large golden milk latte, please." Isabella wore an oversized gray hoodie over black leggings. Brittany couldn't tell if they were expensive leggings or not. She picked up the card and read what it said.

For a woman brave enough to act with integrity, no matter the cost. It's hard to do the right thing. Not everyone has that courage.

How ironic... Brittany peered over the card at the young woman in front of her. Isabella's pale skin made her dark hair seem even richer. Nancy was right; Isabella was abusing the system. But Brittany didn't want to say anything to the girl in front of the other teenagers. She was annoyed with the girl, but not enough to embarrass her in front of her friends.

Although 'friends' might not be the right word in this situation. Brittany had never seen any of the other teens say so much as a word to the girl.

"I'll get that started right away," Brittany said, wondering if Isabella might be lonely. "Go have a seat and I'll bring it to you."

"Thanks." Isabella said, chewing on the end of one of her braids.

While she added the turmeric blend to the mug, Brittany surreptitiously watched Isabella. The young woman found a seat on the outskirts of the communal table. She didn't make eye contact with anyone, but she angled her chair so that any of the other girls could include her in conversation, if they chose to—which they didn't. They were too busy chatting, or looking at their phones, to notice her presence. Isabella gazed at them hopefully for a second, before she hung her head, unzipped her backpack, and removed her computer. She propped it open on her lap and peered at it intently like she was studying.

Brittany sprinkled a dusting of coconut sugar over the latte, and carefully brought the mug over to Isabella. "Here you go," she said kindly. "A large golden milk latte." She set it on the table next to Isabella.

"Great. Thanks." Isabella smiled for half a second before looking back at her computer.

Rude, Brittany thought. Although was it? The girl said 'thanks,' after all. It was only that the whole situation felt off-putting. The Angel Board was meant to serve multiple people in the community, not one teenage girl with expensive taste in drinks.

"Oops," Brittany said, noticing a napkin on the floor next to Isabella's backpack. "Let me get that trash out of your way."

As she bent down to pick it up, Brittany saw inside Isabella's backpack.

Please return to: 16 Sand Piper Lane, Sand Dollar Cove.

Was that where Isabella lived? Brittany had no idea. It was also possible that the backpack had been donated and the address had nothing to do with Isabella at all. Still, something about the address pinged Brittany's memory, but she couldn't quite place it. She'd lived here her whole life, except when she'd traveled, but that didn't mean she could list off every street. Part of her was tempted to plug the address into her phone and drive over there tonight to see what Isabella's homelife was like. But then the front door opened, and four more people came in wanting custom sandwiches, and Brittany forgot all about the address in Isabella's backpack.

It wasn't until closing time, when she was sweeping the floor and blasting 1990s pop music from the stereo, that Brittany's mind returned to the address. She finally remembered where she'd heard about Sand Piper Lane before. That was where Hannah and Guy had purchased the house that they were remodeling! Correction, the *mansion*. Hannah had invited Brittany on a tour to see the place, but the timing hadn't worked out. Maybe now Brittany could make time to see it? She could evaluate the neighborhood and find out if Isabella had hit hard times and was in need of charitable giving, or if she was a self-absorbed teenager who thought the world owed her free drinks.

NINE

Hannah and Guy's new house really did have turrets. Brittany had always loved this house; everyone in Sand Dollar Cove knew about it, even though most people had never been inside. It was so quirky it was iconic. But Mary had strong opinions about the mansion's aesthetics which she conveyed on the drive over. Her boyfriend Steven was chauffeuring Brittany, Mary, and Cheryl to the house in his van.

"This is Sand Dollar Cove, not Disneyland." Mary blew a puff of bangs out of her eyes. "The turrets are a bit much."

"I disagree," said Steven, a tall man with a friendly demeanor. "It's the drama of the house that appeals to me." A former lawyer, Steven had represented Brittany in her wrongful termination suit against the city, but his true passion was movies. He was the new owner of Sand Dollar Cove Cinema and had brought the old theater back to life. "It's like someone went to Neuschwanstein Castle in Bavaria and said: 'I want a house like this.'"

"Or went to Disneyland and rode the Teacups one too many times," said Mary. "It looks like a hard-core Disney fan designed it."

"It wasn't a Disney nut," said Cheryl, from her place in the front seat next to Steven. "If memory serves me right, it was a Japanese businessman who built it in the late 1980s right before the recession. The economy tanked so badly in Japan that he never actually lived there."

"I remember hearing that too." Brittany stretched out her legs in the back seat. The minivan was roomy. She was feeling extra vulnerable at the moment. She'd texted Jeremy last night, asking how he was doing, and he hadn't bothered to respond. She'd tried again a few minutes ago, and still had no response. It was like her own son was ghosting her.

"So, the man built a castle and never moved in?" Steven asked, as he pulled into the circular driveway in front of the house. "Interesting."

"The mansion's been sold five times since then," said Mary, "always to out-of-towners. It was turned into an Airbnb for a while until a wild party over Spring Break a couple years ago trashed the place."

"I remember when that happened." Brittany unclicked her seatbelt since Steven had parked the car.

"The partygoers caused forty-seven thousand dollars in damage." Mary picked up her purse. "Mainly by destroying the wood floor with a Slip 'N Slide and a Jell-O wrestling pit."

"What in the world?" Cheryl exclaimed. "Who does that?"

"It was a frat house from the University of Washington, I think." Brittany used the brush from her purse to tidy her curly hair. "They were put on probation after that."

"Good." Steven opened his door and looked at Cheryl. "I'll be right back with your wheelchair."

"Thanks," Cheryl said, remaining seated. "I don't need to warn you it's heavy, because you've got the muscles to handle it." Cheryl could walk limited distances, especially when she had her walker handy, but used her wheelchair if there was unsteady terrain or if she would be on her feet for a while.

Brittany and Mary got out too, and the first thing Brittany did was turn around and look at the view in front of the house. Sand Piper Lane faced the ocean. Tall grass, as high as her shoulders, grew in the dunes that separated the road from the sand. Brittany could hear waves crashing in a steady rhythm and could smell the salty scent of the Pacific.

"A great thing about this location is that it's far enough away from the lighthouse that you don't hear the foghorn," said Mary.

"You're right." Steven unfolded the wheelchair and locked the footrests into place.

"It's an amazing spot." Brittany looked back at the house and read the number: twelve. Isabella's house, or the house that the backpack had belonged to, must be several houses down, although the homes were so far apart that she couldn't see the neighbors. She wondered what that house looked like and if Isabella really lived in it. It had been a while since Brittany had driven down Sand Piper Lane, and now that she was here, she realized that anyone who lived in one of these houses was unlikely to need any type of food assistance. Sand Piper Lane might as well have been called Millionaires' Row. Or Billion-aires' Row, now that Hannah and Guy were moving in. Guy had inherited an international hotel chain fortune.

After they got Cheryl situated in her chair, they walked up to mammoth front doors, framed by stained-glass windows.

"Jeremy was right," Brittany said, taking in the ornate wood-carving on the door, and the stone gargoyles up above. "It feels like there should be suits of armor standing guard."

"Or Mickey Mouse and Cinderella," Mary muttered.

"Be nice," said Cheryl. "Don't be a design snob."

"She's not a snob, she's aesthetically sensitive." Steven put his arm around Mary. "It's like how strong perfume bothers some people. Mary's triggered by style."

Mary kissed his cheek. "That's why I help you shop for clothes these days."

"I wouldn't want to blind you with wild patterns," he said with a laugh.

"Should we ring the doorbell, or will it electrocute us?" Cheryl asked.

Brittany looked at what Cheryl was pointing at and raised her eyebrows. The button glowed orange and was surrounded by brass filigree. "I'll do it," she said, stepping forward.

"You've got a living will, right?" Cheryl joked.

Brittany rang the doorbell and the musical notes that followed were so loud, and played for so long, that Brittany felt like she was listening to an organ concert.

"Drama," Steven said, when it was over. "I love it!"

"Can you imagine how annoying that would be to listen to every time the Amazon van came?" Mary asked.

"Hush," Cheryl chided. "Green's a bad shade on you."

Mary, who wore a black leather jacket with tight jeans, looked insulted. "I'm not jealous, I'm—"

"Hello!" said Guy, swinging the door open. Hannah was right by his side, holding his hand. They wore matching aprons that said *His* and *Hers* on them.

Never in a million years would Ian have ever agreed to wearing matching aprons like that, nor would Brittany have wanted him to. She thought they were sweet, but silly. Still… every time she was around Guy and Hannah, or Steven and Mary, she realized how wrong she and Ian had been together. He'd tried a little bit, during the first months of their relationship, to make her happy. He'd also spent time when Jeremy was born attempting to be a good father. But Ian never tended any relationship for long. His true love was selling cars, and the only passion he felt was the rush that came from closing the next deal.

Her father had never devoted much time to her either. Alan poured his energy into work and extracurricular pursuits, but always put Brittany and Paul at the bottom of his priority list.

Now it felt like Jeremy was ghosting her too. Was he? Brittany pushed the thought away, unable to deal with it right now.

"Welcome to our humble abode," said Hannah.

"Crumbling abode is more like it," Guy added. "Although the contractor said it's safe enough not to wear hard hats."

"And the kitchen still works." Hannah pulled Guy away from the door so that the others could pass. "We promise to feed you. Or Guy will, anyway. All I did was set the table."

Brittany crossed the threshold feeling curious. Guy had been right; the interior was in shambles. Everywhere she looked she saw gaping holes in walls, bare floor slab, drop cloths, and power tools. Scaffolding stood at the center of the great room rising to the cathedral-height ceiling. The double-paned windows along the back wall were clouded from broken seals.

"It looks like you're gutting the place," said Steven.

"We are." Guy nodded. "Starting from scratch and building it up to code."

"While keeping the exterior," said Hannah.

"Why?" Mary asked, even though Cheryl immediately shot her a look. "Why not tear the whole thing down and start over? You know how I feel about the turrets."

"I like the turrets," Hannah admitted, her cheeks turning pink. "I know you said you hate them, but I think they're fun."

"Oh..." Mary's face froze into a forced smile.

"And the neighbors would have been upset if we'd changed them," said Guy. "Sand Dollar Cove doesn't have a historic register, but if it did, this house would be on it."

"It's only thirty-five years old," said Mary. "That's hardly historic."

"I thought you were happy for me?" Hannah asked.

"I am, but I'd be happier for you if you weren't trying to channel Rapunzel."

Hannah put her hands on her hips. "Well, that's rich,

considering you're the one with longer hair. Have you ever considered that—"

"What is that delicious smell coming from the kitchen?" Cheryl said loudly, even though the only scents Brittany could detect were sawdust and plaster. "I'm hungry."

"So am I," Steven boomed. "So hungry."

"Dinner's not quite ready yet, but I have appetizers out." Guy walked over to Cheryl's wheelchair and began pushing. "Let's get food into these two granddaughters of yours, shall we?"

"The sooner, the better," said Cheryl. "They fight like this when they're hangry."

"We're not hangry!" Hannah and Mary both said at once.

Cheryl was right: spinach artichoke dip and homemade bread made a tremendous difference to sisterly squabbling. The bubbling glasses of Prosecco didn't hurt either. Brittany savored each bite and sip. It wasn't often that someone else cooked for her, and she appreciated the rare treat. Twenty minutes later, Mary and Hannah were both laughing over Hannah's admiration of the arrowslits in the hallway bathroom, and Guy was tapping Brittany's shoulder.

"I have a gift for you," he said, pulling a card out of his apron pocket.

At first, Brittany thought it was one of the Angel Board notecards and was confused. She'd clearly spent too much time behind the sandwich counter that week. But once she looked at it closely, she saw that it was a recipe card.

"This is my absolute favorite, self-developed recipe for vegan pâté." Guy walked over to the refrigerator and pulled out a container. "I made some up so you could try it." He set it on the island.

"You did?" Brittany scanned the ingredients list: walnuts, garlic, olive oil, onions, parsley, and a bunch more. It looked simple enough to make. "Thanks."

Guy opened a package of crackers and sat it next to the pâté. "I thought it might make a good option for vegan sandwiches at your shop, but of course, my feelings won't be hurt if you hate it."

"Wow. That's really thoughtful of you. Thanks." Brittany scooped a cracker into the mixture and took a bite. A flavorful explosion hit her taste buds. "This is delicious," she said as soon as she finished chewing.

"The best part is you can make it ahead of time and it keeps for several days in the fridge." Guy dipped a cracker into the pâté.

"I want to try," said Steven. He served himself a generous helping, took a bite, and nodded his approval. "Yum."

Brittany paused for a second, mindful of the moment. She wouldn't have Safe Harbor without Steven fighting for her as her lawyer. And here Guy was, generously contributing his favorite recipe. She hadn't known many men in her life who treated her well without wanting something in return. *Nobody but Paul...* She was glad that her friends had found good men who made them happy. Hannah and Mary were lucky, and Brittany suspected they didn't fully appreciate how fortunate they were.

"Ooh! You brought the pâté out," said Hannah, walking up to the island. "I love this stuff."

"Let's do the grand tour," said Mary. "I've seen the whole house before, but Brittany hasn't."

"I'd love a tour." Brittany brushed cracker crumbs off her fingertips.

"It might be better for you to stay down here," Hannah said, looking at Cheryl. "Sorry, Gran, but there are lots of steps."

"You can keep me company while I finish cooking dinner," said Guy.

"Fine by me." Cheryl held out her wineglass for a refill. "I shouldn't drink and walk at the same time."

Twenty minutes later, Brittany had finished the downstairs tour, which was where most of the remodeling work was being done at present. The builders had gutted most of the rooms and were working on the wheelchair-friendly attached dwelling unit for Cheryl first. The ground floor of the house was a shell of what it used to be, but Hannah explained the upstairs was pretty much untouched so far.

"Untouched unless you count the place where the frat brothers rammed their heads into the wall while wearing football helmets," Hannah added. They had started the tour with the main turret first, since that was so outlandish that it begged for attention.

"Animals," Mary muttered.

"I'm glad that Jeremy's community college doesn't have a Greek system." Brittany followed Hannah up the stairs, pausing only to look out through another set of arrowslits. Thinking about Jeremy made her worry about him not texting her back. Was everything alright? She hated being incommunicado with her son.

"I like the arrowslits in the guest bathroom," said Mary, pointing to the oddly shaped windows, but I think you should get rid of these because they're blocking the view."

"But what if we were under attack and needed to defend ourselves?" Hannah reached the landing.

"Are you Robin Hood?" Mary peered through the slits for a second, before following.

"I'm more like Katniss Everdeen," said Hannah. Brittany couldn't tell if she was joking or not, until Hannah laughed. "Kidding, of course. We might get rid of those slits. It's under consideration with the architect, but not being able to see the view on the stairs makes the turret room reveal even better, don't you think?"

Brittany hopped up the last step so she could see what Hannah meant. The circular room had windows on all sides.

"Wow!" she exclaimed, her jaw dropping. "I can see all the way to Hawaii!"

"Not really, but I appreciate your enthusiasm." Hannah wiped a smudge off the glass. "It *is* pretty though, am I right?"

"Every time I see it, I'm stunned," said Mary as she joined them. "You're right in that it's a feast-or-famine type situation, since you can see so little on the stairs."

"Here you can see the dunes, the sand, the waves crashing on the shoreline and all the way out to the horizon. Sunset should be any minute." Brittany sighed dreamily. "The sun's dipping."

"Give it ten minutes and you'll see every color in the rainbow," said Hannah.

"You're going to have such a magical life living here." Mary hugged her sister. "I'm so happy for you, and I'm sorry about the Rapunzel jokes."

"There will be an extra bedroom with your name on it if you want it," Hannah told her.

"Ha!" Mary snorted. "No thanks, but I appreciate the offer." She looked sideways at Hannah, and then at Brittany. "I've actually been putting aside money to have my own apartment, or to find an apartment with Steven at some point, when we're ready."

"That's wonderful," said Brittany. "What a great next step for you."

"I agree." Hannah nodded. "Steven's a keeper. But what about you, Brittany? I know you mentioned perhaps moving into the store attic and renting out your house. That sounds cramped. We don't want to leave you in the lurch. I'll keep paying rent for all three of us for as long as it takes so you can find replacement housemates you like."

"I could never find people to replace you three," said Brittany. She looked out at the water. Here, from a safe distance, she could appreciate the ocean's beauty, especially now that the sky was bursting into a million shades of orange. "The attic above Safe Harbor is a good size, but it needs remodeling. Right now, all it has is a shower."

"Really?" Hannah asked.

"Yup." Mary nodded. "I've seen it. No toilet, no sink, no kitchenette—nothing but a shower floating in the middle of the room."

"How strange." Hannah wrinkled her forehead. "But you know, I always thought the previous owner was an oddball. He never took off that hat he wore, even though it had that disgusting sweat ring around the brim."

"Eeew! Yes!" Mary giggled. "I remember he would come to the drive-thru espresso stand where I used to work, and all the baristas would comment on that."

"A shower's a start," said Brittany. "But I'll need a full bathroom above the shop, and maybe a little room walled off so that Jeremy and I could have some privacy if he moved back home." She couldn't think of that right now. It was too overwhelming. "In the meantime, I guess it would be easier to find new roommates."

"But not yet." Hannah started walking toward a window in the turret. "We don't want to move Gran out of your house until her new rooms are ready."

"I'm not moving out anytime soon either," said Mary. "Steven and I have only been dating for six months. I love the adorable hunk, but I don't want to rush into things."

"Come look out this window," said Hannah. "From this side of the house, you can see the rest of the street. The family next door has a pool."

"And the house on the other side of that one is the one I redecorated this past summer before the people moved in." Mary trotted over.

They could see the other homes on Sand Piper Lane? Brittany wondered if they could see house number sixteen where Isabella's backpack lived.

"Was that the client who didn't want any color in the house beside white, gray, and chrome?" Hannah asked. "I remember you complaining about that."

"Yes. At first the lack of color drove me nuts, but once I saw all his modern furniture arrive, it made sense. The place looks like the cover story for *House Beautiful* or *Modern Home*. There's zero clutter at all, not even a toaster on a kitchen counter."

"Where do they keep the toaster?" Brittany asked as she peered through the window, past the backyard with the pool, and at the sleek modern house with a metal roof.

"Yeah? Why would you put the toaster away?" Hannah asked. "That sounds inconvenient."

"The previous owners installed an appliance closet when they redid the kitchen," Mary explained. "You pivot a door, and that's where the toaster and the coffeemaker are found."

"I still say that's inconvenient," said Hannah. "It's adding an extra step to your morning routine."

"Yes, but it also creates a 'low-stimulus environment' house —that's what my client liked to call it," said Mary. "He valued distraction-free living. His teenage daughter, on the other hand..." Mary laughed. "I had a lot of fun decorating her room."

Teenage daughter? "What house number was it?" Brittany asked, her curiosity piquing. "This house is number twelve, right?"

"Yup." Hannah nodded.

"The minimalist house is number sixteen," said Mary.

"Sixteen?" Brittany's curiosity was exploding. Did Isabella live there too, or had she somehow acquired the backpack from the girl who did?

"Yes. Sixteen." Mary stood on her toes and looked straight down the window at the pool next door.

"Is the daughter in house sixteen named Isabella?" Brittany asked.

Mary whipped her head around and stared at Brittany. "Yeah, how did you know?"

Brittany quickly explained about the Angel Board, and Isabella stealing all the cards to feed her golden latte habit.

"Whoa!" Mary said, wearing a shocked expression.

"That family can definitely afford to pay for their own drinks," said Hannah. "The dad drives a Lexus."

"Nancy was right," Brittany said, feeling frustrated. "The girl's been taking advantage of me."

"Nancy's always right," said Hannah. "We still have twenty minutes before dinner. Why not march over there and let Isabella's father know what's going on?"

"Yeah," said Mary. "And peer through the entryway while you're at it so you can appreciate my artistry."

"You think I should?" Brittany asked.

"Absolutely," said Hannah.

Mary nodded. "You don't deserve to be ripped off."

Brittany took a deep breath, already feeling nervous about a potential confrontation. "Okay," she said reluctantly. "I'll give it a try."

TEN

"I'm not a crazy person," Brittany told herself as she walked up the winding private driveway that led to house number sixteen. "I'm a small business owner who's being taken advantage of by a bratty teen."

Right before she reached the porch, her phone buzzed. Jeremy had texted her back!

I'm having fun. Classes are interesting.

Then he'd sent a picture of him leaning against the Mustang, with a huge smile on his face.

He wasn't ghosting her! This was excellent news. Brittany typed quickly on her phone.

Love you so much.

Love you too.

Brittany sighed when she read Jeremy's response. That's as good as it got these days, parenting an adult son who lived far away. He was independent and thriving and didn't need his mom that much anymore. He didn't seem to need her help at all. That's what she wanted, right? Still... she felt proud and crushed at the same time.

Maybe after she dealt with this Isabella fiasco and had gone back to Hannah and Guy's house for dinner, she'd ask for a second glass of wine. She wasn't driving, after all, or responsible to anyone but herself. *That part of my life is over*, she thought sadly. Jeremy was gone.

Brittany stepped onto the front porch of Isabella's house. Sleek slate tile and metal awnings created an aerodynamic aesthetic. She couldn't see through the clouded privacy windows; but she smelled the distinctive aroma of steak cooking. Brittany adjusted her blue and gold necklace and placed the X over her heart. Squaring her shoulders, she knocked firmly on the door.

The delicious scent of the steak dinner grew stronger and made Brittany even more annoyed. She loved steak, but knew it was expensive. Teenagers who lived in beachside mansions enjoying steak dinners should not be ripping off her community service project. The Angel Board wasn't meant for privileged rich girls. Plus, she'd personally funded some of those cards. Isabella was taking money out of Brittany's pocket.

I need to take this ire and channel it, Brittany told herself. She couldn't crumple and walk away, even though that seemed easier.

But when the door opened, and she saw who stood in front of her, Brittany's resolve wavered and then her anger roared to life.

"Ryan?" she exclaimed. "*You're* Isabella's father?"

"Brittany?" Ryan wiped his hands on a dish towel. He wore dark jeans and a gray sweater that hugged his broad shoulders. "What are you doing here?"

"You're Isabella's father?" she repeated.

"How do you know Isabella?"

Brittany looked past Ryan into the sleek but austere entrance of the house. Despite Mary's decorating magic, Brittany thought the entryway looked like a marble tomb. She looked back at Ryan, directly into his coffee-colored eyes. "I know your daughter from—"

Beep! Beep! A loud shrieking noise interrupted her.

"Damn, that's the smoke detector. I left steaks on the grill." He waved her inside. "Come on in while I deal with this."

Brittany followed him inside, past an ethereal painting that looked like someone had slashed silver ink on canvas, and through the foyer into a magnificent room that astonished her. Floor-to-ceiling windows faced the ocean, and the property's elevation allowed the occupants to peer over the sand dunes for a spectacular view. The kitchen was part of the great room and flowed seamlessly with the decor. Cabinets covered built-in appliances.

Minimalist, low-backed couches rimmed the room and a fireplace with blue flames glowed at the side.

Ryan raced to the glass wall, and pulled it open, allowing smoke from the indoor grill to escape, then he unscrewed the smoke detector above the island.

"Sorry about that," Ryan said, as he checked the grill.

Now that Brittany was closer, she saw a pan of asparagus steaming on an induction stove surrounded by a gleaming white counter.

"You said something about Isabella?" Ryan prompted.

"Yes, that's why I've come." Brittany put her hands down in front of her and tried to stand straight. She felt underdressed in her jeans and embroidered hoodie, even though Ryan was wearing jeans too. She'd grown up in an upper middle-class home, but she'd never lived in a house this fancy. Ryan hadn't either. He'd grown up blue-collar. It felt odd to be here with him now, watching him grill steaks that were beginning to burn.

"How do you know my daughter?" Ryan turned off the grill and slid the steaks onto a covered tray.

"It's like this," Brittany started to say. But before she could continue, Isabella walked into the room.

"Why are the window-doors open? It's freezing in here. This house is never warm enough. I wish—" Isabella paused when she saw Brittany. "Oh." Her unbraided hair fell almost to her waist in waves. Without her usually severe hairstyle, she appeared more like a typical teenage girl and less like Wednesday Addams. "Why are you here? How do you know my dad?"

"I knew her brother." Ryan rinsed his hands underneath the touchless faucet.

"My brother who *died*," Brittany added, with an emphasis on the last word.

"How did he die?" Isabella asked.

Brittany whipped around and faced Ryan. "You didn't tell her about Paul?"

"Who's Paul?" Isabella stepped up to the island and pulled out a chair but didn't sit down.

"That's not important right now," Ryan said, gruffly.

"My brother's not important?" Brittany's heart raced.

"That's not what I mean," Ryan sputtered. "What I meant is..." He palmed his forehead and pushed his silver-threaded dark hair up by the roots.

"Take a seat." Isabella pushed the stool closer to Brittany and sat down on the one beside it.

Ryan dropped his hand. "Brittany's not staying."

"Is that your name?" Isabella asked. "Brittany?"

It was odd seeing the girl animated since her demeanor at the shop was usually reserved. "Yes." Brittany sat down, not because she wanted to stay a while, but because she knew it would annoy Ryan. "My name's Brittany Thompson and Paul Thompson was my brother. My one and only brother. Now why don't you tell your father what you've been doing with my Angel Board? It was supposed to be a blessing for people who couldn't afford to order food."

Isabella's owl-like eyes became even wider.

"What's she talking about, Bella?" Ryan put his hands on the counter as he leaned forward and stared at her.

Isabella blinked rapidly but didn't answer.

"Were you unclear what the board was for?" Brittany prompted. After all, she hadn't explicitly written out a one-card limit rule, like Nancy had suggested.

"No, I knew what it was for," Isabella mumbled.

"Could someone please tell me what the Angel Board is?" Ryan looked from his daughter to Brittany.

"It's like a grace-and-favor program," Brittany explained. "Customers donate five dollars and gift that future purchase to someone who could use a pick-me-up. They write a special message of encouragement on the card for the recipient. The whole point of the board is to do good."

Ryan's forehead furrowed. "I still don't understand."

Brittany tried again. "Like for example, I gifted a card that said, 'For a daughter whose parents are divorced,' and that was the first card Isabella used."

"Oh." Ryan nodded. "I'm beginning to see."

"But what's unfortunate in this situation is that Isabella took nearly every card off the board."

"You what?" Ryan looked sharply at his daughter.

Isabella curled forward, her wavy hair making a curtain that fell around her face, blocking her expression from view.

"Is this true, Bella?" Ryan asked. "Were you going to the cafe when you told me you were in the library?"

What? That's what Ryan was worried about? Brittany frowned, as Ryan continued.

"We agreed that for your own safety, you were only allowed three places," Ryan continued. "School, the library, and here."

"My cafe is plenty safe," Brittany said, feeling insulted. "It's literally named 'Safe Harbor.'"

"Yeah." Isabella lifted her head. "It's totally safe, and it's also where everyone from my homeroom hangs out after school. Nobody goes to the library but losers."

"That's not true," said Ryan.

"How would you know?" Isabella countered. "You've probably never been there."

"I've been to the library plenty of times." Ryan stepped away from the counter.

"When?" Isabella asked. "In the last millennium?"

Despite herself, Brittany felt a whisper of a smile brush her lips. Truth be told, she hadn't been to the Sand Dollar Cove Library since Jeremy was in elementary school because the collection was so small.

Isabella looked at Brittany. "I'm sorry I misused the Angel Board. I knew it was wrong, but I don't have any spending money because *he* won't give me any, and—"

"Hey!" Ryan said.

Isabella kept talking right over him. "I just had to go to Safe Harbor because it's really my only chance of making friends, since that's where everyone hangs out, and also because *he* won't let me have a phone." She stared daggers at her father.

"Why aren't you letting her earn spending money?" Brittany asked. "Make her do some chores, or something. And why are you telling people that my perfectly wonderful dining establishment is unsafe?"

"I'm not," Ryan insisted.

"But you are," Isabella said emphatically. "You told me it wasn't safe. Or am I not a person?"

"Of course you're a person." Ryan pushed a button on the stove and the pan of vegetables stopped simmering. "I just want you to be extra careful because of—"

"I *am* being careful," Isabella insisted. "I moved out here like you wanted, didn't I? You said this place would be better, but so far it sucks!"

Again, Brittany felt an urge to smile, especially as she turned away for a second and saw the five-million-dollar view. Oh sure, this place sucked alright. She looked back at Ryan, whose left eyebrow was twitching. Watching Isabella give him a hard time was deliciously satisfying.

"Brittany's cafe is perfectly safe," said Isabella. "I should be allowed to go there, and you should let me use some of my birthday money so I can pay for my own drinks." She clasped her hands together. "Please?"

"Or make her scrub toilets to earn cash," Brittany suggested. "That works, too."

Ryan kneaded the back of his neck with his knuckles. "Fine. You can go to Safe Harbor, but only if you pay Brittany back for all the Angel Cards you stole."

"I didn't steal them," said Isabella. "I mean... I kind of did, but I'm not a thief."

"How many did she take?" Ryan asked, looking at Brittany.

"Five, I think."

"It was six," Isabella admitted. "Thirty dollars' worth."

"Okay then." Ryan moved the pan of vegetables to a trivet. "This is the deal. You owe Brittany thirty dollars' worth of dish-washing, or floor sweeping, or toilet cleaning, or whatever she wants you to do, and then you can have the privilege of being a bona fide paying customer in her store."

Ryan's suggestion surprised Brittany. She thought for sure he would have opened his wallet and paid her in cash. But she also respected it as a parenting decision that taught natural consequences.

Hang on there a second, she realized. *Did I just find something to like about Ryan?* She had, and it shocked her.

"Is that okay with you?" he asked Brittany.

"You mean working her debt off?" Brittany asked. "Sure."

She wondered what Isabella would make of the idea. Scrubbing toilets wasn't a great way to impress potential friends. But Isabella's reaction surprised her too.

"When can I start?" the girl asked. "This sounds like so much fun!"

"It's not supposed to be fun," Ryan said gruffly. "It's a punishment."

"Employment is not a punishment, it's an opportunity," said Brittany.

Ryan let out a puff of laughter. "You sound like my mother."

"I like your mother." Brittany put her elbow on the counter and rested her chin on her hand.

"You know Grandma Patti?" Isabella asked.

"I know everyone," said Brittany. "And you can come work for me tomorrow, if you have the time. Two hours ought to repay your debt."

"Can it be three?" Isabella asked hopefully.

"It'll have to be next weekend," said Ryan. "We're visiting Grandpa Frank tomorrow, and you need to study for your geometry test. Until next Sunday you're grounded for lying to me. Is that understood?"

"Ugh!" Isabella hopped off her stool. "You're so unfair! I hate Sand Dollar Cove. I wish we could move back to Seattle." She stormed off before Ryan could respond.

When Brittany saw the miserable expression on Ryan's face, she almost felt sorry for him. Almost...

ELEVEN

"What should I do first?" Isabella asked, when she showed up to work the following Saturday.

Brittany had been thinking up chores for the girl all week. She'd gotten a few more details about Isabella from her grandmother Patti, and now knew that she was fourteen years old and a freshman at Sand Dollar Cove High. Patti also mentioned that she'd tried to teach Isabella to sew. Isabella had labored for five hours over the sewing machine crafting a skirt under her grandma's tutelage, and it had come out beautifully, but she never asked Patti for a sewing lesson again. Patti didn't know why.

Today, Isabella wore jeans, Converse, and a red hoodie, with her dark brown hair twisted up into a bun. "Do you need help making sandwiches?" she asked. "I've memorized the menu."

"That depends." Brittany handed her an apron. "Do you have your Washington State food handler's card?"

Isabella shook her head. "Never heard of it."

"In that case, I'll have you help with tasks that don't require it, like cleaning the bathroom. Do you know how to clean the bathroom?" Brittany wondered if Ryan's fancy house included a maid.

"We have a house cleaner who comes once a week, but I have lots of experience cleaning toilets at my mom's house." Isabella wrinkled her nose.

"Perfect. Let me show you where the cleaning supplies are."

An hour later, after Isabella had cleaned the restroom, dusted the chair rails, and swept off the front porch, Brittainy gave her an easier job, restocking the napkin dispensers.

Since it was two p.m., and well past the lunch hour, the shop was quiet. A handful of patrons were scattered across the dining area in comfy chairs, reading books, working on computers, or playing board games with friends. Brittany wasn't selling many meals right now, but people did come up to the counter for drinks. She was using the time to prep food for the next day. Brittany showed Isabella how to collect the napkin dispensers off the tables and refill them. Five minutes later, they were both working side by side; Brittany was blending the vegan pâté recipe from Guy, while Isabella tackled the dispensers.

"Where's the other woman who works here?" Isabella asked, as she lined up half-empty dispensers on the counter.

"Nancy has the weekends off." Brittany peeled two cloves of garlic. "She only works here part-time on the weekdays."

"Do you have someone else here on the weekends?"

"Nope." Brittany pulled leaves off parsley. "I'm flying solo."

"Oh." Isabella lapsed into silence.

She didn't say another word until she'd returned all the napkin dispensers back to their tables, and asked Brittany what to do next.

"I have some utensils for you to wash." Brittany showed her the small pile by the prep sink. "They need to be hand-washed and can't go in the dishwasher in the back."

"Can I see the back room? I've always wanted to see behind the scenes."

"Sure. You can go find some fresh dish towels on the shelf next to my desk."

Brittany watched Isabella walk away and noticed she was smiling. Instead of the somber expression she usually wore, the girl seemed happy, even though she was "facing a natural consequence," as the parenting books called it.

A little bit later, when Isabella was up to her elbows in dish suds and Brittany was scooping pâté into a container, she dug for more information. "So, did you end up being grounded all week, or did your dad relent and let you go to the library?" Brittany asked.

Isabella frowned. "My dad? Stop being strict?" She snorted. "That will never happen. This is the first place I've been to that isn't school all week. I was so bored I thought about calling my grandma and asking for another sewing lesson, but I didn't want to torture myself."

"Patti's a professional seamstress. What's so bad about sewing with her?"

"She thinks I'm going to wear what we make, and I don't want to be humiliated again."

"Again?" Brittany put the pâté in the refrigerator.

"I don't want to talk about it," Isabella said, suddenly becoming prickly.

"Well, I'm glad your dad's changed his mind about letting you come here. It's good to have someplace to go after school besides the library."

"Yeah. He's way overprotective. He's always been like that, but it's gotten worse since we moved here. It's like he thinks I'm going to fall down one of those tunnels they discovered under the movie theater or something."

"Those are carefully blocked off, so I don't think that would happen." Brittany handed Isabella the blender to wash. "I'm surprised that Ryan is being overprotective, though. He used to have the run of the town when he was your age. He got into all kinds of trouble."

"Really?" Isabella stopped scrubbing the colander she was holding and looked at Brittany in disbelief.

Shoot. Brittany realized too late that she maybe shouldn't have mentioned that, but since it was Ryan she was talking about, she didn't care. He deserved every lingering bit of his prodigal reputation. "My mom thought he was a bad influence on my brother Paul and me and she was right. One time your dad convinced my brother to release a herd of goats that had been brought in to clear blackberries out of the park. Ryan herded them down Main Street and they ran into the parking lot next to the roller rink and started chewing on the tires of the parked cars."

"My *dad* did that?"

Brittany nodded. "Paul was involved too, but he was more of a sidekick."

"And wait. Where's the roller rink?"

"It's closed."

"That figures. My dad told me when we moved here that there would be fun things to do like that, but there's nothing."

"Nothing but the beach, and horseback riding, and dune buggies, and the movie theater, and hiking in Olympic National Park. Oh, and tide-pooling, and digging for clams, and kayaking, and—"

"Okay, okay..." Isabella rolled her eyes. "Thank you, Ms. Tourist Brochure, I get it. You sound like my dad. But I don't want to do any of those things with him, and besides, he probably wouldn't let me do any of them anyways because he'd say they're too dangerous. He already nixed the idea of horseback riding because he said he knew a kid who fell off a horse, broke his ribs, and had a concussion."

"That was someone in my grade, actually. Freshman year. But that was back in the days when we didn't wear helmets.

Horseback riding is a lot safer now." Brittany passed Isabella a bowl to wash.

"My mom says that my dad is such a cautious rule follower that she could never have any fun while he was around. That's one of the reasons they got divorced."

"Oh really?" Brittany tried to be chill, but she was intensely curious about all the ways Ryan had screwed up his life after ending Paul's. She hoped that his ex-wife had made him miserable, and that the divorce had crushed him. Just like what had happened between her and Ian, so Paul's death hadn't only ruined her life. Realistically, she knew that it couldn't have tortured him too much financially, since he lived in that spectacular beach house, but hopefully he was emotionally wounded. "What's your mom like?" Brittany asked, since that seemed like an innocent question.

"She's great." Isabella accidentally sloshed water as she scrubbed chicken salad off the mixing bowl. "Her name is Melissa and she's an artist. That's how my parents met. My dad's crazy about art. They met at the gallery where she used to work."

Brittany remembered the abstract painting hanging in the foyer of Ryan's house but kept her opinion about it to herself. "It sounds like they both like art," she said, restating what she'd just heard. That was one of the parenting tips she'd read for teenagers. It had never worked on Jeremy very well, but seemed to work great on Isabella, because the girl nodded, and kept talking.

"They *do* love art, only they sold most of their collection when they got divorced so they could buy two more houses."

"Two more houses?" Brittany echoed. Had she heard that right?

"Yeah." Isabella nodded. "A house for my mom, a house for my dad, and a house for me. They were all small houses, because Seattle real estate costs a bajillion dollars, but the good thing was that I never had to move. I had just started kinder-garten and they thought that was easier for me. When it was Sunday, Monday, and Tuesday my dad would stay with me, and when it was Thursday, Friday, and Saturday it was my mom's turn. Then they would take turns every other Wednesday."

"Wow. That must have required a lot of cooperation." Brittany couldn't imagine Ian agreeing to a plan like that for Jeremy, nor would she have wanted to be that tied to her ex-husband. The clean break seven years ago had been good for all of them. Well... good for her, at least. She knew Jeremy had been impacted by Ian taking off for Seattle, and only coming back to see him on rare occasions. "That sounds like it was a positive system for you," she told Isabella.

"It was." Isabella carefully cleaned a knife. "Everything changed when my mom married Troy, though. That was when I was in seventh grade. He has three sons, and they're all under ten, and we have to share a bathroom. It's so gross." Isabella shuddered. "My brothers couldn't hit the toilet even if you painted a target in the basin."

Brittany laughed. "I remember when my son was that age. Luckily Jeremy's hygiene skills improved."

"You have a son?" Isabella put the knife in the drying rack.

"Yes, he's eighteen and just moved away to college."

"He's lucky to have a cool mom like you."

"Where'd you get the idea that I was cool?"

"You have a nose ring, and an Apple Watch, and you have this awesome job, and—" Isabella snapped her mouth shut and stopped talking.

Brittany turned to see what she was looking at, and saw the group of teenage girls who usually hung out at the back table—Lana, Scarlett, and Gabby—walk in through the front door, and step up to the counter. "Customers. Would you like to take their order, or should I?" She was curious to see what Isabella would say.

"I don't know how to work the register."

"I'll enter it for you and prepare the drinks." Brittany found the notepad and pen she used to jot down her shopping list and offered it to Isabella. "You can write down what they want, and I'll handle the rest."

"I don't know..." Isabella said uncertainly.

"That's okay." Brittany didn't want to pressure her, even though she sensed that Isabella was eager to make friends with the other girls. "I'll—"

"Isabella Osborne, is that you?" asked Scarlett. The tall girl wore leggings and a form-fitting sweatshirt.

Lana flipped her blonde hair over her shoulder. "Do you work here?" She carried a sparkly pink Starbucks cup.

"Kind of," said Isabella.

"Lucky." Gabby's soft brown sweater matched her skin. "It would be cool to work at this place."

"Here you go." Brittany passed the notepad and pen to Isabella and encouraged her forward. "You've got this."

Isabella took the pad and went up to the spot behind the counter where she could take their order. She came back a few minutes later. "Can I offer them a discount?"

"Sorry." Brittany shook her head. "That's not in my budget."

"What if I offered to work extra to pay for it?"

"Still no. Friends should want to hang around with you because of who you are, not what you can get them."

"But that's the problem." Isabella ripped off the page and handed Brittany the order. "There's no way for these girls to find out who I am. The only time I see them is at school."

"Well, they know your name. Maybe you could follow them on social media and they might follow you back." Brittany began making the drinks.

"My dad won't let me have a normal phone anymore. It's so unfair."

"Oh." Brittany dumped ice into the Vitamix. "I want to hear all about it once I'm done with their orders. In the meantime, you can dry those dishes you washed."

Ten minutes later, when the teens had paid and claimed the communal table, Brittany and Isabella were restocking the paper to-go cups and lids and Isabella brought up the conversation again. "Would you let me have my iPhone back if I was your daughter?" she asked. "I have a dumbphone, but all it does is call five numbers. It won't even text."

"That depends." Brittany chose her words carefully. She certainly wasn't on Team Ryan, but she knew parenting teenagers was difficult, and that Isabella wasn't necessarily trustworthy. "I couldn't say what I would do since I don't know why your dad took the phone away in the first place."

"Because he's a control freak, that's why. And because he doesn't know what high school is like. He thinks that just because I had a hard time in middle school that it'll all happen again at Sand Dollar Cove High."

Hard time in middle school? That caught Brittany's attention. "What does your dad think might happen again?" she asked.

Isabella stacked another row of lids. "It's a long story, and you have two customers that just walked in."

Brittany turned to look, and was gobsmacked when she saw who stood there, holding a woman's hand, like this was the most natural place to be in the world. *Keith!* "That's my ex-boyfriend," she hissed.

"Why is your face so red? Was it a bad breakup?"

Brittany nodded, barely able to get the words out. "He fired me from my job at the senior center and then I had to sue the city for wrongful termination."

"What an asshole! I hope you won your lawsuit."

"I did. That's what gave me the money to open Safe Harbor."

"Those stupid glasses he's wearing make him look like an owl," Isabella whispered.

Brittany chuckled. Isabella was right. But that didn't stop her pride from hurting. Keith was eight years younger than her, and the woman he was with looked like she was ten years younger than Keith. She was so young that she looked to be Hannah or Mary's age. Why was Keith dating someone in her twenties?

Why did I date someone in his thirties? she asked herself a second later. But she already knew the answer. Because she was lonely. Loneliness was behind all her past relationship decisions. Ian had filled that void in her heart when she'd come back from Europe. He'd sold her a Toyota and the opportunity for companionship. That had meant her becoming an underappreciated girlfriend and wife, but at least she hadn't been lonely at the beginning of their relationship. The men she'd dated after her divorce were just fillers, people to see on the rare weekends when Jeremy was with Ian. Then when she'd met Keith, and he'd been so controlling and clingy, she'd thought: *Yay! He wants to be with me all the time!*

"I bet he's trying to make you jealous," said Isabella. "That woman he's with has her boobs on full display. It's too cold to be wearing a dress like that, and it makes her look like a lumpy potato."

Whoa, Brittany thought. *What would Isabella say about me if I wasn't here?* Fourteen-year-old girls were harsh. Jeremy had given her trouble at that age, but it had never involved fashion snark. "Body-shaming hurts all of us," Brittany said on instinct. "Although I agree with you that it's not warm enough for an outfit like that."

"Where's the notepad?" Isabella put the cups down and grabbed the pen. She picked up the notepad a second later. "I'll take down their order, so you don't have to deal with them."

"Really? You'd do that for me?"

"Of course I would. I'd spit in their cups too, but I don't want to get you in trouble."

Brittany laughed. "You sound like your father," she said, remembering the time Ryan had purposefully squirted ketchup on the guy standing next to them at the old roller rink's snack bar. The person had accidentally dumped sauer-kraut on Brittany's new skates. She'd been nine years old at the time, and promptly burst into tears, until she saw eleven-year-old Ryan hose the boy down with ketchup. Ryan had skated off into the crowd before the owner could catch him, while Paul stayed behind and helped her clean cabbage off her laces.

"My dad would never do something like that," said Isabella. "He'd be disappointed in me for even thinking of it."

"And I'd be disappointed with myself for letting Keith waltz in here and intimidate me." Brittany picked up the X of her necklace and placed it on her heart. "Thanks for the offer, Isabella, but I'll handle this myself."

"I'm right behind you if you need me. To spit, or whatever."

Brittany chuckled again, which meant when she approached the counter and greeted Keith she had a smile on her face, like his presence didn't bother her one bit. "Hi, Keith, what can I get you?"

"You mean what can you get for me and my *girlfriend*? This is Erica." He brought Erica's hand to his lips and kissed her fingertips. "Just two bottles of water for us. I've tasted your cooking before."

Brittany took a deep breath through her nose but kept smil-ing. "Two water bottles, coming up."

"Go get us a seat, babe," Keith told Erica. "I'll pay."

"You spoil me," Erica said, before licking his neck. "Tasty."

"You know it." Keith licked her back.

Gross! Brittany felt the urge to barf. She'd barely turned around to get the water when she heard Erica scream.

"Ahh!" she cried. "I slipped on this piece of lettuce and now I've hurt my back!"

Oh, no! Brittany ran around the corner to see what had happened. Erica was sprawled forward, at an awkward angle, and holding her back like it was in pain. A fat piece of lettuce was stuck to her shoe.

"Should I call an ambulance? Are you okay?" Brittany knelt to help.

"Don't you dare touch her," Keith snarled. "She might have a broken back. I hope you have good insurance."

Insurance? *Damn.* Brittany *did* have business insurance, but she didn't want to have to utilize it in only her second month. That would probably send her premiums skyrocketing. Still, her first concern was safety. "I'll call 911," she said, rising to her feet.

"I'm not sure that's necessary," growled a deep voice. "Unless you're calling a fraud detective."

Brittany looked up and saw Ryan standing in the doorway, wearing black pants and a gray sweater. His silver-threaded dark hair was slightly damp, like he might have gotten caught in the rain.

"What the hell?" Erica cried. "I'm in so much pain. Why isn't anyone calling a doctor?"

Brittany pulled her phone out of her apron pocket, but what Ryan said next made her pause.

"I don't know who you people are, or what you think you're pulling," he said, pointing to Keith. "But I saw you drop that lettuce on the ground, and I saw that actress of yours fall on purpose."

Brittany's mouth gaped open for a moment before she closed it again. "Is that true?" she asked Keith. "Were you trying to fake a lawsuit?"

"What?" Keith jerked back. "Of course not. Don't be ridiculous."

"I'm really hurt down here," Erica mumbled. "*So* hurt."

By now, a crowd of people had surrounded them, including the teenage girls from school.

"It's true," said Scarlett. "I saw him drop the lettuce, too."

"And I got it on video," said Gabby. "I figured they were filming a prank or something."

"Could you send that video to me, please?" Brittany asked. "I'd really appreciate that."

"Sure." Gabby shrugged. "No problem."

Brittany rattled off her phone number for Gabby and then looked at Keith. "Still want me to dial 911?" she asked. Her phone buzzed with the incoming text from Gabby.

Erica hopped to her feet. "That won't be necessary," she squeaked.

Keith's scrawny face turned a greenish color. "Never mind about the bottled waters," he said. "This place probably has rats."

Ryan yanked the front door and held it open wide, even though rain blew in. "Get out!" he yelled. "The both of you, before I throw you out."

Keith held onto his glasses as he hurried out the door, and Erica followed seconds behind him.

TWELVE

It wasn't until after Keith and Erica had left that Brittany realized she was shaking. She felt her chest tighten, like she was sucking oxygen through a tiny tube, and would run out of air any second.

"Are you okay?" Ryan asked, his dark eyes piercing through her.

"Yup," she gasped. "Just dandy." Brittany curled and uncurled her toes within the safety of her wool socks. She felt the comforting fit of her Birkenstock sandals ground her to the floor. She looked down at her jeans and saw the embroidered flowers she'd added earlier that summer, one stitch at a time as she watched travel documentaries on TV. Then she clutched Paul's necklace and felt the X under her palm. "I'm fine," she said clearly, her voice sounding more normal this time. She felt like she owed Ryan an explanation for what had happened. "You're probably wondering what that was all about."

"Nope," he said. "That's none of my business. Get your things, Bella, it's time to go."

"Your dad calls you Bella?" Gabby asked. "Cool."

"I love *Twilight*," said Scarlett, who was a head taller than her friends.

"You do?" Isabella smiled. "Me too. The girls at my old school thought it was stupid."

"It's impossible to live this close to Forks and not love Bella Swan." Lana hooked her blonde hair behind her ear. "Twihard for life, right here."

"Even though it's cheesy," Scarlett added.

Gabby hooked her backpack over her shoulder. "And problematic, since Edward is basically stalking her."

"Still..." Lana shook her head. "I love classic literature."

Classic literature? Brittany felt old. "Thanks for all your hard work today, Isabella. It was much appreciated."

"No problem," Isabella said. "It was fun."

"Hey, Isabella," said Gabby. "We're going to the movie theater next. Do you want to come with us?"

Isabella's eyes lit up. "I'd love to!" She looked at Ryan. "Can I? Please?"

"Well..." Ryan put his hands in his pockets. "I don't know—"

"Please?" Isabella clapped her hands in front of her, begging.

Ryan frowned. "I'm not sure I feel comfortable, considering—"

Brittany coughed loudly and caught his eye. She nodded her head, ever so slightly, and he relented.

"Fine," he said. "What time's the movie over?"

"Eight thirty," said Scarlett. "My mom's picking us up. I'm sure she could give Isabella a ride home."

"That's nice of you to offer," said Ryan. "But I don't know your mother, so—"

"Yes, you do," said Brittany. "Scarlett's the daughter of Stephanie Mathews. Her brother Ben was on your basketball team and we all used to go to the beach together."

"Steph with the Volkswagen Rabbit?" Ryan asked.

"I can't believe my mom used to drive such a cool car," said Scarlett. "It's hard to picture her without a minivan."

"So can I, Dad?" Isabella asked. "Since you know Scarlett's mom?"

"I guess so." Ryan pulled out his wallet and removed two bills. "Here's money for your tickets and popcorn."

"Thank you!" Isabella ran out from behind the counter, snatched up the money, and gave her dad a quick hug.

"We better get going, or we'll be late," said Gabby.

The girls left quickly after that, exiting through the door in such a tight pack that Ryan had to jump out of the way.

"There go my dinner plans," said Ryan as he watched Isabella leave with them.

"You did the right thing." Brittany turned the sign on the door from open to closed. The last few customers had already left. "That's a nice group of girls, and Isabella will be happier here once she has friends."

"If only it were that easy," he said doubtfully, causing Brittany to wonder what he meant.

"As for dinner, can I make you a salad or a sandwich? I still want to say thank you for how you helped me earlier with the lettuce incident. A frivolous lawsuit could have ruined me."

Ryan looked up at the menu board. "I *am* hungry," he admitted. "But I'll pay for my own sandwich. The Osbornes always pay their own way—despite Isabella's abuse of the Angel Board. I'll try a Double Decker, if you don't mind."

"It's no trouble at all." Since Ryan already had his wallet out, she rang up the order first. "That'll be $12.10." She turned the screen toward him so he could pay.

"So that was Ben Mathew's niece, huh?" Ryan tapped his credit card on the screen.

"Yup." Brittany nodded. "The girl in the brown sweater is Gabby Santos, and lives on Eleventh Avenue. Her parents are both teachers at the local elementary school. The blonde girl is Lana Shields, Jason's daughter. Jason was my year, but you might remember him because his dad owned a charter fishing boat."

"Sure. I remember Jason. Small world."

Brittany smirked. "Small town," she corrected. "Jason still runs the charter service with his dad, and his wife is a dental hygienist. They're a nice family." Brittany passed Ryan his receipt.

"Unfortunately, I've learned that some of the meanest girls come from the nicest families."

"What?" Brittany had dealt with a lot of issues parenting Jeremy through the years, but girl drama had never been one of them. She was about to ask Ryan what he meant when he changed the subject.

"Is this the infamous Angel Board?" He walked away from the counter and toward the side wall.

"That's right." Brittany got to work making Ryan's sandwich. "Hopefully the Angel Board's days of infamy are over." She set out three slices of bread for the Double Decker, and then added three more so she could make one for herself as well. It was dinnertime, after all.

"How does the board work again?" Ryan walked back to the counter and watched her spread mayonnaise.

"Customers pay five dollars up at the register, and then I give them a notecard. They write down a message of encouragement to someone who could use a boost. Then, days, weeks, or even months later, someone brings that card up to the register and gets a free drink."

"That sounds like a great system, and I'd like to contribute."

"You don't have to unless you want to."

"I do," he said forcefully. "Want to." He opened his wallet again and pulled out a five-dollar bill. "Here you go. Let it be known that the Osbornes contribute to the board, instead of raid it, from here forward."

"Duly noted." Brittany wiped her hands on her apron before accepting the cash. She walked a few steps sideways, put the money away, and handed him a card and pen. "Here you go."

"Thanks."

Brittany went back to preparing the sandwiches while Ryan wrote something down and pinned it to the top of the board. It was weird being here with him after so many decades. This was the fourth time she'd seen him since he'd moved back to town, but it still felt odd.

Not just odd. Ryan's presence brought a mixture of emotions. It was impossible to see him without feeling things she didn't want to feel: old, hurt, angry, and safe.

Safe? Where had that come from? She didn't feel safe when she saw Ryan, she felt on edge.

Ryan was the boy who stopped what he was doing to put the chain back on her bike when she was eight years old and couldn't fix it herself. But he was also the boy who dumped ice cubes down her back at the field day picnic.

Ryan was the sixteen-year-old who'd let her hop in the back seat of his truck when he and Paul drove to the beach. But he was also the person who pretended like he didn't know her when she ran into him and his date at the movie theater.

When it came to Ryan, she never knew where she stood. When Paul had been alive, Ryan had tolerated her. Once Paul had died, she'd stopped tolerating him.

Well... no... that wasn't being completely fair to Ryan. He'd done more than tolerate her existence.

There was this one time, when Brittany was in eighth grade, that she'd had horrible trouble in algebra, even though she was normally great at math. The teacher had gone on maternity leave and then been replaced by a substitute teacher who wanted to be teaching first or second grade, not middle school math. Brittany tried to teach herself from the textbook but struggled. She was a conscientious student and watching her grade fall into B minus territory freaked her out. Cynthia had tried to help her, but she didn't have the patience for quadratic equations. Alan was always too busy at his orthodontics practice, or out fishing on the *Lovestruck*. Paul was great at math, but couldn't explain how he solved anything, so he was no help.

But one day when Ryan had come over to the house to shoot baskets with Paul, he'd noticed Brittany struggling with her homework at the kitchen table. Ryan was in tenth grade, and well beyond Algebra 1. "Do you want some help?" he offered, as if it were as simple as that. As if someone—anyone—could help her pull up her sinking grade.

"Yes," she'd said, not thinking he was serious. Or if he was, maybe he meant pointing out her mistake in the problem set that was terrorizing her. "I have a test tomorrow that I'm going to fail."

"That sounds important." Ryan looked over her shoulder at her textbook.

"You can just repeat Algebra 1 next year when you get to high school," said Paul. "The teachers there are better, anyway."

"But then I'll fall behind, and that would be embarrassing to have to repeat a class." Brittany cared about her grades. She wasn't especially studious, but she wasn't a slacker either.

"There are still six weeks before the end of the school year." Ryan pulled out a chair next to her and sat down. "That's plenty of time to bring up your grade." He spent the next hour and a half helping her finish her homework and study for the test. He also wrote out a practice set of problems to work on during homeroom the next morning.

Brittany had gotten an A on that test, and the next one, and the one after that, because Ryan had tutored her for the rest of the year. That's when she'd started baking cookies for him, come to think of it. She'd gone through multiple recipes before she discovered that chocolate thumbprints were his favorite.

Yes, seeing Ryan brought back emotions, alright, and she wasn't sure what to do about any of them.

"Isabella did great here today," she said, catching his attention. Ryan was still staring at the Angel Board. "I enjoyed her company a lot. She's a really sweet girl."

"Sweet." Ryan grunted. "She can be, from time to time. If she feels like it."

"What's the story with her not having a cell phone?" Brittany plated the sandwiches and added a serving of coleslaw and a couple of thumbprint cookies to Ryan's for old time's sake. "I heard a lot about that."

"I bet you did."

Brittany walked around the counter holding the two plates and set them on the closest table. "What do you want to drink?"

"I didn't order a drink, and I didn't realize I was eating here."

Brittany wrinkled her forehead. "Of course you didn't. I'll grab a to-go box so you can eat at home." What had she been thinking? She hadn't, clearly. She'd been traipsing down memory lane. Brittany walked back to the counter, feeling disgusted with herself.

"I didn't mean it like that," Ryan said suddenly. "Or to be rude. I just didn't want to put you to any more trouble." He pulled out a chair and quickly sat down. "A glass of water would be fine, thank you."

"I have other things, too," Brittany said, her temper softening. After all, Ryan had kicked Keith out. "Iced tea or a soda, maybe?"

"Whatever you're having. Thanks."

"Two Shirley Temples coming right up."

"What?"

Brittany laughed. "I'm kidding. Diet Coke?"

"Sounds better than a Shirley Temple." Ryan smiled.

A minute later, Brittany was sitting at the table next to him and it was hard not to let nostalgia wash over her. There wasn't an algebra notebook between them, or Paul sorting through his CD collection, or a thousand other things she missed about her youth, when time stood immobile and the future was full of promise. Nostalgia was a tricky witch, making her wish for things that could no longer be, while also feeling like they washed around her at the same time.

"I see you're still making thumbprint cookies," Ryan said, looking at his plate.

"They are quite popular," she said, pleased that he had noticed.

"But do they taste as good as they used to?"

"I would hope so."

"I'll be the judge of that." Ryan picked up a cookie and ate it in one bite.

"And?" she asked. "What's the verdict?"

Ryan finished chewing before he spoke. "They taste different. Less buttery."

"You mean *more* buttery. I don't use margarine anymore."

"Could be," he said drolly. "I should probably try another one for the sake of science."

"Don't let me stop you."

Ryan ate the second cookie and leaned back slightly. "I can see why these are popular," he said. "And I don't miss the margarine at all."

"I should hope not." She smiled slightly, knowing a compliment from Ryan when she heard one. He wasn't effusive with praise, but he spoke volumes with actions, like how he'd eaten the cookies first. "So, what's the deal with Isabella not having a phone? She told me all about that, but nothing about the reasons why."

"You and I survived high school without phones, and we did fine."

Brittany tilted her head to the side. "We went to school with the dinosaurs."

"We're not *that* old." Ryan grinned for a second before his face became serious again. "You're at least two years younger than me, and I still have a long way to go before I hit fifty."

"Enjoy the next few years because fifty's coming for you."

"It's coming for me first, and I'm fine with that." Ryan lifted his glass. "To the privilege of aging," he said gruffly.

Hearing him say that out loud made Brittany understand that Ryan was thinking of Paul too. Her heart dropped into her stomach.

"To growing old," she said, clinking her soda against his.

Ryan took a sip and put his glass down carefully. "Isabella isn't ready to have her phone back yet, because it caused so many problems at her old school. She was bullied so bad that her mom and I pulled her out."

"That's awful! Poor Isabella."

"Luckily, I work from home most days, so I was able to homeschool her, but it wasn't a first-choice solution for any of us. Troy—that's my ex-wife Melissa's second husband, he's a firefighter and was able to help on his days off. Together, between the two of us, we kept Isabella up with her lessons, but she hated every minute of it. Wanted to be back at school with her friends." Ryan shook his head. "But her friends weren't necessarily her friends, if you know what I mean."

"Ah... I see."

"Her so-called *friends* were part of the problem. Sometimes I dream about meeting whoever invented social media and punching them in the face."

"Wait a minute," Brittany said, her mind still stuck on something Ryan had said. "Do you mean to tell me that you and Troy get along so well that you were able to develop and implement a homeschool program together?"

Ryan picked up his sandwich. "We didn't have to develop it from scratch. There's a lot of curricula already out there. But, yeah. Troy's a great guy. Although I think it was harder on him than it was on me because he also had his sons to deal with. I just had sales reps and engineers trying to overschedule me for online meetings the whole time."

"That's amazing." Brittany couldn't quite wrap her brain around it. "Isabella told me you had a complicated three-house system, too, that worked out well for a long time."

"It did." Ryan nodded. "Until Melissa and Troy got married. Then we had to reassess." He looked at the Double Decker. "This is a great sandwich, by the way. Is that stone-ground mustard?"

"Yeah. It goes nicely with the honey ham." She pulled an errant curl behind her ear. "That's really impressive that you, Melissa, and Troy are able to co-parent like that. Once my ex and I divorced, I was pretty much on my own. Ian paid the bare minimum of child support, and that was it."

"That's unfortunate. For you and your children. How many kids to you have?"

"Just one." Brittany told him all about Jeremy, and how he'd moved to Seattle to attend community college and pursue his dreams. "He wants to be a firefighter someday, like Troy."

"We should put them in contact. Maybe Jeremy could visit the station one day."

"He'd love that," Brittany said, assuming it would never happen. Ryan, for all his grumpy and gruff ways, was only being polite. And Brittany wasn't sure she could ever trust him anyway, not where Jeremy was involved. "So, is it the school situation that caused you to move back home to Sand Dollar Cove? I thought it was because of your father."

"Both." Ryan shook his head somberly. "Everyone agreed

that a fresh start in a new school would be good for Isabella. We could have stayed in Seattle and sent her to private school, but by the time we'd made the decision we'd missed the application periods for the good ones. Our next option was for one of us, me or Melissa and Troy, to move to a new house zoned for a different high school. We had to get Isabella away from her toxic friend group. Around the time we started that conversation, Melissa found out she was pregnant."

"Wow!"

"Yeah. She's forty-two, and it was a complete surprise. It'll be Troy and four kids in one house, plus Isabella when she's over there. The house is a decent size by Seattle standards, but Isabella wasn't so keen on the bathroom-sharing issue or sharing her room with a new baby. Meanwhile my mom's not getting any younger, and my dad..." Ryan's voice drifted off, and the pause became noticeable.

"Is doing well in memory care but still needs support," Brittany offered, when she saw that Ryan was having a hard time formulating the words to describe Frank's battle with dementia.

"That's right. So, we came up with a new plan, and it was for Isabella and me to move here, and for her to start at Sand Dollar Cove High as a freshman and spend summers and holidays with her mom."

"That sounds like a good plan on paper, but a hard one in reality when all of a sudden you're the only parent managing a teenager's mood swings and expectations." Brittany spoke from personal experience. Jeremy might not have had girl drama, but he had his share of scrapes.

"Yeah." Ryan let out a huff of air. "You're telling me. Melissa helps as much as she can, talking to Bella every night, but it's turned into this good cop, bad cop situation that's not helpful for any of us. Although Melissa and I are both in agreement that Isabella's not ready for a phone again anytime soon."

"Well, her making friends with Scarlett, Lana, and Gabby is

a step in the right direction. And if you're willing to add Safe Harbor to your list of places Isabella can come after school to hang out with kids her own age, that's another positive thing. I don't provide supervision here, but I'm not *not* supervising either. It's better than being holed up in her room feeling depressed about life in general."

"You're right." Ryan scooped a bite of coleslaw onto his fork. "I know you're right. I just don't want her to fall in with the wrong group again, or get hurt, or do something dangerous or—"

"I know. Believe me, I know." Brittany told Ryan about Jeremy getting caught putting a toilet on the roof of the high school. "When the principal said the words 'senior prank' I thought my heart would explode. I was so afraid."

"I can imagine," he said in a low voice.

"But in general, I think Sand Dollar Cove is a great place to raise teenagers. It's safe here. We don't have big drug or gang problems. For the most part, the locals get along, and the tourists are happy to be on vacation. Moving here with Isabella was a wise choice."

"I appreciate you saying so." Ryan looked down at his empty plate. "And thanks for dinner."

"You paid for your dinner."

"Well, thanks for the drink and cookies, that is. I've taken up enough of your time." He stood. "I'll be out of your way," he said, before saying goodbye. "Bye, bye, Britt."

"Bye." Brittany rose to her feet and watched him go. When the door closed behind him, an emptiness weighed down on the normally cozy space. She took a deep breath before getting to work, knowing that the sooner she could get home to her craft projects and television shows, the better. She'd tried to schedule some relaxation for herself by ordering a new embroidery kit that pictured a shelf of dying houseplants and the words *Killer*

On the Loose, but so far all she'd done was put the fabric in the hoop.

Brittany closed down the kitchen, started the dishwasher, and swept the floor. She was about to turn off the lights and leave when she remembered that Ryan had left a message on the Angel Board and she didn't know what it said. Brittany went up to the board and read the notecard she'd watched him pin on the top. There it was, written in the clear, easy-to-read handwriting she remembered from her algebra notebook.

For someone who's lonely. Your future is full of hope, I promise.

What a poignant thing to write. She stared at Ryan's handwriting, wondering if he still felt lonely himself sometimes. After all, he didn't seem like he'd reconnected with any of his old friends in town.

But then her eyes drifted down the board and she saw another notecard, written in unfamiliar handwriting. She didn't know who had left it, and what she read made her gasp.

For a mom who wears Birkenstocks and wool socks. Good for you for being comfortable, no matter what the fashionistas say.

That was oddly specific. Brittany's gaze looked down at her socks-and-'stocks feet. Who'd left a message meant for *her*?

THIRTEEN

Mondays should have been her day off, but as a brand-new small business owner, Brittany had little free time anymore. Over the past two days she'd stitched the first dying houseplant in her embroidery kit, a depressed-looking philodendron, but that was as much relaxation as she'd managed. Now she was all done putting away groceries and restocking the dish towel pile in the back room of Safe Harbor. The shop felt peaceful in its resting state, which helped set Brittany's mind at ease that yes, she really could take the afternoon off to enjoy herself without worrying about her business. But first she wanted to explore the attic to see how much effort it would take to bring it into a livable condition.

Brittany pulled down the trapdoor, and the stairs descended inches away from the dishwasher. She climbed the aluminum steps and into the attic. It took her a moment, but she eventually located the chain that pulled on the light, and the soft glow from one bare bulb illuminated the space.

The last time Brittany had explored the attic had been summer, and it had been hot. But now she shivered in the unheated space. The floor was stable and sturdy, but the pitched roof didn't have any insulation. Luckily, it was tall enough that she could stand upright when she was in the center of the room, which stretched the entire length of the cafe below, making it a considerable size. She was just inspecting the prefab shower stuck in the middle of the room when the fluttering of wings startled her.

"Ahh!" Brittany cried, nearly jumping out of her skin. When she looked up, she saw tiny brown bodies nestled close together, hanging from the rafters. *Bats.*

Yuck! Not only was there a colony of bats sleeping up there, but the side of the shower that rested below them, as well as the floorboards, were covered in droppings. Double yuck.

This wouldn't do at all. She couldn't have vermin living above her restaurant. Brittany didn't know how to deal with the bats, but at least she could clean up the crud they dropped. She rushed over to the stairs, ready to come back with rubber gloves and bleach. But as she climbed down the rickety steps, she wondered if coming back up to the attic while the bats were still there was a wise idea. What if one of them bit her and she had to get rabies shots? Brittany shuddered. She hated shots, and didn't have time to deal with that—not that she'd have the choice, if there was a risk of infection.

What could she do? Call an exterminator? That would be horrible! If people saw an exterminator truck parked in front of Safe Harbor, she'd lose all her customers. Brittany pushed the trapdoor up, closing off the attic, wishing she'd never gone up in the first place. She washed her hands and wallowed in discouragement. A soft knock on the back door interrupted her pity party.

That was odd. The shop was closed today, and besides, who would try to enter through the alley? Brittany peeked through the side window to see who was there, and was surprised to see Patti, wearing knit pants and a jacket with quilted blocks sewn over the denim.

"Hi, Patti," Brittany said, after opening the door. "We're closed today, sorry."

"I realize that." Patti clutched her purse protectively and looked to the left and right. "But when I saw your car parked back here, I figured now was my chance to speak with you privately."

"Oh. Ah..." Brittany held the door open wider, wondering what Patti had to tell her that was so important she'd sneak in through the back door. "You'd better come inside, then. Can I make you a cup of tea? I don't have a pot of coffee going, but tea is no problem. Or I could brew you an espresso."

"Tea would be fine. Thank you." Patti followed Brittany through the back room and into the storefront. When she reached the register, she took out her wallet "How much is it?" she asked.

"Don't worry about that." Brittany brought out the caddy. "I don't have the register turned on. Which flavor would you like?"

"Chamomile would probably be good, because what I have to tell you is upsetting. But I really do need to insist on paying. Osbornes always pay their way."

Hearing that made Brittany recollect Ryan saying the same thing two nights ago when she made him a sandwich. "Why don't you contribute a dollar to the tip jar, and we'll call it even?" she suggested.

"That works." Patti took out three dollar bills and dropped them into the collection.

Brittany added tea bags to two paper cups and filled them from the instant hot water dispenser. Then she joined Patti, at a table that was far away from the windows. The woman was staring at her hands, which shook slightly, and she spun her wedding band around and around her ring finger. "Here you go," said Brittany as she set down the cups. "They still need two more minutes to brew."

"Thank you, dear. You treat me so well. You always have,

ever since the senior center, even when I know that seeing me must have been hard." Patti looked away. "Because of Paul."

"Paul would have wanted me to treat you well. He always talked about how you mended his letterman's jacket after it ripped on a fence post."

Patti looked back at Brittany. "He was a fine young man and I've always felt horribly sad for what happened."

"It was a tragedy," Brittany said coolly, not wanting to discuss it further. Some conversations were too hard to have, especially on her day off. "Is that what you wanted to talk about?" If so, she'd politely maneuver Patti out the door.

"No, actually, it's Ryan."

"Ryan?" Now Patti had her full attention. It's not that Brittany had been thinking about Ryan a lot since their impromptu dinner. But he'd definitely crossed her mind more than she'd care to admit. Witnessing how he was such a devoted father to Isabella—so protective and involved—had softened her attitude toward him ever so slightly. It was like Ryan was one of those fathers on 1980s sitcoms that she used to watch on television. The type of dad who stuck around and gave wise advice. When it came to parenting, Ryan was the total opposite of both Brittany's father and ex-husband. "What about him?" Brittany asked. "It must be nice for you that he and Isabella have moved back to town."

"It is." Patti nodded and warmed her hands on her tea. "Now when the memory care center calls, because of Frank doing this or that, Ryan can help, too. It doesn't all land on me. Last weekend Frank fell and spent twelve hours in urgent care."

"I'm so sorry to hear that."

"He's okay now," said Patti. "And he doesn't remember what happened. But Ryan was my rock that day. He stayed with Frank the whole time, so I didn't have to." She stared down into the tea. "It's hard for me to be around Frank, you see. Since he's so far gone. My husband's no longer there. Or that's what it feels like, at least."

"How awful." Brittany took her tea bag out and set it on a napkin. She still didn't understand where this conversation was going, although she was heartbroken to hear of Patti's struggles.

"Here's my problem, and why I need your advice." Patti removed her tea bag as well. "How do I tell Ryan about Don?"

"Don?" Brittany repeated. Realization about Patti's predicament hit her all at once. "Oh... I see. Because you're... dating?" she finished, asking it like it was a question. She'd seen the two of them together holding hands, but didn't want to make assumptions.

Patti nodded. "Kind of. Don wants us to make things official. He's even started calling me his 'old lady,' instead of 'dollface,' which is good because he calls everyone dollface, even Cheryl."

"Since you mention Cheryl, what does she think? She's one of your best friends, after all."

"Cheryl thinks that the sooner I tell Ryan about Don, the better. She said I should just get it over with, like ripping off a Band-Aid."

That seemed like good advice to Brittany. In her experience, after living with Cheryl for over a year, her housemate's advice was usually spot-on. "Do you have any reason to think that Ryan won't like Don?" Brittany asked.

"I'm cheating on my husband!" Patti's eyes misted. "My husband of forty-eight years. What will Ryan think of me?"

"I think you should take loaded words like 'cheating' out of this situation." Brittany put her hand over Patti's. "Don's a fun guy and he makes you happy. There's no need to be lonely when, as you already put it, Frank's not there anymore."

But it was more than that. Frank Osborne had never been a good man to begin with, at least according to everyone Brittany knew. Cynthia railed about how awful it was that Frank could never hold down a job. Paul came back from Ryan's house with stories of Frank passed out on the couch in the middle of the day, surrounded by empty Budweiser cans, and Alan used to say that the only thing Frank was good at was playing poker. Why Patti had stuck by her husband all those years was a mystery to everyone, and she certainly didn't owe him devotion now.

"Keep living your life," Brittany told her. "Be brave."

"Me? Brave?" Patti withdrew her hand from underneath Brittany's so that she could blow her nose on a tissue. "That's the last word I'd use to describe me. I've found happiness again and I feel guilty about it."

"Don't feel guilty for living your life."

"Easier said than done, I'm afraid." Patti picked up her tea like she was going to drink it, and then set it down again. "I worry about Ryan thinking he might have made a mistake for moving out here once he finds out what a floozy I've become."

"Again with the loaded words," Brittany chided. "You're not a floozy."

"Liberated woman, then." Patti took a deep breath. "And instead of Ryan being able to live his own life, and do things he loves to do, like hike and travel, he's stuck working all the time and then helping with Frank. I asked Ryan if he had the chance to do anything that was just for him, and he told me: 'Don't worry, Mom, I hung a bat box in my backyard this afternoon.' See what I mean? *That's* his idea of entertainment."

"Does Ryan play baseball?"

"No. Real bats! Live ones. Most people try to get rid of them, but my son..." Patti rolled her eyes.

That's right! Ryan knew about bats... Brittany had almost forgotten that. Could he possibly help her solve her problem? "I have a colony of bats living in my—" she started to say, but then stopped. The seniors at the center loved to gossip, and Patti was no exception. She didn't want half the town to know that Safe

Harbor had winged creatures pooping in the attic. "Living in my shed," she lied. "Do you think Ryan could help with that?"

"Absolutely." Patti pulled out her phone. "Let me give you his number. I should get your number, too, because that'll make it easier when—" Her eyes opened wide.

"When what?" Brittany prompted.

"Well, see... The thing is..." Patti pulled her earlobe. "I hoped that you might come over to my house for dinner one night and help me introduce Don to Ryan, since you know both of them..."

"I wish I could," Brittany said, trying to find a way to politely decline the invitation. "But I'm really busy these days, and—"

"Don't you ever have the chance to put your feet up, let alone have someone else cook for you?" Patti folded her hands and leaned forward. "You've spent the past few years making sure I had wholesome meals to eat at the senior center. Please allow me the chance to cook dinner for you. At least this one time?"

"Well..." Brittany felt torn. She wanted to make another excuse to get out of it, but she couldn't resist Patti's plea. Patti and Don had been so supportive of her and her new business, after all. "Okay, I'll come." Brittany fiddled with the bracelet she'd crafted out of hammered copper and turquoise beads. "I don't know how much help I'll be, but I'll try."

"Thank you so much!" Patti patted her on her shoulder. "I was thinking this Saturday, but I don't want to ruin your social life."

Brittany smiled ruefully. Now that she didn't work at the senior center, the gossip about her must not be very detailed or Patti would know she didn't have a social life. "Saturday night will work for me."

What had the world come to? She was eating dinner with

Ryan Osborne two weekends in a row. She wasn't sure how she felt about that.

"Great." Patti pushed her phone forward. "It's all settled then. In the meantime, here's Ryan's number so you can call him about those bats."

FOURTEEN

Brittany didn't have the opportunity to deal with her bat situation until the following day after work. She was home, in her family room, with her aching feet elevated on two pillows and her embroidery kit on the coffee table beside her. Brittany was too exhausted to pick up the needle, but she took out her phone and texted Ryan.

Hi, she began. *This is Brittany. I've found bats in my attic and wondered if you knew how I could*—she paused, thinking how best to word her request—*safely remove them without attracting attention from my customers.* There, that sounded good. Brittany hit send and leaned back into the cushions. She closed her eyes, not expecting him to answer right away. Ryan was a busy person after all.

But he responded immediately.

I can help. We should deal with this as soon as possible before the colony hibernates.

Hibernates???

Brittany stared at her reply and wondered if three question marks were enough. This issue was becoming more complicated.

Her phone rang a second later, with an incoming call from Ryan. She swung her feet to the floor and sat up straight before she answered.

"Hi," came his gruff voice. "I figured it was easier to explain this over a call."

"Thanks. I appreciate any advice you can offer. What did you mean about bats hibernating?"

"They sleep through winter in a hibernaculum, like an old well, a hollow tree, a cave or—"

"An attic?" Brittany scrunched up her face.

"Exactly. It protects them from predators and bad weather. They usually enter their hibernaculum sometime between late September or early October. That's why it's illegal to exclude bats after October fifteenth."

"Exclude bats? From what, a Christmas party?"

"No, that means safely remove them to a new location."

"Oh, jeez. This is officially becoming a nightmare."

"Not necessarily. Bats do wonders for the environment. They eat mosquitos, for example."

"That's nice." Should she mention the white lie she told Patti to keep her quiet? "By the way, if your mom asks, the bats are in my garden shed. I didn't want everyone at the senior center knowing Safe Harbor has a bat problem."

"Ha!" Ryan chuckled. "I'm careful what I say to her too, sometimes."

"How do I move the bats along to a new location?" What was the word Ryan had used? "I mean, 'exclude' them?"

"What's today's date again?" Ryan asked.

"Tuesday the seventh."

"Right. Okay, that gives us a handful of days to work with."

Us? "You mean, you'll help me?"

"Of course. Bats are a federally protected species and I'm excited to check out your colony. I've always wanted a colony to choose me, but no matter how many bat boxes I've put up, it hasn't happened."

"Some dreams just aren't meant to be." Brittany put her feet back up on the pillows and laid her head on the armrest. Even though they were talking about bats, and even though Ryan was the last person in the world she really wanted to talk to, she was relaxing into the conversation and almost enjoying it. Almost...

"So, you want to check out my bats?" she asked.

"Yes. In the daytime when they are there."

"But without disturbing my customers," she cautioned. "This is a top-secret mission."

"Roger that."

"Mondays would be best, because that's when I'm closed, but I guess we can't wait that long."

"Exactly. October fifteenth is the deadline. Let me look at my schedule and see what my meetings are for tomorrow. Isabella has a half-day at school."

"Maybe she could stop by afterward and then you could come pick her up? After taking a stealthy tour of my attic?"

"That could be arranged. I'm sure Isabella would love another excuse to go to Safe Harbor."

"How did her movie night go with Lana, Gabby, and Scarlett?"

"Great, so far as I know. Of course, now I'm hearing the 'I need a real phone' conversation on repeat because she can't be part of their group chat."

"Which is an issue," Brittany said, delicately. She didn't want to stick her nose in where it didn't belong, but she could see Isabella's point. "If they make plans to meet up after school, how can Isabella be included in that conversation? Email?"

"She *has* a phone," Ryan protested. "It just doesn't have texting or smartphone capabilities."

"Which is great for calling you or Melissa, or if she needed to dial 911."

"Yeah. That's the point of it."

"I think Jeremy once set up an email chain with his friends on his school computer when I took his phone away for a week after he got in trouble on the school bus."

"What did he do?" Ryan asked.

"He was about the same age as Isabella. Jeremy and his buddy were playing catch in the back of the bus with a bag of mandarin oranges."

Ryan laughed. "That sounds like something that—"

"You'd get Paul in trouble for doing?" Brittany finished for him. "I know." She said it in an annoyed tone but smiled. "I took Jeremy's phone away for two weeks, but he earned one week back for good behavior after he cleaned out the garage. I figured that was transportation-related, so it counted as a restorative justice opportunity."

"Restorative justice?"

"Yeah. Earn back privileges through good behavior and making amends. That works great for teenagers. Although I don't know if I should give parenting advice. Jeremy and I have crossed swords over the years."

"If you *were* handing out advice, how would you handle this situation with Isabella and her phone?" Ryan asked. "I'm curious."

"Well, for starters I'd acknowledge her very real need to make friends at a new school, and how challenging that must be for her without a phone. It's like sending a kid to Paris and telling them to have fun but that they're not allowed to speak French."

"Is my daughter paying you to say this?"

Brittany laughed. "No, she's not. But maybe you and Melissa could work together with Isabella to figure out a plan for how she could earn her phone back, and what type of safety procedures you could put in place once she did? Monitoring apps, or time limits, or something along that nature."

"You bring up a lot of good points." Ryan paused for a moment before continuing. "Friendships are important. I get that."

"I know you do," Brittany whispered.

"I kind of miss the old days of landlines and answering machines."

"You're the one to thank for us finally getting call waiting," Brittany said, remembering. "I was in fourth or fifth grade, and my mom missed a call from her accountant because you and Paul had been on the line for so long talking about video games. Can you imagine how bad the two of you would have been if YouTube had been invented? Jeremy *loved* watching other people play Minecraft on YouTube."

"Seriously?"

"It's a thing. Don't ask me why, but it is."

"Paul would have loved giving Jeremy video games at Christmas and on his birthdays," Ryan said, in a somber voice.

"Yeah. He would have."

They both fell silent.

"Okay, so bats," Ryan said, after clearing his throat. "I'll come help you figure that out after lunch."

"I'd appreciate that, thanks." Brittany rolled over on her side and looked at her embroidery supplies spread out over the coffee table. "See you tomorrow."

"Bye, bye, Britt." Ryan ended the call.

Brittany put her phone on the table next to the silk embroidery floss. Ryan was right. Paul would have showered Jeremy with every hot new game release that got buzz. It was hard for her to picture what an older version of Paul would have been like, because he was forever trapped in her mind as a seventeen-year-old. As each year passed, her brother seemed younger.

But her conversation with Ryan just now had given her a

glimpse of what Paul might have been. Forty-seven-year-old Paul would have connected with his nephew in ways that Brittany couldn't, as Jeremy's mother.

And had it been Paul who'd started saying "Bye, bye, Britt," or Ryan? Brittany still couldn't remember. Her memories of Paul were like that. Some were as sharp as the spike of a sea urchin, but others had diluted like brackish water.

Those sharp memories though; oh, how they pierced the heart.

Brittany closed her eyes, thinking of her brother, and a particular scene came to mind.

She had been making Paul's favorite recipe, pumpkin bread, and wearing a tube top and crocheted vest over flared jeans. That must have been when she was a sophomore because her feet hurt from the platform sandals she wore to keep the jeans at the right length. She'd just poured the batter into the bread pan when Paul came into the kitchen spinning a basketball on his fingertip.

"Did you add walnuts?" he'd asked.

"No." She scraped the last bit of batter with a spatula. "You hate walnuts. I added pecans, instead."

"Yum." Paul palmed the ball and turned on the kitchen faucet, drinking directly from the sink.

"Gross!" Brittany shrieked. "What are you, a dog?"

"I'm part Dalmatian. Didn't you know?" he asked with a wry grin. "Promise not to turn me into a coat."

"I promise, but use a water glass, next time. The rest of us live here, too."

The memory made her smile. Thirty years later she'd caught Jeremy doing the same thing, drinking water directly from the faucet. He'd also swig milk from the carton. Had Paul done that as well? Brittany wasn't sure.

The memory settled over her like a warm blanket, making her feel safe, and comforted. But then came the prick of a needle poking skin when she remembered what had happened next.

Cynthia had rushed into the kitchen right when Brittany was sliding the bread pan into the oven. "What are you doing?" she snapped at Paul. "Why aren't you dressed yet?"

"What do you mean?" Paul indicated his sweaty basketball shorts and tank top. "I'm dressed."

"Not for your senior picture," Cynthia hissed. "Your portrait session is in thirty minutes and cost a small fortune. You can't go to the studio looking like that."

Paul sniffed his armpits. "I don't smell that bad. I'll go throw on a clean shirt and—"

"No!" Cynthia pointed her finger at him. "Shower and change, pronto, mister."

"Good idea." Brittany finished setting the oven timer. "Senior pictures live forever."

"I don't need any input from you, missy," said her mother. "I need you to clean this gigantic mess you've left in the kitchen. I swear you have no respect for the family. The rest of us have to live here, too."

Paul caught her eye and gave her a conspiratorial smirk. "Yeah," he said, in a tone that didn't tip Cynthia off that he was mocking her. "The rest of us have to live here, too."

"What are you standing there for?" Cynthia planted her hands on her hips. "Go shower, already."

Brittany surveyed the kitchen. She hadn't made *that* bad of a mess. Had she? Not by her standards as a fifteen-year-old, she hadn't. Cynthia sat at the kitchen desk, checking her email on their mammoth desktop computer while Brittany loaded the dishwasher and wiped down counters.

"What is that delicious smell?" Alan said, when he entered the kitchen a while later.

"Pumpkin bread." Brittany pushed the start button on the dishwasher.

"With nuts or chocolate chips?" Alan turned on the oven light and looked through the window at the baking bread.

"Pecans. We were all out of chocolate chips."

"You spoil me." Alan gave her a quick hug, and when he did, Brittany had detected the scent of a perfume that was popular at the time, Sun Moon Stars by Karl Lagerfeld.

Cynthia didn't wear perfume, and neither did Brittany, because it gave her mother a headache.

Smelling the sickly-sweet scent on her father made her queasy. Where had it come from? A patient, or another woman?

"I'm ready!" Paul announced, and he strode into the room wearing slacks, a button-down shirt, and a tie. His wet hair was slicked back but would probably dry on the drive over to the studio. "The time has come to immortalize me." He struck three funny poses in a row. "The Sand Dollar Cove High School yearbook will never be the same."

And it wasn't.

The following spring when Brittany opened her yearbook, she could barely look at the full-size page dedicated to Paul.

But it was worse than that.

Paul's copy of the yearbook had arrived too, because they'd preordered it when he was still alive. At first, Brittany didn't know what to do with it, but then Ryan had whisked it away and spent the next three days getting signatures from every person in school. Paul's friends wrote long messages, and his acquaintances wrote their sincerest regrets for not having known him better. By the time Ryan returned the yearbook to Brittany, so she could pass it on to her parents, it was a living, breathing memorial of loss.

Brittany reached for a box of tissues on the end table and blew her nose.

She dried her eyes, and picked up her embroidery kit, hoping to push the sad memories away. Then she cried harder when she realized that meant pushing the good ones away as well.

Paul grinning when she'd caught him drinking from the faucet.

The joy of baking him pumpkin bread.

Ryan handling Paul's yearbook so she wouldn't have to. That was a kindness. She could see that now.

And that senior photo that stood on her dresser up in her bedroom... Paul's youthful charm and good looks, immortalized forever.

FIFTEEN

"What's got you all frazzled?" Nancy asked the following day, when they had a tiny break in the lunch rush.

"Nothing," Brittany said evasively. The truth was, Ryan was coming, and she didn't know how she felt about it. "A friend is stopping by to look at what I might do about the attic." She hadn't told Nancy about the bat colony yet. She figured the fewer people who knew, the better.

Nancy raised her eyebrows. "It must be some friend, considering I've never seen you wear lipstick before."

"Oh." Brittany felt herself blush. "This is the problem with being forty-five. I put on a little makeup, and suddenly I look like a different person. I'll go wipe it off."

She started to dart to the restroom, but Nancy grabbed her sleeve.

"Don't do that. You look great. I'm sorry I gave you a hard time. But I hear you on the makeup issue. If it weren't for Maybelline, I wouldn't have any eyebrows at all."

A customer stepped up to the register, ending their conversation.

As Brittany prepared the order, she pondered what she'd

told Nancy. Had she really referred to Ryan as a friend? She had, and that shocked her. The first ten years of knowing him had involved nursing a huge crush. The last thirty years had passed in bitter hatred. Friendship wasn't an adequate descriptor.

And yet... Last night when she'd been thinking of Paul's yearbook, and how Ryan had shepherded it around school, gathering signatures, it had softened her viewpoint on him. Seeing how protective he was of Isabella helped, too. He clearly had good qualities, and as much as she wanted to ignore them, she couldn't. Like when he'd loaned her his coat on the dock because she was freezing cold.

Shoot! She'd left it at home even though she still needed to return it to him. Brittany was contemplating whether or not she'd have time to rush home and retrieve it when she heard Nancy speak behind her.

"Why yes," Nancy was saying. "Brittany mentioned someone was stopping by."

Brittany looked up and saw Ryan standing behind the counter. "You're here."

"I am." He nodded.

"I'll handle the tail end of the lunch crowd." Nancy untied the back of Brittany's apron. "You go do what you need to do."

With her half-fastened apron now dangling, Brittany undid the last strap and hung it on the hook.

"Follow me," she told Ryan, in her most professional tone.

They squeezed into the tiny back room that was barely large enough for two people. The dishwasher and storage shelves took up most of the space. Brittany stood on her tiptoes and tried to reach the handle that pulled down the stairs but couldn't reach the loop without stepping on her desk chair.

"Here." Ryan raised his arm. "Allow me." He was tall enough to reach it easily.

"Thanks. Watch yourself." Brittany pressed herself against

the dishwasher to make room for the ladder. It rattled down with a clatter and clicked into place. "I'll go first so I can turn on the light." She grabbed the handrails and hauled herself up one step at a time.

"After you," Ryan said.

Knowing he was behind her, staring directly at her backside, made her nervous. If only she had started a lunges and squats program six months ago. Instead, all she had lifting her butt was a generous percentage of Spandex in her jeans.

"Get ready for a disaster zone." Brittany pulled the light bulb chain. "This attic needs some love."

"I see what you mean," Ryan said, as he ascended through the trapdoor. "It looks like a cozy place for bats, though." He could stand straight in the center of the room, but the eaves were so low that he stooped as he walked past her. "Where'd you say the colony was?"

"Behind the shower." Brittany pointed but didn't follow. She wasn't keen on seeing them again and needed a moment to steel herself. "See them?"

"I do." Ryan's face softened. "And what a good number of them. Little brown bats. So cute."

Cute? "Yeah, uh... What if they have rabies?"

"That's possible, but highly unlikely." Ryan scratched his chin, still admiring the bats. "Only about one in twenty thousand bats actually carries rabies. You know, I said I thought these were brown bats, but now that I'm getting a better look at their ears, they might actually be Townsend's big-eared bats." Ryan looked down at the shower. "Did you know this pipe is leaking? That must be their water source."

"No, I didn't. Once I saw the bats, I went the other direction." Brittany stood rooted to the spot, still not moving.

"Come on over and look," Ryan encouraged. "I'll be right here the whole time."

"Okay..." she said, hesitantly. Brittany crept closer until

she stood slightly behind him, peeking around his torso. Her hair brushed against his wool sweater and instantly frizzed from static. Her eyes focused on the cluster of brown lumps nestled close together. Every now and then, one of them would wiggle, and the surrounding bats would wiggle back, like they were cuddling. Ryan was right, they were cute... kind of.

"I think what we need to do is seal off entry points," he said.

"How do we do that?" Brittany poked her head out one more inch past Ryan's side, her curly brown hair still attached to his sweater.

"I've got a ladder back at the house I'll bring over. Then I can look for places they might get in, like pipes, wires, corners, roof edges, or even gaps beneath the shingles."

"How can I help with that?"

"You won't need to. But as far as relocating the colony, that'll be a job for an expert, and it'll need to be done before the fifteenth. I know someone I can call about that. I'm not sure how much he charges."

"Whatever it costs, I'll pay." Brittany shivered. The sooner the bats were gone, the better. "How'd you learn so much about bats?"

"That's a long story. I should take some pictures to send to the exclusion expert."

"Of course." Brittany stepped back. "I'll... look for gaps in the construction where they might be sneaking into the attic."

"Good idea." Ryan took out his phone and began snapping pictures.

Brittany walked around the room in a slow circle, crouching down when the eaves became too low. "There's a tiny space right here," she said. "It's barely the size of my fist."

"That's big enough for them, alright."

"It's also big enough for weather to get through, too. I'm lucky the roof's not leaking."

Ryan took another picture of the colony. "Maybe the shingles overlap in such a way that rain can't get in, but bats can."

"Could be."

He turned in her direction and snapped her picture.

"Hey!" she protested. "Give a girl some notice, first."

"Sorry." He grinned. "I wasn't taking a picture of you, though, I was taking a picture of the entry point."

"Oh." The answer made sense, but she wasn't entirely mollified. "So how did you learn about bats? I can handle a long story."

"How about a depressing story, can you handle that?"

Brittany raised her eyebrows. "Try me."

Ryan let out a deep breath. "Well, it's like this..." He lifted his arm up and braced it on a rafter, which caused Brittany to notice how strong his biceps were. She could see muscle definition through the tight sweater. "After graduation, I was out of here. I never wanted to come back to Sand Dollar Cove again." He looked down at the dusty floorboards. "Too many bad memories."

"I get that." They were bad memories that Ryan was responsible for, as far as she was concerned, but that was beside the point.

"I didn't have college money or the basketball stardom it would take to earn a scholarship, but I had that old truck my dad helped me fix up."

"Your Ford Ranger."

"You remember it?" Ryan looked surprised.

"Of course. It had those jump seats in the back of the cab that I'd squeeze into when you and Paul let me ride along."

"The seatbelts worked. I made sure of that."

"They did," she nodded.

"Anyhow, I drove to Tacoma first, and got a job working in construction. I lived in my truck for a few months, before I found a roommate and stable housing. It took me a while, but I worked my way through community college and transferred to the University of Washington where I studied business. I graduated right around when the dot-com boom was taking off."

"In the 2000s."

"Yes. That's right."

"What's the depressing part of this story? So far, it's a 'pull yourself up by your bootstraps' tale."

"Because I just told you the good parts."

"What are the bad parts?" Brittany sat down on one of the camping chairs and pushed the one next to her an inch closer to Ryan.

He sat down a few seconds later, and slumped forward, resting his elbows on his knees. "I don't know how much you want to hear." The anguish in his voice surprised her.

"As much as you'd like to tell me," she said plainly.

"Well..." He massaged his right temple with his thumb. "I started off in construction, like I said, but that's a glorified way of saying digging ditches. They paid in cash at the end of each day."

"Interesting. I've never had a job like that."

"I'm glad." Ryan brought his hand down. "A lot of my 'co-workers,' and I use that term loosely, were ex-cons, or deadbeat dads. People who wanted cash payment because otherwise their wages would be garnished for child support. It wasn't a great group to be around."

"Especially after what you were used to with your friends back home."

Ryan nodded. "But... after everything that happened, I pretty much fell apart and figured this was all I was good for. Digging ditches. Sleeping in my truck or on someone's couch. If Paul wasn't alive, why did I deserve to live? Most days I wished I had drowned with him." He looked down at his hands.

"What?" Brittany was shocked.

"I felt worthless, utterly worthless."

"I'm so sorry." The words slipped out of her mouth unconsciously. After all those years of hoping Ryan rotted in misery, it had turned out he had been in worse straits than she could have ever imagined. It was as if the intense amount of vitriol she'd harbored against him had shot forth into the world and found him.

She paused to consider that, and felt shame.

Deep shame.

Because no matter what had happened, she knew in her soul that Paul wouldn't have wanted Ryan to suffer.

She placed a light hand on his shoulder. "Paul would have wanted you to live life to its fullest."

"Live enough for both of us," he grunted.

"Right."

"I eventually realized that, but it took me a while to get there." Ryan sat straight, and Brittany withdrew her hand.

"What happened next?" she asked.

"One of my housemates asked me to help him pick something up with his truck. I thought it was going to be a TV or a mattress or something, so I said yes. But he took us to this storage center in Tacoma, and when we got there, it was all his stuff. Things he'd stored when he was in prison, and now had to sort through because he couldn't afford the fees anymore."

"How sad for him."

"Yeah. But that's what changed my life."

"What do you mean?"

Ryan gestured with one hand, as if pointing to a memory. "While we were there, I noticed a crowd of people bidding on an unclaimed storage unit. It was an auction. I was curious, so I went over to see."

A faint memory resurfaced in Brittany's mind. "Your dad used to buy things at auction too, right?"

"Vehicles, mainly. That's how he acquired my truck." Ryan

paused. "And that's also how he bought the boat that we renamed the *Carpe Diem*."

"That's right." Brittany spun her bracelet around her wrist in circles.

"Anyhow, as soon as I saw there was an auction going on, I thought what the hell. It must have been a bit of my dad coming through. I placed a bid—and I won."

"You did? What was inside the unit?"

"Junk, mainly. But that was good for me. The internet was taking off, and I sold most of it online. I made more money from that storage unit than I did all month digging ditches."

That was the Ryan she knew. The good part of Ryan, that is. The part of him that was smart, resourceful, and tenacious. The Ryan that identified challenges that needed to be solved, like eighth grade Brittany failing in algebra, and then patiently, step by step, walked toward victory.

"Good for you," Brittany said, meaning it.

"Thanks. I bid on another storage unit, and then another. Soon I was earning enough that I could quit my job and move into my own apartment. That gave me enough confidence to go back to school and graduate from college. The storage unit biz is also what got me interested in art, which is how I met Isabella's mother. I sold art I'd acquired to her gallery and asked for her number." He grinned. "I got Isabella out of the transaction, as well as Melissa's friendship, so I always joke that that was the best storage unit auction I ever won."

"I should say so." Brittany smiled. "But how does this relate to bats?"

"I encountered bats in more than one unit, especially the older ones that were more likely to have access points. I also encountered my share of rats." Ryan shuddered. "Bats were always a cool discovery, but rats, not so much."

"Yuck."

"Yeah."

"And all of this was because you took a chance and bid on an abandoned storage unit?" Brittany asked, looking at him with awe.

Ryan nodded. "Yes. I remember seeing that crowd of bidders and thinking, why not me? So I opened my wallet, counted the cash, and went for it."

"*Carpe diem*," Brittany whispered.

"Seize the day. That was Paul's favorite expression, and every time I placed a bid, I felt like he was there with me."

"He would have loved knowing he'd helped encourage you." Brittany looked at Ryan with newfound respect, her opinion of him softening. He'd turned his life around with hard work, smarts, and ingenuity. Paul would have been so proud of him.

Ryan cleared his throat. "Melissa would tell you that all that trauma when I was young has made me way too overprotective of Isabella, and maybe she's right. But some scars don't heal all the way, if you know what I mean."

"I do." Brittany had her battle wounds too.

"Um... well... I've got all the photos I need." He rose to his feet. "I'll contact the bat relocation company right away and ask when the owner thinks it's best for me to seal up the holes. Saturday, maybe." Ryan stooped because the eaves were so low. He rested his hand on a beam so he wouldn't hit his head.

Brittany stood too, only she was short enough that she didn't need to duck. She thought about stepping to the side, so she wouldn't be so near Ryan, but she didn't. It felt like one of those rare times back in high school when he'd lean against her locker and mumble that he'd give her a ride home from school with Paul. Usually, Ryan had ignored her at school, but when he didn't, she'd felt so seen that it was like he'd shone a spotlight on her.

She felt like that now.

Noticed.

Valued.

He thought she was important enough to confess his deepest secrets to. Had any man ever been that honest with her?

Despite her best intentions, her old crush on him flickered slowly back to life.

Ryan hadn't faded with age; he'd become more handsome. A tiny part of her wanted to rake her fingers through his hair and finally feel what it was like to have his strong arms surround her. She pushed that thought away because she had no room for any man in her life—especially Ryan.

"Speaking of Saturday," he said slowly. "My mom said you were coming over to her house for dinner."

"That's right." Brittany nodded. She wasn't exactly looking forward to the event.

Or was she?

"Isabella is excited you're coming. I think she's getting burned out on Grandma's house already, but you're a big draw."

Brittany chuckled. "I'm happy to be your teen magnet."

"That's something you've always been good at." He stepped to the side. "But heads up, her house isn't like yours was growing up."

"What do you mean?"

"Clean. Your mom always kept things so orderly."

"My mom does like a clean house," she agreed. "I'll see you on Saturday."

As Brittany descended the stairs, the flutter in her heart was as quiet and as rapid as bat wings.

SIXTEEN

It was mid-morning the following day, and Brittany was paying the invoice for the bat exclusion company while Nancy handled the counter. She'd just finished the payment when her phone rang with a call from Alan.

"Hi, Dad. What's up?"

"Probably nothing, but have you seen Tansy?"

"No, I haven't." Brittany was surprised by the question, since Alan and Tansy lived together, and Tansy was also the receptionist for his orthodontic practice. "Was she supposed to stop by to get some coffee or something?"

"No, darn it. I knew it was a long shot that she was with you, but I was hoping."

Hoping for what? Brittany wondered. "Dad, what's going on?"

"Tansy's missing."

"What!" Brittany and Tansy weren't close, but she didn't wish her any ill will. "Since when? Did you file a police report?"

"It's not a missing persons type thing," Alan clarified. "She took off two nights ago after we had a huge fight about money."

The door between the tiny back room and the shop was

cracked open. Nancy poked her head in. "Is everything okay?" she whispered.

Brittany nodded and placed her index finger against her lips as she concentrated on what her father was saying.

"Tansy's run up a sixty-thousand-dollar tab on our credit card," Alan said. "I had no idea our balance was that high. She's the one in charge of the checkbook."

"Why weren't you viewing your account balance online?" Brittany asked. "Almost nobody uses checks anymore."

Nancy's eyes opened wide, and she pointed to herself. "I use checks," she whispered.

Brittany frowned and flapped her hand like she could shoo Nancy away.

"Sorry," Nancy whispered, before leaving.

"Now Tansy's gone," said Alan. "And two of my credit cards are frozen because she's hit the limit."

"Two credit cards? I thought you said the balance was high on one of them."

"I'm still untangling it all," Alan admitted. "And then to top it all off, the office is going nuts without her there to work the front desk."

"Oh, boy. I'm sorry things are such a mess. Is there anything I can do?" Brittany offered, thinking she might stalk Tansy's social media or something.

"Yes," said Alan. "You can call your mother and convince her to come into the office and help."

"Mom doesn't work the desk anymore." Brittany stood and leaned against the doorjamb for support. "She handles the practice's financial accounting, and that's it."

"I need her to hold down the fort. She takes money from me, too."

"Mom earns money from the practice as a co-owner who helped build the business from the ground up." Brittany felt irked that she was being asked to be her parents' go-between, yet again.

"Which is why she needs to come in," Alan insisted. "I texted her five times, but she hasn't responded."

I'm too old for this, Brittany thought to herself. But she didn't see any way out. "Did you tell Mom about Tansy leaving you?" she asked.

"Tansy didn't leave me, she went on a road trip, or something. That's between her and me, not your mother."

"I know, but Mom would be more likely to come in and help if she knew that Tansy... ah... wasn't there to do her job properly."

"I don't need to reveal personal details about my relationship with Tansy to your mother. I need Cynthia to get her butt in here and prove that she is actually a part owner of this business and not another leech in my life bleeding me for money."

"Mom's not a leech!" Brittany said. "She works hard."

"Yeah? Well, call her right now and tell her to prove it." Alan hung up, without saying goodbye.

Brittany let out a huge breath. What should she do? If the orthodontist practice faltered, that would impact both her parents. Cynthia wouldn't want that to happen because it would be lost income for her. Maybe she should call her mom and explain what was going on. But before she could place the call, Nancy came over.

"I'm so sorry to have eavesdropped." Nancy wiped her hands on her apron. "That was tacky of me."

"Don't worry about it. I was talking kind of loudly. Sorry about that."

"Why are you apologizing? You have nothing to be sorry for. I was the person being rude."

Brittany sighed, and squeezed her eyes shut for a moment. She always felt the need to apologize where her parents were concerned. She opened her eyes and looked at Nancy, realizing that the woman often gave good advice. Maybe she would have something to offer about the situation. It wouldn't hurt to ask, would it?

"My dad's fiancée and receptionist has taken off on an impromptu road trip and left the orthodontist practice in the lurch. He wants me to call my mom and convince her to come help, since she's a co-business owner, and used to run the front desk."

"That sounds complicated. Why are they involving you?"

"Because..." Brittany didn't know how to explain it. "They just do, that's all."

"Well, I think you should put a stop to that nonsense. You're their daughter, not their secretary."

"If only it were that easy."

"It is that easy. Text your father back and tell him you love them both a lot but that you're not going to be caught in the middle of their drama. If he needs your mom's help, then he should ask her himself."

"He *did* ask her, and she ignored him."

"Perhaps he didn't ask her in the right way, then. With enough politeness."

"Or begging," Brittany muttered. She *knew* Cynthia would come charging into the office on a hero's mission if she learned about Tansy's financial indiscretions. But Nancy was right, there was no reason for Brittany to get involved in this mess.

"Thanks, Nancy. I appreciate your good advice."

"And I'm grateful to you for offering me this job, because it gets me out of the house. Herman's poker club is tonight, and if I were home right now, he'd expect me to cook a bunch of appetizers."

"My dad used to play poker," Brittany said. Tansy wasn't the only one who made financial mistakes. "My mom made him quit after he lost a whole load of money."

"How much money?" Nancy asked. "I don't let Herman bet more than five hundred dollars."

"I think my dad lost closer to ten thousand dollars. At least, that's what my mom said."

"Holy cow! Who'd he lose that much money to?"

"Frank Osborne."

"The guy who ran the old pawnshop? Or was he a handyman? I can't remember."

Brittany nodded. "That's the one. Frank was a jack-of-all-trades, or no trades, according to my mother. Frank used the poker winnings to purchase the boat that later sank and caused my brother's death."

"Oh, sweet girl. I remember that. Everyone in Sand Dollar Cove does. His name was Paul, right?"

Brittany nodded, not wanting to talk about it further.

Later on, when she was back working the front counter, she thought about her parents and money. Cynthia had always run the family's budget with an iron fist. A huge battle had been brewing right before Paul died. He wanted to go to Northwestern, which was Alan's alma mater, but Cynthia said it was too expensive and Paul should go to an in-state school instead. Between her mother's hot temper, and Alan's cheating, she could see why they got divorced. It's too bad that they were still connected financially through the business, though. Their fighting continued non-stop.

Just then a woman about Brittany's age who wore a house-cleaning uniform for the Motel 6 came up to the counter holding an Angel Card. Her blue hair had faded, but complemented her sapphire nose ring. "Could I cash this in for the largest coffee you've got?" she asked in a raspy voice. "I just got off the overnight shift and now I need to pick up my son from daycare."

"Sure thing." Brittany picked up a cup. "Would you like coffee or something fancier, like a latte?"

"You can do that?" The woman leaned against the counter like she was dead on her feet.

"Absolutely. I can even add some vanilla syrup if you want."

"Sugar would really help. I'd love that, thanks."

Brittany crafted the latte and snapped on a to-go lid. "Have a great day," she said, as she handed it to the woman.

"Thanks, hon. I really appreciate this."

Brittany watched her go and then turned over the Angel Card to read the message on the back.

To a forty-five-year-old woman with a nose ring. It looks cute but be careful when you blow your nose.

What? Brittany touched the stud in her nose. What a weird message to write on the Angel Board. The messages were supposed to be encouraging, not passive-aggressive...

SEVENTEEN

Brittany wore the chunky sweater she'd knitted a few years ago which was extra warm, over soft brown corduroy pants, and leather booties. She also hoped it would be suitable attire for dinner at Patti's house. Patti had told her to arrive at five p.m., and Brittany was two minutes late. She parked her car, collected Ryan's coat that he'd given to her on the dock a while back, and walked up the mossy steps to a one-story craftsman cottage with a small front porch covered with pots. Mums and pansies, in orange, yellow and purple, spilled over the terracotta rims. Brittany lifted the knocker and rapped three times.

The door opened a moment later, and Ryan stood in the doorway, freshly shaven, wearing dark blue jeans and a long-sleeve black T-shirt. "Hello," he said in that deep voice of his. "Glad you could come."

"Thanks."

"You brought my coat." Ryan stepped backward so she could cross the threshold.

"Thanks for lending it to me. I'm sorry I held onto—" She paused, mid-sentence, at a complete loss for words by the shocking sight in front of her. Every inch of Patti's tiny living room was covered with knickknacks, pictures, and stuffed animals.

Collectible Dutch plates rimmed the room, right next to the ceiling. As her gaze traveled down, Brittany saw shelving units displaying dolls, porcelain figurines, music boxes, snuff boxes, pincushions, and wooden shoes. There were two, no, *three* china cabinets. Brittany could see the third one behind Ryan's shoulder in the dining room, which was also packed with stuff. The small couch and two armchairs had so many pillows and stuffed animals that there was barely any room to sit. Despite the overwhelming amount of display items, the room was organized. Brittany could see vacuum lines in the ancient carpet, but it also bore a musty odor from old things and dust.

"It's a lot to take in," Ryan grunted. "To put it mildly."

"I'm sorry it took me so long to return this," Brittany said quickly, finally remembering what she was going to say. She handed his coat back to him.

"Thanks." Ryan hung it on the coat stand. "Come, take a seat. My mom will be right out. She's teaching Isabella how to baste a turkey."

"That must be the delicious smell coming from the kitchen." Brittany could detect that aroma now, the rich scent of turkey cooking, but after breathing in deeply she sneezed from the dust.

"Here." Ryan picked up what looked to be a doll from the cluttered end table. "Take a tissue." He pushed back the cloth figure and revealed Kleenex underneath.

"Fancy. Thanks." Brittany helped herself.

"My mom used to sew these and give them away as teacher presents. Which was... uh... exactly what I wanted to be known for in school."

Brittany chuckled. "I don't think you were known for Kleenex dolls."

"Oh yeah?" He grinned. "What was I known for? Wait. Don't tell me. I don't need to relive past failures."

"Not even the parachute pants you wore in elementary school? Or your acid-washed jeans? Or that neon-green shirt you loved that glowed in the dark?"

"Oh, are we talking about fashion failures?" Ryan lifted his hand above his head. "I seem to recall your bangs being this tall and sprayed with so much hairspray they could handle a windstorm."

She giggled. "Maybe we shouldn't relive elementary school fashion. It's safer for both of us that way."

"What's so funny?" Isabella asked as she came into the room.

"Is that Brittany?" Patti called from the back of the small house. "I'll be right out."

"Grandma's acting super weird," Isabella whispered. "She's wearing mascara."

Ooof. Apparently, people noticed when you suddenly wore makeup in your seventies, too.

"Maybe she's nervous about having company." Ryan sat ramrod straight.

"I can be terrifying." Brittany tugged down her marigold sweater. It was a tad too snug since she'd knitted it a while ago. "But I appreciate the effort Patti's gone to." She looked across the living room into the dining room. "It seems she even set out her china."

"Oh, Grandma has lots of china." Isabella plopped into an armchair. Her hair was braided in one long braid down her back tonight. "She has at least six sets."

"Six sets?" Brittany wasn't sure if she'd heard that right.

"One from her wedding, one for Christmas, two sets her friends gave her when they moved to a retirement home and nobody wanted their dishes, and..." Isabella looked at Ryan. "Do you want to tell her about the last two sets?"

"Oh boy." Ryan shielded his face with his hand. "I'd rather not."

Isabella snickered. "Mr. Softie here bought her a new set for her seventieth birthday a few years ago, and then another one when we moved Grandpa to memory care, just to cheer her up. I think that's the one on the table tonight."

"That was sweet of you." Brittany looked over at Ryan and noticed him flush.

"It was shortsighted of me, because the last thing my mom needs is more—"

"Brittany!" Patti entered the room in a swirl of pink fabric. She wore an A-line dress with a wide belt, and a long, flowing coat in a floral pattern that matched. "I'm so glad you came. I hope you can forgive my tardiness. That bird was a real beast to wrestle out of the oven."

Ryan rubbed his chin. "Ma, I told you I'd help. Why didn't you take me up on my offer?"

"Because you needed to be in here greeting Brittany." Patti sat in the remaining armchair. "This is such a special evening, and I wanted everything to be perfect. Did you offer her a drink?"

Too late, Brittany realized she should have brought a bottle of wine or a hostess gift or something. She'd been so exhausted after a long day at the shop that it hadn't occurred to her.

Ryan jumped to his feet. "What can I get you? White or red? Soda's also an option."

"What type of white?" Brittany asked, knowing that she didn't like Chardonnay, but that red wine gave her hot flashes. *Thanks, perimenopause.*

"There's Pinot Grigio chilling in the fridge, but I could also open a bottle of Chardonnay if you'd like that better."

"The Pinot Grigio would be great, thank you."

"Coming right up," said Ryan.

"I'd like some too," said Isabella.

He shot her a look. "Ask me again in seven years."

"Nice try, though," said Patti. As soon as Ryan left, Patti leaned forward conspiratorially. "If it were up to me, I'd give you a teeny-tiny portion in a sherry glass."

Isabella raised one eyebrow. "You just want to use your sherry glasses."

Patti shrugged. "Guilty as charged."

"I like your Nirvana T-shirt," Brittany told Isabella. "Did your dad ever tell you about the time we ran into Kurt Cobain at a gas station?"

"Only about a million times." The girl smiled. "But you can tell me again. I want to hear your version."

"Good, because I was going to tell you anyway." Brittany leaned forward with excitement. "It was my freshman year and your dad was giving me and my brother Paul a ride home from school in his truck. We stopped for gas, and the car in front of us was a four-door sedan. At first, nobody noticed anything unusual, and your dad went in to pay for the gas. But then Paul realized that it was a 1965 Dodge Dart, and he said, 'Hey, I heard that's the type of car Kurt Cobain drives.'"

"How did he know that?" Isabella asked. "My dad never told me this part of the story."

"Because Paul was a huge grunge music fan," Brittany explained. "And also because even though Kurt Cobain was about ten years older than us, he grew up in Aberdeen, which isn't that far away. People used to run into him all the time. We just never had."

"Until that day," said Isabella.

"Right." Brittany beamed. "Paul and I got out of the car just as your dad was coming back from the convenience store, and sure enough there was the lead singer of Nirvana pumping gas right next to us."

"Did you get his autograph?" Isabella asked.

Brittany shook her head. "Paul was too cool for that. He just gave him a head nod and said, 'Hey,' and Kurt said 'Hey,' back."

"What did my dad say?"

"He told Kurt that his taillight was out. Your dad was always good about noticing things like that."

"Still is," Patti said proudly. "Ryan's always been observant."

"True." Brittany's gaze skimmed the room, without being able to focus on any one thing. The sheer volume of trinkets was overwhelming.

"I see you've noticed my collections," Patti said proudly.

"Yes." Brittany jerked her gaze toward Patti. "They are quite impressive."

Patti rose to her feet and carefully walked over to a shelf stuffed with figurines. "This is my kitten collection. That's how it started. For my first wedding anniversary Frank gave me this adorable tabby cat. It looked just like our first tomcat, Tiger." She held up a figurine. "We couldn't afford it, I knew that. But he paid for it somehow." She set it carefully back on the shelf. "The collections grew from there. First it was cats, and then I got interested in music boxes, and after that, Frank took an interest in antique pipes, and spoons."

"Wow," said Brittany.

"Frank was always scouring estate sales and bringing me home a trinket or two." She smiled wistfully, but then her peaceful expression melted into sadness.

"Here you go," said Ryan, entering the room carrying an ornate crystal wineglass in one hand and a can of Diet Pepsi in the other. He gave the wine to Brittany and passed the soda to Isabella.

"Thanks, but are you making me drink alone?" Brittany asked.

"No." Ryan shook his head. "I'll be right back."

"So, Isabella, how's school going?" Brittany asked.

The teenager shrugged. "Fine, I guess. I have world history with Scarlett, and Spanish with Lana, and Gabby is in my English and yoga classes."

"Yoga?" Patti asked. "That's what you're doing for PE?"

"Times have changed," Brittany said. "Jeremy took sports for PE, but he said he wished he had taken yoga because that's where all the pretty girls were."

Isabella fluttered her eyelashes. "I hope that people still say that."

"And I'm back," said Ryan as he re-entered the room holding two more wineglasses, one for himself and one for his mother. "The turkey smells delicious, Ma. The timer says it has eight more minutes."

"That's perfect, just perfect." Patti checked her watch and then looked knowingly at Brittany.

When was Don arriving? Brittany didn't know. Maybe she could help the woman out. "How are things at the senior center these days?" she asked. "Cheryl tells me the food is still awful, and that everyone is upset that Keith canceled the Halloween party."

"That's right," Patti muttered. "The nerve of that man. I'd already sewn our costumes, too, for me and my... friend."

"What were you going to go as, Grandma?" Isabella asked.

Patti smoothed her skirt. "Cleopatra. And my friend Don was going as Antony."

"Like a couples costume?" Isabella popped open the tab of her soda.

"Dawn must be a good friend, seeing how she's willing to be Antony to your Cleopatra." Ryan sipped his wine.

"Well, the thing is..." Patti began. A knock at the door interrupted her.

"Could that be Don now?" Brittany asked innocently.

"I was wondering why there was an extra place at the table," said Isabella. "I thought you'd miscounted."

"I'll get the door." Ryan set down his wineglass.

"No, I'll get it." Patti hurried over to the door and opened it.

From her place on the couch, Brittany couldn't see Don, but she could hear his voice.

"Why hello there, old lady. Aren't you a sight for sore eyes."

"Oh, Don," Patti cooed. "It's good to see you too."

Isabella coughed on her soda, and accidentally sprayed it over the carpet.

"Here's a tissue," Brittany said, offering her the doll box. She looked over at Ryan to see his reaction. Don and Patti were entering the living room, holding hands.

Ryan's mouth dropped open, and his eyes grew wide. He looked so shocked that Brittany worried he'd forget to breathe.

"This is Don?" Isabella asked. "A man?"

"The last time I checked," said Don. "Nice to meet you. I take it you're Isabella?"

"Yup." Isabella gulped her soda.

Ryan stood.

"And this is my son, Ryan," said Patti, still clutching Don's hand.

Ryan held out his own to shake. "Nice to meet you, sir."

Don shook Ryan's hand heartily. "Just plain Don is fine. Or you can call me Pops. That's what my kids call me."

Ryan's expression froze and Brittany knew that under no circumstances would Ryan ever be calling Don "Pops." Ryan might have worked out an amicable divorce and co-parenting relationship with his ex-wife, but this was clearly new territory for him.

"It's good to see you again, Don," Brittany said. "I miss my friends at the senior center."

"And we miss your fine nutrition program," he said graciously.

"Bella, why don't you come sit on the couch and give Don your chair?" Ryan suggested.

"Sure." Isabella sat on the opposite end of the couch to Brittany and patted the middle cushion. "There's room for you right here, Dad."

"Uh... thanks." Ryan crossed the room and squeezed into the center of the sofa. He sat so close that Brittany could feel his arm press against her sweater. She could feel his jeans rub against her corduroy. She could smell the woodsy scent of his soap that clung to him like pine needles.

Maybe it was his nearness, or perhaps it was the wine, but suddenly she felt like she was in high school again, and her heart was going into convulsions because Ryan was sitting next to her. Her childhood crush simmered so intensely that she began to perspire. This sweater had been a poor choice. The acrylic yarn didn't breathe. Had she put on enough deodorant? She wasn't sure.

And why was she nervous? This wasn't *her* awkward family dinner. She was the neutral party Patti had invited to make the evening easier, not harder. It was just that being so close to Ryan had made her picture those hearts she'd drawn on her binder, the one with his and her names entwined.

She glanced to her left, to look at him, and her heart thumped harder. Damn, he was good-looking. She couldn't believe that she was squished next to Ryan Osborne, and that after all these years he was still so yummy that she secretly wished he'd drive her home.

As if he sensed her thinking about him, Ryan turned his head and looked at her. It was a pleading look, like he was asking for help.

Shoot, instead of helping Patti smooth things over, Brittany had been daydreaming about Ryan like she'd decided to forgive him, or something. *Which she hadn't.*

"I've known Don for a while through my work at the senior center," Brittany said, suddenly businesslike. "You've lived here for two years now, right, Don?"

"Two and a half," Don corrected. "I worked for Boeing for thirty-nine years, and retired a year before my wife was diagnosed with cancer." He sighed heavily. "After she died, I just couldn't stay in our house anymore without her, so I talked to my kids about it, and they suggested I move out here for a fresh start."

"Don's house has three spare bedrooms and one of them is a playroom for his grandkids," said Patti.

"My daughters come visit often." Don grinned. "Grandpa's house is like a vacation paradise for them because it comes with cable television and free childcare."

"Sounds swell," Ryan said stiffly.

"All that's missing is a hot tub," said Don. "But that's being installed next month."

"You're going to need to go swimsuit shopping, Grandma," said Isabella, hiding her smile behind her soda can.

"Why yes, I will," Patti nodded. "Swimsuits are one garment I've never been good at sewing."

"Same here," said Don. "That's why I prefer skinny-dipping."

For the second time that evening, Isabella spewed out her soda, only this time she was laughing.

Brittany tried to ease the situation by laughing too. "Oh Don," she said. "I've missed your humor."

"Bella, please go get a rag to clean up your grandma's carpet."

"Yes, sir," Isabella said, as she tried to regain her composure.

"Speaking of men with a sense of humor, how is that teenage son of yours?" Don asked. "I used to love hearing stories about Jeremy."

"Jeremy's doing fine, I think." Brittany shrugged. "He texts me, but never calls. I don't think he needs me at all anymore."

"Oh, that can't be true. Teenage sons are just like that." Patti looked at Ryan. "Right?"

"Every teenager's different," Ryan said gruffly.

"Ain't that the truth." Don slapped his thigh.

"The timer's about to go off." Patti stood. "I better check the turkey."

"I'll come help." Don rose to his feet. "My mouth's already watering."

As soon as they left the room, Ryan shook his head. "You knew about this?" he whispered, not moving from his super-close position next to her on the couch. "Don and my mom?"

"Yeah..." Brittany twisted her bottom lip for a moment and bit down, trying to think of what to say. "Does their relationship bother you?"

"No, not really." Ryan stopped whispering and spoke in a quiet voice. "This explains the spring in her step. I was really worried about her these past couple of years, but she seems much happier now. Maybe that's Don's influence."

"It probably is, but she was worried how you'd react. Patti invited me so I'd be a buffer guest."

Ryan chuckled, surprising her. "That's not why she invited you," he said.

"It's not?"

"Of course not. She's trying to set us up. I wouldn't be surprised if Isabella's in on it. She made name cards for the dining room table and sat us together."

"Oh... Huh." Brittany turned toward him slightly. "Why?"

"Because my mom knows I had a thing for you in high school."

"What?" Brittany gasped.

Ryan folded his arms across his chest. "Not that I could have ever done anything about it. You were my best friend's little sister."

"I wasn't *that* little. I'm only two years younger."

Ryan shook his head. "Yeah, well, two years is way too

much of an age gap in high school, and Paul would have kicked my ass."

"That's a little harsh."

"Is it?"

Brittany chewed her bottom lip again. "Paul was pretty protective of me," she admitted.

"Yeah, so anyhow, that's why I ignored my feelings and never said anything."

"Until now," Brittany pointed out. "You're telling me now."

"I guess I am." Ryan scooted to the left, away from Brittany, giving her more space.

Brittany scooted to the left too, so she was smack up next to Ryan again. "I had a crush on you, too, in high school," she admitted. "Since we're baring all."

"Baring all, huh? Speaking of which. Did Don really insinuate that he intended to go skinny-dipping with my mom in his hot tub?"

Brittany laughed. "I think so."

Ryan threw his arm around the back of the couch and leaned closer, his face inches from Brittany's ear. "What else do you know about the guy?" he asked quietly. "Is he good enough for my mom? She's got a lot on her plate, and I want her to be happy and treated well."

How sweet. Brittany was impressed by how well Ryan was taking Patti springing her new relationship onto him like this, while also maintaining a concern for her well-being. "Don's a fun-loving guy and popular at the senior center," she said. "My housemate, Cheryl Turner, has said he's a bit of a player, but Don seems to have settled down now with your mom. Every time I see the two of them together, they look to be having a great time."

"Cheryl's your housemate?" Ryan asked. "She's been my mom's best friend for years."

Brittany quickly explained her living arrangement and how

Mary had mentioned being Ryan's interior designer. "Is it true that you've hidden your toaster?" she asked.

"*I* didn't hide it. The previous owners installed the kitchen before I bought the house. But yes, the toaster, and all the small appliances, are in their own cupboard." He flicked his hand. "After growing up with this, I've gone the opposite direction. I can't stand clutter. It makes it impossible for me to concentrate or relax."

Brittany nodded, finally understanding. His minimalist house made sense now.

Ryan made more sense, too.

He'd come from humble beginnings and forged a life for himself and his daughter that was miles away from this one.

He'd made one fatal mistake that night on the *Carpe Diem*, and devoted the rest of his life to redemption.

Maybe it was the half a glass of wine she'd drunk while talking, but Brittany leaned closer. "If I had a hot tub, would you come skinny-dipping with me?" she asked, feeling bold.

He raised his eyebrows. "Do you have a hot tub?"

She shook her head.

Ryan's forehead softened. "It doesn't matter," he said with a grin. "The answer would be yes either way."

A bell rang from the dining room. And then another. And then one more. A whole chorus of bells rang as Isabella worked through the collection on a shelf next to the tallest china cabinet.

"Dinner!" she hollered.

Ryan and Brittany both laughed and made their way to the table.

EIGHTEEN

The bat removal specialist had come and gone, and Brittany faced a fresh new week with the assurance that her cafe no longer contained winged guests. Today, Ryan had stopped by to install a bat box under the eaves, next to the hole they used to access. Hopefully, if the bats came back, they'd find shelter in their cozy new home.

"Are you sure you don't need me to hold the ladder?" she asked Ryan as she looked up at him, perched above her, carrying his toolbox. The Monday morning was gray and misty. Frost coated the ground, and Brittany worried that the ladder might slip. She also wanted to spend more time with Ryan, so that she could untangle her complicated feelings about him. They'd had such a good time at dinner Saturday night. Could their easy rapport continue without a bottle of wine and Patti's delicious home cooking?

"The feet of this ladder have a good grip." Ryan rose one more step. "Go on inside where you can stay warm. There's no need for you to be outside in the cold on your day off."

"Okay..." Brittany hesitated. "Shout if you need anything."

She took one last admiring look at Ryan's backside, before

entering her restaurant. Safe Harbor was closed today, which made for the perfect opportunity to pay bills.

She was just turning on her computer when her phone trilled with an incoming call from Jeremy. *He was finally calling her instead of just texting!*

"Hi Jeremy, how are you?"

"Awful, Mom, just awful."

"Oh no! Are you safe?"

"Yeah, but my car isn't."

"Uh-oh..." She knew Alan giving him that Mustang was a bad idea. "What happened?"

"Someone slashed the ragtop while I was parked outside of Kenzie's dorm. My convertible's ruined!"

"I'm so sorry. How bad is the damage?"

"I don't know. The top is destroyed, the interior is all wet. I think someone was sleeping in there or something, because I found hamburger wrappers and a soaked hoodie."

"Oh dear... Seattle is one of the most amazing cities in the world, but it does have its challenges."

"What do I do, Mom? I don't know what to do."

Brittany felt secretly thrilled that Jeremy was asking for her advice. *He still needs me*, she cheered. "Is your car drivable or does it need a tow truck?" she asked.

"I can drive it. I brought it home to Dad's house."

"Your dad has a garage, right?"

"Yes, but it's filled with junk."

"Does the junk include a tarp? The first thing to do is find a way to cover it. The second is to call the insurance company. Take a bunch of pictures so you can show the agent what happened. This will make our rates go up, but the insurance should pay for repairs."

"How much will they go up?"

"I don't know. But Jeremy, you're also going to have to pay

the deductible. The insurance won't pay for anything until we meet the deductible."

"How much will that be?"

"I can't remember. A thousand dollars, I think." She was tempted to pay it herself, even though her budget was stretched thin. But she was already helping with the insurance. She'd been against this car from the beginning but didn't want to look like the bad guy. "Will you be able to come up with that much cash?" she asked, worried about what he would say.

"Yeah. I have my savings from McDonald's I can use." Jeremy sighed. "I'd been intending to use it on moving out of Dad's house and getting my own place someday."

"That can still happen. It just might take a little while longer."

She wanted to tell him a million things.

Give the car back to Grandpa.

Use public transportation.

Don't waste money on luxury goods you can't afford.

But she didn't. Jeremy was eighteen now, and needed to learn things on his own, without her spoon-feeding him.

The sound of hammering outside reminded her that Ryan was up on the ladder installing the bat box. "Do you have any more questions about your car?" she asked.

"No. I'll call the insurance company right now. I'm really sorry about this."

"It's not your fault. Cars get broken into, especially in the city."

"Yeah, but if I had been driving my old piece-of-shit car, it might have been left alone."

"Possibly, but we don't know that for sure. The important thing is that you're safe."

"Yeah, but I don't feel safe. I feel like somebody injured my baby."

A smile curled on her lips. "You really love that Mustang a lot, don't you?"

"I do. I really do."

"Well, that's why we have car insurance. Good luck, and text me when you have more information."

"I'll do that. Love you."

"Love you, too." Brittany hung up and paused at her desk for a moment, reflecting. Jeremy had sought out her advice but hadn't needed her to bail him out. Was this what parenting an adult felt like? She'd raised a baby into a functional human being and had put herself out of a job in the process. She felt proud, but also empty, like part of her soul was missing.

Brittany looked at her phone, wishing she could hear Jeremy's voice again, or see his face splash across the screen. But then she noticed the time. It was almost noon. Ryan hadn't mentioned if he'd eaten lunch or not, but it would be nice to offer him some.

It would be nicer still to eat it with him, and not just because she was feeling lonely.

Ever since their mutual confession a couple of nights ago, Brittany had been thinking crazy thoughts, like what if teenage crushes meant something? What if, thirty years later, those adolescent feelings of attraction could grow into something real and meaningful? Ryan had obviously changed. He wasn't the same seventeen-year-old boy who captained the *Carpe Diem* thirty years ago; he was a grown man who took considerable care with his family. But what hadn't changed was how she could sense his nearness. How she had a radar for all things Ryan Osborne. It was like an energy field hummed in the air whenever they were in proximity.

Even here, sitting at her desk in the tiny back room of her restaurant, she could sense that he was on the other side of the wall, up on that ladder installing the bat box.

And who went out of their way to protect bats? Caring for

one of the most misunderstood creatures in nature was something special, although Brittany was happy her establishment was now bat-free. For Ryan to care so much about them meant that despite his gruff demeanor, he had a tender heart.

But she'd always known that about him.

Always...

Brittany rose from her desk and opened the back door. "I'm making lunch," she called loudly so Ryan could hear her up on the ladder. "What type of sandwich do you want?"

He paused, mid-hammer. "Something that's not turkey. My mom sent us home with a ton of leftovers."

"Same." Brittany laughed. "How about ham?"

"Sounds great. Thanks." Ryan nodded his head.

Brittany went back into Safe Harbor and prepared lunch. She was all out of thumbprint cookies, but she added chips and apple slices to the plates and took two bottles of pear kombucha out of the fridge. She'd just set the dishes on a table when she heard the back door open, and then the sound of the faucet running in the restroom. Ryan came out a minute later, after washing his hands.

"Thanks for making lunch." He caught her gaze and smiled. "I don't know if I could have faced another meal of leftover turkey."

Brittany chuckled. "If your mom makes that much turkey on a normal Saturday night, what's she like at Thanksgiving?"

"You don't want to know," Ryan said with a groan.

They both sat down and began eating.

"I didn't know if you liked kombucha or not." Brittany unscrewed the cap. "I can get you something else if you're not a fan."

"I like it a lot. Troy makes it, from a starter. Or he used to until Melissa complained that their kitchen always smelled like vinegar."

"I think that's so cool that you are on such good terms with your ex-wife."

Ryan opened his drink, too. "There's no reason not to be. She's a great person, we just weren't right for each other."

"Why not?" Brittany was curious.

"She thrives on chaos and making intuitive decisions. I like things calm and orderly. One kid was fine with me, but Melissa wanted a whole houseful. That's the main reason we divorced. Meeting Troy a little while later was the best thing for her, because he came with three young boys under the age of ten."

"Whoa. Chaos is right. Mothering one boy was enough for me. And now Melissa's pregnant?"

"Yeah. So, that'll be a blended family of five kids total, when Isabella visits." Ryan put down his sandwich. "Did you ever think of having more kids?"

Brittany shook her head. "No, because Ian was always working at the car dealership, or out fishing with his friends. Almost all the childcare fell to me. I love Jeremy with my whole heart, but he was a lot of work when he was little. Plus, Ian and I were constantly fighting—mainly about him never being around. I knew our tiny family couldn't handle more drama. It was a relief when we got divorced, seven years ago, because things could finally calm down. I don't do well in chaotic environments either."

"I always admired how well run your house was growing up."

"What?"

"Your mom ran a tight ship. The house was always clean. She had dinner on the table at six each night, and there was always enough extra if I ended up staying. Your dad worked hard building his practice and Paul always had his basketball fees paid on time. That really made an impression on me."

"Yeah, well, all those things were good, and my mom earned money too, by the way, because she helped run my dad's practice. But you must have gotten the wrong impression about us, because our home was full of chaos."

"You mean the arguing?"

"Yes. Our house might have been clean, but my parents literally can't agree on anything. It was a horrible way to grow up."

"I *did* notice that. I think Paul had it easier than you because he was in so many sports that he had a built-in escape."

Brittany nodded. "But that meant I was stuck at home caught in the middle of my parents' battles. At least when Paul was there, he'd serve as a buffer." She looked down at her bag of Lay's potato chips, which were her brother's favorite brand. "My parents were usually better behaved around him. Paul was their favorite, after all."

She didn't know why she had said that just now, but it was the truth. Paul *was* Alan and Cynthia's favorite. They gave him more spending money and freedom. They showered him with praise for his sports accomplishments. Cynthia would say that after-school activities that Brittany enjoyed, like jewelry making, pottery, or collage were hobbies that she'd have to pay for herself out of her allowance. Meanwhile, they spent enormous sums sending Paul to basketball camps, competitions, and professional games, not to mention buying all the sports gear he needed. Brittany was required to get a part-time job as soon as she entered high school, but Paul wasn't because he had basketball.

The message at home was always clear: Paul deserved more resources because he was the oldest, the favorite, and the son. As for Brittany, she had a nice life, so what did she have to complain about?

"Paul *was* their favorite," Ryan confirmed. "And he felt awful about it."

"He did?" This was news to Brittany. She and her brother had never addressed Cynthia and Alan's favoritism.

"Yes, like that time they canceled your tenth birthday party because our team was in the playoffs."

"Oh. That..." Thirty-five years later and the memory still hurt. "I did have my birthday party, eventually. It was at the roller rink."

"I remember. But your mom insisted on letting Paul invite our teammates, too, since she'd rented out the whole place, and Ben Mathews was kind of rowdy, and it turned into more of a team celebration than your birthday."

"Paul told Ben to shut up when I was opening presents."

"And I hosed him down with ketchup when his hot dog spilled on you in the food court."

Was *that* when it had happened? At her tenth birthday party? "I remember that happening, but I thought I was nine. Someone spilled sauerkraut on my new skates, and you chased him away."

"Yeah, it was your tenth birthday party, and our entire team was there because we'd just lost in the final round of the play-offs. Paul was upset with your parents for giving you roller skates as your main present, because for his tenth birthday they'd given him a television for his room. He didn't think it was fair."

"Paul was always justice-oriented. He couldn't stand cheaters, or people who ran yellow lights, or—"

"Didn't come to a complete stop at four-way intersections," Ryan added.

"Yeah." Brittany smiled. For the first time in a long time, it felt good talking about her brother, instead of sad. Talking about her childhood was helping, too, because there was nobody else she could do that with. She had friends, of course, but none who had borne witness to the inner workings of her family life like Ryan had.

"Paul was really worried about leaving you when he went off to college." Ryan sipped his kombucha.

"Really?"

"He wanted to go out of state somewhere and get as far away from Sand Dollar Cove as possible, but he felt guilty for abandoning you."

"I wish he hadn't felt guilty. Paul had his heart set on going to Northwestern, in Illinois, and I really wanted that dream to come true for him."

"I did too." Ryan put down his drink. "Paul was concerned because your mom thought it was too expensive. Northwestern would have cost five times as much as the University of Washington."

"I remember her saying that. My parents saved money for us to attend college, but not enough to cover Northwestern without them making sacrifices like selling our boat. But Paul could have taken out loans or found a part-time job. That would have helped."

"I'm sure he would have figured something out. In fact, that's why Paul wanted to get to the lighthouse so badly that day. It wasn't only about painting our class year on the rocks. Paul wanted to think things through about Northwestern and escape your parents' arguing, even if it was only for a few hours."

"He did?" Brittany asked.

Ryan nodded.

The longing to escape resonated with Brittany. She'd had the urge to escape her parents' bickering her entire childhood. But now she had a longing for something else, too: forgiveness. For Paul's sake. At the very least she wanted to be able to move past her anger toward Ryan. That meant learning the truth and addressing her anger, once and for all.

"Why did you stay out on the *Carpe Diem* when the storm came?" she asked. "Was it so Paul could have more time away from my parents?"

"No." Ryan shook his head. "It was because of the sea stars."

"Sea stars?" Brittany twisted her napkin.

"When we sailed off to the lighthouse, the wind was picking up, but the conditions were fine. It took longer than we had expected to paint the rocks. We had to scrape off slime, and carefully remove sea stars."

"Paul loved creatures of all types."

Ryan nodded. "We barely had time to finish painting before the rain started. That's when things get hazy for me." He rubbed his temples with his thumbs before raking his fingers through his hair and looking her straight in the eyes. "You have to know, Brittany, as soon as it got stormy, I insisted we go back."

"Wait... You did?" Her heart stopped in her chest.

"Yes," Ryan said emphatically. "But the storm came so quickly that it was too late. We boarded the boat. I remember that. Nothing seemed wrong yet. But we'd barely sailed a minute before the boat took on water at an alarming rate. I yelled to Paul to put on his life vest. A wave knocked us over, and we took them out of the bench seat in back, but we got them on."

Brittany's body froze as she listened.

"I radioed for help like my dad had taught me," Ryan continued. "'Mayday, mayday, mayday! This is the *Carpe Diem*. Our position is east of the Sand Dollar Cove lighthouse, and we are sinking.' I kept at it until we capsized. Then I swam toward Paul so we could stick together. It wasn't that far to the harbor. We were both strong swimmers and could have made it. But a wave crashed against us before I could reach him. It smashed Paul against the rocks. Right against the rocks we had painted." Ryan's face splotched red with emotion. He took a ragged breath before continuing. "The Coast Guard came quickly. They were only a few minutes away. It was the impact against the rocks that killed him. That's what they told me at the hospital when I asked."

"That's what my parents told me, too." Brittany shivered.

This was too much for her to process. But she forced herself to face the facts.

And the facts were too awful to bear.

Ryan had tried to save Paul's life, and all these years she'd hated him unfairly. Her heart felt like it was splintering all over again.

"I'm sorry, Brittany," he said quietly.

"No, *I'm* sorry," Brittany insisted. "I've spent all these years blaming you for what happened when it really was a horrible accident. It wasn't your fault."

"That's not true. I could have studied the weather report ahead of time. I could have told Paul to forget about the sea stars, or the prank altogether, and just sailed home. But I didn't."

"Paul didn't either," Brittany whispered, even though it felt terribly disloyal to her brother to say so. "It wasn't his fault that he died, and it wasn't your fault either." Her body unfroze as forgiveness thawed her. She felt tension in her neck release and her shoulders relax into their normal position.

They lapsed into silence until Ryan finally spoke. "I didn't know I'd get a side of absolution with my sandwich."

"It took me long enough to put it on the menu." Brittany rested her chin on her hand and looked at him. All the talk about Paul had left her feeling worn out, so she changed the subject. "How's Isabella doing? Are things with Gabby, Lana, and Scarlett still going well?"

A smile twitched on Ryan's lips. "They are, and in fact, I think you'll be proud of me about how I've loosened the reins a bit. Today's a half-day from school, and she asked me if she could hang out with them, and not only did I say yes, but I suggested a place where they could go."

"That's great. Where did you send them?" Brittany picked up an apple slice.

"Rhododendron Lane."

"What?" Brittany dropped the apple onto her plate.

"I know it used to be make-out spot, but Isabella and her friends will just go and enjoy the view. I figured the walk would be good exercise for them."

"No, it's not that." Brittany picked up her plate, and Ryan's too, even though they weren't done eating. "Oh no, this is awful! We need to get over there now and stop them." She dumped the dishes in the sink.

"Why? What's going on?"

"Rhododendron Lane is a death trap. The cliff has become unstable and is at risk of sliding into the ocean."

"Shit!" Ryan grabbed his coat from the back of his chair.

"Come on," she said, as she rushed to get her purse. "I'll drive, and you can call her from the car. Let's go!"

NINETEEN

"Any luck?" Brittany asked as she turned right onto the state highway that bordered the ocean. Ryan was calling his daughter from the passenger seat of her SUV.

"It's just going straight to voicemail," he said, with a frown.

"Well, try leaving a message, at least."

"By the time she hears the message it might be too late. This is all my fault!" Ryan squeezed his eyes shut and then opened them again. "How could I have been so stupid?"

"You're not stupid. You had no way of knowing that Rhododendron Lane is no longer safe."

"I could never forgive myself if something happened to Isabella. Life wouldn't be worth living." Ryan buried his head in his hands.

"Don't say that. Stay calm," Brittany cautioned. "It's going to be alright." She pressed down on the accelerator and her Subaru went faster. To the left was Olympic National Park. To the right, was the Pacific Ocean. Daylight had burned away most of the frost except for where shadows made the pavement glisten with deadly black ice. "Try calling again," she instructed. "Only this time leave a voicemail."

"Okay." Ryan lifted his head. "I'll try... Hi, Bella, this is Dad," he said, his voice almost breaking. "Can you call me when you get this? Rhododendron Lane is not, I repeat *not* a safe place to go anymore because of the risk of cliff collapse. So please don't go there. *Please*. Bye."

"Good." Brittany nodded. "That was nicely done. Now, can you text her? Jeremy often has his ringer off, but can still see when texts come in, so that's often been a better way for me to catch his attention."

Ryan rested his elbow on the side of the door. "Her phone doesn't have texting capabilities. I thought that was too dangerous."

Brittany sucked in air through her teeth. "That's right. I forgot." She didn't want to stick her nose into his business, but she thought it was dangerous *not* giving Isabella a phone she could text from. Hell, if she had a pretty fourteen-year-old daughter roaming the beaches of Sand Dollar Cove, she'd give her a smartwatch too, so that she could always track her whereabouts.

"Okay, new plan," she said, calling upon her reserves of mothering resourcefulness. "I don't have Stephanie's number, but I'm Facebook friends with her. Isabella is with her daughter Scarlett, right?"

"Right." Ryan nodded.

"Great. Well, I'll message Stephanie and she can text Scarlett and we'll reach them that way." Brittany clicked on her blinker so she could pull into the viewpoint that was coming up, Blackfish Point. It was a narrow strip along the side of the highway that only had three parking spots, but which offered breathtaking ocean views. Brittany parked the car and pushed open her door. "You drive, I'll contact Stephanie," she said as she jumped out and ran around her Subaru.

Ryan followed suit, and they crossed paths awkwardly at

the tailgate, each one of them moving in the same direction so that they almost smacked into each other.

"After you," Ryan said, pausing so that Brittany could circle around him.

Once they were back on the road, Brittany found her old friend on Facebook and sent Stephanie a quick message about what was going on.

"Did it work?" Ryan asked. "Can she reach the girls?"

"Steph hasn't responded yet. I have Gabby's mom's email though, because she used to be Jeremy's third grade teacher. I'll contact her that way."

"Thanks."

Brittany cut and pasted the same message she sent Stephanie and forwarded it along to Mrs. Santos. After that, she tried calling Lana's dad Jason, who owned the fishing charter. She spoke to the booking service, who promised to pass the message along after Jason returned to port.

"I appreciate you trying," Ryan said.

"It's going to be okay. We'll find them."

The turn to Seaside Resort was coming up, which was the best place to park to reach Rhododendron Lane, but Ryan wasn't slowing down the car.

"Whoa there, cowboy." Brittany pointed through the windshield. "There's the parking lot."

"I thought we were parking at Seaside Resort?" Ryan asked, while also decelerating.

"That *is* Seaside Resort. They replaced the sign last year and have also majorly improved the entrance, so it looks more upscale and less faded."

"Wow. I see what you mean." Ryan turned past huge displays of hydrangeas, smoke bush and lilacs, into the newly refreshed parking lot of Seaside Resort. "I haven't been here since homecoming senior year."

"You took your homecoming date to a hotel?" Brittany asked, surprised that he'd share such a personal detail with her.

"To the restaurant, not the hotel," Ryan clarified. "Paul came too, with that girl he was dating. What was her name?"

"Carly. Her family moved away, and I haven't heard from her since."

Ryan parked and put on the emergency brake. "Let's go find my daughter."

"You got it." Brittany jumped out of the car to follow him.

"At least the trail hasn't changed," Ryan said, as he strode past parked cars. "That's the sign, right?"

Brittany looked where he was pointing. "Yes, the Beach Bluff trail should take us there." She followed Ryan onto the trail, which climbed a hill covered by alder trees, cottonwood, and big-leaf maples, as well as evergreens like fir and cedar. When they reached the top, they could see a paved path to the right that entered the hotel complex. Seaside Resort boasted fifty unique cottages that guests could rent, perched on the bluff overlooking Sand Dollar Cove. To the left, the trail veered off into the edge of the forest. Further down the path, it crept closer and closer to the cliff's edge.

Rhododendron Lane was only a short ten-minute walk away. It was technically on the resort's property but was also a beloved location of everyone who grew up in Sand Dollar Cove.

"You know your mom's friend Cheryl Turner?" Brittany asked.

"Yeah." Ryan stuffed his hands in his pockets.

"I told you how Cheryl and her granddaughters Hannah and Mary live with me, right?"

"You did."

"Okay, so Hannah is the general manager of Seaside Resort, and her fiancé Guy Blanchet owns the place."

"I believe my mom told me something about this. He's rich, right?"

Brittany nodded. "And a really sweet person. Anyhow, Hannah's made sure that Rhododendron Lane has been erased from the resort map for years because of safety issues, and early this spring Guy's company, the Blanchet Maison hotel conglomerate, sent out a team of engineers and naturalists to assess the cliffside. It's cordoned off with fencing now, to keep people out, but Jeremy told me that high schoolers still sneak in there all the time. He showed me pictures on the unofficial Sand Dollar Cove High School trash account."

"Trash account?"

"On Instagram. Kids post all sorts of things they shouldn't. Fellow students sleeping in class, vaping in the bathrooms, toilet-papering the principal's house, climbing on the roof of school to install a toilet…"

"That was Jeremy, right?" Ryan chuckled.

"Yeah." Brittany cringed. "Anyhow, that's how I know that kids still visit Rhododendron Lane, and so far, nobody has gotten hurt. I just wanted to share that, in case it helps reassure you."

"The only thing it's made me think is that I'm doubly glad Isabella doesn't have a smartphone. That trash account sounds like trouble waiting to happen."

"If she doesn't have a smartphone or social media, she won't be able to know as much about her peers." Brittany repositioned her purse strap so it wouldn't pinch her shoulder. "What if the cute boy she likes in math class is posting pictures of himself vaping in the bathroom during passing period? Wouldn't you want Isabella to know that?"

"Well, yeah, but what if she posts snarky comments on other people's posts, or her so-called friends do that to her? Before you can say 'unfriend me' I could be back in the principal's office trying to defend my daughter from another parent accusing Isabella of 'passive-aggressive hearting.'" Ryan lifted his fingers to make air quotes.

"I don't know what passive-aggressive hearting is."

"Apparently it's something thirteen-year-old girls do to terrorize each other."

"Yikes. But Isabella's fourteen now, right? And she's not in middle school anymore, she's a freshman in high school."

"Your point?" Ryan asked.

"Hopefully she's grown since then and learned her lesson. But you know your daughter better than me, obviously. If you don't think Isabella is mature enough to handle a phone, then she's not."

Wind whipped a lock of hair across Brittany's face, and she pulled it away from her eyes. The weather had warmed up to the low fifties, which was still cold, but the brisk walk and her thick coat kept her warm. The foghorn moaned from somewhere far away. It wasn't the best weather for a short hike, but it wasn't awful, either. At least it wasn't raining.

"Let me see if Stephanie has messaged me back." Brittany pulled out her phone. "No, still nothing." She checked her mail. "Gabby's mom hasn't contacted me either." After stashing her phone in her pocket, she looked at Ryan. "How were the girls going to get here to begin with? None of them can drive."

"The school bus stops near the hotel. I confirmed that with the school district's transportation office last evening." Ryan shook his head. "I thought I was being so safe."

"It's not your fault. You didn't know."

"I packed her a thermos of hot chocolate to share with her friends, too."

"See?" Brittany patted his back. "You were really trying."

Ryan shook his head. "That doesn't mean I'm not an idiot." He walked faster, and his long strides were almost too much for Brittany to keep up with. But she understood his urgency and picked up her pace. If Jeremy was in danger, she'd hurry too. A minute later, they reached a slight bend in the trail that would have looked completely normal to an outsider. But Brittany remembered what that crookedness meant, and so must have Ryan, because he stopped, next to an enormous outcropping of Himalayan blackberries.

"This is it," he said gruffly.

"Yeah." Brittany stared at all the thorns and wondered how they'd cut through.

Then she wondered how the *girls* had cut through. Blackberry vines were nasty and could slash a teenager's expensive Lululemon jacket faster than you could say "ouch."

"How did they—" Ryan started to say, but he was interrupted by Brittany's phone ringing.

She pulled it out of her pocket and answered without looking to see who was calling, because she was so focused on the brambly impasse. Ryan canvassed it from the left and right, trying to find a way in. "Hello," she said, as she watched Ryan's progress.

"Hi, it's me," said Mary. "Guess what?"

"Hi, Mary. Now's not the best time."

"Sorry, I'll let you go. I don't mean to bother you."

"That's okay, I can talk to you later when I get home. I'm with Ryan, looking for his daughter."

"Isabella?" Mary asked. "But that's why I'm calling. She's here at the movie theater with me. I just gave her and her friends free popcorn."

"What?" Brittany asked. "Isabella is with you?"

Ryan, who had plunged through the first foot of blackberries, stopped in his tracks and looked back at Brittany. "Isabella's safe?"

Brittany nodded. "She's at the movie theater," Brittany explained. Then to Mary she said, "Mary, could you put Isabella on the phone? I think Ryan would like to talk with her."

Ryan nodded and climbed out of the blackberries.

"Sure," said Mary. "She and her friends are taking pictures at the selfie station with Godzilla."

A few minutes later, a much-relieved Ryan was ending his conversation with Isabella and handing Brittany's phone back to her. "Lana's mom found out where they were going and told them it was a bad idea," Ryan explained. "They changed their plans and went to the movies instead. Isabella's phone was out of juice or she would have called me."

"Which is a perfectly reasonable explanation." Brittany's gaze zeroed in on Ryan's cheek, which was bleeding. "It looks like the blackberries attacked you." She unzipped her purse. "I don't have a first-aid kit with me, but I do have tissues." She offered him a Kleenex.

"Thanks." He dabbed his cheek. "I don't think my jacket was safe from the attack, either." He held up his elbow and she saw a giant rip.

"Oh, no. Maybe it could be repaired? Your mom's a whiz with a needle."

"And she loves to be helpful." Ryan let out a deep breath. "You've been so helpful today too, and I brought you on a wild goose chase."

"Thank goodness for that, because it's better than the alternative. Every time Jeremy's gotten into a scrape I've flipped out. I seriously cannot handle the thought of my child being in danger, no matter how old he gets."

"Me neither." Ryan took a deep breath and shuddered.

"Hey." She rested her hand on his elbow. "It's okay. Everything's fine."

Ryan nodded, and his breathing steadied. "Seriously, Brittany," he said, his voice raw. "I can't thank you enough for today. You dropped everything to come help me, even though it was your only day off."

"Of course I did. I mean, it's..." She paused, not knowing how to articulate her thinking. "*You*," she finished lamely. "It doesn't matter how many decades it's been, or what I've thought about you since high school. Of course I'd be there for you in an emergency, and that includes your daughter."

"Really?"

"Yes, really. You'll forever be in my inner circle, because of Paul." She dropped the hand that had been touching his elbow and tilted her head upward so she could see him better.

Ryan looked at her solemnly. "I feel the same way about you, which is one of the reasons I was uncertain if I should come back to town."

"Why?"

Ryan looked at the blackberries for a moment, before looking back into her eyes. "Every time I look at you, I remember how much I liked you in high school but never felt like I was good enough. And you make me think of Paul, which is like having him ripped out of my life all over again."

"You remind me of him too. Talking about Paul with you makes me feel as if my brother is alive once more." Brittany bent her head. "And I didn't think that was possible." She looked up and hugged him spontaneously. "Thank you for that."

Ryan hugged her back and it felt good. "No, thank *you*. I feel the same way."

"It's not just about Paul. I don't have anyone to talk to about what my parents were like when I was younger, except my parents."

"That's hard."

"It *has* been hard." Brittany closed her eyes and listened to the thump-thump of Ryan's heartbeat under his coat. She couldn't believe they were embracing, but on the other hand, it felt like the most natural thing in the world. Neither one of them moved to end the hug. In fact, when she let her arms slide down a little bit to his waist, she felt his hand rub her back and something inside her stirred.

Ryan rested his chin on her head. "I worried that if I moved here, you'd never want to see me again, and every time we'd cross paths it would be awkward."

"It *was* awkward, at first." Brittany gazed at the blackberry vines. "For me at least. What about you?"

"So awkward. Compounded by the problem that you are every bit as smart, creative, and beautiful as I remembered." He stroked her hair for a moment.

She could have stepped back and ended the hug, but she didn't. Instead, she tightened her hold on his waist and looked up at him shyly. "How's that a problem exactly?"

Ryan gently pulled a windswept curl off her face and hooked it behind her ear. "Because it makes me remember that time at the beach, summer before my senior year, when Paul caught me ogling you in your red and white bikini and he punched me in the arm and told me you were off-limits."

"He did not."

"Did too."

"For real?"

Ryan nodded.

"I might have accidentally-on-purpose bought that bikini hoping to catch your attention when I wore it." Brittany felt flutters in her stomach. "I didn't think you did."

"Oh, I noticed alright." Ryan abruptly ended the hug. "Thanks again for your help today," he said, his voice strained.

Brittany felt abandoned. One moment she was in the warm shelter of Ryan's embrace, and the next she was standing in the cold, alone again. This wouldn't do. Forget Paul and his arm-punching, and his ghostly "my sister's off-limits" nonsense. She might not be able to rock her sophomore bikini anymore, but she could absolutely make Ryan Osborne want to hug her again, and perhaps even up the ante with a kiss.

"If we're going to talk about being helpful," she said, pulling her shoulders back so she stood up straight. "Don't forget to mention installing my bat box. As well as contacting the bat removal specialist." She took a step closer to him and poked at the rip in his sleeve, pushing the stuffing back inside. "Isabella's safe and made a smart decision with her friends' help. Take that as a win." She patted his bicep and then let her palm rest there. "You're doing a good job."

"I had a friend's help, too, today." Ryan took a shuffle step forward, closer to Brittany. "I cut my face, ripped my coat, and I'm missing the work meeting I'm supposed to be at right now, but I got a crash course in parenting high schoolers 101 from someone who's smarter than me about things like that, for which I'm grateful."

"I wouldn't say smarter, just more experienced." Brittany gazed up into his dark brown eyes. Out in the daylight, the silver streaks in Ryan's hair appeared lighter, like blond highlights.

"Oh, I'd definitely say smarter," Ryan reaffirmed. "You've always been a go-getter."

"Me?"

"Yes, you. Tackling your schoolwork. Not giving up. Plotting out your future trip to Europe with all those guidebooks and maps pinned on the walls of your room."

"You were never in my room, were you?"

"Nope." Ryan grinned. "But every time I walked past your room on my way to Paul's, and your door was open, I'd try to sneak the best view that I could."

Brittany laughed. "I *might* have guessed that, which is why I *might* have made sure I always left my door open when you came over."

"Clever. And look at you now, too." He brushed the back of his fingertip lightly across her cheek. "Still a go-getter. Starting your own business that's not only doing well but is also serving your community. That's as impressive as hell."

Brittany felt her pulse race when he touched her. Was she impressive? Maybe... She'd been so used to the men in her life tearing her down. Keith berating her. Ian ignoring her. Alan's patronizing ways. Even Jeremy gave her a hard time when he was younger. It felt strange having a man as accomplished as Ryan saying something positive about her.

"You're impressive, too," she said, as if the compliment was easier to manage if she acknowledged he was worthy of it as well. "You're a wonderful father, a good provider, and it's amazing how you've managed to stay on good terms with your ex."

Forget about encouraging Ryan to kiss *her*, she'd kiss *him*. Her lips parted and she lifted her chin slightly. She wasn't an innocent teenager anymore; she was a grown woman with experience under her belt. She had choices. She'd always had choices, but now she was brave enough to use them.

"You really are something, aren't you?" Ryan tilted his head down. "Wise. Capable." He cupped her face with his hand. "Beautiful."

Ryan Osborne called me beautiful. The teenager in her swooned. The grown woman in her took action. "I'm a damn good kisser, too. Or so I'm told."

Before she could hesitate.

Before she could talk herself out it.

Brittany pressed her lips against his and slipped her arms behind his neck, letting her fingertips roam freely across his solid back muscles. The kiss was gentle, but passionate, as if all her bottled-up emotions were coming to the surface and being released in one ardent moment. Ryan's feelings seemed to be surfacing too.

It turned out Ryan was a damn good kisser, as well. Just like she'd always dreamt he would be.

TWENTY

This must be what people meant when they said they were on Cloud Nine. For the past forty-eight hours, Brittany had felt like she was floating. Her heart soared every time she thought about her romantic moment with Ryan on Monday, and last night they'd talked on the phone until the wee hours. Ryan told her about his business trips to Germany, China, India, and Singapore. He still enjoyed traveling but found it difficult to vacation for pleasure due to his busy work schedule. Brittany told him about backpacking through Europe after college, her road trip to Ensenada, Mexico in her mid-twenties, and the trip to Ireland she'd planned and then canceled after she found out she was pregnant with Jeremy. Ian had said it cost too much money, and him not understanding how much the trip meant to her still stung.

Now it was Wednesday, and her phone buzzed with a text from Ryan as she wiped crumbs off the counter in front of the register. Safe Harbor hummed with diners, the seats half filled, which was a nice amount for the afternoon crowd.

How's my favorite attic? Ryan texted. *Still vacant?*

Yes, Brittany responded. *I looked up there this morning and didn't see a single tenant.*

What about the bat box? Is anyone in there?

I'm not sure. Brittany was grateful that nobody was in line at the moment, so she could text. *Isabella's here, though.*
Does it look like she's having fun? Ryan asked.

Yes. She's hanging out with her friends. Your mom was here for lunch earlier, but she's gone now.

Did my mom come alone?

Patti came with Don.

Ahh. I see. Mr. Dollface.

Ha! Brittany added a laughing emoji for good measure.

Would you like to come over for dinner this Saturday?

Brittany felt like her feet had wings. *Yes*, she said. *What can I bring?*

I wouldn't say no to cookies.

Brittany was just about to reply when a customer came to the register. *Got to go. Will get the details later*, she texted.

Still smiling, she turned her attention to the woman in front of her, whom Brittany recognized as one of Jeremy's former co-workers at McDonald's. Luna was a single mom with two jobs. She worked as a paraeducator at the local elementary school, supervising recess and helping support children with learning disabilities, and then spent her evening hours working the grill at McDonald's. Her son worked there, too. He was a year younger than Jeremy.

"Hi Luna, it's good to see you. What can I get you?" Brittany asked.

"I was hoping to treat myself to one of your salads I've heard people raving about." Luna adjusted the zipper on her jacket so that it fully covered her McDonald's uniform. "There was one container left." She placed a salad from the grab-and-go fridge on the counter.

Brittany looked at the label. "Green Goddess. That's one of my favorites."

"Great." Luna smiled. "I'll pay for that one myself, but I was wondering if I could also use one of these coupons for a free mocha."

"Coupons?" Safe Harbor didn't issue coupons, so at first Brittany was confused. But then she saw that Luna was holding a card from the Angel Board. "Oh yes. Absolutely."

Luna read the message on the back. "'To a woman whose son seemingly doesn't need her, please know that he still does. Sons always need their mothers.' That sounds like it was written about me and Jorge."

"Or me and Jeremy," Brittany said, feeling intrigued. Why were the Angel Board messages becoming so specific? It almost felt like they were directed at her.

After she'd finished Luna's order, Brittany called Nancy, who had already gone home for the day. She knew that Nancy was a giver of good advice and had been closely monitoring the entire Angel Board situation.

"Hi Nancy," Brittany said, as soon as her friend picked up. "I'm sorry to bother you after work, but something odd happened and I wanted to get your opinion on the subject." She conveyed what had transpired and read the most recent Angel Board message.

"That's bizarre," Nancy muttered.

"Do you remember who might have given you five bucks for the board recently?"

"Lots of different people," said Nancy. "That board's been popular."

"I don't think I could name everyone who has sponsored one either," Brittany admitted. "Customers have been very generous."

"What does the handwriting look like?" Nancy asked. "Can you compare it to the other cards?"

"I don't know. I don't have them."

"Yes, you do. I've been collecting them in a basket next to the dish towels."

"You have?" Brittany asked.

"I thought we could string them together into a garland at the end of the year to celebrate community giving."

"That's a fabulous idea! I love it." Brittany scanned the dining area to make sure that her customers were happy, and then raced into the back room to find the basket of cards. She hurried back to the counter a moment later. "Okay, I have the cards." Brittany laid them out next to the register. "There have been eight cards so far, and three of them seem to have the same handwriting, including this one."

"Read them to me."

"It's the first lines that really jump out." Brittany read them over the phone. "'For a mom who wears Birkenstocks and wool socks.' 'To a forty-five-year-old woman with a nose ring.' 'To a woman whose son seemingly doesn't need her.' So?" she asked. "What do you think this means?"

"Three cards is probably a coincidence at this point. Lots of forty-plus-year-old women in Sand Dollar Cove have nose rings. Nobody in the Pacific Northwest wears Birkenstocks in fall without socks, and I don't know of any mother in America who hasn't worried about her son. I hate to break it to you, kid, but you're not that special."

"Having a stalker wouldn't have made me special." Brittany still felt peculiar about the notes, but Nancy's wise counsel had reassured her a little bit. "But thank you for your analysis of the situation. That makes me feel better."

"Don't forget to put the cards back in the basket," Nancy reminded her before they hung up.

Brittany was just returning from the back room when Isabella came up to speak to her. Her long hair hung loose today, and she wore flared jeans and white Nike high tops with a tiny white T-shirt and pink cardigan. Isabella was looking less like Wednesday Addams and more like a typical Sand Dollar Cove High School freshman by the day. Brittany didn't know if that was good or bad, but understood that it took teenage girls a while to settle on their signature look.

"What can I help with?" Brittany asked.

"Scarlett, Gabby, and Lana have been talking about Halloween. It's only two weeks away."

"That's right." Brittany had been thinking about hosting a party at Safe Harbor but had been so overwhelmed with running her business that she hadn't planned anything yet. "You're just barely in the age range where it's still socially acceptable to go trick-or-treating, if you want."

"Exactly!" Isabella's dark eyes brightened. "They've invited me to go with them but there's no way my dad will say yes. He'll think it's too dangerous."

Brittany scoffed. "You're not in Seattle anymore. Trick-or-treating is perfectly safe here. The worst that could happen would be you'd hit five Airbnbs in a row and nobody would be giving out candy." *Which was another reason Safe Harbor should host a party.*

"So, you'll talk to him for me?" Isabella clasped her hands together. "Pretty please?"

"Sure. You and I can both discuss it with him when I come over to your house for dinner this weekend."

Isabella's mouth gaped open. "Dad invited you to dinner? He never does that. He hardly ever goes out on dates, let alone invites a woman over."

"It's not a date." Brittany felt her cheeks flush pink. "We're old friends. That's all." But she pictured those passionate kisses in front of Rhododendron Lane and blushed harder.

"Whatever this dinner is, my dad must really like you," said Isabella.

"I'm not sure about that..."

"He's been talking about you non-stop."

"He has?"

Isabella lowered her voice an octave in a hilarious impression of Ryan. "'Brittany always did her homework first before she watched television. That's why she got excellent grades and was accepted at the University of Washington.'"

"Oh gosh. Please tell me you're joking." Brittany pressed her fingertips to her forehead like she was trying to stop her head from exploding.

But Isabella kept going. "'Brittany has been experimenting with recipes since she was in middle school. That's why she's such a good cook.'"

"True, but why is he telling you this?"

"I'm not done," said Isabella. She dropped her voice again. "'Brittany never tried to copy what other girls were wearing. She made her own jewelry and developed her own look.'"

"Okay, that one's only partially correct. Yes, I made my own jewelry, but I also wore clothes that helped me fit in. I've never been a person who wanted to stick out." She touched the clasp of her necklace. "I still don't understand why your dad is rambling on and on about me like this."

"I already told you," Isabella said with a grin. "He likes you, which is exciting because my dad barely likes anyone. He's *so* cautious and paranoid."

"But hopefully not too cautious to let you celebrate Halloween with your friends, right?"

"Exactly! Thanks, Brittany."

"Don't thank me yet." Brittany held up her hands. "I haven't convinced him of anything."

But as Isabella walked away Brittany realized she'd convinced herself of something. Two things. Hosting an all-ages Halloween party at Safe Harbor was a fabulous idea. And also... it felt good knowing that Ryan was talking about her with his daughter.

TWENTY-ONE

Tonight was supposed to be fun and exciting, but Brittany already felt nervous. She sat in the driveway of Ryan's mammoth beach house and looked at the Angel Board cards she'd stashed in her purse. Besides the ones about her Birkenstocks, nose ring, and the mother–son relationship, now there were two more in the same shaky cursive.

To the woman who feels lost, forgotten, and unloved; you are not alone.

To the woman who could have been so much more if relationships hadn't tied you down, I see your true worth.

What did these messages mean? Were they specifically directed toward her?

With a heavy sigh, Brittany stashed the cards back into her purse and climbed out of her car into the wind, holding a plate of thumbprint cookies. She pulled her coat's hood over her head, but it was too late for her hairdo. Rain pelted her shoulders. Skipping puddles as best she could, Brittany darted up the path to Ryan's front door and rang the bell. As she waited, she pulled down her hood and combed her curls with her fingers.

Brittany wore faded jeans, a soft off-white sweater, and a

hammered copper necklace she'd made. Her brown hair was bouncy and full of body, and the under-eye cream concealer she'd put on gave her the illusion of being well-rested. She'd taken care with her outfit, not wanting to dress up too much or too little for dinner with him and Isabella. The most important thing to her was that she felt comfortable. She hadn't seen Ryan since Monday at Rhododendron Lane. Sure, they'd spoken on the phone or texted every day since, but they were still in uncharted relationship territory.

When Ryan opened the door and smiled at her, she saw that he was wearing jeans too, as well as a dark brown sweater. His thick hair was damp, and he carried a delicious soapy scent like he'd just come out of the shower. "You braved the weather," he said as he opened the door wider.

"I did."

"And you brought my favorite cookies."

"Of course." Brittany stepped inside and everything seemed fine for half a second. But when she shifted her weight, the wet soles of her boots slipped on the slate floor. Her feet flew forward, her butt fell back, and the plate of cookies went flying. The only thing that stopped her from falling was Ryan's strong hands reaching out to catch her in the nick of time.

Brittany scrambled to get up, but her boots kept slipping. Plus, her backside was still connected to Ryan's hand, which felt surprisingly good. She grabbed onto his biceps and stared up into his coffee-colored eyes.

"You're okay," said Ryan, as he lifted Brittany to her feet. "Oh, sorry." He let go of her jeans. "I didn't mean to manhandle you like that."

"You can manhandle me anytime you want, if it keeps me from breaking a hip." She brushed her hand down the side of her body, like she was checking for injuries. "All good."

"I was thinking your hips looked good too, especially in those jeans." Ryan's eyes twinkled mischievously.

Brittany stepped closer to Ryan and hooked her thumb in the belt loop at the right side of his waist and tugged. "I don't know about your hips, but these jeans feel a bit loose to me." She let go a second later, not wanting to come on too strong.

"Probably because I need more of your homemade cookies." He bent down and collected the baked goods. "Thankfully the plastic wrap saved them."

"Almost all of them." Brittany plucked the one that was falling off the plate. "This one might have touched the floor. We should probably—"

"Five-second rule," Ryan interrupted. "I'll save it." He opened his mouth.

"What? No, I brought you a whole dozen. You don't need to—"

"Oh yes I do." He nipped the cookie out of her hand before she could stop him.

"Ryan!" Brittany laughed as his lips touched her fingertips. "I would have brought you a replacement."

"Saving that cookie was the least I could do," he said after swallowing. "Sorry the floor's so slippery. I need to get a mat."

"I'm surprised Mary didn't order one for you."

Ryan retightened the plastic wrap. "She said it ruined the aesthetics of the entryway, but I should have protested because functionality comes first."

"I'll take off my boots, so I don't track mud across the floor."

"You don't have to do that."

"It'll keep me from slipping again." Brittany was already unzipping her right boot. When she stepped onto the ground she was in for a lovely surprise. "The floor's warm!"

"Yup. The previous owners put in some nice upgrades, including heated floors. Can I take your coat?"

Brittany lined up her boots by the front door and shrugged out of her coat. So far, her grand entrance hadn't been very smooth, but that was okay because she'd expected things to be a little awkward. "Here you go," she said, holding her coat. "Sorry it's wet." She wasn't sure where he'd hang it. There wasn't any sign of a coatrack or closet, nor was there a staircase banister to throw the garment over, like Jeremy often did. "Where should I put it?"

"I'll show you." Ryan leaned backward on the wall, and the entire surface pivoted, revealing a hidden room. He set the cookies on a shelf next to the door. "Welcome to my lair."

"Whoa! That's cool, I didn't know the wall did that." Brittany bent down and scooped up her boots. "We can add these while we're at it." She followed Ryan into the tiny room and found a place for her footwear while he hung her coat on a wooden hanger. The space smelled like wool and cedar. She turned around at the same time he did, and they faced each other, crammed together in the tight quarters.

Brittany thought about stepping back, to give Ryan more room, but she didn't. She noticed that he didn't move backward either, although he could have.

She thought of a lot of things, in fact, squeezed into the tight space next to him. She remembered how he'd always been taller, older, wiser, and more mature. Ahead of her by two years and eons away when they were younger. But now that age gap meant nothing. What didn't mean nothing was the fluttery feeling in her stomach standing this close to him. Or how the piney scent of his shampoo was driving her wild and she couldn't pinpoint the fragrance. What was it? Something expensive, probably.

Everything about Ryan was expensive now, from his understated wardrobe to his minimalist mansion. He'd gone from rags to riches like the hero of a movie. Did that mean he was still out of reach? If so, that was a big problem, because after those kisses at Rhododendron Lane... After the texts and phone calls this past week... After feeling his lips on her fingertips when he rescued the cookie just now... After all those things, Brittany wanted Ryan to be within her reach. She just needed to be brave enough to show him.

"The floor's just as hot in here as it is out there," she said, her toes curling and uncurling in her thin socks.

"Hopefully not too hot. I set the floor's thermostat to eighty-three degrees. Well below body temperature."

"But still cozy."

"Exactly." Ryan lifted his arm up and rested his hand on the wall next to her. "Thanks for coming tonight," he said in his deep voice. He gazed down at her lips, but didn't bend closer, like he was waiting for her to make the first move.

"Thanks for inviting me." For a moment she was transported back in time and became her fifteen-year-old self, star-struck that Ryan Osborne leaned against her locker to speak to her. But then she remembered that she was an experienced forty-five-year-old woman who knew exactly what she wanted—Ryan Osborne's lips against hers. "That sweater looks scratchy," she said, brushing her palm lightly against his chest, and leaving it there. "What is this, lambswool?"

"It's merino, and it's not as scratchy as it looks." Ryan's eyes traveled from her lips down to the cowl-neck of her cream-colored sweater, and back again. "But I guess that's comparative considering what you have on." His hand rested against her low back, and his thumb rubbed against the yarn. "What is this?"

"Angora. Or a blend, at least." She leaned closer, and they breathed in unison for moment until Brittany felt her courage build. She slid her hand up Ryan's firm chest then rested it behind his neck. "Ever made out in this closet before?" she whispered, hoping that he wouldn't share details if he had.

Ryan crooked his head closer to her own. "Nope." His hand on her waist became like iron as he pulled her toward him. Their lips were inches apart. "Never," he murmured.

Brittany wrapped her other arm around his shoulder and closed the circuit between them. When their lips touched, she felt a jolt like she'd downed a double espresso. Energy washed over her, making her feel alive. Ryan deepened the kiss and her tongue danced with his. She lifted up on her toes to be nearer, enjoying the strong weight of his hands pushing against her back, pulling her in for a tighter embrace.

Brittany forgot for a moment that they were surrounded by coats and jackets. She forgot where she was at all. All she knew was that she was in Ryan's arms, and the boy she had crushed on for years was now the man who was kissing her, and oh what a fine kisser he was. Her pulse raced. Her tongue caressed his and heat flushed her cheeks. Ryan's strong hands held her steady as her knees went weak. Brittany pressed against him, hungry for contact. She tilted her head, exploring the kiss from a new direction and felt her temperature spike.

The ivory sweater she wore, which had seemed like such a comfortable choice a moment ago, felt too hot. Her breathing, which had been normal, now sounded slightly out of control. She knew she needed to cool herself down so that she could think clearly. But did she want to think clearly? *Not in the slightest.*

Brittany's palms wandered down Ryan's back until they looped around his waist. She closed her eyes and moaned as his kisses wandered from her lips, down to her neck, and back again. She slid her fingertips underneath his sweater and felt the warmth of his bare skin. Her hands traveled up and felt the strength of his back muscles.

In all her adolescent fantasies involving Ryan, he'd never felt as irresistible as he did now. But then a voice echoed through the outside hallway, and they both froze.

"Dad?" Isabella called. "Are you there? Brittany's car is in the driveway."

Brittany jumped back and jostled the raincoats hanging behind her. She plucked out her curls with her fingertips. Ryan hastily pulled down his sweater.

"I'm hanging up Brittany's coat right now," he hollered through the closet opening. He grinned at Brittany. "Or something," he whispered.

She chuckled. "Something is right."

"Ladies first." Ryan scooted over so she could pass.

Brittany picked up the cookies and walked through the door and into the entryway where Isabella stood waiting. "I still don't understand how the hydraulics work on this thing," she said. Brittany spun around so she could see the place where Ryan had pushed the door to pivot. "Why didn't they build a normal door?"

Ryan emerged a second later. "Cleaner lines this way." He tapped the edge of the wall. "It's also how they did the appliance garage in the kitchen."

"Hi." Isabella smiled and surprised Brittany by hugging her.

She hugged the teenager back. "Good to see you."

"Can I show you my room?" Isabella asked.

"Sure." Brittany passed the cookies back to Ryan. "Lead the way."

"Dinner's not for fifteen minutes, so take your time," said Ryan.

Brittany followed Isabella through the hallway, across the great room, and down another hallway lined with incredible artwork. Her feet felt cozy thanks to the heated floors, but the white walls and modern artwork were out of Brittany's comfort zone. Not that she didn't like them, or think the house was beautiful, it just wasn't what she was used to. She was accustomed to houses that all looked the same. In her neighborhood, the same exact four houses were built over and over again, and all of them were probably furnished by the same big-box stores. This type of luxurious, ultra-modern individuality was new to her.

"There's the bathroom in case you need it." Isabella stuck her arm inside the room and waved her hand, activating the motion sensor light. "Everything's touchless so don't be confused."

"What?" This wasn't supposed to be a tour of the bathroom, but now Brittany was curious.

"The faucets, I mean. The bidet has switches." Isabella kept walking down the hallway and turned a corner. "That's my dad's room," she said, pointing through double doors to a California king-size bed facing a balcony. "My room's upstairs next to the guest room and office."

A flight of stairs later, Brittany felt like she was standing in the middle of a fairy tale. Isabella's four-poster bed had fluffy pillows and a velvet duvet. A sheer lace canopy draped to each side.

"This chair's my favorite part." Isabella sat in a hanging basket and spun around.

"That's beautiful, but I bet the view is even better." Brittany walked over to the telescope pointing at the window. "Too bad the sun already set."

"Yeah. It's really starting to get dark here, fast."

"This entire room is stunning." Brittany looked around. "The white desk is gorgeous. I love the decorative woodwork."

"We had a designer help us. Her name's Mary."

"I know Mary Turner. She's my housemate."

"Really?" Isabella seemed impressed. "Mary's great. She knows how to make latte art, too. She tried to teach me on our espresso machine, but I could never get the foam right."

"I've never learned how to do that either," Brittany admitted. "I can make all the fancy drinks, but when it comes to hearts or smiley faces, I'm out."

Isabella climbed out of her basket chair. "Now that I have you up here away from where my dad can hear, I need your help."

"Help with what?"

"Right before you arrived, Scarlett called and invited me over for a sleepover with Gabby and Lana. I really want to go."

"Oh. When is it?"

"Tonight. Scarlett's mom said she could pick me up."

Brittany felt that jolt again, only it was like a triple shot of espresso this time. "It won't bother me if you go," she managed to say in a casual tone. "A sleepover sounds like fun." *Lots of fun.* She pictured Ryan's lips against hers in the tight space of the closet. Her cheeks became as warm as the heated floors. "But I don't know your dad's thoughts about overnights." *Yet.*

"So, you'll help me convince my dad that I can go?" Isabella asked hopefully.

"I'm not going to interfere with your dad's parenting, but if he asks my opinion, I'll say I think it's a good idea. I assume you have a sleeping bag?"

"I do, and I already packed my duffle bag, just in case." Isabella pointed to a bundle on the ground next to her desk.

"Great." Brittany's pulse fluttered nervously. "I guess we'll go see what your dad thinks about sleepovers."

TWENTY-TWO

"Well, look who finally came home," Cheryl chirped, as Brittany closed the front door behind her. It was Sunday night, and she'd just left Safe Harbor. Cheryl had an easy view of the entryway from her customary position in the living room recliner. Hannah and Mary sat on the couch, with their cat Ferdinand resting between them.

"Hi." Brittany hung her purse and coat on the rack.

"Not only did she not come home last night," said Hannah, "but she's wearing the same outfit she left for dinner in."

"Ooh, la, la!" Mary clucked her tongue. "This is what I miss out on when I'm at Steven's apartment—analyzing Brittany's love life."

"Very funny." Brittany entered the living room and sank down cross-legged on the carpet, since there was no place else to sit.

"You don't need to sit on the floor." Hannah picked up Ferdinand, and patted his spot next to Mary, holding the cat in her lap. "Come put your feet up."

"And tell me how impressed you are with my decorating

prowess, now that you've seen every corner of Ryan's house." Mary wiggled her eyebrows.

"I haven't seen *every* corner." Brittany sat on the sofa and sank into the cushions. She unzipped her boots and put her feet up on the coffee table, like Hannah and Mary were doing.

"Which corners have you seen?" Hannah stroked Ferdinand's fur.

"Ryan's bedroom, for example?" Cheryl asked.

"I don't kiss and tell," said Brittany, wanting some secrets to remain private. The joy she'd experienced with Ryan had been that much sweeter because the past year had been so hard. "Isabella had an unexpected sleepover at her friend's house."

"And so did you." Mary leaned across Hannah and gave Brittany a fist bump. "Way to go putting Keith behind you."

"This wasn't about getting over Keith," Brittany protested. "I've known Ryan practically forever. He's..." Brittany tried to find the right word. "Special," she said, because that was the truth of it. Ryan Osborne held a special place in her heart. She hadn't seen him in three decades but there had been a Ryan-sized hole the entire time.

"What's so special about him?" Mary asked. "Besides being handsome, and rich, and having ridiculously good taste in interior designers?"

"He's observant." Brittany leaned back into the couch. "Ryan notices things. He pays attention to people, and he isn't so stuck in his own head that he's oblivious to other people's problems." She thought of all the ways, little and big, that Ryan had helped her when she was younger. She could see that he was like that with other people, too. "Ryan's smart, and a self-starter, and when he sets a goal he goes for it, just like me."

Saying that out loud about herself made Brittany feel good. She *was* self-motivated. She'd accomplished a lot of things that were important to her, like divorcing Ian, stabilizing her finances, and starting her own business. Brittany wasn't the type of person who sat on the couch thinking *woe is me*; she kept moving.

"It sounds like Ryan will make for a great neighbor once Guy and I finish our renovations on our Sand Piper Lane house," said Hannah.

"I'm not holding my breath for that house to be completed soon," said Cheryl. "Contractors always underestimate how long it takes to finish things."

Hannah sighed. "You may be right. The code inspections take a while, too."

"Which gives us plenty of time to continue living here with you, Brittany." Mary hugged a throw pillow. "And for me to save up money for when Steven and I eventually move in together."

"Changes are coming," said Cheryl. "But not quite yet."

"I'm glad for that," said Brittany. "This is the happiest, most peaceful household I've ever been a part of."

"Aw..." Hannah frowned. "That's both sweet and sad."

"I was thinking the same thing," said Cheryl. "Your home wasn't happy growing up?"

"Not really." Brittany shrugged. "Mary's seen how my parents are when they are together."

"Like caged animals," Mary confirmed.

Brittany looked out the window at the canal. The sun had set, but she could see the dark water. "When my brother Paul was alive, my parents were on slightly better terms, but not by much. I used to blame my mom's anger problems for driving my dad away, but now I realize that my dad didn't care that much about me to begin with. He could spend time with me now if he wanted to, but he doesn't." She looked back at the Turners. "Then with my marriage, Ian was self-absorbed and focused on his own wants and needs. Jeremy and I were always an afterthought to him. I didn't feel true peace until our divorce."

"Divorce must have been a hard decision, but it sounds like the right one." Hannah pushed Ferdinand's tail out of her face.

"You couldn't control your experience when you were little, nor can you rewrite the past," said Mary. "But you're in charge now. I think you put up with Keith way too long."

"Yeah." Hannah nodded. "I agree. He wasn't good for you either."

"The way that man chipped away at your self-esteem was horrible to watch," Cheryl muttered.

"I can see that, looking back," Brittany admitted. "I guess I was afraid of being lonely. But now I can see that it's better to be alone than with someone who's mistreating you." Brittany looked around the room at her happy little found family. "This has been my first real experience with drama-free living. Thank you for helping me learn how freeing that is."

"You're welcome," said Hannah.

"We're grateful for this living arrangement, too," Mary added.

"I don't know what you're talking about," Cheryl quipped. "You must be living with a different woman and her granddaughters, because the Turner family has never been without drama."

"Gran has a point." Hannah adjusted the cat's collar. "Ferdinand brings his share of drama as well. He's decided he no longer likes Fancy Feast, even though we have an entire case of what used to be his favorite."

"By the way," said Mary. "Your mom called me on Friday. I forgot to tell you."

"What?" Brittany asked. "My mom called *you*?"

"Yeah, to get a quote on my interior design service. She thought a hundred eighty dollars an hour was way too much, even though I told her the going rate was two hundred dollars, and I was giving her a friends and family discount."

"My mom's middle name is Frugal," said Brittany.

"I realize that," Mary continued, "which is why I was surprised that she hired me anyway even though she thought I was too expensive."

"Really? You're working for my mom? I didn't know she had a project. Which room does she have you redoing?"

"Her entire condo," said Mary. "All 1,800 square feet. She said that Tansy shouldn't be the only one who gets a new kitchen or anything else she wants."

"I thought Tansy was out of the picture?" Hannah asked. "Isn't that what you said, Gran?"

Brittany looked at Cheryl. "How did you find that out? The only person I told about that was Nancy."

"Nancy doesn't blab," said Cheryl. "Don't blame her."

"I'm not." Brittany stretched out her toes. "But I am wondering how you found out." She suspected it was from the senior center, since the members loved to gossip.

"I heard it from Ann, who heard it from Nugget's vet, who heard it from her sister who is one of the hygienists at your father's clinic," said Cheryl.

"Oh jeez." Brittany rolled her eyes. "I bet my mom loves it that half of Sand Dollar Cove is talking about Tansy running off on him."

"And apparently your father loves it that your mom is back at the practice, managing the reception desk," Cheryl added.

"That's impossible." Brittany shook her head. "I mean, yeah, he's probably glad that their business isn't imploding, but I'm sure he hates having to see her each day."

"I don't know about that," said Hannah. "My friend Jasmine told me they came into The Summer Wind the other night for dinner."

Mom and Dad eating at Seaside Resort's restaurant? Impossible. Brittany stood. "It sounds like I need to give my parents a call and find out what's gossip and what's the truth. But first I need a shower and a good night's sleep."

"When you talk to your mom, sing my praises," said Mary.

"Are you sure you want me to do that?" Brittany raised her eyebrows. "My mom can be difficult."

"I'm already hired. I just want to start out on the right foot. And you want to talk difficult? Difficult is designing a whole house where every last thing needs to be hidden, even the door handle. Did you see Ryan's coat closet?"

Brittany felt blood rush to her cheeks. "Why yes, I did."

"So, what's next with you two?" Hannah asked. "Are you going to ask him out?"

"Probably." Brittany picked up her boots. "I haven't thought that far ahead."

"I hear the Sand Dollar Cove Cinema makes for a great dating venue," Mary said with a twinkle in her eye.

"Says the girlfriend of the owner." Cheryl harrumphed. "I'm not saying that's not a good choice, but why don't you do something more modern, like invite him on a hike or something?"

"Since when have you seen me hike?" Brittany asked.

"Good point." Cheryl tapped her chin. "How about a picnic on the beach?"

"In this weather?" Hannah asked. "It's supposed to be in the mid-forties all week."

"But clear," Mary added. "You could invite him for a car date on the beach."

"What's a car date?" Brittany asked. "Is that a Gen Z thing?"

"No, but it's a Sand Dollar Cove thing," Hannah explained. "We're trying to promote it at Seaside Resort, actually. Pick up a picnic lunch from The Summer Wind restaurant, and drive onto the beach for a romantic escape."

"That *does* sound lovely," Brittany said, considering.

"You can order a lunch box on the website if you're interested." Hannah slid Ferdinand over onto the free space on the couch. "Jasmine just needs twelve hours' notice to have them ready."

"I appreciate the suggestion." Brittany said goodnight and headed toward her room. She'd barely closed the door when her phone buzzed with a text from Ryan. As soon as she saw his number, she flopped onto her bed and snuggled into the pillows to read the text.

Is it too weird to say that I miss you? Ryan texted.

No, Brittany responded. *I miss you too.* She wished she didn't have to work on the weekends.

How about lunch tomorrow from 11:30 to 12:45?

That's oddly specific.

Sorry about that. I have meetings all day but carved out a window.

Just for me? Brittany asked.

Of course.

Isabella will be at school?

That's right, Ryan texted.

Thank goodness for the Turner women's dating tips. Brittany was already prepared with an idea. She was about to suggest lunch on the beach when Ryan surprised her.

I made reservations at The Summer Wind for 11:30. Will that work? he asked.

Yes! The beach picnic could wait. Dining at The Summer Wind sounded even better.

Unfortunately, I'll have to meet you there, because of the timing.

That's fine. See you tomorrow.

After they'd said goodnight, Brittany put her phone down on her dresser and looked at Paul's picture. The necklace she'd made with the Roman numeral ten draped over it. Brittany kissed her fingers and touched the X. Paul's immortal smile beamed back at her. "Guess who's going on a date with your best friend?" she whispered. She wondered what Paul would think of that. Hopefully, he wouldn't punch Ryan in the arm.

TWENTY-THREE

Waves of nostalgia hit her like rough seas dashing on rocks. Brittany noticed the autumn colors as she walked up the winding paths of Seaside Resort, snaking her way past the lobby and the wellness center on her way to the restaurant. Vine maples burned a brilliant orange, and purple and yellow glacier pansies lined the well-trodden sidewalks. The flowers were different, and the cottages didn't look like she remembered, thanks to extensive renovations, but this whole experience of walking to The Summer Wind, in the middle of an ordinary Monday, felt eerily familiar.

Why?

Brittany tried to shake off the feeling but couldn't. Nor could she understand the sense of dread that weighed down each footfall. She was excited to see Ryan. Truly, she was. But this moroseness that hit her as soon as she entered the resort property was hard to comprehend.

Then, she remembered, all at once. The last time she'd eaten lunch here on a weekday had been seven years ago, when she'd met her lawyer to complete her divorce. Yes, that was it. Brittany's shoulders heaved as she let out a huge puff of air. The divorce had been worth it; parting from Ian was one of the best things that had happened to her, but that didn't mean she walked away without regrets.

Was she foolish to begin a brand-new relationship with Ryan? Maybe she should call it quits from the get-go before she got hurt. Safe Harbor could be her soulmate, not that she believed in soulmates.

She *wanted* to believe in soulmates, but in her experience, true love was only something that happened in fantasy books. Most men turned out to be trolls or executioners, and the only dragons worth fighting were the ones that messed with your kid. That's why she'd spent all morning on the phone with the insurance agent insisting that they replace, not repair, the ragtop of Jeremy's Mustang. She'd emerged from that battle victorious, but now she was running three minutes late.

Brittany charged up the path, barely noticing the crooning song of the foghorn. She could see The Summer Wind now, and its beautiful wraparound deck and pavilion. Hannah and Guy were to be married there in a year, weather permitting. At least that was the plan. Brittany felt pleased for the young couple, and her joy for their future union was undiminished by the bitterness she felt for her own. Some fairy tales came true, after all. Hannah and Guy were a happily-ever-after. Mary and Steven looked to be that way too. But Brittany was on the road to crone status, and that was fine with her.

Or so she told herself.

Somewhere deep in her heart, a seed of hope grew, tenderly watered by the knowledge that she was having lunch with Ryan Osborne. *The* Ryan Osborne. And that Ryan was every bit as wonderful as she'd imagined him to be, back in girlhood.

He was waiting for her now. She could see him on the deck, arms braced on the railing, staring at the Pacific. His dark slacks and slick black raincoat looked reliable. But when he turned around and smiled, it gave away his roguish side.

"You made it," Ryan said, before she'd even stepped onto the deck.

"Sorry I'm late." She climbed the steps. It was only eleven thirty-three, but she felt the need to apologize.

"Don't worry about that. I was enjoying the view." He reached for her hand and gently pulled her toward him. "I've been missing you."

"Same." She put her free hand on his broad shoulder and lifted her lips for a kiss.

Ryan leaned forward and caressed his lips against hers.

"Happy Monday," he murmured.

"So far this week has started out pretty good." Mindful of their public setting, and the hotel guests that might be watching, she brushed her lips against his one more time and settled for holding his hand.

He squeezed her fingertips and led her to the entrance of The Summer Wind, holding the door for her as they entered.

An instrumental version of "You Learn" by Alanis Morissette was playing on the sound system, which made Brittany think of high school, and how that song had played non-stop on the radio the year after Paul died. The real version, where Alanis sang it, not the elevator music version that was playing now. What would Paul have thought of that song, or "You Oughta Know" from the same album? He'd probably have had a firm opinion on it. Paul had strong opinions about every song that came across the radio. He also hated Brittany's own taste in music back in high school, which was a mixture of Indigo Girls, Amy Grant, and Lisa Loeb.

"Would you consider Paul to be a music snob?" Brittany asked after they'd been seated.

"Yes, absolutely," Ryan said, without giving it a second thought. "Remember his CD collection? That was his most prized possession."

"He kept it in a plastic tower next to his boom box." Brittany smiled. "I haven't thought about that thing in ages."

"He loved that collection."

"He sure did." Brittany pictured the stack of CDs. "My parents kept Paul's room intact for a few years, but when I came back from college on winter break, his entire room had been cleared out and turned into a guest bedroom."

"That must have been a shock."

"It was." Brittany nodded. "Everything was gone, even his letterman's jacket. I asked what happened to it, and my mom said she'd put that, and a few other things, in a storage box for safekeeping, but that she'd given all his other things away."

"And your dad was okay with that?"

Brittany shrugged. "I have no idea. They yelled about everything. They couldn't stop arguing long enough to celebrate Christmas." She looked down at the menu, embarrassed that she'd brought up ancient history that Ryan wouldn't want to hear about.

But he surprised her.

"Did anyone suggest grief counseling after Paul died?"

"What?"

"Or family counseling, to help you all process what you'd been through? Maybe that would have helped."

"No. We never saw a therapist. But I did bring a therapist on board when Ian and I started having trouble, and Jeremy and I kept seeing her after the divorce."

"That's sad that your family didn't have professional support after the accident." Ryan pushed his menu away so he could fully concentrate on her. "The school counselor came to speak to our basketball team and met with me one-on-one for weeks. He didn't come see you, too?"

Brittany shook her head. "No, he didn't."

"I wonder why not? I don't think his sessions helped that much, but at least it was something."

"Something's better than nothing." Brittany picked up her menu again, trying to focus on the too-small print. "I'm sorry to bring up depressing subjects on our date." As soon as she said the word "date," she tensed. Did Ryan consider this to be a date? Or was this a thank-you-for-waking-up-with-me-yesterday-morning meal?

"Brittany, you can talk with me about whatever you want, especially about Paul. I hope you know that."

Mollified, a smile twitched on her lips. "Can I talk to you about how bad my eyesight's getting now that I'm forty-five? I can barely read the menu."

Ryan chuckled. "I can see the menu just fine, but don't ask me to read that clock across on the wall."

Brittany turned to see where he was looking. "Eleven forty-one. Shoot! We better order something fast so you can make it out of here in time. When's your next meeting again? Twelve forty, did you say?"

"Twelve forty-five. But I can take it in the car."

Brittany unzipped her purse and brought out her reading glasses. "Much better," she said as the menu came into focus.

"I like you in glasses." Ryan bumped his foot against hers, making her giggle.

"I call them my cheaters." She ran her finger down the menu and settled it on what she wanted. "I'll have the pan-fried oysters and side salad."

"And I'll go for the grilled seafood platter." Ryan signaled to their waiter.

After the server left, Brittany put her glasses away and looked through the floor-to-ceiling window they were seated against to admire the view. The ocean mirrored the gray sky, but at least it wasn't raining. "This view is beautiful," she said, "but I like the one from your house better."

"Same. Every day I wake up and look at the water and I can't believe I live there. Isabella has an entirely different life than what I had growing up, but I don't think she appreciates it."

Brittany looked from the window to him. "Because the poor, deprived girl doesn't have a smartphone," she teased.

"It's a rough life."

Brittany chuckled. "Although I think you should give her one, so she doesn't become a social outcast."

"Is Bella been coaching you to say that?"

"No. But I remember how hard it is to be a freshman girl, and Isabella doesn't have a big brother or his best friend there to look after her."

"I don't know if I'd say I looked after you. Looked *at* you is more like it."

"Oh really?" Brittany knocked her foot against his and he wrapped his leg around hers, touching her calf.

"Especially those cropped-top sweaters you used to wear. Paul caught me staring once and knocked me upside the head."

"He did not!" Brittany exclaimed, laughing.

"He most certainly did." Ryan laughed with her.

Now that they were talking about Paul again, Brittany asked a question that had been bothering her. "Do you think if Paul had been accepted at Northwestern he would have gone? Even if the tuition was so expensive and it meant leaving me behind?"

Ryan's smile faded and was replaced by a somber expression. "Yes. He would have gone."

"I think so too, even though we'll never know if he got accepted or not since he died in fall before the letters went out."

Ryan locked eyes with her. "Actually, Paul didn't tell anyone but me, but he'd applied to Northwestern's early decision program. He received their acceptance letter the day he died."

"What? Paul got accepted to his dream school?"

"He did. And he was excited."

The server arrived and quietly put down their plates. Brittany and Ryan's conversation paused until after the waiter had departed.

"Why didn't Paul tell me?" Brittany asked. She smelled the delicious aromas coming from her oysters but didn't eat one bite.

"He was going to tell you," said Ryan, "but..."

"Paul was worried about how it would impact me, wasn't he?"

"He was." Ryan cut a bite from his salmon. "When we were painting the rocks, we talked it over and came up with how he could afford Northwestern without pissing off your mom. Paul was going to use his Advanced Placement credits to graduate a year early."

The tightness in her chest released, and Brittany relaxed. She slid an oyster onto her fork. "I didn't have a dream school. I was so messed up after he died that I went away to the University of Washington on autopilot, and that worked out fine because it's a great school as well."

Ryan set down his knife. "That day at the lighthouse, he said he would tell your family... He just never got the chance."

"And you've held onto Paul's secret all these years?" Brittany gazed at Ryan and saw the grief set there. His clenched jaw and lined forehead showed the tension he carried.

"I didn't know what else to do," Ryan admitted. "If I'd told your parents about Paul's acceptance letter, would that have made things better or worse?"

"I don't know." Brittany considered the paradox. "My dad would have been over the moon that Paul was going to his alma mater, but my mom would have been angry that he wasn't intending to go to an in-state school like she'd wanted."

"Exactly. And what would you have thought?"

"I would have been glad for him." She looked down at the oysters. "As it turned out, I got *all* of the college money. All of it. And then when it came time for my son to go to college, I didn't have as much money saved for Jeremy as my parents gave me, because of how much my divorce wrecked my finances."

"Paying for college is a mess in this country. Don't beat yourself up over not being able to save more."

"Ian won't contribute to Jeremy's tuition at all. Meanwhile, I send Jeremy every penny I can, paying for his tuition and his car insurance. He's using his savings from his old job at McDonald's to pay for books and gas. If he's lucky, he'll graduate with his associate degree debt-free, and then sign on with a fire department that will pay for his academy training."

"Nice." Ryan scooped up a spoonful of rice. "That's more than my parents gave me."

"Sorry to rant. I don't know why I started telling you the messy intricacies of Jeremy's non-existent financial aid package." Brittany took a drink of her Diet Coke.

"No, I'm glad." Ryan reached across the table and held her hand. "Being eighteen, nineteen, twenty... Those years can be hell. These questions of did our parents help us when we really needed assistance, or did they kick us to the curb as soon as we turned eighteen... they are really important." Ryan let go of Brittany's hand and picked up his fork. "Just like, I think..." He didn't finish what he was saying.

"You think, what?" Brittany prodded.

Ryan put down his fork and looked at her. "Favoritism. That leaves scars too."

"You were an only child. What do you know about favoritism?"

"Only what Paul told me, and what I observed eating dinner at your house. Like how you always helped your mom with the dishes, but Paul didn't."

"Because he had basketball practice."

"Yeah, and so what if he did?"

"Yeah, but dishes aren't such a big deal," she said, mainly in defense of her brother.

"What about that time we were there studying for your algebra test and your mom discovered the screen saver had been changed on your family's computer?"

Brittany flinched. "Oh... That..."

"She berated you for twenty full minutes for changing the desktop settings and 'ruining her computer.'"

"But I hadn't, and I told her that."

Ryan frowned. "And then she accused you of lying. It was so awkward for me to witness her rant at you like that, but I didn't want to abandon you."

Brittany looked down at her unmanicured hands and let out a puff of air. "I was kind of used to her treating me like that, to be honest."

"By the time Paul got there, she had grounded you, put you in charge of cleaning the house for the next two months, and taken away all your phone privileges. Then Paul walks in and admits that *he* was the one who changed the screen saver."

Brittany nodded. "And my mom said, 'Really? That's clever of you to know how to do that.'"

"I was shocked that she didn't apologize to you," Ryan said, with deep sympathy in his voice. "Completely stunned."

Old wounds split open inside her. "It wasn't just my mom. My dad didn't bother hiding his favoritism either. Paul never had a summer job, or a part-time job, but I had to clean the orthodontist office each weekend as soon as I turned thirteen. My dad gave Paul new skis for his sixteenth birthday but when I turned sixteen, I got a hairdryer. He gave Paul as much money as he wanted to build his CD tower, but I had to work for every allowance dollar I spent." Brittany rested her elbow on the table for just a moment before she realized what she was doing and slid it off.

"Melissa grew up with favoritism in her house, too, which is why she's extra careful with Isabella and her stepsons. She, Troy and I talk about it all the time."

"That's good." Brittany smiled for half a second until she realized her eyes were blurring with tears. She fished a tissue out of her purse and blotted them away.

"I don't know how you ended up so normal, and not totally screwed up," Ryan said. "I mean normal as a compliment, by the way. Although you're not normal, you're extraordinary."

"Thanks." This time, Brittany smiled for real.

"Your house might have been spotlessly clean, but perfection stopped there. At least I knew my mom loved me, even though she couldn't do much to help."

"My mom loves me," Brittany said, on instinct.

"Unconditionally?" Ryan asked.

"Well..." Brittany didn't know what to say. Both of her parents treated her like a chess piece they could move across the board as a proxy shoulder in their own fights.

Ryan bunched his napkin in his fist, crumpling it into a little ball. "I'll never forget at Paul's funeral, when I walked into the vestibule of the church with my parents, and your mom flipped out and yelled at us to get the hell out. Remember that?"

Brittany nodded. "She was really upset. She blamed your dad for the accident." Brittany squeezed her right fingers around her left thumb. "Just like I blamed you."

"I get that. I really do." Ryan swallowed. "Anyhow, I left the church, but I didn't leave the property. I wanted to be there for Paul." Ryan's eyes clouded, and his neck became splotchy like he'd eaten something too spicy. "After the service started, I snuck into the back, where it was standing room only."

"I didn't know you were there."

"Well, I was." Ryan tugged his collar. "You and your folks walked in last. I saw your mom eviscerate you for wearing that basketball necklace you made to cheer Paul on at our games. The one with the X for his jersey number."

Brittany touched the empty space on her throat where the necklace wasn't. "She said it was tacky and not appropriate and made me take it off."

"That's right." Ryan nodded. "She didn't love you unconditionally. She loved you if you made her look good."

There was a lot of truth in that statement, and it was difficult for Brittany to digest, but it pinged another memory. "That was right before the argument about the music," she said.

"Yes. I was there for that, too."

"My parents told me I could pick one song for the funeral's playlist, and I wanted to pick 'Come As You Are' by Nirvana, since that was Paul's favorite song, but my mom vetoed that because of the lyrics, so I chose 'Runaway Train' by Soul Asylum instead. But then the funeral director came up to us right before the service and said that the organist needed sheet music for it."

"And you said you didn't have sheet music," said Ryan.

"And that it would sound stupid on the organ, and that no way would Paul want an organ playing at his funeral, anyway." Brittany felt tears roll down her cheeks. "He'd want his CDs, but my dad argued, 'That's why we're playing Celine Dion at the end.' That's when I freaked out and cursed and said: 'Paul hates Celine Dion!'"

"He really did. He refused to go see *Titanic* just so he wouldn't have to listen to 'My Heart Will Go On' again."

"And that was the song they played." Brittany wiped her eyes with the tissue. "It was the only thing in the whole service they could agree upon, a song Paul would have hated."

"*Did* hate. Detested, actually. Got one more of those tissues?" Ryan brushed tears off his cheeks.

"I do." Brittany handed him the package from her purse.

She could see it all so clearly now, with the wisdom of adulthood. It had taken the clarity Ryan offered her as a witness to help her fully understand that Cynthia and Alan were deeply flawed people who put their own selfish wishes ahead of their children. Brittany had borne the brunt of it since Paul was their favorite and had died so young. She had forty-five accumulated years of putting up with her parents' awfulness. It was no wonder she'd struggled in relationships. Brittany hadn't really learned what it meant to be part of a healthy family until therapy.

When she'd been married to Ian, she hadn't known how to say: "I need you to make Jeremy and me a priority in your life," without shouting it like Cynthia or making nasty snide comments like Alan. And it's not like Ian was any better. He used work as an escape to avoid his family commitments altogether. Ian liked having a family to come home to but didn't want to put in any effort to sustain one. He had been more than happy to let Brittany do all the housework, child-rearing, and bill paying on her own even though she was also working full-time. Thank goodness she and Jeremy were on solid ground. Bringing him with her to therapy when she'd divorced Ian had been a good decision.

"'Runaway Train' would have been an awesome choice, by the way," Ryan said. "Although I would have picked 'One' by U2. Paul was obsessed with that song. He played it on repeat when he broke up with Carly."

"I remember that!" Brittany smiled. "I told him to switch over to his Walkman because his boom box was so loud that I could hear it in my room, and it was driving me nuts."

Ryan lifted his water glass. "Here's to Paul driving us nuts."

Brittany raised her Diet Coke. "Cheers to that."

They clinked glasses and took a sip.

"Sorry to ruin our first official date with a bunch of sad memories," Ryan said, as he put down his glass.

"No, don't apologize." Brittany reached across the table and squeezed his hand. "This conversation was exactly what I needed. Truly."

TWENTY-FOUR

Ever since her date with Ryan the day before, Brittany had wanted to speak with both of her parents. Separately, of course. She didn't have a death wish. But she was determined to sit down and discuss—like mature adults—how she refused to be sucked into their toxic drama from this point forward. She mentioned this to Jeremy on the phone Tuesday night, and they discussed how a conversation with Cynthia and Alan might go. Sharing her troubles with her son felt good, especially because he was old enough to give her meaningful advice.

"Tell Grandma that you don't want to hear her insult Grandpa in front of you anymore," Jeremy suggested. "Grandma can rant about him to her friends, not you or me."

"I like that." Brittany wrote down the talking point on a notepad. "What else?"

"Sometimes Grandpa asked me to pass messages to Grandma, and I hate that."

"He does that with me, too." Brittany jotted that on her paper.

"But the most important thing," Jeremy said, "is to catch them in the act."

"Doing what?"

"Belittling each other. When you're there witnessing them being awful, that's the best time to say something, and make them stop."

"Right..." Brittany wrote that down, too.

"Squirt them on the nose with a water pistol, or say in a really loud voice, 'No. Stop that!'"

"Wait... what?"

"I'm just kidding. Dad's girlfriend lent me a book on puppy training since she brings Hudson over so often."

"That sounds fun."

"It *is* fun. Except when Hudson pees on the carpet and chews my shoes. I'm beginning to understand why we never had a dog."

"How has it been living with your dad after so many years apart?"

"Dad's always at work, so I hardly ever see him."

That sounds familiar, Brittany thought to herself. But she didn't say that out loud. "You and he both have a strong work ethic," she said instead.

"Yeah, I just wish he'd spend more time with me now that I'm here, you know? I like his girlfriend, but when he's home they're always together, and he never makes any time for me."

"Making time for the people you love is important."

"Like when you dropped everything to come help me at school, even though it meant losing your job."

"Worth it," Brittany said, surprised that Jeremy had brought it up.

"I'm sorry my stupid prank made Keith fire you."

"*I'm* not. If that hadn't happened, I wouldn't have Safe Harbor. And looking back, I think the prank was funny and the school overreacted. There should still be room left for fun in this world, without everyone freaking out."

"Thanks, Mom."

"I love you and miss you so much, and I'm proud of you for striking out on your own in Seattle."

"I love you, too."

After they hung up, Brittany's emotions felt sweet and warm like apple pie. These past eighteen years of parenting Jeremy hadn't been perfect, but she felt like their relationship was healthy and respectful. She wanted that with her parents, too, but didn't know if it would be possible. The only way to find out was to try. Brittany texted Cynthia and invited her to Safe Harbor the following day for a visit.

"Thanks for stopping by," Brittany told Cynthia as she brought her mother a blueberry muffin and a cup of tea. It was Wednesday afternoon, half an hour before closing time, and Safe Harbor only had a handful of customers.

"Boy, it looks like your foot traffic has really died down." Cynthia surveyed the room. "The novelty must have worn off already. Maybe you should lower your prices or mail out coupons."

"Business has been fine, thanks." Brittany sat down and scooted her chair closer to her mother. "It's usually quiet around closing time, and that's okay because it gives me a chance to prep for the next day."

"What happened to that woman you hired?"

"Nancy's working out great, thanks for asking. She goes home at three." Brittany dunked her tea bag in her mug and watched color seep into the water.

"Have you spoken to your father recently?" Cynthia peeled the wrapper off her muffin.

"I texted this morning but haven't heard back."

"Probably because he's up to his eyeballs sorting out the financial mess Tansy left."

Here we go, Brittany thought. She sensed one of Cynthia's rants coming on.

"That tart is such an idiot that she—"

"I'd rather not discuss Dad's personal relationships," Brittany said quickly, cutting her off. "How are you doing? Do you still love your Peloton?"

"I adore it." Cynthia showed Brittany her Apple Watch. "I've been completing my rings every day."

"Nice. Good for you."

"Now that I'm back working at the practice, it's harder to hit the standing goal." Cynthia peered down at her watch. "But I stand up every hour so that I can be sure to close that ring."

"So, Dad talked you into it? You're holding down the fort at Thompson Orthodontics?"

Cynthia nodded. "Just until we can hire someone else. I told your father that it was my business too, and if it was in trouble then that reflected poorly on me. Which is entirely unfair because it's his dipshit decisions and horrible choice in women that got us into this situation."

Catch them in the act, Brittany remembered Jeremy saying. It was too bad that squirting her mom on the nose with water wasn't an option. "Venting to me about Dad isn't helpful," she said. "I'm not the right person to talk to about that."

"What do you mean, you're not the right person?" Cynthia put down her muffin. "You're his daughter, after all. His only surviving child—that we know about, at least."

"What's that supposed to mean?" Brittany asked, shocked that her mother's acrimony could still surprise her.

Cynthia sniffed. "I'm just saying you're his only legitimate daughter. He probably has bastards all over this town."

"That's not true." Brittany slapped her hand on the table. "Stop trash-talking Dad in front of me and in front of Jeremy. It's not healthy for any of us."

"Don't be so dramatic. You sound like a teenager."

"No, I sound like a grown woman setting healthy boundaries." Brittany paused for a moment to choose the right words. "If you don't have something nice to say about Dad, please don't talk about him at all. Not to me. It's not fair."

"Spare me your clichés."

"I will, if you lay off Dad. There are other things I'd rather talk about. Like, how is it being back in the office, for example?"

Cynthia patted her freshly cropped hair and straightened the collar of her button-down shirt. "Fine, except for how filthy the reception desk was until I cleaned it up. You should have seen the mess Tansy left. Her computer monitor was so dusty I could barely read the screen." She shook her head in disgust. "Thank goodness I'd been handling billing and insurance reimbursement this whole time, or else the business would have gone under."

"Office management isn't for everyone." Brittany picked up her tea. She was willing to draw a line in the sand for Alan, but not Tansy.

"Your father was even in danger of losing that damn boat of his."

"What?"

"The bill for the *Moonstruck*'s payment plan comes to the office, apparently, and Tansy hadn't been paying it."

"Oh no! Dad loves that boat."

"I know." Cynthia sniffed. "Not that it's anywhere near as good as the *Lovestruck*. They don't make boats like they used to."

Brittany was glad that her mom had at least *some* happy memories from the past. The only time she could remember her family being truly joyful was when they were waterskiing. She could still picture their happy faces. Paul gliding across the water; Alan driving the boat; Cynthia wearing her bathing suit and an extra layer of suntan lotion.

"Did I tell you how Tansy had decorated the reception desk with pictures of her childhood dachshund?" Cynthia asked.

"Sparky?"

"Oh, was that his name?"

"I think so." Brittany repinned a stray curl that had loosened from her bun. "He died from back problems."

"How sad." Cynthia frowned. "What a poor, poor, adorably sweet dog."

"I thought you hated dogs. That's why we couldn't have one growing up. You said they made messes. That's why I told Jeremy we couldn't have one either."

"And I stand by that. I had enough to manage what with you kids, work, and your father's—" Cynthia stopped herself. "Never mind. So, what's new with you? I see you're still doing those crafting projects. Your apron looks nice."

"Thanks." Brittany touched the brooch she'd pinned to her apron. It was a hammered copper teapot pouring beads into a button-sized teacup. "I made this a while ago and recently found it in my jewelry drawer. As for me, and what's fresh..." Brittany paused, not wanting Cynthia to know about Ryan. Their romance was too new, too precious, to risk exposing it to her mother's scrutiny. Instead, she spoke about work. "I'm planning a Halloween party here at Safe Harbor." She pointed to the poster by the front door. "It'll be from six thirty to eight thirty, and have games, pumpkin decorating, and pre-made sandwiches for sale."

"Clever." Cynthia nodded her approval. "I hated having to rush home from work to get dinner on the table in time for trick-or-treating. Sandwiches would have been nice."

"Yeah, that's what I was thinking, too. Then families can head off trick-or-treating or to the Sand Dollar Cove Cinema for the free showing of *Zombie Prom at the Disco* at nine."

"Maybe you could put up a poster about the candy buy-back at Thompson Orthodontics the first week of November. I always thought your father was smart to offer that."

"I agree," said Brittany, stunned that Cynthia had complimented Alan. Was setting boundaries about not bashing him working already?

"Did I tell you I'm redecorating my condo?" her mother asked.

"No. Mary mentioned that you'd called her, though."

"Yes. I decided I needed professional help. Home design is so tricky. One minute eggplant counters are the hot new kitchen trend, and the next, it's out of style faster than you can say 'Silicone Floozy.'"

Now *that* was the Cynthia she knew. "I know my kitchen's out of date," said Brittany. "But I've got enough financial obligations to tackle before I can worry about renovation."

"That's my practical girl." Cynthia patted her on the back. "I taught you well." She looked over at the counter. "You appear to have customers."

"Do I? Oh, gosh. Got to run. It's been nice chatting with you."

Cynthia blotted her lips with a napkin. "I need to leave, too. I have dinner plans."

With whom? Brittany wondered but didn't ask, figuring her mom would tell her if it were important.

"Love you, Mom." Brittany gave Cynthia a quick hug before she rushed over to the register. Ann from the senior center stood in front of the counter. Thankfully Ann had left Nugget at home this time. Brittany didn't see any sign of the poodle in Ann's purse.

"Hi Brittany," said Ann. Always elegantly dressed, today Ann had on slacks and a cashmere sweater with a tiny moth hole near the shoulder that was barely noticeable.

"Hi Ann, how lovely to see you again. I'm sorry to have kept you waiting."

"No, I'm the one who should be apologizing. You close in fifteen minutes." Ann held out a piece of paper. At first, Brittany thought it was an Angel Board card because it was the same stationery that she used in the shop. But then she saw it was a name and address.

"I have a great idea for you." Ann rested the paper on the counter. "At least *I* think it's a great idea. You might think it's rubbish, and that would be okay."

"What's your idea?" Brittany asked, feeling curious.

"My neighbor Juan owns three Airbnbs, all over town, and he was telling me about how he has binders in each one that list fun activities to do, and places to eat."

"Oh... Neat. Do you think he'd include Safe Harbor in his binder?"

"I do, which is why I wondered if you had a takeout menu that I could give him."

"I don't have a takeout menu yet," said Brittany. "But it's on my to-do list. I need to create a website, too."

"I'm amazed that you have time to sleep when you're starting a new business like this." Ann fingered the clasp of her pearls. "I wish I go could back in time and make my dream come true."

"What was that?" Brittany asked.

"I wanted to open a floral design studio, you know, like for weddings and funerals. But my husband said that I had enough work to do at home without adding more to my plate."

"Oh."

"My husband was right. I *was* busy at home, especially with our three boys to take care of." Ann sighed. "My husband passed away, my kids have grown up and moved to other states, and now it's just me and Nugget."

A life like that sounded lonely. "I'm glad you have the senior center to help fill your days with fun things to do," said Brittany.

"Right? It's my happy place, even though the food's awful since you left."

"Maybe you could speak to Keith about teaching a floral arrangement class? I bet the other members would love that."

"What a great idea!" Ann smiled. "Anyhow, here's Juan's contact info so you can mail him some takeout menus when you have them."

Brittany picked up the card. "Thanks so much for this. I'll send those off as soon as I create them."

"Glad to be of service. I need to get home to Nugget, now. His dinnertime is coming up."

Brittany waved goodbye and looked around the room. All but two customers had left, and it was five minutes until closing time. She began her shutdown process, and when the clock read five p.m., she turned the OPEN sign to CLOSED on the front door. Since the two remaining customers didn't take the hint, she made an announcement. "Sorry, friends, but I'm closing."

"Oops," said a man wearing a fleece jacket and hat. "I got lost in this book I was reading and didn't realize the time." He pushed in his chair and brought his soup bowl and mug to the soapy-water tubs.

The other customer, a teenager Brittany didn't know, cleared away her things as well, and left, wordlessly.

But just before the door closed behind her, Isabella and Ryan slipped through.

"That CLOSED sign doesn't mean us, does it?" Isabella asked. She wore an enormous coat that matched her dark hair.

Brittany gazed into Ryan's eyes and grinned. "Of course it doesn't mean you two. I'm closed, but I could still whip you up a..." She glanced at the now-kaput sandwich bar. "A something."

"No need for that," said Ryan.

"Yeah." Isabella smiled. "We're here to take you to the T Bone Bluff with us."

"If you want, that is," Ryan said, with a hopeful look in his eyes.

"Really? I'd love to." She could finish her prep work for tomorrow after dinner. "I just need to lock up."

"Take your time." Ryan put his hands in his pockets. "We're not in any rush."

"Speak for yourself, Dad. I'm starved." Isabella looked at Brittany. "Anything I could do to help?"

"That's sweet of you to offer. Do you think you could wipe down the tables while I cash out the register?"

"With the disinfectant spray, right?"

Brittany nodded.

"You can put me to work, too," said Ryan. "I'm good for sweeping, at least."

"I'll show you where the broom is, Dad," said Isabella.

"I appreciate the help." Brittany felt happy. Delighted, even. After a fulfilling day at work, and a productive conversation with her mother, she was headed out to dinner. Whisked away by the handsome Ryan Osborne and his incorrigible daughter.

Ten minutes later, just as they were leaving, Isabella picked up a note that had fallen on the floor. "What is this?" she asked, staring at the card. "I'm not sure it's even English. It looks like it might be from the Angel Board."

"Read it to us," said Ryan, as he helped Brittany into her coat. "Thanks for eating dinner with us," he murmured in her ear.

"Thanks for inviting me." Brittany's skin tickled from where his breath had touched.

"I can barely read it because the cursive is so awful, but I think it says '*Carpe diem*,'" Isabella spun around. "Is that Italian or something?"

"What?" Ryan stepped in front of Brittany like he was blocking her from oncoming traffic.

"*Carpe diem?*" Brittany asked. "Is that what you said?"

"Yeah." Isabella pointed to the card. "I think so."

Brittany shuddered. "Saying '*carpe diem*' is the number one way to get my attention."

"It's Latin," Ryan said gruffly. "For 'seize the day.'"

Brittany stepped around him and crossed the room. "I need to see the handwriting." She took the note from Isabella. When she saw the familiar scrawl, chills raced down her spine. "Shit," she muttered.

"Shit?" Isabella stepped closer and looked at the card again. "Why shit?"

"It's a long story, that I've been meaning to tell you, Bella," Ryan said in a somber voice.

"No, it's more than that." Brittany opened her purse and pulled out the other cards, that she still had stored there. "You've got to see these." She sat down at the closest table and spread them in front of her. Ryan and Isabella sat down too. She read them out loud in no particular order: "To the woman who could have been so much more if relationships hadn't tied you down, I see your true worth. For a mom who wears Birkenstocks and wool socks. To the woman who feels lost, forgotten, and unloved; you are not alone. To a forty-five-year-old woman with a nose ring. To a woman whose son seemingly doesn't need her, please know that he still does. *Carpe diem.*"

"Shit is right." Isabella whistled dramatically. "Somebody is stalking you."

"I don't get it." Ryan picked up a card. "Why would you think that?"

"Because the cards are about Brittany, Dad. Clearly." Isabella pointed at Brittany's feet. "I mean, look at her shoes."

Brittany curled her toes in her wool socks and Birkenstocks. She should start wearing her sneakers more often.

"And Brittany just said that saying '*carpe diem*' is the

number one way to get her attention," said Isabella. "Whoever wrote that must have known that phrase was significant to her."

But Ryan didn't agree. "Those cards aren't about Brittany," he said.

"They aren't?" Brittany asked.

"'To the woman who could have been so much more...'" Ryan read. "Don't disparage your accomplishments by thinking that's meant for you. You have a house, an education, a grown son in college, and a booming business. I mean sure, maybe if you'd stayed single you could have cured cancer or become president, but the same could be said about me. Who knows what great things I would have done if I hadn't become a father?"

"Hey!" Isabella protested. "I'm sitting right here."

"I would hate life in the White House." Ryan gave Isabella a quick side hug. "Life with you is much better."

"Than curing cancer?" Isabella asked skeptically. "Don't answer that." She picked up the card about the nose ring. "This is clearly about Brittany. If you take this one, and add it to the message about the Birkenstocks, then that's Brittany Thompson." She placed the two cards together.

"That's what I was thinking as well." Brittany rubbed her arms to tame the goosebumps. "But *Carpe Diem*... Isabella, that's the name of the boat my brother died on."

Isabella's eyes grew wide. "The one my dad was on too?" She looked to Ryan for confirmation.

He swallowed and nodded. "I really do need to tell you the whole story."

"But not now," said Brittany, shuddering. "Let's go out to dinner and have a lovely meal. I'll figure out what to do about the creepy Angel Board messages later."

Isabella stood. "Maybe you should call it the Fallen Angel Board. Like, for Halloween."

"It does feel like I have a dark angel following me." Brittany belted her coat.

"Don't worry," said Ryan, as he opened the door. "We'll figure out a way to deal with this. It's not okay for someone to make you feel uncomfortable in your own restaurant."

"Yeah." Isabella nodded. "This is like passive-aggressive Instagram hearting to a whole new level."

"Thanks." Brittany felt better, but only for a moment. As they walked out of the shop her eyes drifted over to the board one more time. *Who's targeting me*, she wondered. *And why?*

TWENTY-FIVE

"So, are you and my dad, like, dating now?" Isabella asked as she sprinkled coconut sugar on her golden milk latte. Lana, Gabby, and Scarlett were already seated at Safe Harbor's communal table, with a pile of papers and computers in front of them, using the Saturday afternoon to study. Brittany was pleased to know that Isabella's school items were among the mess, and that she was now a bona fide member of the friend group. "He's been talking on the phone to you non-stop," Isabella continued. "And he said you went out to lunch earlier this week, and then last night you went to the movies without me."

"We invited you, but you had plans with your friends." Brittany scooped flour into a bread machine insert.

"I know, but my dad hates going to the movie theater."

"He does?" That was news to Brittany. Ryan had seemed to love every minute of the Oscar contender they'd watched last night. They'd shared a tub of popcorn and a box of candy and talked about the film's plot the entire ride home.

"And now he's bugging me about what he should wear as a Halloween costume for your party, and I don't think I've ever seen him dress up."

"Ryan's planning a costume?" Brittany was touched. "You're right. He hates being a spectacle." Every year growing up Patti would sew him the most amazing costume ever, which would make Ryan the center of attention—much to his chagrin. "The only time I ever saw your dad truly comfortable in a Halloween costume was when he and my brother dressed up like the skeletons from *The Karate Kid*."

"Huh?" Isabella put a lid on her latte.

"You've never seen *The Karate Kid*?"

"Never heard of it."

"What about the remake, or spin-off, *Cobra Kai*? Jeremy loves that show."

"I watched the first two episodes but thought it was stupid," said Isabella.

"Same," Brittany admitted. "But I stuck with it because Jeremy loved it so much and it was something we could do together."

"So anyhow, are you and my dad dating?" Isabella asked again.

"I believe we are." Brittany made a divot in the dry ingredients in the bread machine pan and sprinkled in a packet of yeast. "At least, I hope we are officially dating. Are you okay with that?"

"Yeah. That's cool." Isabella looked over her shoulder at her friends and then leaned forward over the counter, so that she was right up in Brittany's face. "Just be nice to him, okay? He might look tough on the outside, but he's a real softie."

"I'm aware." Brittany said, the corners of her mouth turning up into a smile.

"And maybe you can talk him into letting me have a sleepover at Gabby's house tonight?" Isabella asked hopefully. "We're going to watch as many versions of *Scream* as we can until we collapse."

"That sounds like fun." Brittany smiled. "Go have fun with your friends. I'll talk to your dad about the sleepover."

"Thanks, Brittany. You're the best." Isabella grinned and walked away.

Isabella might not be home tonight? All of a sudden Brittany's plans to decorate Safe Harbor with cauldrons and fake cobwebs seemed like they could wait until tomorrow. She'd see what Ryan thought when he got here. He was on his way over with a security camera system to install.

The plan was to put in a lens that was positioned so that it encompassed the entire front room, with the ability to also zoom in on the Angel Board. That way, Brittany's business would not only have more protection, but she'd also be able to catch the prankster behind the creepy notes.

Brittany wasn't sure if "prankster" was the right word for the culprit. It felt like she had eyes watching her. Brittany wasn't scared by any means, but she did feel unsettled. She and Nancy had tried to remember who all had brought cash up to the register to sponsor cards, but nobody stood out as someone who might have a bizarre sense of humor.

What if Keith was paying someone—or multiple people—to sponsor the cards, just to freak her out? But no... Brittany would have recognized his handwriting, and besides, Keith printed; he didn't write in cursive.

Huh... A thought just occurred to her. She'd only seen Keith's printed handwriting before, so actually, she had no idea what his cursive looked like. Which meant that it was possible these cards were some sort of wicked plot against her, coming entirely from Keith. It was a good thing Ryan was fitting those security cameras tonight, because she wanted to deal with this situation once and for all—especially if her ex was involved.

The line at the counter picked up, and Brittany spent the next forty-five minutes keeping up with the Saturday lunch crowd. When she finally had five minutes with no people to help, she chopped vegetables and tidied up. Then she collected the overflowing used-dishes tubs and brought them to the back room.

She was just making a second trip for the silverware receptacle when she walked past the communal table and heard a snippet of the girls' conversation.

"That's why people say that the ghost only comes out on Halloween night, when there's a half-moon," said Scarlett.

"It's true," Lana said. "My dad's crewman saw the ghost on a charter boat once. He tried to take a picture, but his phone had a crappy camera."

What in the world? Brittany wondered as she deposited the silverware in the back room and started the dishwasher. She returned to the front room in time to hear the story continue.

"It *has* to be a half-moon," said Gabby. "That's what I heard. And the ghost only shows himself to virgins."

"Whoa!" Isabella exclaimed. "That's sick."

Brittany couldn't help herself. "What are you girls talking about?" she asked, even though she knew she risked embarrassing Isabella by butting in.

"The ghost of Sand Dollar Cove," said Scarlett. "My mom said it wasn't a thing when she was our age, but now it's legendary."

"*Everyone's* been talking about it." Lana flipped a page of her notebook.

"Especially since this Friday will be a half-moon," Gabby added.

"Here's a picture." Lana held up her notebook. "A composite picture, at least. I created it based on everything we've learned so far."

Brittany checked to make sure nobody was standing in line waiting to be served, and then sat down next to the girls so she could look at the artwork. She pulled her reading glasses out of her apron pocket to see better. "This is a sophisticated picture, Lana. You have real talent."

"Thanks." Lana smiled. "I take lessons online."

"That's the ghost right there," Isabella pointed. "He wears long black robes but doesn't have a face."

"Completely faceless," Scarlett echoed. "Except for eyeballs."

"Floating eyeballs?" Brittany couldn't tell if the girls were being serious or not, so she focused on the drawing. "I love how you drew Main Street, and the lighthouse and marina. Your handling of perspective is amazing."

"There's Safe Harbor right there." Isabella tapped the paper. "See?"

"I do." Brittany smiled. She felt like an official business owner now that Safe Harbor was immortalized like that. "I bet you'd get an even better perspective if you painted from my attic. It has one tiny window that looks down over Main Street."

"I'd love to do that someday," said Lana.

"So, tell me more about this ghost," said Brittany. "How do you know it's a he?"

"We don't," said Gabby. "But if we see him, we'll ask about pronouns."

"Sounds like a plan." Brittany heard the front door open and stood. "Tell your ghost that I give free coffee to ghouls on Halloween."

"Ha ha," Isabella said. "We'll be sure to mention that when we find him."

When Brittany saw who entered the restaurant, she felt a zip of excitement. It was Ryan, holding a stack of small boxes. She rushed up to him to help. "That looks like quite the load." She lifted the smallest one off the top so that he could see better.

"I ended up buying cameras for the back room and attic, too."

"Thanks for that. I hope you saved the receipts so I can pay you back."

"I did." Ryan continued walking through to the back room, where he placed the boxes on the now-humming dishwasher. "But I also bought a game camera for the bat box, that I will happily pay for myself, if you'd be willing to let me install it."

Brittany smiled. "Your daughter just called you a softie, and this proves her point."

"Me, a softie? Never." Ryan wrapped his arms around her and rested his head against hers in a warm hug. "I'm tough as nails."

"I take it you're not coming to my Halloween party dressed as a giant teddy bear, or a bunny rabbit, or some other adorable woodland creature?" Brittany listed off as many of Ryan's childhood costumes as she could remember. Patti had loved sewing with fake fur.

"That would be a no, seeing as how my mother won't be involved in the creation of this costume at all."

"But you'd make such a snuggly teddy bear," Brittany said as she burrowed her head on his shoulder.

"What are you going as?" he asked.

"The same thing I go as every year, if I can still squeeze into it: Queen Guinevere from Camelot. It doesn't really work now that Ian's Lancelot outfit is out there in the middle of Seattle somewhere, but the costume was expensive and makes my butt look good, so I bring it out each year."

"Your butt always looks good." He gave her a playful pinch.

Brittany laughed. "Glad you noticed. By the way, Isabella wants to know if she can sleep over at Gabby's tonight."

"Yes," Ryan said, in a growly tone. "The answer is yes."

TWENTY-SIX

"Hi, Cheryl." Brittany escorted Ryan into her kitchen Sunday morning. They'd stayed at her place last night because she needed a fresh change of clothes before work today. But she hoped that Cheryl wouldn't scare Ryan away with her teasing.

"Morning, handsome." Cheryl raised her World's Best Grandma mug. "Help yourself to the fresh pot of coffee I put on."

"Good morning to you, Cheryl. Nice to see you again," Ryan said cordially. "The coffee smells delicious."

"It does, doesn't it?" Cheryl sniffed her cup. "Maxwell House gets me every time. But try telling that to the coffee snobs I live with."

Maxwell House? Brittany remembered Ryan's fancy Italian espresso machine hidden inside the appliance garage of his gourmet kitchen and felt mortified.

But store brand coffee didn't faze Ryan one bit. "You and my mom have the same taste in beans," he said. "I feel right at home."

"I bet you do," Cheryl quipped. "Brittany's very welcoming."

Now Brittany *was* going to die of embarrassment. "Can I get you a mug, Ryan? Or some cereal?" She didn't have time to make breakfast since she was due at Safe Harbor.

"Coffee, yes. Cereal, no."

"Black, right?" She took two mugs from the cabinet.

"Don't pretend like you don't remember his coffee order, Brittany. We all know where you were last weekend."

That did it. Brittany spun around. "Cheryl, please—"

"Tell us all about my mom and Don," Ryan interrupted. He kissed Brittany's cheek. "Cheryl and I go way back, and there's not much she could say that would shock me." He sat on a kitchen chair next to the older woman. "Right?"

"Oh, really?" Cheryl clicked her fingernails on the table. "What about if I told you I texted your mom at three a.m. this morning when I got up to go to the bathroom for the second time and realized you were still here?"

"I'd say you were full of it." Ryan leaned his arms on the table. "You wouldn't dare wake my mother up because you know she hasn't been able to sleep well since my dad went into memory care."

Ryan and Cheryl locked eyes in a staring match that was so engrossing Brittany almost overfilled the second coffee mug. She stopped pouring just in time and brought both mugs to the table.

"Maybe that's why I knew your mother would be awake and available to read my text," Cheryl deadpanned.

"Or maybe you knew she was at Don's house?" Ryan dipped his chin slightly but continued staring directly at her. "Was she?"

Seconds passed with no one touching their coffee.

Finally, Cheryl broke eye contact. "Of course I'd never dare interrupt Patti's sleep. Once you dance with menopause, sleep's not a partner you ever want to strike from your dance card." She sipped her coffee but said nothing else.

"You didn't answer my question." Ryan picked up his mug.

"Did you ask a question?" Cheryl asked. "My hearing's not what it used to be."

Ryan looked sideways at Brittany and grinned. "I asked if you knew if my mom was at Don's house last night. When I dropped Isabella off at her friend's house, I stopped by Ma's to see her, but she wasn't there."

Cheryl cupped her hand around her ear. "What? Sorry. I can't hear you."

"Ma's car was in the driveway, but she didn't open the door. I texted her and she said she was baking cookies," Ryan continued.

"Still can't hear you," Cheryl said. "Funny how those ears of mine work."

The doorbell rang.

"Could you hear that?" Brittany asked.

"Why yes." Cheryl nodded sweetly. "I could hear that just fine."

"Who could it be?" Brittany stood. It was seven in the morning. Mary was still upstairs, fast asleep. Brittany knew it was Mary up in the sisters' shared bedroom, and not Hannah, because Mary's car was parked in front of the house. The sisters took turns spending time with their grandma and their boyfriends, so that there was always one sister present if Cheryl needed help.

Brittany walked to the front door, grateful she was already dressed for the day, and peered through the peephole. It was Alan! She opened the door for him. "Dad, what are you doing here? This is a surprise."

Alan wore slacks, a collared shirt, and a fleece jacket. His summer tan had officially faded. "Sorry to come over like this without calling first, but it's important. Can I come in?"

"Of course. Can I get you a cup of coffee?"

"No thanks. My stomach is queasy enough as it is. Stress will do that to you."

Brittany had two options. She could have brought her father into the living room, right in front of the entryway, but that was the Turners' official domain. Her space was the family room on the other side of the kitchen. For a split second Brittany thought about ignoring all that and choosing the living room. But she didn't. She knew the Turners wouldn't have minded if she'd used their space but decided to be bold and walk her father directly through the kitchen—past Ryan—and into her family room.

"Ryan Osborne," Alan exclaimed as soon as he saw him. "How's it been, young man? I haven't seen you in years."

"I'm not so young anymore." Ryan patted his hair. "Every time I look in the mirror, I see another strand of gray."

"Wait until you're my age and feel lucky to have any hair at all," said Alan.

"You can say that again," said Cheryl. "Hi, Alan. Want some coffee?"

"Thank you, but no. I came here to..." Alan looked at Brittany for support, but she didn't know what the matter was.

"Dad and I were just going to have a chat," she said. "Cheryl, would you mind keeping Ryan company?"

"Oh, I'll keep him company alright." Cheryl patted Ryan's hand. "Wait until I brag to everyone at the senior center about my Sunday morning coffee date with a younger man."

"I bet my mom will love gossip like that," Ryan said with a laugh.

Feeling confident that Ryan could handle himself despite Cheryl's best efforts at teasing him, Brittany brought her father into the family room, and they sat on the couch next to the window that looked out at the golf course. "So, what's going on?" she asked.

"I can't tell you specifics." Alan wiped his palms on his knees. "There are details that I absolutely cannot reveal because then you might be complicit, too, and I could never let that happen."

"Complicit? What are you talking about?" Now Alan had her attention.

Her dad looked at the golf course and back at her. "Let's say that a friend discovered that his significant other had run up an enormous debt on their joint credit cards."

"Like a sixty-thousand-dollar debt?"

"Yes." Alan nodded. "Exactly. And also moved money from their joint account into a personal account he couldn't access."

"What? That's theft!"

"I wouldn't say theft." Alan tugged his collar. "The significant other was confused about how banking worked and didn't realize she was accidentally transferring funds into her own account, and—"

"Bullshit. That's embezzlement." Brittany wasn't sure where Alan was going with this. What was he hiding behind the "friend" story? She knew he meant himself and Tansy.

Alan frowned. "The money was in a joint account and legally hers to move even if she hadn't earned it. But now my friend is broke. Luckily, he has another person in his life, one that's an excellent money manager, and she came in to help clean up the mess."

"That sounds like a good idea." Brittany eyed the clock on the wall. Hopefully her dad hurried this tale along because she had Ryan waiting for her in the kitchen, and Safe Harbor to open soon.

"And the friend's friend, the one who's an excellent money manager, realized she could hack into the significant other's personal accounts because the security questions were so easy."

"What?" Brittany squeaked. Did she hear her father right?

"Name of your childhood pet... High school mascot... Kindergarten teacher... Things like that."

"Are you saying Mom hacked into Tansy's bank account?"

"Shh!" Alan held a finger to his lips. "I said no such thing. I haven't told you anything that would legally require you to share any of this information with anyone."

"I don't know about that..." Brittany thought fast. "I think I should give you the name of the lawyer who helped me with my employment lawsuit. His name is Steven Clarke."

"*I* don't need a lawyer," said Alan. "But I'll pass that information along to my friend."

"Oh, my goodness." Brittany closed her eyes and massaged her temple. "Let me get that phone number for you." Brittany rushed to her bedroom, found her phone, and jotted down Steven's contact info. Before she returned to the family room, she gave herself a pep talk. *I don't need to be part of my parents' toxic relationship. They are them, and I am me. My job is to protect myself and Jeremy.*

"Here's Steven's info," she told Alan as she handed him the paper. "From now on, please communicate all stories about your friend to a lawyer, and not me. I don't want to be involved in any of this. And do not, under any circumstances, repeat any of this to Jeremy. Leave him out of it, too. Got it?"

"Loud and clear." Alan pocketed the paper. "Again, I'm sorry to bother you this early. But it was nice running into Ryan. What's he doing over here, anyway?"

"Waiting for me to take him home."

"Oh. Huh..."

"You can say goodbye to him on our way through the kitchen." Brittany grimaced as she led the way. Cheryl and Ryan were eating cinnamon toast and laughing about something.

"It was good to see you, Ryan," Alan said as they passed by. "Tell Frank I said hi."

"I will do that." Ryan nodded to Alan and looked over at Brittany like he was questioning if she was okay.

Brittany raised her eyebrows in response, picked up her coffee mug, and took a strong drink as she walked her father to the front door. She was so desperate for relief that even Maxwell House tasted good.

TWENTY-SEVEN

It was a good old-fashioned Halloween party. Brittany turned on the twinkling pumpkin lights and smiled. She'd closed Safe Harbor an hour early and used the time to transform the cafe into a spooky destination. A hay bale and corn stalks created an impromptu selfie station next to a scarecrow—that had been Mary's idea. Brittany hoped people would tag Safe Harbor's fledgling social media accounts with costume photos and give her free publicity. There was also a cauldron for bobbing for apples, a pumpkin-decorating station with stickers and googly eyes, and four dozen donuts hanging on strings from a horizontal broom handle. Nancy would manage that activity. Players would need to eat the donuts without using their hands.

As for money-making opportunities, Brittany had stocked the grab-and-go fridge with sandwiches and would sell espresso drinks all night. That was her plan, at least. She'd need to sell out of sandwiches to break even on party costs. Anything extra she earned from drinks would be profit. It was a financial risk, for sure, but the weather was in her favor.

The skies were overcast, and a storm was predicted for later that night. Pacific Northwesterners were hardy, but trick-or-treating wasn't much fun in the rain. If the heavens opened, that might send more customers her way. The party would start at six thirty p.m., which was twenty minutes from now. Brittany barely had enough time to change into her costume. She rushed into the back room, closed the door, and pulled down the blinds.

Last night she'd decided that her Guinevere costume was out. Brittany didn't want to be one half of a couple's costume with Ian anymore. Instead, she'd used glow-in-the-dark paint to spiff up a comfy pair of black jogger pants and a long-sleeved athletic shirt. There was face paint and a pointy hat to go with it too, as well as fairy lights and a battery pack that slipped into her pocket. Once Brittany was in her full regalia, she pressed a switch and glowed, becoming her travel dreams incarnate. She was the Eiffel Tower.

"Well, look at you!" Nancy said, five minutes later, as she came in through the back door. She wore a long white dress with red hearts stitched around the hem, and a pointy crown with red rubies. "You twinkle."

"Thanks! I love your Queen of Hearts costume."

"Wait until you see Herman." Nancy stomped her feet on the doormat. "He's a poker dealer."

"Where is he?" Brittany looked over Nancy's shoulder to spot him. She'd never met Herman, but had heard so much about him that she felt like she knew him well.

"He'll be here at the last minute." Nancy stashed her purse under Brittany's desk. "We get such an influx of trick-or-treaters that we bought thirty pounds of candy."

"Thirty pounds? I only bought five for our house. Cheryl's passing out Snickers."

Nancy smoothed her skirt. "I don't know what happened, but somehow our neighborhood developed a reputation for being *the* place to go. People drop their kids off by the truckload. Of course, with the storm that's been predicted, who knows if we'll get that many. I might be hiding candy from Herman for weeks, so he doesn't make himself ill."

"Wow. We're lucky if we get twenty trick-or-treaters at my house." Brittany tucked the elastic strap of her Eiffel Tower hat behind her ear and took out her phone. "Cheryl's staying home tonight to manage the front door. Mary's helping Steven at the cinema and Hannah had to work. Let's go take a picture of the two of us at the selfie station before we open the doors, and it becomes a zoo in here."

"Good idea."

"At least, I *hope* it becomes a zoo," Brittany said as she walked into the main room. "I really want tonight to be a success."

"It will be. We put signs up all over town, and I posted in all the neighborhood Facebook groups." Nancy sat on the hay bale and scooted over so there'd be room for Brittany next to the scarecrow. "Hopefully, nobody's allergic to straw."

"Yeah." Brittany felt her nose tickle. "It smells good, but might be sneeze-inducing."

It took several tries, but Brittany snapped a photo that was flattering to them both. She posted it on her social media accounts and felt proud of what she'd accomplished. Safe Harbor had only been open for two months, and this felt like a well-deserved celebration. Her work–life balance was out of whack, but she was doing something she loved that earned money and helped make her community a better place. Brittany was worlds away from where she'd started out at the beginning of summer.

"There's already a line formed outside," said Nancy. "I saw storm clouds on my way here. The weather's turning, I can tell."

"Hopefully that doesn't keep people away. I just need to flip on the Halloween playlist and then we can open the doors." Brittany cued the music from her phone and the surround sound came to life. As she looked at the screen she checked to see if the security cameras were working and was glad to see that they were. "Okay, we're ready."

"Let's get this party started!" Nancy hurried over to the door and flipped over the OPEN sign.

Once customers spilled in the doors, Brittany sold out of sandwiches fast. The first arrivals were families with small children, trying to start and complete Halloween early so that nobody stayed up too late past bedtime. The bobbing for apples station ran itself, but Nancy kept busy restringing donuts on the line. Brittany didn't sell quite as many expensive coffee drinks as she'd hoped, but she could tell that she was at least making a profit. Drink orders picked up as the evening grew later, and an older clientele arrived. Now there were fewer young children and more young adults.

When the door opened and Brittany saw Isabella and Ryan walk in, she smiled as brightly as her Eiffel Tower lights. "You made it," Brittany called, waving across the counter to them. She was in the middle of processing a cappuccino order. She didn't have time to talk yet, but she looked at them long enough to admire their costumes.

Isabella was almost unrecognizable in a blonde wig and black eyeliner, but she looked quite a lot like Taylor Swift, which Brittany knew was what she was going for.

As for Ryan, his costume had been a closely guarded secret, but now that Brittany saw him, she realized she could have guessed. He was dressed as Batman: cape, pointy ears, mask, and all. Brittany waved to them at the back of the line and greeted the next person.

Brittany assisted several customers she didn't know, vacationers who were staying at short-term rentals, and newcomers who'd moved to town. Then a friendly face showed up in line.

"This place is hopping," said Ann, who was bundled in a long wool coat with a sash that read *Votes for Women*. She had on an elaborate hat as well. "I've got Nugget with me, so I can't stay." She clutched her purse protectively, and Brittany saw the poodle's fluffy head stick out. "I was hoping I could get a sugar-free vanilla latte to go. I would rather have a hot chocolate, but that wouldn't be good for my diabetes."

"A sugar-free vanilla latte is a wise choice. You can doctor it up with a sprinkle of cinnamon." Brittany processed the payment and crafted the drink. As she was topping off the foam, she heard familiar voices.

"Votes for women," Don boomed. "My great-great-grandma was a suffragette. I love it, dollface."

"Brilliant," Patti added.

Brittany turned back toward the counter and saw Don and Patti, dressed as Antony and Cleopatra, talking to Ann.

"Women didn't fight the patriarchy so you could call everyone dollface, Don." Ann shook her head in disgust. "I've told you that before."

"You're right." Don shrugged. "Mea culpa." He threw his arm around Patti, almost knocking off her wig. "My old lady told me that, too."

"Here you go, Ann." Brittany handed over the latte. "You and Nugget stay warm, okay? Especially with that storm coming."

"He's wearing his fisherman's sweater, so I think he'll be fine." Ann blew her poodle kisses.

"Are you going to the free movie at the Sand Dollar Cove Cinema after this?" Patti asked. "It starts at nine."

Ann shook her head. "I'll be in bed long before it starts. What about you two?"

"Wouldn't miss it," said Don. "The more places to show off my gorgeous queen of the Nile, the better." He lifted Patti's hand and twirled her around.

"But we're going to hang around here, first," said Patti. "A bunch of friends are coming from the senior center. You really saved the day, Brittany, since Keith refused to let us have a party."

"Yeah," Ann grumbled. "Keith said it wasn't in the budget, but everyone knows he didn't want to do any extra work."

"He's such a jerk." Don shook his head in frustration.

Ann said goodbye and Patti and Don placed two orders for decaf coffees.

A teenager wearing jeans and a hoodie showed up after that and handed Brittany an Angel Board card. "Could I get a double shot of espresso?"

Brittany turned the stationery over and read the message.

For someone who is lonely. Your future is full of hope, I promise. It was the card Ryan had left!

"Sure," Brittany said, surprised that the teen had revealed something so personal for an espresso drink. She didn't recognize him. He must have been two or three years younger than Jeremy. Probably he was closer to Isabella's age than Jeremy's. When Brittany came back with the double shot of espresso, she offered him a warm smile. "Are you going to the movie theater tonight to see *Zombie Prom at the Disco*?" She knew a bunch of teenagers would be there and it might be an opportunity for him to make friends.

"I might." He pulled up his hood. "Or I might head down to the harbor to look for the ghost of Sand Dollar Cove."

"You've heard about the ghost, too?"

The young man nodded. "Hasn't everyone? Supposedly he haunts the lighthouse looking for souls to suck into the void."

"Whoa." It made Brittany feel old knowing that there was a trendy town ghost story that she was too mature to care about.

"I know, right?" the teen asked, before he walked away.

"It's finally our turn," Isabella said, as the guy left. "We've been waiting almost fifteen minutes. I was beginning to think we'd stand in line forever and that I'd be late to meet up with my friends."

"Sorry about that," said Brittany. "I would have had Nancy help me run the counter, but that donut game is just barely under control."

"It's okay." Isabella flicked back a chunk of her wig's blonde hair. "Taylor Swift's not a prima donna, and neither am I."

Ryan grunted. "Oh really? Says the girl who complains every time she takes out the trash."

Isabella rolled her eyes. "I don't know why I can't just take out the recycling instead. There are two of us living in that house you know, and the trash is icky."

Brittany decided to change the subject. "I love both your costumes." In fact, she was unable to keep her eyes off Ryan. The tight shirt he wore showed off his broad shoulders.

"Are you supposed to be the Eiffel Tower?" Isabella asked.

Brittany nodded.

"Cool. My mom and dad took me to Paris before they divorced, and it was super fun."

"I'd love to—" Brittany started to say, but Nancy rushed over and interrupted her.

"We are officially out of donuts." Nancy adjusted her jewel-encrusted crown. "How about I take over at the register here so you can enjoy the party?"

"That would be great," said Brittany. "Thanks. Just let me prepare drinks for Ryan and Isabella first."

"Make mine a golden latte," said Isabella. A large, please."

"I'll have the same, since I'm curious to know what they taste like," said Ryan. "A small, though." He took out his credit card and Brittany didn't protest taking it. She knew the rules, *An Osborne always pays their way.*

Once she was relieved of her barista duties, Brittany soaked in the fun atmosphere of her party. Old people mingled with young ones, and quite a few people came in off the street just to use the restroom, which was fine with her. Safe Harbor had turned into the living room of Main Street. People felt welcome, lots of them spent money, and everyone left with a smile on their face. Brittany and Ryan took turns bobbing for apples, but Isabella refused because she didn't want to ruin her makeup. Brittany sensed that she thought the whole party was lame, in fact, but the girl definitely perked up when her friends arrived.

"Scarlett's the Statue of Liberty, Gabby's a bride, and Lana's a cat," said Isabella. She rushed over to greet them.

"Do any of them have a coat?" Brittany asked Ryan.

"I couldn't convince Isabella to bring one either," he grumbled. "Despite the fact that it's in the low forties and supposed to rain."

"At least it's not raining yet." Brittany checked her watch. "It's seven forty-six. That gives them over an hour to trick-or-treat before the movie starts. The people who live near Main Street are pretty generous with candy."

"I better nail down the pick-up details before she darts off." Ryan made his way across the room.

Brittany followed him. "Great costumes," she told the girls. "You'll freeze your tushes off, but you'll be cute human popsicles."

Scarlett pointed at Brittany with her torch. "You sound like my mom."

"Probably so." Brittany grinned. "But as I recall, Steph dressed up as a murdered cheerleader freshman year, and she didn't wear a coat either."

"My mom did that?" Scarlett's jaw dropped. "I really need to dig through the pictures the next time I go to my grandma's house."

"Come on." Gabby waved her arm toward the door. "We better get going or we'll run out of time."

"That's right," said Brittany. "The movie starts in an hour."

"You all have pillowcases?" Ryan asked.

"Huh?" Lana asked. "Why do we need pillowcases?"

"I told you, Dad," Isabella grumbled. "Nobody trick-or-treats with pillowcases anymore."

Gabby held up four Lululemon bags. "I brought enough Lulu for everyone."

"Oh. Okay, well..." Ryan squared his shoulders. "Stay on well-lit sidewalks, and be careful when you cross the streets, and—"

"We know, Dad." Isabella shielded her face from her horribly embarrassing father.

"I'll meet you at the movie theater at eleven p.m. to pick you up," said Ryan.

"But you're not coming, right?" Isabella asked. "Please tell me you're not coming."

"No, zombies aren't really my thing." Ryan looked sideways at Brittany. "I'll stay here and help Brittany clean up from her party. But Grandma will be there."

"She will?" Isabella pulled down her hand. "Great. Just great."

Brittany looked across the room to where Patti and Don were smooching in the corner. "I'd find a seat in the movie theater as far away from them as possible if I were you."

Isabella cringed. "Good plan."

"Is that your grandma French-kissing someone?" Scarlett's eyes grew wide.

"Hello, PDA." Lana snickered.

"Can I be far away from my mom, too?" Ryan asked. "Because I'm feeling like this is too close."

"Oh?" Isabella asked. "Grandma making out with Don makes you uncomfortable, does it?" She jabbed him in the shoulder with her finger. "Consider this a taste of your own medicine from when you and that pharmaceuticals rep you were dating showed up at my band and orchestra recital and—"

"Okay, that's enough of that." Ryan took out his wallet.

"Here's twenty bucks, so you can buy popcorn and soda at the theater."

"But wait." Brittany laughed. "I want to hear more about the pharma rep you dated."

"Same," said Gabby. "My parents have been married forever. They're so boring."

"His old girlfriend specialized in IBS medicine," said Isabella. "And was constantly asking me about the quality of my poop."

"This is true." The part of Ryan's face not covered by the Batman mask turned red.

"I started calling it the 'let's-go-ten-minutes-without-talking-about-poop challenge,'" said Isabella. "I'll tell you more later, Brittany, but I got to go."

"To the movie theater, not the bathroom," Scarlett clarified.

"Have fun." Brittany waved. Isabella was a handful, but Brittany enjoyed every minute of her company. She enjoyed seeing Ryan embarrassed, too. He was usually so stoic and serious.

"Sorry about that," Ryan mumbled.

"No, I'm sorry." Brittany picked up his hand and held it to her heart. "Here we've been dating a whole week and I haven't even asked you once about your bowel movements." She busted up laughing.

Ryan chuckled along with her. "Rude," he said. "But what can I expect from France?"

"Romance and food?"

Ryan lifted her hand to his lips and kissed her fingertips. "I should hope so. But what can you expect from Batman?"

Brittany didn't need a second to think. "Intelligence and protection."

"That sounds fair."

"There's still half an hour left of the party." Brittany looked around the room. "I need to restock the bobbing-for-apples cauldron and tidy up the pumpkin-decorating station. Why don't you go visit with your mom and get to know Don better?"

"That sounds like wise advice that I don't want to follow but will anyway, because it's the right thing to do."

"I knew I liked you for a multitude of reasons." Brittany slipped her arm under his cape and hugged him.

"Right back at you, Paris." Ryan kissed her behind her ear.

Brittany spent the next twenty minutes making sure that the end of her Halloween party was as successful as the beginning. The crowd had changed, now. Instead of young families, there were older folks. A lot of people stopped off for drinks before the movie. Brittany was delighted to see so many friends from the senior center, and tried to visit with as many as she could, before moving over to the counter to help Nancy with the large volume of orders.

"We're just coming over to say goodbye," said Patti, as she walked by the register. "Don and I are headed over to the movie now. I love that Mary stars in it as the lead zombie."

Ryan followed Patti, holding his drink.

"We're huge Mary Turner fans," said Don. "If she ever gives up interior designing to become an actress again, Hollywood better watch out."

"That's right." Patti looked at Ryan and then at Brittany and smiled wistfully. "Happy Halloween, you two."

"Happy Halloween," said Brittany.

"Love you, Ma," said Ryan. "Be careful driving home after the movie. It's dark out there."

"That's why I had cataracts surgery," said Don. "I'm like a nighthawk now."

"And I'm your prey." With a girlish giggle, Patti held his hand and they left.

"Don being a self-professed nighthawk doesn't make me feel any better," Ryan muttered as they watched them go.

"I'm glad my costume glows in the dark." Brittany rested

her head on his shoulder. "Better visibility."

"I'd better stick with you, then." He put his arm around her waist.

"You'd better." Brittany closed her eyes and savored the feeling of happiness. She'd taken gigantic leaps of faith this year. Starting her own business. Forgiving Ryan. Taking a risk on a new relationship with him. But thankfully, the risks had been worth it. She hadn't been this happy since the day she'd brought Jeremy home from the hospital. Thinking of her son made her realize she hadn't checked in with him today.

"I should send Jeremy a quick text," she said, pulling her phone out of her pocket. "Just to make sure he's okay."

"Good idea. Depending on where he goes tonight in the city, it could get pretty wild. Seattle's known for some epic Halloween parties."

"I'm glad you said 'epic' and not 'chaotic.'"

"That word works, too."

"Great." Brittany laughed soundlessly. "That doesn't make me feel better either."

"Join the club." Ryan grinned.

Hey there, she texted Jeremy. *I hope you're having fun tonight. Here's me:*

Brittany sent him the picture she'd taken with Nancy on the hay bale.

Since Jeremy hadn't immediately responded, she sent one more text. *If you need an Uber, take an Uber. I'll pay. Love you!*

Brittany was seconds away from putting her phone back in her pocket when it buzzed.

She smiled when she saw the photo of Jeremy and Kenzie dressed as a firefighter and surgeon, standing in a crowd of people their age.

Happy Halloween, Jeremy texted. *Don't worry about me. I'll be safe. I love you.*

Love you too, she replied.

Tears misted her eyes, but they were happy tears. Her son was grown up and living life on his own terms. That was what mattered. And he texted her back right away. That was a win, as far as she was concerned. Brittany felt grand about everything, including her party, which was about to end.

The line had died out at the counter, and most of the customers had left or were in the process of leaving. Brittany walked over to where Ryan sat at a table. "I need to close the register and tell Nancy she can go home," she told him.

"No rush on my account. I'll just be sitting here, forcing down the rest of this yellow sludge."

"You don't like the golden milk latte I made you?"

"Not really. It's not as bad as the time you made those butterscotch cookies that burned, but close."

"I was in eighth grade and learning to bake. I can't believe you remember that."

"The cookies were memorable. That's all I'm saying." Ryan grinned. "As was the girl who made them."

"I can get you a coffee. Would you rather have a coffee?"

"I'm good." His gaze drifted to her lips. "I don't want to have coffee breath."

"I'd better get Nancy and the rest of the people out of here then." Brittany kissed his cheek and took off.

The first thing she did was turn the OPEN sign to CLOSED on the front door, and next she flicked the lights. "Thank you all for coming tonight. I really appreciate your business. Safe Harbor is closing now, but will reopen at eight o'clock tomorrow morning."

"Tonight was awesome," said a customer, a man in his forties holding a newspaper. "This building used to be my favorite place to buy bait, but now it's my favorite place to drink coffee."

"Uh... thanks." Brittany smiled. "Thanks for your business."

She said goodbye to a few more folks and then walked over

to the counter, where Nancy waited for her, wearing a pinched smile.

"What's the matter?" Brittany asked. "And where's Herman? Did I miss him?"

"He ended up not being able to come because we had so many trick-or-treaters." Nancy held her hands behind her back. "He called to tell me he passed out all the candy and moved on to giving away a bag of potatoes because that's all that was left to give."

"Potatoes? Is that a thing now?"

"I don't think so, but the kids who got them thought they were cool."

"Well, I won't keep you from Herman any longer. I can close the store. Thanks so much for your help and—"

"Wait. There's something you need to know."

"What?"

Nancy brought her hands from behind her back and showed Brittany an Angel Board message. "This showed up tonight. A woman in her twenties redeemed it, but I don't know who wrote the message. Do you?"

"Nobody's given me money for an Angel Board donation in days." Brittany picked up the card and instantly recognized the spidery cursive writing.

For a woman who can't get it through her thick skull that she has no right to be dating.

"Holy crap!" Brittany exclaimed. "This one's scary."

"I was just thinking the same thing." Nancy frowned. "Should we call the police?"

"Over a donation card?" Brittany took off her hat and felt the instant relief of the elastic band no longer pinching. "I don't know. That seems extreme. It's probably just a twisted prankster." Still, the card made her nervous. She looked over her shoulder at Ryan. "Hey, Batman! You're going to want to see this."

TWENTY-EIGHT

"What the hell!" Ryan took off his mask and stared at the card. "Who would leave such an unhinged message?"

"And why is the handwriting so shaky?" Nancy asked. "I've been wondering about that."

"Maybe whoever is leaving the messages is trying to disguise their handwriting?" Brittany guessed.

Nancy's phone chimed. "That would be Herman probably wondering when I'll be home. He doesn't like for me to be driving at night in a storm."

"Go," said Brittany. "And thanks for your help tonight."

"Call me if you find out who your trickster is, will you?"

"Will do," Brittany promised.

"Hi, Herman," said Nancy as she answered her call. "I'm on my way." She pulled the door shut tight behind her.

"I'm going to make sure that's locked." Brittany glanced warily at the Angel Board as she crossed the room and checked the deadbolt. What began as a night of Halloween fun had turned sour. "Who would try to frighten me like this? This last message feels almost like a threat."

"I agree," Ryan said with a grunt. "But we've got those security cameras in place now. Let's see what they tell us."

"That's right. Hopefully they caught the person in action."

Brittany and Ryan crammed into the tiny back room and turned on her computer. There was only one chair, and Ryan offered it to Brittany. He knelt beside her and worked the mouse.

"This is like my system at home," he said. "With the monthly subscription service you have right now on the free thirty-day trial, we have access to many features including a timestamp."

Five separate videos appeared on the screen. One camera was angled at the register, the second panned out toward the front door and the Angel Board. The third camera captured the back door and hallway. The fourth showed the attic, and the fifth video looked slightly different and didn't appear to show anything at all.

"What's that feed for?" Brittany asked, pointing to the outlier.

"That's the game cam angled at the bat box. So far it's empty, but that doesn't mean the colony is in danger. They probably found another place to hibernate—away from my camera."

"Not everyone loves for their picture to be taken."

"I know, but I'm still hoping I'll get bat footage. Those little critters are cute."

"You say cute, I say vermin."

"Let's hope they are having a good rest somewhere, and are hunkered down for winter."

"Yes," Brittany agreed.

Ryan clicked on the video feed that showed the Angel Board and dragged the mouse so that the video went in reverse. "Do you remember if the message was there at the start of the party?"

"I don't." Brittany clicked off the battery pack in her pocket and her fairy lights went out. "But I inspected the board this morning, and that card wasn't there."

"Okay. Let's start in the morning then. This might take a while."

"I feel bad that you're on your knees. Why don't you squeeze in the chair with me?"

"The only way that would work is if you sat on my lap."

"Good point. I might squish you."

"I don't mind being squished." Ryan stood and Brittany gave up the chair so he could sit down first. Then she sat on his lap as lightly as she could.

"This *is* better," Ryan said as he gave her a hug.

"Much." Brittany smiled for a moment, enjoying the safe feeling of Ryan's embrace. "This would be better still," she said, brushing her lips against his. A quick kiss wasn't enough for either of them and they rapidly grew distracted.

"We'll never find the culprit like this," Ryan murmured, when they parted for air.

"You're right." Brittany reluctantly climbed off his lap. "I'll grab a second chair from the cafe."

As she walked into the main room, her gaze drifted over to the Angel Board, and she remembered the new message. *For a woman who can't get it through her thick skull that she has no right to be dating.*

What if her trickster was right? What if she had no right to date Ryan? No right to date anyone at all? What if this fledgling romance was an exercise in stupid futility? Brittany had an awful track record with men. Who was to say that her relationship with Ryan would be any different?

Doubt crept in followed by dread for what would happen if they broke up. *When they broke up.* Who was she kidding? Brittany was relationship poison, not just with boyfriends but with every man in her life, including her father.

No, that wasn't true. Brittany remembered her sweet text exchange with Jeremy that evening. She and her son were on solid ground.

Plus, Ryan wasn't Keith, or Ian, or Alan. He was a mature adult with an emotional toolkit bigger than any of the previous men in her life could imagine. Not once had he yelled at her or abandoned her. Ryan was steady and reliable; a man who would protect her, not rip her self-esteem to shreds.

Dating Ryan isn't a mistake, she told herself. *I'm a different person than I used to be. I've matured too, thank goodness. Every experience in my past has prepared me for my life today.*

She returned to the back room a minute later, and wedged the extra chair inside, next to the dishwasher. "Okay, back to the bat cave." She sat next to him and looked at the monitor.

It was tedious work, and as they searched, they talked about the evening.

"I'm glad Isabella seems to have made some good friends," said Ryan. "But I still worry about her. I wish there was a way I could get to know Lana, Gabby, and Scarlett without it being weird."

"Weird how?"

"Would *you* have wanted Alan hanging around you and your high school friends trying to get to know them?"

"Eew! No. I see your point." Brittany considered his predicament. "Here's an idea. Why don't you invite the girls' families over for dinner in November? You could host a chili feed. That would be easy. I'd loan you my Crock-Pot, unless you have one hidden away in that appliance garage of yours."

"I like that idea. I'm not sure Isabella will like it, but I want the other parents to know that our house is a safe place for their girls to hang out."

"Isabella would love showing off her room, too. She and Mary did a great job designing it."

Their conversation roamed beyond Isabella. Work, cars,

past relationships, and health concerns. No topic was off-limits. Time flew by almost as fast as the video feed that sped past them on the monitor. Ryan told her more about his divorce from Melissa and how difficult it was buying two extra houses in the middle of a hot Seattle housing market. Brittany explained how Hannah, Mary, and Cheryl moving in with her had come to be, and how much of a blessing that arrangement had been.

Ryan asked her if she'd ever been up the Eiffel Tower, and Brittany told him yes, after college when she went to Europe by herself. She also explained how she'd planned a ten-year wedding anniversary trip to London and Paris, and she and Ian had ended up canceling because they decided to pursue divorce instead.

"Ian never enjoyed traveling the way I did," she said. "Which is ironic because when we were married, we had money to go anywhere we wanted, but divorce wrecked both of our financial situations for years. I've only recently clawed my way out of that mess and built up my savings account again."

Ryan clicked on the computer screen, as the video continued to scroll. "I still enjoy traveling for pleasure, but my last job burned me out on work travel. I'm lucky that Melissa and Troy were there for Isabella because I was gone more than I wanted to be. But my new company has environmental sustainability goals to meet, and one of the ways they accomplish that is by limiting business travel. That's been good for me because it means I can stay home with Isabella."

"I'm sure she appreciates that."

"Wait a second." Ryan paused the mouse. "Is that something? That dot right there?"

Brittany peered forward. "I don't see anything. But that could be because I don't have my glasses on." Brittany found her glasses case on her desk and slipped on her "cheaters."

"I think if I push this button, it'll let me zoom in on the board," said Ryan.

"Great." Brittany felt the world had opened up now that she had her glasses on. She could see clearly again.

"I'm not seeing the card on the board yet. Are you?" Ryan asked.

"No. So far, this is what the board looked like this morning."

"I'm speeding up the feed, so we won't be here forever." Ryan pushed Brittany's hair off her neck and kissed the tender spot underneath her ear. "Not that I'm in any hurry to leave."

"That tickles." Brittany giggled. "Wait! Stop!"

"Kissing you?"

"No, stop the feed and go back. I think I just saw something."

"I must have missed that." Ryan moved the mouse. "I was distracted again."

"Funny how that keeps happening." Brittany turned her head and kissed his cheek, before looking back at the screen. "There. Right there. The board looks normal and then someone with dark hair walks past it and puts up the card."

"I'll be damned, you're right." Ryan set the video to slow motion. Frame by frame, they saw a person with dark hair wearing a coat walk up to the board and pin the card.

"Who is that?" Brittany asked. "I don't recognize the person at all."

"Me neither. I'll pan the camera out and maybe we can tell who it is from context."

"This looks like it happened during the end of the day, but before the shop closed for me to decorate for the party." Brittany pointed at the screen. "See? I hadn't hung the pumpkin lights yet."

"You were there the whole time, though, so how did the person get the card from the register? I'm assuming at this point that they didn't pay for it."

"Probably not. But I've seen that stationery before. I can't exactly remember where..." Brittany thought hard. "Wait a second, I think Ann from the senior center had a notecard like that, and she was here tonight."

"Does she have dark hair?"

"Kind of. It's more of an auburn color, depending on how she's dyed it."

Just then, Brittany's phone rang. She stood and answered the call. "Hi Mary, what's up?"

"Hopefully nothing," said her housemate. "I thought about calling Ryan, but it's not really any of my business, so I'm telling you instead and if you think he should know then—"

"Know what?" Ryan asked loudly.

"Ah, Mary," said Brittany. "Ryan's here with me and it's a small room, so he heard every word you said."

"Oh... Well, in that case, this is what happened," said Mary. "I'm at the theater, with Steven, and the place is packed. Patti and Don said that Isabella and her friends were coming too, but they never showed up. Patti ordered Isabella a popcorn combo and it's still waiting for her."

"Could you have missed her?" Brittany asked. "Maybe she didn't know her grandma had ordered her popcorn."

"That's what I thought, too," said Mary. "So I went into the auditorium and looked for Isabella, but I didn't see her, or her friends."

"That is odd." Ryan's forehead creased with worry. "Isabella should be at the theater by now."

"Probably she's still trick-or-treating," Brittany suggested.

"That's a good bet," said Mary. "Anyhow, like I said, I don't want to get Isabella in trouble if she stayed out too late, which is why I called you, not Ryan, but I guess that didn't quite work out like I'd planned."

"You can call me anytime," Ryan said loudly, so Mary could hear. "Don't worry about getting Isabella in trouble, she does a fine job of that on her own."

"Have fun at the movie, Mary," said Brittany. She hung up

and looked at Ryan. "It's probably nothing. They're just having a trick-or-treating marathon, is all. Those Lululemon bags looked like they could hold a lot of candy."

"Isabella's not where she told me she would be," Ryan said with a grunt.

"Which is a problem, but one that can be solved. Why don't you call her?"

"Good idea." Ryan took his phone out of his pocket and dialed. "She's not picking up."

"Okay, well…" Brittany thought the problem over. "I have Stephanie's phone number now. She gave it to me after I messaged her about the Rhododendron Lane debacle. I'll call Steph and see if she knows anything."

"Good idea." Ryan nodded. "I appreciate it."

Brittany searched through her contacts and called her former school chum. "Hi Stephanie, this is Brittany Thompson."

"Brittany, how are you? Did your party go well? I saw flyers for it all over town."

"It was great, thanks. I loved Scarlett's Statue of Liberty costume."

"She worked hard on that. Her history teacher gave her extra credit."

"Cool. Hey, I'm here with Ryan Osborne, Isabella's father, and we were wondering if you might know where the girls are?"

"What do you mean? I thought they were at the movie theater. I'm supposed to pick Scarlett up in an hour and ten minutes."

"We thought they were at the movie theater too, but apparently they aren't."

"Wait. What?" Stephanie's voice rose with alarm. "Where are they then?"

"We're not sure. Probably they are trick-or-treating and forgot to check in, but—"

"Sorry, Britt, I'm getting another call and it's Gabby's mom. I'll be right back."

Brittany covered the receiver. "This is why Isabella needs a cell phone with a GPS locator," she whispered. She knew it was none of her business, but she couldn't help offering the advice. Then she worried she was butting in. "I mean... sorry. You know what's best for your daughter, not me."

"No, you're right." Ryan pushed hair off his forehead. "I agree with you. Since it's illegal to jab Bella with a locator pin like she's a timber wolf being tracked, an iPhone would be the next best thing."

"Brittany?" Steph came back on the line. "The girls are at the marina."

"What?" Brittany looked at Ryan and saw panic in his eyes. "In this weather? Why would they do that?"

"Gabby told her mom it was something about a ghost," said Stephanie.

"The ghost of Sand Dollar Cove?" Brittany asked.

"Yeah. That's it," Stephanie confirmed. "I'd never heard about it until Scarlett explained it to me. Gabby's mom told her in no uncertain terms that she was not allowed to be there, because it's not a great place to hang out at night, but Gabby argued with her and hung up the phone. I'm going to call Jason and let him know what Lana is up to."

"Good." Brittany looked at her watch as she followed Ryan into the front room. "It's nine fifty-one. Ryan's putting on his coat. We'll walk down there right now and make sure the girls are safe. The marina's only three blocks away."

"That makes me feel better," said Stephanie. "My fourth grader's here counting candy, but we can pile in the car and come get Scarlett at a moment's notice."

"How about we collect the girls and drive them home?" Brittany suggested.

"That would be awesome," Stephanie replied. "Thank you.

I don't know what in the world got into Scarlett's brain that she would try a stunt like this."

"Teenage brains aren't fully formed." Brittany grabbed her coat and keys. She said goodbye to Stephanie and hung up.

Ryan opened the front door, into a blast of wind. "Why is parenting a teenage daughter a million times harder than raising a little girl?" he asked.

"It just is." Brittany stepped into the cold. "But don't worry —" Lightning cracked, interrupting what she was about to say. "Oh shoot! Here comes the storm."

"It's still a way off." Ryan shut the door behind them. "We haven't heard—"

Boom! Thunder crashed from above and it felt like all of Main Street rattled.

"Let's take the shortcut on foot." Brittany zipped up her coat. "It'll be faster than the sidewalks if we cut through the park and down the path."

Lightning cracked again, and thunder shattered. Raindrops the size of Hershey's Kisses fell on their heads. Despite the full moon, the storm made visibility poor, and a car almost hit them when they crossed Main Street.

"Hey!" Ryan hollered at the driver. "Watch where you're going!"

Brittany reached into her pocket and turned on her battery pack, causing her costume to glow to life. Her coat covered the top of it, but at least her legs could stop traffic.

"What's this about a ghost?" Ryan asked loudly above the wind. "Have you heard about this before?"

"Only recently." Brittany picked up her pace. "It's supposed to be a teenager who haunts Sand Dollar Cove and seeks the company of teens under the light of a half-moon."

The rain pounded harder, and it became impossible to talk for the next few minutes. They leaned into the wind and walked quickly through town. Brittany wished she'd brought a jacket with a hood, because her hair was soaking wet, but there was nothing she could do. Ryan's coat didn't have a hood, either.

The foghorn blew loudly as they entered the park, just before ten p.m. The storm was noisier still. Brittany didn't hear her phone ring, but she felt it vibrate in her pocket. "Hello?" she shouted to be heard over the wind.

"Brittany, it's Steph. We think the girls are headed to the lighthouse."

"What?" Brittany shrieked. "In this weather?" She broke into a run, and Ryan followed.

"It gets worse," Stephanie continued. "Jason says his rowboat is gone. One of his crewmen called and told him this evening. He didn't think anything of it until I called him about the girls being missing. That's when he put two and two together. Lana was talking about the ghost of Sand Dollar Cove haunting the lighthouse every Halloween with a half-moon."

"And now the girls are at the marina." Brittany's heart pounded in her chest as she ran.

"Exactly. I've tried calling Scarlett and can't reach her. Jason's called Lana. The Santoses can't reach Gabby. None of the girls are answering their phones. I'm climbing in the car right now. Jason's driving down to the dock as well. I called my mom, and she's posting pictures on her neighborhood Facebook group. Everyone in town will be looking for them."

"Good!" Brittany cried, her lungs pounding. "We're almost at the marina. I'll call you when we find them."

"What's going on?" Ryan asked, jogging next to her. "Why are we running?"

Brittany realized he hadn't been able to overhear Stephanie's conversation above the roar of the storm. "The girls might have taken a rowboat out to the lighthouse."

"What? Why?"

"To see the ghost of Sand Dollar Cove." It felt stupid saying something so ridiculous out loud. "Apparently he haunts the lighthouse." Saying that second part caused something to click in her brain.

A ghost who haunted the lighthouse and sought out the company of teenagers...

Was this silly yarn based on the true story of her brother's accident?

"Shit!" she cried. "They're searching for Paul! They're headed to the place he died!"

"Oh my God!" Ryan yelped like a wounded animal and shot forward into the park, bolting down the path toward the marina so fast that Brittany couldn't keep up.

TWENTY-NINE

Her heart banged like a drum.

Her legs ached.

Every muscle fiber in her body strained with exertion.

Brittany, who wasn't a runner, sprinted as fast as she could.

She didn't begrudge Ryan for running ahead of her; she understood his fierce need to protect his child.

With each heavy footfall, her fear grew worse.

Would the girls really be so stupid? Would they seriously sail to the lighthouse in the middle of the storm?

She didn't need a crystal ball to answer that question.

She knew it in her heart. In her bones, and in her soul.

There was always the chance that every teenager, no matter how smart, capable, or trustworthy, might make one spur-of-the-moment decision that ruined everything, especially if their friends were involved.

As she ran toward Isabella, she couldn't help but think of Paul.

Paul, who was so athletic and smart. Paul, who loved music and watching out for his sister. Paul, who would be here, right now, except for one terrible mistake.

When she emerged from the path and saw the marina lights in front of her, and the long fishing pier stretching out into the water, she looked at the lighthouse and shivered.

Isabella, Gabby, Lana, and Scarlett were headed to the lighthouse to seek out a ghost. Was that Paul's legacy? Had he become a rumor bandied about town, whispered from one adolescent to another? Was Paul the ghost of Sand Dollar Cove? If so, that was Brittany's fault. It was her fault for not talking about Paul more. It was her fault for not keeping his memory alive. Instead, she'd allowed his death to transform into superstition.

Why hadn't she moved Paul's picture from her bedroom dresser to the family room where everyone could see it?

Why hadn't she searched the thrift stores to find a CD tower just like the one Paul had cherished, and spent the past thirty years rebuilding his music collection? Jeremy could have helped her. Her son would have loved that.

Why hadn't Brittany thought to put pumpkin bread with pecans on the Safe Harbor menu? She could have named it after him: Paul's Favorite Pumpkin Bread. Then, when customers asked her who Paul was, she could have told them. *Paul was the most wonderful brother in the world, and he died too soon.*

If Paul had become a ghost story it was because she'd let him become a ghost in her own life. Paul was the loss that haunted her and carved deep wounds on her soul.

"Isabella!" Ryan shouted from somewhere in the mist. "Isabella, where are you?"

Brittany ran up to the edge of the pier and stepped onto the slick wooden planks. The marina was well lit at least, but she didn't see any sign of the girls, or Ryan.

"Isabella!" she cried. "Scarlett! Gabby! Lana!"

I know you're gone, she whispered to Paul. *But if you can hear me, please help.* She needed to overcome her fear of the water if she was to ever step foot on the dock.

Brittany took one shaky step and then another. With a courage she didn't know she had, her strides grew stronger. Soon she was charging forward down the pier, hollering at the top of her lungs. "Isabella! Scarlett! Gabby, and Lana!" The boats to the left and right of her bobbed madly in the water.

"Bella!" Ryan shouted, from the end of the pier. Brittany could see him now, a lone wolf in the rain, shouting into the wind.

Should she call the police? Or the Coast Guard? What if the girls had gone back to the movie theater by now and she called the authorities for nothing? Fear coursed through her, making her queasy.

Help me, Paul, her heart begged. *What should I do?*

Paul wasn't there to answer her, but it didn't matter. She had her own wisdom guiding her now. She was a mother who knew what it meant to parent teenagers. Brittany took out her phone and dialed 911.

THIRTY

"Bella!" Ryan shouted. "Bella, where are you?"

The anguish in his voice broke Brittany's heart. She rushed as fast as she dared across the slippery dock toward Ryan and handed him the phone. "It's the 911 dispatcher," she said. "He needs more information. I already explained what costumes the girls were wearing."

"Hello?" Ryan spoke loudly over the raging wind. "Yes. Her full name is Isabella Pauline Osborne. She's four feet four inches tall and weighs 103 pounds."

Hearing Isabella's middle name cut Brittany's heart wide open. *Pauline*. Ryan had never forgotten Paul. He hadn't erased his best friend's memory. Could she say the same about her own brother?

Turning away from Ryan, Brittany peered over the choppy black water, looking for any sign of the girls. She staggered up and down the dock, hoping to see them tucked away on one of the boats, sheltering on the deck of a houseboat, or having a private Halloween party with just the four of them in a cabin. When she came to the *Sockeye Express*, Jason's charter boat, she called out their names again. "Lana! Gabby! Isabella, and Scarlett! Are you there?" But she didn't see any trace of them.

Turning around, Brittany saw her father's boat, the *Moonstruck*, smack against the rubber dock bumper. The marina was supposed to protect the boats in the harbor, but the weather was so fierce that nowhere was safe. Her costume's battery pack flickered off for some reason.

What can I do for the girls? she wondered. *How can I help?*

Ryan needed her help. At the very least, she could stand by his side. Brittany ran down the dock at full speed, no longer afraid of slipping. The movement must have jostled the battery pack in her pocket to turn back on, because her costume lit up, right before she reached him. The glow of the fairy lights cast to the left and right of her caused her to gasp.

Was that a life jacket floating on the water? *And a blonde wig?*

"Ryan!" she screamed, pointing at the surface. Brittany hurried to the edge of the dock and fell to her knees, peering over. She zipped open her coat so that the lights on her sweatshirt could glow too. There, floating in the water, were two empty life jackets and a cooler. Right next to them was a broken, overturned rowboat with the *Sockeye Companion* written on the side, and a tangle of hair attached. "It's Jason's rowboat!" she shrieked. "And Isabella's Taylor Swift wig!"

"What?" Ryan lunged forward onto his hands and knees, staring at the water. Brittany's phone clattered onto the boards. "Bella!" he cried.

Brittany picked up her phone and turned on the flashlight app, shining it down toward the broken rowboat. "She's not here. It's just her wig. Maybe it blew off. What if they're stuck out on the lighthouse rocks?"

Ryan jumped up and looked toward the lighthouse. The foghorn sounded, barely audible over the storm. "That's it!" he called. "They could be stranded!" He sprinted to the edge of the dock and screamed, "Bella!"

Brittany looked frantically around, trying to find a way to save the girls. Lightning split open the sky and thunder roared a few seconds later. When Brittany looked up at the moon, she had an idea—a horrible idea, but it was their only option. She leapt to her feet and grabbed Ryan's sleeve. "Let's take my dad's boat!" she cried, pulling him toward the *Moonstruck*.

"What?"

"If they're out there, we need to get to them!"

"Yes!" Ryan nodded his head emphatically. "I'd swim, if I had to."

The two of them ran down the dock toward the *Moonstruck*. Brittany had only boarded her father's boat one time to go crabbing, back when Jeremy was three years old and difficult to entertain. It was before her panic attacks began about the ocean. Jeremy had been so whiny on that trip, that Alan had never invited them again.

"How will we operate the boat?" Ryan asked. "Do you have a key?"

"No," she admitted. "But my dad always hid the key to the *Lovestruck* in a waterproof box in the built-in cooler." They ran the last few steps toward where the *Moonstruck* was docked. Brittany stopped abruptly, staring at the aft.

Could she actually do this?

Face her fear of the water?

She had to.

Her courage couldn't fail her now.

Brittany boarded the motorboat and walked directly to the bench that contained the cooler. *Please let this work*, she prayed, as she slid her fingers underneath the cushion and felt the latch that unhitched the compartment below. Clicking it open, Brittany lifted the seat and stared into darkness. The lights from her costume helped her spy a tiny box below.

"I found it!" Brittany popped the box open and held the key. "Let's go save your daughter!"

"I'm one step ahead of you." Ryan untied the ropes connecting the *Moonstruck* to the dock. "Do you want to captain this thing, or shall I?"

"You do it. But give me your phone. I'll keep calling Isabella."

Ryan handed his phone over and sat down in the captain's seat.

"Wait!" Brittany opened the bench seat with the PFDs. "Put on a life jacket first." She passed him the largest vest.

"Good idea." Ryan zipped up the vest and tightened the cord.

Once Brittany was wearing her life jacket too, Ryan put the boat into gear and navigated them away from the dock. Brittany dialed Isabella's number repeatedly, but it went straight to voicemail. As they sailed out of the marina and through the harbor, Brittany scanned the water for any sign of the girls. She didn't see anything in the harbor, but people were arriving on land. "A truck just parked at the boat launch," she shouted. "That must be Jason!" Flashing lights tore through the park, and the wail of a fire engine cut through the storm. "And the first responders!" She clung to the gunwale as the *Moonstruck* picked up speed.

"Isabella!" Ryan hollered.

Waves rocked the boat harder and harder, the further they got from the marina. Brittany's hair whipped around her, making it difficult to see. *Please don't let history repeat itself,* she prayed. When she turned back toward the shoreline, she saw another boat enter the search. A larger boat with huge flood-lights—the *Sockeye Express*. She knew Jason was out searching for the girls, too.

"People are coming to help," she shouted over the wind.

They were approaching the lighthouse now. Ryan cut the

engine and the boat drifted toward the rocks. "Do you see them?"

"No. Is there a better light we could turn on?"

"I have no idea. I haven't operated a boat in thirty years."

The *Moonstruck* was fancier than the *Lovestruck*, the boat of her childhood, and Brittany was out of her element. But she looked at the helm of the boat searching for switches. "What does this one do?" She pulled a small lever. Floodlights lit up the water all around them.

"Yes!" Ryan exclaimed. "That helps!"

But did it? Was any light powerful enough to shine through this horrible situation?

The foghorn boomed, sounding a low, mournful noise that resonated across the water. Brittany stared at the rocks where Paul had died and felt the icy tentacles of panic strangle her lungs. Her breathing grew shallow, and she couldn't swallow. Drifting on the water like this was terrifying.

"Bella!" Ryan cried, his voice breaking. "Bella, where are you?"

But there was nobody there. All they saw was the historic lighthouse, which had been unmanned since the early 1950s.

"She's not here," said Brittany. "None of them are here. That's a good sign, right?" She held onto Ryan's arm and turned him to face her. "I have to believe this is a good thing."

"But the smashed rowboat. And Gabby calling her mom. And—"

"Lana Mathews, where are you!" called a bullhorn. "Lana, are you okay?"

"That's Jason's boat," said Brittany.

"Which means they're still out there." Ryan yanked off his shoes.

"What are you doing?" Brittany cried.

"I'm swimming over to those rocks and climbing onto the island. It's too dangerous to dock the boat in this weather."

"But the water's freezing! It's deadly cold!"

Her phone buzzed deep within her pocket. Brittany pulled it out and saw a text from an unknown number. As soon as she read what it said, it felt like she was the one submerged in icy water.

"What the hell is this?" she screamed.

She passed the phone to Ryan so he could read what it said: *Carpe diem.*

THIRTY-ONE

It felt like Paul's ghost was speaking directly to her, but Brittany knew that was impossible because ghosts didn't exist, and even if they did, her brother wouldn't haunt her.

"What the hell?" Ryan shouted over the wind. "Is this your Angel Board sicko?"

"I have no idea. I'll just ignore it."

"No, wait." Ryan handed back her phone. "What if it's about the girls? What if the two things are connected?"

"Like my sicko kidnapped your daughter?" Brittany gulped.

"Shit! The boat's drifting." Ryan took the helm and powered the engine, pushing them away from the rocks.

"I'm texting the person back and ending this once and for all." Brittany sat at Ryan's feet and wedged herself with her feet so she wouldn't be in danger of falling overboard.

Who is this? she texted.

You know who this is, the person replied.

I don't, Brittany typed. *Please tell me.*

I have a secret.

I don't like secrets, Brittany responded.

"What's the person saying?" Ryan asked.

"They're playing mind games with me." Brittany read the text exchange out loud.

"What an asshole," Ryan muttered.

Brittany passed Ryan his phone, which was still in her pocket. "Call 911 and tell them what's going on with the creepy texts. This could be important. And let's go back to shore. I don't think they're here."

I bet you can guess my name, the texter wrote.

I'm not playing games, Brittany replied, her fear turning to anger.

I don't want to get my friend in trouble. That's why you need to guess.

No way, Brittany typed angrily. *I'm calling the police.*

No!!! Brittany it's me.

"The person knows my name for sure," Brittany told Ryan. "It's not a random caller."

"Keep them texting," said Ryan. "That's what the dispatcher says to do." He had one hand on the phone and the other on the throttle.

Who's me? Brittany typed. *I don't recognize this number.*

Did you see the video?

"They claim there's a video!" Brittany scrolled up through the texts until she came to an image she had overlooked when her phone buzzed.

"Of what?" Ryan yelled frantically.

Brittany tapped the screen and saw... Keith dropping a

lettuce leaf on the floor of Safe Harbor. Huh? It took a second for her memory to click into place.

"I've seen this video before," Brittany exclaimed. "This is the video Gabby sent me when Keith tried to trick me!"

"What?" Ryan shouted.

Brittany dialed the number, still uncertain who would pick up on the other end of the line.

"Hi," said the voice. "Did you guess it was me?"

"It's Isabella!" Brittany shrieked.

"What?" Ryan shouted. "Oh, thank God. Where is she?"

"Isabella?" Brittany asked. "Are you okay?"

Isabella's voice was hard to hear against the roar of the boat engine. "I'm safe."

"Give the phone to me," Ryan held out his hand. "Please."

"I'm passing you over to your father," said Brittany.

"No, please, don't!" Isabella begged. "He's going to be so mad at me."

"Why were you playing guessing games with me like that?" Brittany asked. "Why didn't you tell me who was texting?"

"Because I'm using Gabby's phone. She's been letting me borrow it for all sorts of things. But her mom reads her messages each night, and I don't want to get Gabby in trouble. Her parents told her she couldn't lend it out. That's why I used the code words *carpe diem*. You said that was the number one way to get your attention. I figured you'd know who was texting you without me having to spell it out and alert Gabby's mom."

"I see." Brittany ignored Ryan's outstretched hand and turned away from him slightly. "And you're in a safe place right now?" she reiterated.

"Yes, we're safe. Scarlett, Lana, and Gabby are with me. But we're freaking out. An ambulance went by, and it sounds like the whole town is looking for us."

Judging by the number of boats Brittany saw coming into the harbor, that assumption was true. The girls' faces were probably plastered in every Sand Dollar Cove Facebook group by now.

"Are you still on the line with the dispatcher?" Brittany asked Ryan. He nodded. She grabbed his hand and pulled it down, squeezing his fingers to let him know the girls were okay. "Tell them the girls are safe and that I'm talking to Isabella right now."

"What was that?" Isabella asked. "I couldn't hear you."

"I was telling your dad that you're safe," said Brittany. "Now take a deep breath and tell me where you are."

"We're in the attic."

"What attic?"

"The attic of Safe Harbor!" Isabella exclaimed.

Ryan pulled the boat into the marina and steered it toward the slip. A crowd of people, including Stephanie Mathews and her husband, waited on the dock with flashlights.

"They're in the attic at Safe Harbor," Brittany repeated to Ryan.

"Yes, that's where we are," said Isabella. "And it's freezing up here. How do you turn on the heater?"

"There is no heater. Come down into the cafe where it's warm."

"But we can't!" Isabella cried. "That's just it. We're trapped up here!"

"What?" Brittany asked. "How?"

"I don't know, but the ladder won't budge and it's really dark up here, and our phones are dying, and—"

"Stay calm," Brittany urged. "We'll be right there."

THIRTY-TWO

"That second chair must be the problem," Brittany said after flinging open the door to the back room. "It looks like it caused the trapdoor to jam." She was dripping wet and felt like she'd run a marathon, but she was finally here, in Safe Harbor, with Ryan by her side, ready to rescue the girls.

"Why'd they put it on the dishwasher instead of out in the cafe?" Ryan hauled the chair away. "Bella!" He called up to the roof. "We're here."

Brittany stood on her tiptoes and reached for the handle, but it took Ryan's extra height to pull it down. "Maybe they moved the chairs to reach the trapdoor?" she wondered out loud.

As soon as the stairs descended, Isabella climbed down, fast as a chipmunk, and threw herself into her father's arms. "I'm so glad to see you!" She gave him a tight hug.

"I'm so relieved to be out of that attic." Scarlett dropped her Statue of Liberty torch to the ground, before hitching up her skirts and climbing gingerly down the stairs.

"I thought I was going to have to pee in that creepy shower," said Lana, her cat tail twisted over her arm.

"Is my mom here?" Gabby poked her head down first, before she came down the ladder. "I'm going to be in so much trouble."

"Don't worry about that now," Brittany advised. "We're all just glad that you're safe."

"So glad." Ryan rumpled Isabella's hair. "When I saw your wig floating in the water I about died. How did it get there?"

"Let's save the explanations for later," said Brittany. "Come on into the cafe because there are some people who are eager to see you." She led the way into the storefront.

"Scarlett!" Stephanie cried, throwing her arms around her daughter. "Never scare me like that again!" Her husband and Scarlett's little brother joined the family hug.

"I swear, little lady, you're in one heap of trouble," Jason told Lana. "How'd you like to be grounded for life?" But then he burst into tears and gave Lana an enormous bear hug that lifted her off her feet.

Gabby's parents spoke to her in rapid-fire Tagalog, and Mrs. Santos wrapped her in a fuzzy beach blanket, even though her daughter wasn't wet.

Brittany saw a firefighter enter the building, along with the two patrol officers from the police department.

"Time to face the music." Ryan put his arm around Isabella's shoulders and walked with her to the authorities to give a statement.

After greeting the officers, the girls sat down and shared their story.

"We were going to look for the ghost of Sand Dollar Cove," Isabella began.

"Everyone's been talking about it," said Gabby.

"It was supposed to be a simple trip," said Lana. "I've taken that rowboat out a million times."

"Not in a storm," Jason blustered. "Not without my permission. I—"

"Let her finish," Brittany said, interrupting him. "There'll be time for discussion later."

The girls nodded gratefully.

Lana took a deep breath before continuing. "We'd only been on the rowboat for a few minutes when I realized that the water was too choppy, and we should head back."

"So that's what we did," said Scarlett. "We tied the boat up by the rocks next to the park."

"I tied the knots," said Isabella.

Not very adeptly, Brittany thought, as she pictured the capsized rowboat. But she didn't want to burden Isabella with that knowledge right now.

"What happened next?" Ryan asked.

"We figured we couldn't go to the movie because the tickets were probably sold out," said Gabby.

"It was my idea to go to Safe Harbor and warm up." Isabella looked at Ryan. "I figured you would be here with Brittany. But when we got here, the back door was open, and you were gone."

"I remembered what you said about your attic being the perfect place to see a larger view of Main Street." Lana picked at the fur of her cat costume. "That's why I suggested we go up there—in case it made it easier to see the ghost."

"But all we saw was rain," said Isabella.

"We didn't realize everyone was looking for us until about ten minutes later," said Gabby. "All of a sudden, I had a million messages on my phone."

"So did I." Scarlett nodded.

Isabella twisted the Kleenex she held until it ripped in two. "Once we saw all the fire engines go by, we worried we might be in major trouble, so we tried to come down from the attic."

"That's when we got trapped," said Gabby.

"The trapdoor was jammed." Lana looked at Jason. "I was worried we'd be stuck up there forever without a bathroom."

Isabella waved her hands around excitedly. "We all

panicked and didn't know what to do, but I said that Brittany would help us without flipping out like our parents would."

Brittany pulled a wet curl behind her ear. "I would never freak out," she lied.

Stephanie hugged Scarlett. "Thank goodness you four girls are okay."

"This calls for hot chocolate," said Brittany. "Who wants some?" After a quick count of hands, she tied an apron around her still-soggy costume, washed her hands, and flicked on the instant hot water machine. Working as quickly as she could, Brittany scooped hot chocolate powder into a dozen paper cups and waited for the water to heat. Meanwhile, the first responders said goodbye and left.

"Need some help with that?" asked a friendly voice.

Brittany turned around and saw Nancy wearing a puffer coat over her pajamas. "Nancy! What are you doing here?" Seeing her co-worker brought unexpected tears to Brittany's eyes. The stress from the evening's outrageous adventures finally caught up with her.

Nancy looked at her with concern. "I was scrolling Facebook and saw the news. I came as soon as I could."

"Thank you." Tears rolled down Brittany's cheeks.

"You poor thing." Nancy hugged her tightly.

"I'm all wet," Brittany said, her chest frozen. She was willing herself not to cry.

"Now I'm wet too, but that's okay." Nancy squeezed her one more time and then pushed her away gently. "Do you still have the clothes you wore today before you changed into your costume?"

Brittany nodded. "Yeah. I never made it home this evening."

"Go change into those dry clothes while I finish the hot chocolate."

"Thank you so much. I don't know what I'd do without you."

"You'd manage somehow." Nancy smiled. "You always do. That's why you're so impressive."

Brittany went into the back room and put on her jeans, shirt, and sweater. There was nothing she could do about her wet underwear, besides go commando. But being in dry clothes felt good. Best of all was clasping the X necklace around her neck. Blue and silver beads, and the number ten for Paul. He had looked out for her on that boat as she faced her fears, she knew it. Brittany pressed her fingertips to her heart and closed her eyes, honoring her brother's memory, before she looked straight in front of her, ready to face the world again.

She walked back into the cafe and saw even more people than there were before. The movie must have let out. Patti, Don, and Mary were there too.

"My phone was blowing up with messages," said Mary as she rushed toward Brittany's side. "Are you okay?"

"Yeah. I'm good." Brittany pulled a wet curl behind her ear. "This night has been a lot, though."

"Have some hot chocolate." Nancy put a warm cup in her hand.

"I still can't believe you did this, Isabella," Ryan said in a stern voice. "After all the safety lectures I've given you about boats and the ocean."

"We were wearing life jackets," Isabella protested. "I'm not stupid."

"It doesn't matter." Ryan rested his elbows on his knees and curled forward in his chair. "I never want you to go out on a boat like that again, not without an adult present, and especially not with a storm coming on." His jaw clenched, and his voice shook. Brittany could see and feel the fear in his eyes.

"We wanted to see the ghost," Isabella whispered. "That legend and my new friends are the only good thing about moving here."

"What ghost?" Patti asked. She looked at Don. "Did I hear her say ghost?"

Brittany took a deep breath and touched her necklace. She knelt on the wood floor in front of Isabella and picked up the girl's hands. "Isabella," she said in a solemn voice. "Do you realize that my brother Paul drowned near that lighthouse?"

"What?" Isabella gasped.

"Did you say drowned?" Scarlett asked.

"I didn't know you had a brother," said Gabby.

"Me neither," Lana added.

Brittany dropped Isabella's hands and looked at all four girls at once. "My brother—my remarkably smart, kind, athletic, and wonderful brother who was two years older than me—died his senior year when the boat he was on, the *Carpe Diem*, sank by the lighthouse in awful weather just like tonight. His name was Paul Thompson."

"The ghost of Sand Dollar Cove," Isabella murmured. "That's exactly like the legend."

Scarlett bit her lip and looked at her mom. "Some people call it *Carpe Diem* rock, now. I didn't know it was from a boat. I thought it was just a ghost story."

"It's not a ghost story or a legend," Ryan said abruptly. "Paul was my best friend."

"And Ryan fought valiantly to save Paul's life." Brittany looked at him with gratitude. "Ryan risked his own life trying to save Paul. Just like he would have done tonight, if he'd needed to." She knew that to be one hundred percent true.

"Yes, I risked everything to save him," Ryan said in an anguished tone. "But Paul wouldn't be dead if I hadn't taken him out on the water. I've lived with that guilt my entire adult life."

"Do you hear that?" Jason pointed at Lana. "Make better choices."

"Yes. Make better choices." Patti stood and strode to the

front of the room. She slowly removed the metal asp bracelet that coiled around her arm and looked it dead in the eye before putting it on the table next to her. "Ryan, my darling son," she said in a clear voice. "I know you blame yourself. But it's not your fault Paul died."

"Patti," Don exclaimed. "You don't have to do this."

Patti looked at him sadly before shaking her head. "Oh, but I do. In fact, I'm decades past due. I should have spoken up ages ago instead of letting my son carry a guilt that wasn't his." She turned to face Ryan. "You don't bear one ounce of blame for Paul's death. It's your father's fault, and I'm through with covering up for Frank any longer."

Brittany gasped.

"Mom." Ryan jerked back like Patti had sucker-punched him. "What do you mean?"

THIRTY-THREE

"Thirty-one years ago, Frank and I were broke." Patti spoke clearly, facing the small audience. "But that was nothing new. We were always out of money. The faster I made it hemming dresses and sewing drapes with my alterations business, the faster he spent it. That man could never hold down a steady job, not that he even wanted to."

Brittany felt gobsmacked. She'd never heard Patti speak ill of Frank. She listened closely as Patti continued her story.

"One of Frank's favorite get-rich-quick schemes was to buy vehicles at auction, fix them up, and sell them for a profit." Patti took off her deep-black Cleopatra wig and passed it to Don. "Usually he did this with cars, and sometimes he made a profit." Patti looked at Ryan. "Which he'd gamble away before I could use it to pay any of our bills."

Ryan grimaced and looked at the floor.

"Like I said," Patti continued. "Frank typically did this with cars, or trucks, but there was this one time... this one fateful time... He'd won some money playing poker with Brittany's father. Ten thousand dollars! Cynthia was furious, but Alan paid up. Frank decided to try his scheme with a boat, even though he had limited shipbuilding skills."

"The *Carpe Diem*..." Brittany whispered.

"Originally it was called something else." Patti took off her heavy necklace and placed it next to the asp. "Frank was determined to change the boat's name as fast as he could. So fast, it made me suspicious. I wondered if maybe the boat was hot property. I wouldn't have put it past him to make a shady transaction like that."

"It was Paul who came up with the name for the *Carpe Diem*." Ryan surprised everyone by speaking. "That was one of Paul's favorite expressions."

"Ryan's right," Brittany confirmed. "Paul loved telling people to seize the day. It was the motto he lived by."

"Changing the name so fast was the first red flag for me," said Patti. "The second was the enormous insurance policy Frank took out on the boat. The payout was fifty thousand dollars, even though he'd bought the boat for ten thousand dollars."

"How did that even go through?" Nancy asked.

"I'm not entirely sure," Patti admitted. "But I think Frank claimed the boat was his business and livelihood. If the *Carpe Diem* sank, he would not only get property reimbursement, but wage reimbursement as well."

Shady as hell... Brittany clenched her fists in her lap.

Patti took a deep breath before continuing her story. "One day Frank placed an envelope on the stack of bills I was mailing and said to be sure to get it into the mailbox that morning. I *did* mail those envelopes, but what I didn't realize was that the postage rates had gone up the day before. The letter didn't make it. Frank's final payment to the insurance company never went through." Patti turned slightly and gazed directly at Ryan and Brittany. "The *Carpe Diem* sank six days later. When the insurance failed to pay out, Frank blamed me for ruining everything." Patti's voice cracked, and she melted into tears. "Frank said it was my fault we had to declare bankruptcy. And I couldn't say anything, because how could I? I suspected my husband was guilty of insurance fraud."

"Not just insurance fraud," said Nancy. "Manslaughter."

"Murder..." Brittany rasped.

"Not murder," Patti quickly interjected. "I don't think Frank meant to kill anyone—just to milk the insurance company."

"Oh, Mom..." Ryan's voice broke. "You should have said something. You should have gone to the police. Was the *Carpe Diem* even seaworthy? Had Dad tampered with it?"

"I'll never know." Patti's face was red and blotchy. "I was too much of a coward to speak up."

"My poor dollface." Don handed her a handkerchief. "Frank placed you in an impossible situation."

"But it wasn't impossible." Brittany rose to her feet. "You suspected the boat had issues. You stayed silent while Paul died, and your own son nearly drowned with him." Anger bubbled up in her like boiling water. "How could you do that? How could you live with yourself and the consequences of your decisions all these years?"

Patti hung her head, seemingly unable to meet Brittany's gaze. "I wasn't brave, like you. I couldn't stand on my own without a man beside me. I couldn't start my own clothing store, like I wanted. I never had the courage. But then—" She looked at Don. "Then Don came into my life, and I realized that the only way I could move forward was to make amends."

"Make amends?" said Brittany. "How would that even be possible?"

"Yeah, Grandma, explain yourself," said Isabella.

Patti jerked back at the sound of her granddaughter's voice, but then she stood straight and looked Brittany in the eye. "By apologizing to Brittany the only way I felt I could, through the Angel Board."

"What?" Brittany and Ryan said at the same time.

Patti lifted her chin and spoke in a clear voice. "'For a mom who wears Birkenstocks and wool socks. To a forty-five-year-old woman with a nose ring. To a woman whose son seemingly doesn't need her, please know that he still does. To the woman who feels lost, forgotten, and unloved; you are not alone. To the woman who could have been so much more if relationships hadn't tied you down, I see your true worth.'" Patti walked slowly forward. "Brittany, I've been trying to tell you for months how much I admire and respect you. Trying to encourage you after everything you've been through. I left those messages to heal my emotional wounds, but also to cheer you on, and to heal your wounds, too."

"Cheer me on?" Brittany echoed. "Those messages didn't encourage me, they rattled me."

"Yeah, Grandma, I thought they were creepy too," said Isabella.

"What about the last one?" Nancy asked. "The one that said: 'For a woman who can't get it through her thick skull that she has no right to be dating.'"

Patti pressed her palm over her heart. "That last one was for me." She turned toward Don. "I'm trying to get over my guilt for being so happy with you, I really am."

"Mom, I'm shocked," Ryan said. "And why didn't I recognize your handwriting?"

"That would be my thyroid medicine." Patti held up her shaky hand. "It causes tremors."

"Wait a minute." Nancy marched up to Brittany and stood beside her, staring Patti down. "Wait just a minute. How did you pay for the Angel Board cards, because if you didn't pay for the donation, that's basically stealing."

Patti frowned and lifted her chin. "Osbornes always pay

their own way. I put five-dollar bills in the tip jar every time I took a card from behind the counter when you weren't looking."

"Oh, well..." Nancy looked at Brittany. "Are you alright, sweetie? How are you doing?"

Brittany felt gutted. "I'm numb," she managed to say.

"And you, Ryan?" Nancy asked.

Ryan opened and closed his mouth several times, clearly incapable of saying anything at all.

"Ryan, my sweetheart, I'm so sorry." Patti shook her head sadly.

"Grandma, this is really messed up," said Isabella. "Like, seriously. All of it."

Don stood and put his hand on Ryan's back. "It must feel good knowing that the boating accident wasn't your fault. Right? You have your mother to thank for that sense of relief."

Ryan unfroze. He jerked Don's arm away and grunted. "Take your hand off me."

"Yeah," said Isabella. "Don't make excuses for my grandma's awful behavior. That's almost as bad as her making excuses for Grandpa." She looked up at Ryan. "Can we go now? I just want to go home."

Ryan nodded. "Absolutely. Come on, Bella. Let's go."

"Wait!" Brittany called after them. She felt bad that they were leaving like this.

Ryan shot Brittany a tortured look. The pain in his eyes was so intense it burned her soul. "I'm sorry, Brittany. I'm sorry for everything my family has done to you." Without another word, he walked out the front door, with Isabella chasing after him.

THIRTY-FOUR

"I think it's totally fine to open the cafe late today." Hannah refilled Brittany's coffee cup and sat next to her at the kitchen table. "Have another blueberry muffin. Guy baked them fresh this morning just for you."

"Thanks." Brittany folded her muffin wrapper into quarters. "That was really sweet of him."

Mary rubbed Brittany's back. "And Steven told me to tell you he's happy to consult on any legal matters you want to pursue. Frank and Patti have covered up a crime for thirty years."

"Leave Patti out of it." Cheryl scooted in her chair. "She's my best friend, and if you'd seen how Frank treated her when his mind was still working, you'd know that she's a victim in this situation, too."

"Really, Gran?" Hannah narrowed her eyes. "You're comparing Patti's suffering to Paul's death?"

"I don't have a son or a brother, but I know that Patti being stuck in a terrible marriage and Paul drowning are two entirely different levels," said Mary.

Brittany felt the same way.

"Well, I've lost a son." Cheryl nodded emphatically. "And I still found it in my heart to forgive the people whose reckless-ness killed him." She meant Guy's grandfather, and his mistress, who accidentally ran into her son Max's truck and drove him off Blackfish Point when Hannah and Mary were little girls. "I'm also old enough to understand that people can grow and change. Patti's not the same person she was thirty years ago when the accident happened, and she protected her husband."

Hannah smacked her hand on the table. "But she's been protecting Frank for thirty years! She could have come forward at any time and told the authorities what she knew about why the boat sank."

"It wasn't only about her and Frank." Cheryl looked at Hannah intently. "It was also about Ryan."

"Ryan was completely innocent," Brittany said. "He had no idea the *Carpe Diem* was dangerous. I truly believe that."

"Yes, but if Patti had exposed Frank for his insurance fraud scheme, he might have also been convicted for manslaughter," said Cheryl. "And as hard as Patti worked doing piecework alterations in her living room, she didn't earn enough money to support her and Ryan. She would have really struggled without Frank's financial help, as unreliable as it was. Then who knows what would have happened after that? Maybe Ryan wouldn't have left town to pursue his own dreams."

"Ryan didn't leave Sand Dollar Cove to 'pursue his dreams.'" Brittany made air quotes. "He left in a cloud of shame and depression that almost destroyed him. It was his own pluck and perseverance that brought him out of it. His intelligence and solid work ethic made him successful."

"Plus, it must have been incredibly difficult for Ryan all these years, not having clarity about how Paul died," said Hannah. "He *thought* he knew what had happened, but he didn't." She looked at Brittany. "For you, as well. For Ryan though, it must have been more visceral. More nightmarish. Because he was there, and he almost died too."

"What we're talking about is trauma and protecting loved ones from trauma." Cheryl folded her knobby hands and placed them on the table. "Mothers will go to great lengths to protect their sons, and I think this is at the heart of why Patti did what she did."

"Just because you want to forgive Patti doesn't mean the rest of us have to," said Hannah. "Especially not Brittany."

"Thank you for that." Brittany tensed. The muscles in her neck were so tight they felt like they could snap.

"Poor Ryan," said Mary. "This must have been devastating news for him to hear."

"His own mother lying to him for thirty years." Hannah shook her head. "It's despicable."

"And his father's scheming causing the death of his best friend." Mary picked a blueberry out of the muffin she held.

"All these years I blamed Ryan for Paul's death when it turns out he was totally innocent." Brittany rested her elbows on the table and buried her face in her hands. "Not only that, but Ryan was a victim, too." She felt so bad. Paul wouldn't have wanted her to have hated Ryan all those years.

The sound of a car pulling up in the driveway captured everyone's attention.

"Who could that be?" Cheryl asked.

"Steven said he'd drop by later with some movies for us to watch," said Mary. "In case Brittany wanted to unwind in front of the TV. But that doesn't sound like his van."

Brittany tightened the belt on her bathrobe and finger-combed her hair in case it was Ryan. She wanted to see him and have a chance to talk things over after the awful way they'd parted last night, but she worried she looked like a hag. She hadn't brushed her teeth yet.

But then, the sound of the lock turning in the front door

rattled through the downstairs, and Brittany heard a familiar voice that melted her heart.

"Hello, hello!" Jeremy called. "Mom? Are you there?"

Leaping out of her chair, Brittany flew to the entryway and threw her arms around her son. "Jeremy," she cried. "What are you doing here?"

Mary and Hannah were close behind her, and Cheryl's walker shuffled along the floor as she came at her own pace.

Jeremy hugged Brittany tightly before letting her go. "Mary texted me last night and told me you'd had a terrifying experience out on the water." He put his arm around her shoulder. "Mom, you hate the ocean. That must have been so scary."

Brittany nodded, tears filling her eyes. She wiped them away with the sleeve of her bathrobe. "You drove all this way just to check up on me?"

"Of course." He tilted his head to the side. "Wouldn't you have done the same for me?"

"Absolutely." Brittany nodded. "I'd do anything for you."

"I know it." Jeremy smiled and the way his eyes crinkled made her think of Paul.

"I'm glad you're here." She took a deep breath as she realized what needed to be done—what she could use Jeremy's help to do. "Would you help me talk to Grandma and Grandpa today? I need to tell them something important about how your uncle Paul died."

"That sounds like something I want to hear, too." Jeremy guided her into the kitchen. "But first I'd like some coffee. Your Halloween might have sucked, but mine was a rager."

"You've come to the right place," said Cheryl. "I just brewed a huge pot of Maxwell House."

THIRTY-FIVE

They started with Alan, first, because Brittany thought that the conversation with her dad might be easier than with her mom. Jeremy drove, and Brittany had to admit that the Ford Mustang was a fun ride. She only felt a little bit carsick when he took the corners too fast.

"I love hearing about Uncle Paul." Jeremy parked in Alan's driveway. "Every story you told me about him was special. I always wondered why you didn't talk about him more."

Brittany unclicked her seatbelt and picked up her purse. "Because it was too hard. Every time I talked about him, it made me sad. Also, because I put Paul on this pedestal, an impossibly high pedestal, which made it hard for anyone else to reach. Your dad, my father, every man I ever dated—none of them could compete with Paul, and that wasn't fair to anyone, Paul included."

"Do you think Uncle Paul would have liked me?"

"He would have loved you."

"Yeah, but would he have liked me?" Jeremy removed his seatbelt.

"Of course he would have." Brittany smiled. "There are so

many ways you're like Paul. You're both clever, and quick-witted. You love a good prank. You're knowledgeable about music. Remember that awesome playlist you put together for the party at the senior center earlier this year? And you're both excellent at planning out a practical course of action for how to get from point A to point B in your lives. You have your fire academy dreams, and Paul was headed off to Northwestern, no matter if Grandma approved of that or not."

"That's cool to hear." Jeremy got out of the car and Brittany followed.

"The only thing Paul wouldn't understand about you is how much you hate pumpkin bread."

"Bleh! It's like squash turned into a pastry product." Jeremy stuck out his tongue.

"Yeah, well, Paul loved the stuff."

"What are you going to say to Grandpa?"

"I'm going to tell him about Ryan and I commandeering his boat last night, and then..." Brittany sighed. "Then I'll just wing it, I guess."

"I'll be here to help." Jeremy pushed the doorbell.

It felt weird standing on the porch of what was once her childhood home and waiting to be admitted. Brittany noticed the cobwebs in the corners of the steps, next to where their old milk delivery box had once stood. A faded wreath hung at the door, which must have been Tansy's addition, because Brittany couldn't imagine it occurring to Alan to buy a wreath. She wondered what had become of Tansy, and the credit card fiasco, and whether her parents would suck her into their drama like usual. But then Brittany remembered she was made of sterner stuff, now. Her backbone was forged in steel. She was here to share pertinent information, that was all. Brittany refused to be part of her parents' conflict.

The door opened a minute later, and Alan stood in front of them wearing slacks and a bright green sweater. He was wiping his hands on a dish towel. "Jeremy, and Brittany. What a surprise. Come on in."

Brittany followed her father into the house and realized it was she who was in for a surprise. There, sitting in the living room, was Cynthia! "Mom, what are you doing here?" Brittany felt her eyes all but pop out of her head.

Cynthia crossed her ankles and sat primly on the black leather couch. It was a different couch than the one that she'd purchased for the living room back when she'd still lived here. The whole room was different, in fact, except for the 1980s wallpaper with the tiny blue hearts that Tansy used to complain about.

"Hi, Grandma." Jeremy kissed Cynthia's cheek and sat down on the loveseat, leaving room for Brittany to sit next to him.

"Hi." Cynthia laced her fingers together and rested her hands on her knees. "Your father and I had some financial matters to sort out, but that's all settled now."

Alan plopped onto the couch next to his ex-wife and leaned into the cushions. "It's okay, my dear, you can tell them."

"Are you sure about that, Alan?" Cynthia turned her head and looked at him. When Alan nodded, she looked back at Brittany and Jeremy. "When I returned to the reception desk at Thompson Orthodontics, I discovered Tansy had been embezzling money from the practice."

"Dad mentioned something about that," said Brittany.

"Can someone please tell *me* what's going on?" Jeremy asked. "Because I have no clue."

"Gladly." Cynthia inspected the cuticles of her right hand. "Tansy siphoned off money from the supply budget to the tune of tens of thousands of dollars."

Alan frowned. "She also ran up an astronomical credit card bill without my knowledge on our joint account."

"What did she spend the money on?" Jeremy asked.

"Ha!" Cynthia exclaimed. "That's the best part."

"You mean the *worst* part," Alan corrected.

"Potato, po-*ta*-to." Cynthia shook her head. "Tansy ran up your grandpa's credit card bill buying merchandise at the Best Buy she used to work at in Seattle. She was trying to gloat to her former co-workers about how she'd landed a sugar daddy."

"I wouldn't say 'sugar daddy.'" Alan grabbed the throw pillow next to him and hugged it. "We were two mature adults in what I thought was a committed relationship."

"Only one of you was way more mature than the other," said Cynthia. "You say 'mature,' I say 'old.'"

"I'm the same age as you, dear."

"Don't call me dear!" Cynthia snapped. "I'll accept the term 'financial savior,' though."

"I still don't understand what happened," said Jeremy.

"Yeah." Brittany felt confused too. "Mom, what did you do?" She decided then and there that if her mother admitted to a crime, she wouldn't cover for her. Brittany wasn't Patti, and she was through with tolerating her parents' bad behavior.

"I transferred the debt balance from Tansy and Alan's joint credit card to her solo credit card."

"How did you do that?" Brittany asked, her eyes bulging.

"Oh, it's not so hard to answer those 'who was your kindergarten teacher' security questions when you have all your daughter's old yearbooks." Cynthia smiled coolly. "Then when Tansy threatened to report me to the police, I explained to her how I had documentation of *her* stealing from *our* business."

"That's blackmail," said Brittany.

"Double blackmail." Jeremy gasped. "She can't report you without you reporting her."

"That's right." Cynthia nodded proudly.

"I had to hand it to your mom," Alan said. "She tied up this situation with a neat little bow on top. The exact amount Tansy stole from us, is the amount Cynthia transferred to her credit card."

"Everything's fair and square now." Cynthia smoothed the collar of her shirt. "And I've decided to return to work in the office full-time to keep an eye on things."

"I'm so glad I'm done with braces," said Jeremy.

"You and me both," Brittany said, with wide eyes.

"What a sense of humor you two have." Alan frowned. "I'm glad my devastating breakup and financial situation amuse you."

"I'm not amused, Dad, I'm horrified," Brittany said plainly. She looked from Alan to Cynthia. The truth was she was horrified with both of her parents, and proud of the work she'd done these past few weeks to protect herself from their drama. But this morning her goal was to tell them about Paul, not fortify the wall she'd built to defend herself from Alan and Cynthia.

"Why don't you tell them what we came to tell them?" Jeremy suggested.

"Good idea." Brittany nodded, glad for his support. Having an adult son was turning out to be an enormous blessing. Just because she'd collected a string of bad men in her life, didn't mean all men were bad. She saw that now. Who knew how Jeremy had turned out so well despite her and Ian's inexpert co-parenting, but here he was, offering wise advice, and boy was she grateful.

"What did you come for?" Alan asked.

Brittany's mind spun in circles, trying to find the right words. "Let me start by saying that last night, I borrowed your boat without asking because it was an emergency situation involving the Osbornes."

"What?" Cynthia sucked air between her teeth. "The Osbornes were involved?"

Oh jeez, Brittany thought to herself. *This will be hard for Mom to hear.*

THIRTY-SIX

Brittany held a bottle of wine in one hand and sparkling cider in the other. For once, she wasn't showing up as a dinner guest empty-handed. That made her feel less nervous, but only a little. She closed the door of her SUV with a hip bump and walked up the driveway to Ryan's front door. It was Sunday night, but she'd given herself time to stop by her house on the way home from work so she could shower and change.

When Ryan called yesterday, to apologize for storming off on Halloween, it hadn't been a good time to talk. Jeremy was devoting a whole day to her, and that didn't happen often. Together, they opened Safe Harbor four hours late, and got the cafe sorted out after the party from the night before. She and Jeremy had a million things to discuss having just come from Alan's house. As for her phone call with Ryan, Brittany worried that she'd been short with him, and not given him her full attention. There was so much she wanted to say to him that couldn't be said over the phone. But she'd agreed to see him Sunday night for dinner. At least she'd managed to arrange that.

Still... she couldn't stop the nagging worry that maybe she'd misheard him. Perhaps he'd been trying to break up with her over the phone. What if him apologizing was an "I'm sorry this isn't working. We should end things," and she'd misunderstood?

Brittany gripped the bottles tightly and felt her heart pound fiercely in her chest. The possibility of Ryan ending things made her feel faint. She didn't know how much she wanted him in her life, permanently, until she stared down his sleek front door and had no idea what was waiting for her on the other side. When the front door opened, and she saw Ryan stand in front of her wearing jeans and a gray sweater, she searched his eyes for any hint of what he might be thinking. Did he care for her as much as she did for him?

"Brittany," he said, opening the door wider. "You came."

"Hi, Ryan," she said, her voice as soft as a gentle fall of rain. "I come bearing gifts. I figured we could use a drink."

"I could use more than that." He scooped his arms around her waist and kissed her. "Brittany, I'm so sorry," he said when their lips parted.

"Why are you apologizing? You're not to blame for your parents' actions."

"Yes, but I feel guilty by association." He rested his forehead against hers. "I wasn't sure you'd show up after the way I acted. Come on inside out of the cold."

They entered the house and Ryan took her raincoat from her and set the bottles on a bench. He reached for her hands a moment later. "I shouldn't have run off Halloween night the way I did. I should have stayed by your side and dealt with the mess my family had caused."

"You stood by your daughter, and that's the most important thing." Brittany leaned closer. "Isabella survived one ordeal after another that night, and hearing her grandmother's confession was the last straw. You made the right decision taking her home and away from that mess."

"Yes, but *you*." Ryan shook his head. "It meant leaving you."

"I'm a big girl who can take care of herself. And I'm a

mother, too. That's why it was important to me to spend the day with Jeremy yesterday, while he was here, instead of coming over to see you right away, which would have been nice."

"So, we're okay then?" Ryan asked, a hopeful look in his eye.

"Gosh, I hope so." Brittany threw her arms around him and felt the delicious sensation of his body next to hers. "I hope we're more than okay."

It had taken her forty-five years to realize the truth, but she finally did. Good men weren't only found in fairy tales. They weren't mythical creatures like wizards or dragon riders. Good men were found right here in Sand Dollar Cove. Ryan, who would sail into the middle of a storm to rescue a loved one. Jeremy, who would drive all the way from Seattle in the wee hours of dawn because he knew his mom needed him. Guy and Steven, who treated her royally simply because she was Hannah and Mary's friend. Paul wasn't the only good man to ever walk the sandy beaches of Sand Dollar Cove. Brittany might have collected a string of duds over the years, but that didn't mean good men didn't exist. And the best man of all was right here, in her arms.

"Is that Brittany?" called a voice. "Can I come out of my room, now?"

"Isabella's stuck in her room?" Brittany asked.

"No, but she *is* grounded. She's just being dramatic." Ryan sighed heavily. "The last twenty-four hours have been an intense combination of me being grateful that she's alive, and also absolutely furious at her for doing something so risky."

"I bet."

"But maybe now that you're here, Isabella will stop stomping around the house and sighing theatrically." He picked up the wine and cider.

"Didn't *you* just sigh theatrically?" Brittany asked.

Ryan grunted. "Point taken."

He led her into the living room where the fireplace burned,

and Brandi Carlile's "The Story" played softly from hidden speakers. The rich scent of chili filled the air, and a platter of guacamole, chips and salsa waited for them on the island.

"You *do* have a Crock-Pot," she said, surprised. "At least, I think this is a Crock-Pot. What the heck is this thing? I've never seen one so fancy."

"It was a housewarming present from Melissa and Troy." Ryan opened a drawer and took out a corkscrew. "Would you like that glass of wine?"

"Yes, please." Brittany helped herself to the chips.

Isabella joined them just as Ryan uncorked the wine. "Hi, Brittany. I'm glad to see you. I haven't been allowed to see anyone all weekend, thanks to the ogre I live with."

"I would say your dad's more 'knight in shining armor' material than ogre-like, but it's good to see you, too." She held out her arms. "Hug? I won't be offended if you say no."

"It turns out I could use a hug." Isabella embraced her.

"Mmm... Your hair smells like coconuts," said Brittany.

"Did you just sniff my hair?" Isabella looked at Brittany and laughed.

"Sorry. Force of habit. Jeremy's hair never smelled that good."

Isabella made herself a small plate of chips and guacamole. "I'm going to go back upstairs and keep watching *Grey's Anatomy*, since that's the only fun thing I'm allowed to do."

Ryan checked the chili. "I'll call you when dinner is ready."

"I brought sparkling cider," said Brittany.

"Cool." Isabella picked up her plate. "I'll have some with dinner."

After she headed back upstairs, Ryan and Brittany sat on the long, low-backed couch in front of the fire. It wasn't especially comfortable, but it was cozy being snuggled up next to Ryan with a blanket over their laps. "Something In The Way" by Nirvana was playing, which made her think of Paul.

"I'm going to recreate Paul's CD tower," she blurted out. "One album at a time. Will you help me? I'm not sure I remember all the titles he owned."

"I can do better than that." Ryan slid the blanket off and got up from the couch. He crossed the room and pushed a button on the wall next to the fireplace. An enormous TV screen descended. "Shoot. Wrong button." Ryan pressed it again and the automatic blinds on the floor-to-ceiling windows went down. "Dang it." Ryan punched the keypad until the screen rose and the ocean view was once again revealed. But so was a hidden cabinet. The wall next to the fireplace was secret shelving, and once the panel slid open, a slew of electronic products was revealed: video consoles, remote controls, and... a plastic contraption that Brittany recognized. "I didn't know how to tell you when you mentioned it at The Summer Wind, but..."

"Paul's CD collection!" she cried. Brittany raced across the room and knelt on the floor. "This is it! This is the same exact tower." She pulled the plastic cases off one by one and read the titles. *"Nevermind... Ten... Vitalogy... Loudest Love... In Utero... Automatic for the People..."* There were dozens more. "You have them all! How'd you get them?" She held several of the CD cases reverently.

Ryan knelt next to her. "Apparently, your mom donated all of Paul's things to the thrift shop. My mom was there in the back room, volunteering, when the boxes arrived. She actually hid, so Cynthia wouldn't see her, because she wanted to avoid the confrontation." Ryan took the copy of *Nevermind* from Brittany's hands. "My mom felt bad for Cynthia. She felt horrible. And you know my mom, she can't let anything go, not one possession. So, when she saw those boxes of things that belonged to Paul, she bought the best things she could scrape the money together to afford: these CDs, and Paul's basketball shoes. I have those in a closet somewhere."

Brittany couldn't stop her tears from flowing. She wanted to hug the CD tower, but she didn't. What she really wanted was to hug Paul, but she couldn't. So she hugged Ryan. She felt his strong arms around her as she cried. Brittany realized she'd cried more for her brother in the past few weeks than she had in the past ten years. Paul wasn't a ghost anymore. He was a real-life person living and breathing in her heart again. And he was living in Ryan's heart, too. That made Brittany love Ryan all the more.

"I've spent my whole life since Paul died trying to be careful," Ryan said, in a somber tone. "I took a risk to get my feet on the ground and go back to school, but once I graduated, I stopped taking any chances at all. No to being spontaneous. No to having too much fun. I could never be daring, I had to be controlled. Measured. Conservative. It drove Melissa crazy—that's one of the many reasons we're better as friends. But you know what? We're great as friends, and that's because one of the most valuable lessons I learned from Paul was friendship. I would have walked through fire for him, and I know he would have done the same for me."

"He would have." Brittany wiped her tears. "He absolutely would have."

Ryan nodded. "If all you and I can have is friendship, I'll take it, and I'll be the best friend you ever knew. But the thing is, after meeting you again after all these years, I'm finally ready to take a risk again. Because it's a risk worth taking. Brittany, I need to tell you how I feel about you. How that crush I had on you when we were kids has turned into something so powerful, I can't control it. When you stood on the boat with me that night, sailing out into the storm, I knew. I just knew." He placed her hand on his heart. "I want to hang onto you for as long as possible and see where this goes."

Brittany stared up into his eyes and knew that she was ready to take a risk, too. She'd trust a man one more time, even though she'd been let down before. But this time, she felt confident that it was a safe bet. Ryan was honest and true. He would treat her kindly and with respect. This wouldn't be a relationship that involved yelling or neglect. Ryan would protect her heart like it was his own.

"I've taken a lot of wrong turns in my life," she told him. "But the one that I'll never regret is running into you in the alley that day and coating you with ten pounds of flour."

Ryan chuckled. "Oh really?"

"I'd do it again in a heartbeat. Only next time I'd be sure the eggs hit you, too."

"That sounds... sticky."

Brittany kissed the tears that had formed on his cheeks. "Sometimes I'm messy. But I always clean up after myself." She trailed her kisses down his neck and back again. She paused when their lips were inches apart. "Friendship would be easy, but loving each other will be more complicated."

"Who said anything about loving?" Ryan asked, huskily.

Do it, her heart whispered. *Carpe diem.*

"I did," she said. "I'm seizing the day."

Ryan's hands slid behind her waist and pulled her onto his lap. "So am I," he whispered, before he crushed their lips together with a fiery kiss that melted her tears away.

Right there, kissing Ryan in front of the fire, Brittany felt like her whole life was opening up into a beautiful second act. One where instead of being the sponge absorbing her parents' anger and acrimony, she was released from the toxicity of her past. Instead of tying herself to immature men who didn't respect her, she had learned to make better choices. But best of all, the deep wound that had marred her spirit ever since Paul died had closed over. It wouldn't fully heal, because grief never went away completely, but she was a whole person again, capable of great things. And the greatest thing of all that she wanted to do was to live a life that included loving Ryan. He was her dream come true.

EPILOGUE

ONE YEAR LATER

"Great news." Ryan strode into their bedroom. "I checked the game camera just now, and the colony hibernating in the bat box at Safe Harbor is doing well." He held up his phone. "Do you want to see? They're so cute."

Brittany put on the glittery chandelier earrings she'd made. "Are they as cute as the last time you showed me?"

"Even cuter." Ryan showed her the screen.

"Aw. Look at them, asleep in their little hibernaculum. You did good, Ryan." She bent over and slipped on her shoes. The flowing emerald-green dress was so long it required three-inch heels so she wouldn't trip. It looked fabulous on her. So fabulous, that Ryan whistled once he stopped admiring the bats.

"Wow!" he exclaimed as he sat down on the bed. "You're gorgeous."

"Thanks." Brittany twirled in front of the mirror and watched the fabric flow out. They were attending the double wedding of Guy Blanchet and Hannah Turner, and Steven Clarke and Mary Turner. Brittany was their matron of honor. "I'll look even better with you next to me. You're mighty handsome in that tuxedo."

Ryan smoothed his bow tie. "This is my first black-tie wedding in Sand Dollar Cove."

"I don't think our little town has ever seen a wedding this fancy. They even brought in a live orchestra for the reception."

"It's a good thing we practiced dancing on the cruise ship this summer." Ryan caught Brittany's hand and spun her around, before pulling her in for a quick box step.

"That was a magical vacation." Brittany closed her eyes as they danced cheek to cheek.

"Not to spoil the mood, but do you know where my mom and Don will be seated?"

Brittany opened her eyes. She hadn't been able to completely forgive Patti for her role in Paul's death, but appreciated that Patti had spoken up and had tried to make amends.

Patti had turned herself in to the sheriff's office and confessed to what Frank had done. However, the statute of limitations for insurance fraud was long gone, and the county prosecutor decided not to press manslaughter charges against Frank because his dementia made him unfit to stand trial. Now, Patti was working hard to make amends in other ways, too. She was using her sewing skills to create job interview outfits for moms re-entering the workforce who lived at a homeless shelter in Aberdeen.

"Nancy was in charge of the seating arrangements," said Brittany. "She put your mom, Don, and my parents at her table with Herman. The rest of us are at the family table with Cheryl."

"That's good." Ryan hadn't forgiven his mom all the way yet either, but Brittany knew he would someday, because he had such a deep love for his family.

She looked at the clock. "We'd better be going, or I'll be late. I'm supposed to get there early for pictures, and Jeremy is in charge of grandma-sitting Cheryl."

"I'll gather the kids while you fix your lipstick."

"But my lipstick's perfect. I just checked."

"That's because I haven't kissed you yet." Ryan flashed a mischievous grin.

"Oh, no you don't, mister. I have a double wedding to attend." Brittany held out her fingertips. "You can kiss my hand. That's all you get right now."

"I'll take your hand." He brought it to his lips. "And how about a bit of neck as well?"

"Well, okay." Brittany relented with a giggle. "There's no makeup there, so I think we're safe." She tilted her head back and laughed even harder when Ryan picked her up off her feet and spun her around before kissing her beneath her ear. "Not fair!" she cried. "I was already dizzy."

"I'll put you down *very* carefully," he said. "I promise."

"Dad!" Isabella shouted down the hall. "Are we going, or what?"

"Mom!" Jeremy hollered. "I can't be late. Cheryl's counting on me."

"This is our fault for raising responsible kids." Ryan set her down gently on her spiky heels. "They're so punctual."

"Coming!" Brittany shouted out the door. She plucked her wrap off the back of a chair and found her clutch. "We really *do* need to be going."

"You're right. I'm just dragging my heels a bit."

"Why?" Brittany asked. "Don't you like weddings? Free food, booze, and dancing, what's not to like?"

"Uncomfortable clothes, small talk with strangers, and boring speeches." Ryan followed her out the door. "But these are our friends, so I'm sure it'll be wonderful."

"Of course it will be wonderful." Brittany smiled when she saw Jeremy and Isabella standing in the living room. The space was slightly—only slightly—more colorful now. She'd softened the palate by adding a few houseplants, which miraculously were still alive. Unfortunately, her *Killer On the Loose* embroidery kit was still unfinished, but that's because she was busy.

At Safe Harbor, business was booming. She'd hired three more employees and expanded the hours to be open seven days a week. After the Turners moved out and Brittany moved in with Ryan and Isabella, she'd rented out her house for a tidy profit. Life at the beach was so great that Jeremy opted to come home more often now, especially since he had his own room, and he was learning to kitesurf. That hobby made Brittany nervous, but she kept her mouth shut. A life without taking risks to do the things you loved was no life at all. Which is also why she said yes, every time Ryan offered to whisk her away to one foreign destination after another. Sometimes Isabella came with them, and sometimes she stayed with Melissa and Troy.

"How about I drive since my car is faster?" Jeremy asked, as they headed toward the front door.

"What?" Brittany asked. "I don't think—"

"He's kidding." Ryan looked sideways at Jeremy. "Right?"

Jeremy busted up laughing. "Of course I'm kidding."

"Good." Isabella patted her hairdo. "I love riding in your convertible, but I don't want to mess up my hair."

"Seriously though," Jeremy checked his watch. "We really need to leave now, or we'll be late."

"Wait!" Brittany threw up her hands. "The cards. Do we have the cards?"

"What cards?" Ryan asked. "I sent them gifts off their registry."

"I know, but I also wrote handwritten notes to both Hannah and Mary. It'll only take me a minute to find them."

"Cheryl will destroy me if I'm late," said Jeremy. "No, actually, she'd be totally nice about it, but she might not wait for me to push her wheelchair. She might insist on using her walker, which would be too much activity for her, and then—"

"You go ahead," Brittany suggested. "Your car *is* faster, anyway."

"Can I come too?" Isabella asked. "If you keep the top up?"

"Sure," said Jeremy. "Fine by me."

Brittany raced to the desk in the office and came back just as Jeremy and Isabella were driving away.

"Is this what our life will be like someday?" Ryan asked. "Our kids driving off and leaving us behind?"

"Yes." Brittany linked her arm with his. "That's the goal, actually."

"At least Isabella's still fifteen. We have a few years before she leaves for college."

Brittany looked at Ryan and smiled. "I like how certain you are that we'll still be together when Isabella leaves for college."

"I *am* certain." Ryan squeezed her bicep. "But not as certain as I'd like to be."

"What?" Brittany felt a jolt of panic.

"I meant to ask you when we were in Athens, a few weeks ago, but then I ate that bad shrimp."

"Are you ill? Oh my gosh, Ryan. Do you have food poisoning again?"

"No." He grinned. "I feel fine, in fact. Never better." He dropped to one knee.

"What? Why are you...? Oh!" Brittany covered her mouth with her hands and her eyes grew wide when she saw Ryan take a small velvet box out of his pocket.

"I love you, Brittany. With all my heart, all my soul, and every fiber of my being. I want to spend the rest of our lives making beautiful memories together, if you'll have me."

"Yes! Yes!" Brittany cried.

"I didn't ask you yet."

"Oh, right, of course." Brittany sobered up.

Ryan removed the ring from the box. "Brittany Thompson, will you do me the great honor of becoming my wife?"

Brittany held out her left hand and stretched her fingers but said nothing.

"Well?" Ryan asked, looking up at her with hopeful eyes. "Don't leave me hanging."

Carpe diem, her heart whispered.

"Yes, Ryan Osborne. My answer is yes." She felt the enormous thrill of joy, love, and happiness all rolled into one when he slipped the diamond ring over her finger. She was forty-six years old and her life was just beginning. She'd finally healed from the traumas that had toughened her heart like scar tissue, and she'd grown the skills she needed to embrace true love. The future was sweet and full of promise. It glistened like sunshine on water.

"I love you so much," Ryan said, as he gazed up at her.

"I love you too." She tugged his hands, lifting him to his feet. "Who cares about my makeup? Give me a kiss!"

It would probably take Brittany ages to fix her lipstick, but she didn't mind one bit.

A LETTER FROM JENNIFER

Firstly, I wanted to thank you for diving into the world of Sand Dollar Cove and following Brittany along on her journey. If you enjoyed joining Brittany while she overcame her past in order to find a happier future with Ryan, then stay tuned. You can keep up to date with all of my latest releases by signing up to my newsletter. Your email will never be shared and you can unsubscribe at any time.

www.bookouture.com/jennifer-bardsley

Now, I'm letting you in on an industry secret. A common bit of advice writers hear is: "If you want this book to sell, make the main character younger." Many publishers are hesitant to release books centering on middle-aged characters, even though middle-aged people love to read books. Does this make sense? No, it doesn't, but this is the way of the world—or the publishing world, at least. It's ageism in the bookstore.

Over the course of my career, I've written stories about teens, twenty-year-olds, and thirty-somethings, but this is my first story about a woman exactly my own age: forty-five. A huge thank you goes to my publisher, Bookouture, for letting me do this. At no point did anyone in London tell me: "Forty-five? Eeek! Rewrite Brittany so she's a hot young thirty-year-old with a son in first grade." Instead, I got to write the story I wanted to write, and that means everything to me.

I loved sharing Brittany's story because she's old enough to know what she wants, and her lived experience gives her the tools to make her dreams come true. I also enjoyed writing about Ryan and Isabella because fourteen-year-old girls with phones can be terrifying and passive-aggressive Instagram hearting is a real thing. Live in fear of the group chat lurker!

But my favorite part of this book is bringing readers into the heart of Sand Dollar Cove. Sand Dollar Cove is a fictional place but the beauty—and danger—of the Pacific Northwest is real. Summer is glorious, but when the temperature drops and the weather picks up, you need a cozy place to go like Safe Harbor to boost your mood. Warming up with something hot to drink is never a bad idea either.

Speaking of which, here's an Easter egg for you to hunt for in my Sand Dollar Cove books. A particular beverage plays a scene-stealing role in each book. Do you know what drink I'm talking about?

Here's another Easter egg to search for. I mention the same breed of dog in each book. Did you notice that too?

One more thing, because I love guessing games. *Postcards from the Cove, Photographs from the Cove,* and *Notes from the Cove* each feature a different misunderstood critter. In this book, it's bats, but do you remember the creatures from the previous books?

If I've piqued your interest, and you haven't had the chance to read the rest of my Sand Dollar Cove series, I hope you will. You can find out more by subscribing to my newsletter as mentioned earlier in this letter, or by following me on social media. Facebook is my favorite way to connect with readers. In my VIP reader group Jennifer Bardsley's Book Sneakers, I give away free books every Friday.

Finally, I'd like to say a huge thank you to everyone who takes time to write a quick review on Amazon and Goodreads. Reviews make a big difference in terms of helping my books reach new readers.

KEEP IN TOUCH WITH JENNIFER

www.jenniferbardsley.com

facebook.com/JenniferBardsleyAuthor

x.com/JennBardsley

instagram.com/jenniferbardsleyauthor

tiktok.com/@jenniferbardsley

ACKNOWLEDGMENTS

Thank you to my agent, Liza Fleissig, my editor, Lucy Frederick, my critique partner, Penelope Wright, my copyeditor, Jenny Page, my proofreader, Liz Hurst, and the wonderful team at Bookouture for bringing the world of Sand Dollar Cove to life. Thank you especially to my readers who have traveled with me from one little town in the Pacific Northwest to the next. I appreciate you tremendously, and hope that if you ever get the chance to visit Washington State, my books help you remember to bring layers, sturdy walking shoes, and a highly competent raincoat.

PUBLISHING TEAM

Turning a manuscript into a book requires the efforts of many people. The publishing team at Bookouture would like to acknowledge everyone who contributed to this publication.

Commercial
Lauren Morrissette
Jil Thielen
Imogen Allport

Cover design
Emma Graves

Data and analysis
Mark Alder
Mohamed Bussuri

Editorial
Lucy Frederick
Imogen Allport

Copyeditor
Jenny Page

Proofreader
Liz Hurst

Printed in Great Britain
by Amazon